TOGETHER

Book II of the Janaforma Trilogy

TOGETHER

Book II of the Janaforma Trilogy

Martha Fawcett

JANAFORMA PRESS

Davidsonville, Maryland

Together

This is a work of fiction. All characters and events portrayed in this novel are fictitious and not intended to represent real people or places.

Although some of the locales where this story takes place could be real the author took liberties and this book does not purport to offer an exact depiction of any particular place or location.

Janaforma Press

Davidsonville, Maryland

www.marthafawcett.com

Cover image created by Duncan Long

Library of Congress Control Number: 2013908414

ISBN: 978-0-9890636-1-6

Printed in U.S.A.

First Edition

DEDICATION

To my special friend, Nancy Toner Weinberger, for her creative feedback
and her encyclopedic knowledge of all subjects esoteric.

To my son for his editing skills and to my husband for his belief in my
talent, his critical eye, and the many hours he spent to make sure Together
was published.

CONTENTS

One

Set me as a seal upon your heart,
as a seal upon your arm;
for love is as strong as death.
Song of Solomon

Only in dreams does hope have the daring to come out and play. Wandering through dreamscapes of dusky and circuitous byways, I become hope's eye. Night after night, my quest for fulfillment never ends; yet upon awakening, I find I am still lost on the flat, Midwestern plane of my existence. It's daybreak after just such a night. With my morning cup of stimulant in hand, I barefoot my way toward the scratched, foggy windows of my space pod to check the weather.

Outside, a November dawn paints its dingy palette of misty grays across the Ohio landscape. Through the gap in the curtains, I spy Gertie, my neighbor, best friend, and fellow lackey at Atlas Map. She snuggles deeper into her old red-plaid jacket as she waits for Poppy, her neurotic dog-child to find his perfect spot. Poppy sniffs, squats, and takes his morning dump on our communal turf before finishing off with a backward scratch to the ground. Then it's on to his next perfect spot.

Up and down the uniform blocks of the Erie Pod Park, Earth's somnambulistic risers are stretching and yawning their way into another day. The Erie Pod Park is one microcosm among the billions of pod parks that sprinkle our Orion Spur. Over in the Cedar Point section of our development row after perfect zigzag row of pseudo-distressed pods, squat along the horizon. I don't live in the new section. My days and nights play themselves out in the old section, called The Fields, where the pods appear

1

to have dropped from the sky and landed helter-skelter in the middle of an acre plot of farmland. At various times, I've sensed a bit of snobbery among the residents of The Fields, a feeling of legitimacy concerning their pods. I share none of my neighbor's civic pride and care only enough that my pod is worth more than a factory-distressed model.

Succumbing to the lucrative bait cast forth from newer worlds, most Humanity left Earth ages ago. Me? I remain Earthbound. My closest brush with modern travel happened three years ago when Gertie and I splurged and went on a whirlwind trip around the planet Earth. Bolting through the saturated reds and oranges of Mexico City and Rio de Janeiro, we danced with natives in the streets until dawn. Soaring over the silver arches of Melbourne and the linear skyscrapers of Beijing, left us in crystaglass awe. Near the end of our tour, Tricomet Tours stranded us in a marginal hotel in Mumbai for three extra days where Gertie came down with an authentic case of amoebic dysentery. We managed to survive and when we finally landed in Chicago, Gertie said, "We've done it! We've proven through direct experience that the Earth is round and that protoburgers taste like cardboard no matter where you eat them."

****

Why leave home when I sit in front of my multidex and coax it to unfurl the entire Human drama from cave to space? The multidex tells me that Human wars no longer occur on Earth. Religious and tribal fervor of the fundamentalist sort now seem absurd to all but a brawny few. Yet Earth's new peace has nothing to do with the enlightenment of Humans over their baser instincts. Earth's new peace is the result of apathy, stagnation, and the collapse of our Human dreams.

In the year 2501, Earth faced a series of economic crises and crippling recessions. Alien business conglomerates, in a series of decisive yet clandestine mergers, executed a quick series of corporate takeovers. Seven-months later, Earth declared bankruptcy. Earthlings endured the layoffs and shutdowns and Humans began deserting Earth by the millions to seek their livelihood on yet unexploited worlds.

In June of 2525, the same interplanetary business conglomerates financed the formation of a new political party, called NEW VISION. Suddenly NEW VISION: EVERYWHERE OR NOWHERE posters were as common on the streets of Madang, New Guinea as they were on the Champs Elysées. NEW VISION would assume many faces in its effort to retain power—a revolution, a renaissance, and even a peace movement. In the end, NEW VISION was nothing more than another persuasive voice urging the remaining Humans on Earth to fulfill their dreams on other planets.

By 2565, major cities on Earth were ghost towns. For seventy-five years, the infrastructure continued to crumble and sink into rot. By 2575, Earth's population was a shadow under a billion. Between the years 2580 and 2585, the caretaker governments of the Orion Spur Alliance (OSA) began arriving on every continent and promising that nebulous "something better" as a solution to the 750 million Humans left behind. Tyrowsians began moving to Earth in droves, buying up land at rock bottom prices.

At first, Earth's remaining Humans were humble, claiming they were grateful for alien intervention, accepting that now they were a minority on their native world. Despite NEW VISION'S promises, "something better" never materialized for Humanity. Earth still has its permanent underclass, the uneducated, the superstitious, and the cynical (me). Contemporary historians speculate whether NEW VISION was an unscrupulous plot aimed to siphon off Earth's genius. Nobody really cares anymore because we can't fix the past and we can't find anyone to blame. Revisionist history long ago obscured the question of who were the bamboozlers and who was the bamboozled. The one truth we know for sure—a few people became obscenely rich and Earth now is a cultural vacuum. Forgotten history cannot speak but as the android entertainer, Ramjet, screams through his kakos music, "What'd ya gonna do?" and, "So fucking what!"

In my time, Humans are dying from a new, "so fucking what." Medical experts appropriately call the disease Fundamental SocioPsychic (FSP) breakdown. Everything from suicide to someone unable to roll with the times carries the FSP stigma. FSP is a real and devastating illness, which affects more than an individual's body and mind. FSP destroys communities, institutions, and governments. FSP is a plague brought about by chronic nihilism that consumes our life and leaves us to rattle around the emptiness inside ourselves. FSP spawns attitudes in our culture such as, "Some messes are too big to be cleaned up."

One aspect to survive the NEW VISION blitz is our English language, which has evolved into the monster we now call, "Universal." Amused by Earth's varied history of languages, non-Earthlings sometimes refer to Earth as, "The World of Words." Earth has the unique distinction of being the one planet in the Orion Spur Alliance that's invented thousands of languages. As the comic Stevie Stress quips, "Earth has two hundred words meaning doorknob, but still can't figure out how to open the door." That's because Humans use language not only to elucidate, but also to dilute feelings, shade truths, and hide the guilty.

Who might have guessed that in the prehistoric fifth-century Earth, a tribe of Germanic barbarians would invade and conquer Romano-Keltic England and their combined linguistic seeds would spawn a language now used on other planets? Of course, English has evolved right along with the people that speak it and it would be easier for me to understand an individual speaking Universal than for me to understand one of my prehistoric ancestors. Universal words, phrases, nuances, and a million

3

words explaining other words, swamp Orion Spur planets. As humanoid races extend their tendrils farther out into the galaxy, Universal continues to engorge itself on a million new expressions and catch phrases. Everyone speaks some kind of Universal; Universal is the official language of the Orion Spur Alliance. Despite this dubious honor, nobody understands anyone else. Nevertheless, I can eat fiber fries and sip Coke in an automated drive-thru in Toledo, Wonder World, or the far reaches of Uraino Allure and order in Universal every time. And I can sit in front of my multidex screen, live my life through its filter, and have the ease of listening to a language of meaningless blather. And I don't mind telling you—that's exactly what I do. Convenience is my god and Convenience is the true light at the end of every Human tunnel.

In this bleak new time, Earth's Humanity remains mute. We've been scrutinized, dissected, psychoanalyzed, and market-surveyed down to our last organelle and we have nothing new to say. We lie complacent, like well-used cadavers, with our last secrets splayed open to the market needs of the Orion Spur. The irony lies in the fact that despite all the studied analysis of Earth and its native people, we are more enigmatic, lost, and lonelier than ever; and I confess, of late, even I have felt the cold, disembodied hand of isolation upon my shoulder.

My name is Jane Smith. In a surge of pregnant creativity my mother decided to call me Jane, believing Jane went perfectly with Smith. My Irish grandmother, Lily Weaver Smith, saved me from complete anonymity and suggested Hibernia as a middle name. Eventually, Hibernia turned into Hi. Once I became Hi, I spent years with the erroneous belief that anyone saying "hi" to another person within my earshot was addressing me. Now that I'm a sober thirty-two years of age, I identify myself as Jane H. Smith OSP3467.

****

In a habit ground in by years of Midwestern repetition, I found myself opening the door of my space pod to sniff the winter air. Outside, water laden stratus clouds already were blanketing the northwestern sky. Poppy began barking the instant he saw me, letting loose with a series of ear-piercing little-dog yips. "Come here Poppy. Come to mommy," Gertie called after her problem child. Gertie's pleading voice revealed all the nervous indulgence that had translated into Poppy's delicate digestion problem.

"What's up with Poppy?" I yelled across our communal turf.

"He just saw a squirrel and wants to do some police work," Gertie yelled back. I smiled and gave her an upturned thumb.

When I decided to check my delivery box, Poppy executed a quick U-turn and came running toward me. He looked so cute with his white ears flapping, but I knew Poppy's tricks because I had been his victim an embarrassing number of times. His barking was a ploy. While people worried that this spastic little Bich-poo was going to bite their ankles, Poppy was heading straight for their crotch. If dogs chronicle their successful sniff assessments of peoples' asses, Poppy had many secrets to tell. This morning, I blocked him with my knee. "Go home," I said in my best alpha tone. "Go and get your own butt cleaned before you pass judgment on mine." Defeated, Poppy dropped his head and trotted off toward Gertie, showing me his shit-stained white fur. "I think Poppy needs his backside wiped," I yelled.

"I know, he loves those rawhide bones, but they always give him the runs." Gertie squinted and peered at me. "Are we still on to play cards tonight?"

"I can't. I have a Monday deadline for that moon map I'm redrawing." I ignored Gertie then. I also ignored Poppy, the thought of rawhide bones, and his dirty butt. I opened my delivery box hoping my December holospool from the Universal Geographic (UG) had arrived. I'm a travelogue junkie and love to learn about the unique civilizations still peppering our universe. The delivery box was empty. I raised my fist to the approaching storm to the northwest and mumbled, "Just another shitty day here in paradise on the southern banks of Lake Erie."

At least ten hours of unfinished work waited my focused attention. Back inside, I procrastinated by shuffling through an old deck of cards lying on the kitchen table. When I can't concentrate, sometimes I waste time by playing solitaire. When I play, I prefer paper cards because the multidex discourages cheating with its constipated pre-programmed rules. I fingered the slick cards, arranging them into seven rows, turning over the ace of hearts, the two, three, four, and five of hearts. Damn! I'm winning. Winning disturbed my stupor, made me excited, and demanded that I play the game. Sliding the cards across the table, a few skated and fell over the edge to the floor. Ignoring the lost cards, I rearranged the abbreviated deck, which began taking its own peculiar shape. Then I thought about Poppy suffering a bout of rawhide diarrhea and felt a wave of nausea. For a moment, I did not breathe. I had experienced a similar episode two weeks earlier. Awakening from a bad dream, the shadow of something or someone slipped back into darkness. My mouth tasted of acrid metal and a weight seemed to be pressing through the middle of my chest. Is this my genetic time bomb? As always, I popped another neoanodyne, which is my solution to everything wrong with my life.

Eleven years ago, I was pregnant when a DNA counselor informed me that my genetic profile had a glitch. Confronting my mother about my problem, we had several painful discussions, which ended in her telling me, "When I was eighteen years old, I did something rather impulsive. On the eve of the Earth's endorsement of the World Genetic Accords, I joined with five thousand other Human women in protest, and impregnated myself with the sperm of a randomly selected Human male." In my mother's case, her anarchy produced a slightly toxic soup. The genetic engineers wore their serious professional expressions when they informed me, "You're a genetic time bomb." Mom said that she considered me a blessing, but I have dealt with our mutual genetic embarrassment by deciding that I will be the last Smith.

Sometimes, the Genetically Correct (GC) call conception accidents such as me Casuals, the term suggesting our parents were morally corrupt. Casuals are a rarity nowadays. Estimates put our number at around 25,000 here on Earth. That's small potatoes in the sphere of social and political influence. Casuals don't have a lobbying group, special charity, or handy acronym to describe our predicament. Global Newsday recently referred to Casuals as, "...throwbacks to genetic anarchy, betrayed and deprived by their parents...their trust in life destroyed intrauterine." That may be the GC's reality but my reality tells me Casuals make the GC uncomfortable because we are a constant reminder of the Human imperfections the GC ignores with their perfectly symmetrical faces. Soon, none of this will make a difference because Casuals will be as extinct as bluebirds. Five years ago, the provisional Earth government adapted the precepts of the Intergalactic Genetic Accords making it a crime for genetically engineered individuals to procreate with Casuals. Since then, the GC petitioned and won preferential job rights for their children in fields where their children possess genetic enhancement. When I feel lousy, I think, *the GC is right!* Mom cheated me. In better moments, I pacify myself with the notion that perhaps, I am one of the few Humans left on Earth with an edge of unpredictably left in my life.

My particular genetic glitch has medical experts fascinated with "my case." Eight years ago, a genetic cardiologist scrutinized his crystal ball and predicted that somewhere down the line I was going to experience problems with my heart. As a preventive measure, he suggested I have my natural heart replaced with something a bit more reliable. In the end, I decided that carrying around a Polyplex 4000 Pumper, instead of my physical heart, would not make my life any easier. From then on, I stayed as far away from medical experts and genetic engineers as possible. Still, as my life chugs along, like a hypochondriac, I wait with increasing trepidation for the sky to fall. I popped another neoanodyne and decided I was a depressed FSP neurotic after all. I shuffled the cards and rearranged them a dozen times. Nothing makes any difference. I can't win. Half my cards are under the table, discarded, unknown. I lost the next three games in a row.

"The time is nine a.m.," announced the multidex from across the room.

"No need to nag," I replied to the machine that scheduled my life.

Most reluctantly, I sat down in front of the multidex and called up the charts destined to be my weekend's companion. I work for the Atlas Map Company and it is my *seule raison d'être.* I'm an associate cartographer in the corporate maze at Atlas, exactly like Gertie, and about five hundred thousand other Atlas employees scattered across the Orion Spur. A couple of times, in my lackluster career at Atlas, my boss, Mr. Wantanabi, assigned me to do detail work for Kinsey and Clidmore, a team of cartographers doing the initial mapping of the region of Tau Ceti. This is my one claim to fame. Ninety-nine percent of my work is humdrum and uninspiring, something I do with one eye closed.

This morning, I was supposed to be modifying a map of Earth's moon, specifically, the Mare Imbrium Plain. It was the fifth time I was reworking this particular chart. Eventually, Atlas would sell this map as a souvenir to the thousands of tourists who visit the site of the first crash-landing of the Russian rocket, Luna 2. Calling up the program, the half-finished map drew itself on my screen, the valleys, peaks, craters, and finally the hachure lines. My new assignment was to superimpose the locations of all the new restaurants, concessions, shops, and rest rooms on the old map. No sooner did I open the file than a sudden pain shot down my left arm.

"Multidex, stop and store program. Show me the Toledo doctor directory." I picked one, any one, someone new, someone who did not know I was a Casual.

A moment later, Dr. Patel's office logo appeared onscreen. An idiotic grinning face, of a person who never existed, a multidex facsimile of what happiness should look like, smiled at me. "For an emergency select one and wait for your call to be answered. For an appointment select two," the image said with mind-numbing sweetness.

Selecting two, Dr. Patel's appointment schedule appeared. I reserved thirty minutes of his time on the 23 of November, repeating, "J.SmithOSP3467arm pain." It just fit in the ten-second slot allowed.

The reply returned immediately. "Make an appointment at the Sandusky Clinic for an Internal Body Scan (IBS) and iridic scan. Fee of 25 credits debited to J.SmithOSP3467. Thank you for using the referral services of Dr. Patel."

I sat for a long time staring at "J.SmithOSP3467," printed across the screen without tabbing send. "Do I really need an IBS or iridic scan?" I decide again, for the tenth time, to do nothing.

Each morning, I crawled out of bed, checked the weather outside the door of my space pod, and wandered over to the multidex with my cup of morning stimulant in hand. My two-dimensional, flat-screen life at Atlas Map punctuated my simple three-dimensional world with clockwork regularity. I left home only to buy food and staples.

It was February 2, Ground Hog Day. The groundhog and I arose at dawn to check the weather. The sky was bright and clear except for blue-black stratus clouds near the horizon, so I mumbled something about six more weeks of severe winter weather and the groundhog and I went back to bed. At noon, the meteorological satellite, a hundred miles up in space, scanned Northwestern Ohio, and confidently predicted over Weathervane, "Folks out in the Midwest can expect some spring-like weather in the next twenty-four hours that will last through Thursday." By early evening, the temperature plummeted to just above freezing and an icy wind blew off Lake Erie. By seven o'clock, a fine mist of snow blanketed our corner of the world.

Zigzagging her way between the half-frozen puddles, Gertie dashed across the turf with Poppy under one arm and a box-o-wine under the other. "Hurry, open the goddamn door," she shouted and she stomped snow off her shoes on the doormat as she told me with great excitement, "This one is turning into a blizzard!" She put Poppy down on the floor and he executed an energetic shake to get the snowflakes off his fur. Then he ran around the room like a nutzoid, into the kitchen, down the hall to the bedroom, and finally into the bathroom where he got a quick drink out of the toilet before returning and collapsing on the floor.

"What makes you think we're in for a blizzard?" I asked. "Weathervane's been predicting spring-like weather all day long."

"That's because the goddamn Weathervane satellites have not been properly calibrated in ten years. The sensors for northwestern Ohio are pointing toward Vancouver."

"Oh!" I shrugged. "Stupid of me to assume anything on Earth might actually work."

Most Sunday afternoons, Gertie and I would get together and play a few rounds of two-handed Zeppelin, listen to some music spools, and get tipsy on cheap wine. Sunday afternoons had lost their spark the last few months and seemed more a routine we reenacted to hold our mutual loneliness at bay. I popped open the box of sweet, pink liquid—sold as Chablis—and poured it into two stemmed glasses while Gertie demonstrated her shuffling skills by letting the cards fall from one hand to the other as a waterfall. "How many cards do you want?" I shrugged to demonstrate my obstinacy. "Start with five," she said, playing the game for me. She peeled off five cards and slid them across the table to the rowdy sound of Gathosian folk music coming from the multidex.

When I turned over my uninspiring cards, I said, "Let's skip Zeppelin tonight. What do you say, Gertie? I'll bake some oatmeal raisin cookies while the snow accumulates. We could listen to some of those romantic love songs by Dulce Cœur."

"I'm on a diet," she said and she set her cards aside—face down. Obviously, she had a good hand that she did not want to waste. For all her shuffling skills, Gertie was a predictable card player.

Gertie was an authentic GC, but her father loved her mother, perhaps too much, and told the genetic designer that he wanted his daughter to look exactly like his wife. We all suffer the indiscriminate taste of our fathers and Gertie took the brunt of her father's lovesick eyes.

Gertrude Louisa Martinez was thirty-five years but she looked like a middle-aged senior citizen. She once showed me a picture of herself with her pet rabbit Floppy when she was eight and Floppy looked like Poppy and Gertie looked exactly as she does now. Despite her numerous cosmetic procedures, her eyelids drooped and her mouth had a pinched appearance on one side. Her grooming was minimal. Her hair was a butchered mess and she didn't care. I entertained a grudging respect for her ability to blow off disappointment and when it came to the bottom line, she was able to paint a brighter picture than I could. She was out there with her nose in the wind looking for something good to happen. "Late winter blues kicking up again?" she prodded me.

How could I spit out the bitter taste of my disappointment when I presented only a well-behaved reflection of myself to the world? Ribbons of history unwound within me, showing me that once I was part of something bigger than my cynicism. Lost in timeless moments of inherent memory, I knew togetherness was my natural state. After all these centuries, the ease of The Flow still beckoned, offering me my own innate wisdom as bait. "Yahoo," Gertie said as she waved a hand in front of my face. "You got a FSP body split or what?"

"I'm a lost cartographer." I whined, but I wanted to say I did not want to end up like her, with nothing but a shit-ass, neurotic dog for a companion.

Gertie chortled with an appropriate breathless huff. "Who's that popular comic that tells those neurotic jokes? What's she say? 'I'm a frog in the stagnant pool of my own existence and I'm drowning on pond scum?'"

"Stevie Stress. I hate her, especially right now."

Gertie reached across the table and patted the back of my hand. "I told you before and I'll say it again; if you don't like your life, change it. Reinvent yourself! Get a new face, a new body, a new attitude."

"That's cosmetic poof." I knew the routine because I frequently had powdered my life with poof. In my twenties, style was my religion. I crammed my body into an acceptable mold, an impossible ideal worn by millions of other women. I bought my redesigned face, choosing the sweet and innocent look from a multidex file called Beautiful Feminine Faces. Just as the women of today are buying their redesigned faces with a harder edge, I chose wide-eyed wonder. Time has proven that trade-offs exist with both faces. Sweet and innocent hides the anger and pain just as harder edges keeps everyone at bay. For years, I ignored age as I ignored my inner truth. I treated both time and truth as if I had an eternity to decide my fate. Now in my thirties, life goes faster and today follows yesterday without so much as a memory to hold in the treasury of my heart. Still, nothing mars my surface. My face remains smooth, cool, and reflective as a well-polished stone.

"You're feeling a little depressed because of the cold and the darkness," Gertie was saying. "Go spend some time in the solar chambers. The sunshine will cheer you up."

"I hate those places, all those Tyrowsians lying around on deckchairs and frying themselves yellow. They look like overripe bananas in their swim trunks."

"Forget the overripe bananas and look for a pleasure prince."

"Not that crap again."

"You have to admit, I haven't seen any new faces coming in or out of this pod for a hellava long time." I was a phantom limb going through the motions, pretending I still was alive and Gertie was suggesting a jog around the bedroom as a cure. "A pleasure prince will know how to cheer you up—'pronto prone,' as the kids say nowadays."

"I don't want to be cheered-up. The mere notion of being cheered-up is nauseating. Besides, there's more to life than pigeonholing with a different pleasure prince every other night."

Gertie assumed an indignant expression. "Like what Miss Persnickety? If you think I'm going to dive into a bowl of pity porridge for you, you're mistaken. Come on Janey-Brainy, re-lax! You're such a bore every time February rolls around. You have to snap out of this latest nosedive. Your mind's as dense as a black hole. Listen to Auntie Gertie, if not a pleasure prince—what about the real thing?"

"What's the real thing?"

"You know, a capricious bio, a man. The point is you have to jog your libido, that is, if you want to stay healthy. In my experience, one of the fastest ways to burn up depression is by creating some friction between the sheets. One good orgasm results in a completely new outlook! Fix yourself up. Put on some sparkly eye shadow, go over to Cedar Point to one of those fancy-pants dance clubs, and meet somebody. Who cares about genetic status or whether someone is a bio, biodroid, or android? Bottom line is—are you interested in fucking. You'll see! A couple of months ago, I picked up this biodroid. When I got him into bed, found he had a micovibrator implant."

"No kidding? Where?"

"Where do you think, dummy? It was one hellava good ride too, true innovation. In my opinion, every man over eighteen should have the option to have a micovibrator installed. Hell, I'd support the program with my tax dollar. Think of all the women it would make happy. I say if it is good enough for a pleasure prince than its good enough for our run-of-the-mill, limp-dick Ohio hicks."

Once I was a regular at the clubs. I put in my desperate years filled with drugs, drink, and pleasure princes. A kaleidoscope turned in my memory showing me a morning of nausea and disorientation. An angelic, blonde biodroid slept peacefully beside me in a featureless, motel room. A microchip embedded in his bicep tattoo flashed, "Cleveland Cowboys!" His well-worn western boots lay tossed beside the bed. I picked up my wrinkled clothing on the floor and left the tip on the bedside table. My Cleveland cowboy sleeps on in my mind as the omega of my sexual desires.

Gertie's big brown eyes lit up. "You know what? You should try to find someone through one of those multidex hookup sites like Heart Throbs. It would give you some space to see who you really like."

"Yeah, I can paint that picture in a flash. They would match me with another Casual and we could sit around and hate society together."

"Why do you always says such negative things?"

"I say negative things because we live in a negative society."

"You never want to try anything new."

"What's new about a pleasure prince or what you call, the real thing? If the bio is a Human male, guaranteed, eventually his hair will be growing in all the wrong spots."

"I thought we both still believed in Mr. Right."

"Mr. Rights are fairytales, especially for Casuals."

Gertie held up a hand. "I still believe in Mr. Right because I've met him." Her voice hushed and assumed a reverent edge. "His name was Burke but everybody called him Buddy. I still think of him as Beautiful Buddy. The entire time we were together, I couldn't believe that someone as good-looking, kind, and understanding as Buddy loved me."

"You never mentioned Burke or Buddy before."

"Memories of Buddy are special and I don't like to talk about them."

"What happened to him?"

"He took an engineering job on Mars. He asked me to go along. Made it sound easy, as if all I needed to do was throw some clothes in a suitcase and go. My mother was sick at the time, depending on me to take care of her. Atlas had just made me an associate cartographer and it was too damn hard to just pick up and go." Gertie shrugged. "At the time, when I weighed the pros against the cons, going didn't make sense. Buddy's mind was made up and he did leave and that was the end of our relationship." Gertie's eyes turned glassy. "I guess he was the footloose type. He was different, adventurous, a true Sagittarian."

"You weighed the pros against the cons? Where was your heart in this major decision? You're GC and a talented cartographer. You can get a job anywhere. You could have taken your mother with you. You gave up love and an opportunity to escape this dying world—for what?"

"I guess I was scared."

"That's it? You're going to sit there shuffling your cards and tell me you let Buddy go because you were scared. I don't believe you, Gertie. I don't believe you loved Buddy as much as you claim or you wouldn't have let him go."

Gertie caught her breath. "When you are in one of these foul moods, you turn into a diamond drill bit—do you know that?" She shuffled the last few cards remaining in her hand. "I was scared because the truth is—I didn't know if it would last. Frankly, it seemed too good to last." Gertie sniffed and wiped her nose on the back of her hand. "Still, for a short time, Buddy was my Mr. Right. I swear he was, Jane."

"I'm sorry, Gertie; I didn't mean to upset you. I have no right to question you or your life. I guess I'm merely jealous that you once had the real thing. All my years of riding this planet around the Solar System, I haven't inspired ten seconds worth of honest love in another person."

"That's not exactly true. Your mother loved you."

"My mother? I'm not talking about my mother, especially not tonight." I still wasn't sure what my mother or her death meant to me. To society, she was simply one more FSP sufferer, but to me she gave up her fight too soon.

"Her decision to end her life had nothing to do with you. She was ill, afraid, and in emotional pain. Eventually, you are going to have to realize she did the best she could under the circumstances. Be patient, Jane. Your time is coming. Sometimes when situations seem the worst is when they start to get better."

I hated Gertie at that moment. I hated her for her pathetic optimism and her empty clichés. "It's been—maybe six years—since I've been with any kind of man and I no longer care. Even if Mr. Right appeared out of nowhere, I would fuck up the relationship. I come from a long line of fuckups. The Smiths have fucking up down to a science. Do you know my great-grandmother felt that she had screwed up her life so badly that she isolated herself out in space for eighty-one years? Grandma Lily used to talk about her sometimes. My own mother once told me, 'The Smiths have been isolationists for generations.' She called us, 'the progenitors of the final male/female split.' And you know what? I think the Smith penchant for isolationism is a growing contagion. I have it; you have it; and, if we both weren't so blind, we would see that we are at the forefront of a cosmic pandemic. Do you know what's going to wipe out Humanity? Isolation. How many planets do you think there are in our galaxy—a zillion? Picture it, Gertie, one planet so every sentient creature in our universe could have her own world. Maybe we should each grab a planet, sit it out until the end of time, and avoid the hurt we cause each other."

Launching another cliché, Gertie promised, "Someday, something magical, something like Buddy, will happen to you."

"You're optimism is so pathetic," and yet I knew my cynicism was equally pathetic. Both optimism and cynicism were blind groping and neither viewpoint possessed the robust health of experienced joy. At that moment, I needed an unprecedented experience I could neither question nor deny. I reached over and touched Gertie's hand. Then in awkward silence, we both pulled away from each other.

"You and I are a lot alike," she said in her woman-of-the-world voice. She filled her hands with some playing cards. "We have a wild card in our nature and it makes us loners. We need to figure things out for ourselves."

Gertie was wrong about us. We both had lost our way, but we were not loners. No one is ever alone. "I may be sick," I confessed. My words startled even me. Words that bubbled up from my unconscious had ended up on my lips.

"So that's what this is all about," and she threw her cards down on the table where they splayed and formed a collage of the Virgo Constellation on the tabletop.

"Sometimes, in the middle of the night, I wake up terrified and feel as if I can't breathe."

"Have you seen a doctor?"

"I was going to but—"

"See a doctor, Jane."

"I don't want to lose my physical heart."

"Take charge. Put things off and all your options will fast fade like words off a multidex screen."

Gertie was right. I promised to call a doctor the following morning. Poppy got up from under my chair and rubbed against my leg. Tonight we were comrades in spirit. I felt as shitty as Poppy's backside.

****

The next day I contacted the Sandusky Clinic and spoke with a disembodied voice that arranged my appointment. The next week, when I arrived at the clinic, the staff was robotically upbeat and clinically polite. I sat around a drafty room for two hours, dressed in a blue seersucker gown and brown paper slippers, waiting to undergo an interior body scan, a blood screening, and an iridic scan. Right before my tests, I went through a short, impersonal probing and poking session with a real doctor who seemed to have no name. For twenty minutes, I sat inside an ancient scanner waiting for a mobile android to attach some contact pads to my chest as I breathed in the smell of minty glue. Inside the humming scanner, I kept thinking about the millions of bodies stored in cryogenic chambers. I wondered if they would suggest this option to me if I were going to die from something for which no cure existed. I wondered about emerging in a hundred or even a thousand years to some different world, but knew postponing my life could not change my reality. Truth hit like a hammer against an anvil and I knew my remaining days, be they five minutes or fifty years had to be lived through the energy of my physical heart.

For the blood tests, no Humans were involved. Humans had learned a long time before, the hard way, that blood was the most dangerous of bodily fluids. An automated cart ferried me to the hematology unit where I awaited a robotic phlebotomist, to roll in and take my blood. The left limb of the robot was a claw-like device for holding an arm in place and out of the right limb popped a hypodermic syringe. The claw took my arm and held it in place and I was surprised because the touch was warm. It said, "Relax, one, two, three, little prick," and deftly punctured the vein on the inside on my left elbow.

I clenched my teeth and said, "You would think, after all these years, someone would have invented something easier than this." The robot jiggled slightly when I said that. Perhaps it was old and needed servicing or was adhering to its robotic protocol. If it had sentient implants, it might even have resented that something better than it might cause its demise. A moment later, it held up two vials of dark, red blood. A compartment opened on its leg-like bottom and the used syringe dropped off and disappeared into an incinerator. Then another compartment opened on its belly where it stored and analyzed the two vials of blood.

In the fifth floor ophthalmology unit, the iridic scan took only a moment of holding still. I had no time to become bored. I found the February issue of the Universal Geographic in the delivery box when I arrived home. I ignored my work and spent a pleasant afternoon watching a holospool about a Ganat research team studying the genetic mutations on a newly discovered planet, Herculean.

Two

Three weeks later, a message from Dr. Patel popped up on my multidex. Up to then, I assumed no news was good news; however, when I read, "Contact Patel's office for your test results as soon as possible," my worst fears ballooned into a nightmare. Then in a startling premonition, the multidex screen went black and little starbursts from my screen saver flickered as Gertie's words echoed inside my head. "Wait too long and all your options will fast fade like words off a multidex screen." I promptly made an appointment for the following day and that night I did not sleep. I was afraid to take a neoanodyne because I knew Doctor Patel would not approve of my liberal self-dosing of tranquilizers. That night, I lay in bed pretending to sleep, trying to fool myself into believing I was resting. Up at dawn, I shuffled around the pod for hours. Throughout the day, the message screen flickered a few times and I knew Gertie was attempting to check on me but I ignored everything filtering through the multidex. At 15:00, I swallowed two theobromine tablets to perk me up for the long trip into downtown Toledo. Twenty minutes later, reality rocketed into fast-forward.

By 16:00, I was nervously waiting at the traveltube station for the train to downtown Toledo. Trains were running on schedule so I arrived at Patel's office early. Patel was running late, so I waited another forty-five minutes while my legs jumped up and down from the effects of the theobromine.

****

When Dr. Patel and I met face to face, he was entrenched behind a wide desk and a thick black mustache. He neither looked at me nor spoke directly to me. He merely kept clicking from one screen to the next on his multidex as he scanned my life-file. I felt strange and disconnected as if Jane

Hibernia Smith was somebody else. Yet I was my panic. Every small body movement produced a thousand shocks that pulsed through my arms, legs, and neck. *All this is my fault. I could have changed things. Now it's too late.* I sat there second-guessing my life waiting for the bad news to come out of his mouth. *I could have accepted that position as chief cartographer for that small company on Calypso last year. A long time ago, I could have become an artist instead of a cartographer. I could have married Tom Sellers eleven years ago. How different things would be if I were able to have a child. Now my options are on fast fade.*

Patel played with the wisps of his mustache. He looked smug and calm fortressed behind his desk. He was genetically correct and was not dying in the near future. "You say you are tired?" he questioned.

"I have trouble sleeping."

"Tell me about it," he said. The tone of his voice reflected thinly veiled sarcasm. It was another way of saying, so fucking what! "Your body scan and blood screening are perfectly normal."

"That's good. How's my heart?"

"So far, you're heart seems stable."

"Then why am I experiencing chest pains?"

"I think you might be experiencing a mild case of FSP that can be easily controlled with proper medication." Then he started talking about a new drug called Somatime that was being used to treat FSP."

Fuck Somatime! I thought, and all of a sudden I felt almost giddy. "Then I'm still okay?"

"I do have some concerns about your stress levels," Patel continued. "Stress can be a real detriment to someone with your genetic history. Your iridic scan shows a deterioration of responses between certain neurons, suggesting possible synapse stress."

"Is that serious?"

"Get more rest, more exercise, and eat a balanced diet. That's about all." Dr. Patel leaned forward in his chair and looked sincere in a well-rehearsed gesture he had mastered in front of a mirror in medical school. "I see you have a history of suicide in your family. If personal problems are arising from your Casual status, the Sandusky Clinic has an excellent staff of therapists."

"My family does not have a history of suicide," I insisted, defending every Smith since time immemorial.

"Your records state that your mother took her own life—is this information incorrect?"

"Extenuating circumstances existed in her case."

"With your family history and your genetic contamination, coupled with the fact that you are mildly FSP, please consider the staff at the Sandusky Clinic." Moving to the edge of my seat, I anticipated my first opportunity to escape but I already knew it was not going to be easy. Patel had some weird theories that he was trying to apply to me. He droned on, his voice lacking the peaks and valleys of spontaneous and authentic feeling. "The mind can be a bridge or a barrier. It's up to you, but deny the body or deny the mind and the weaker of the two will create trouble. It's a fundamental law of our Human state that the weakest link of a chain breaks first. For many, the weakest link is their body while for others it is the mind. Your pain does not come from your body therefore it must come from your mind."

"Are you telling me the physical pain I've experienced for the past four months has been an illusion?"

"I'm merely suggesting your mind is stronger than your body. I suggest you pay attention to your physical problems while you still have options." There was that word again. Options! Was this a conspiracy?

****

Escaping from Dr. Patel's office, I wandered around the downtown area of Toledo. I could not go home, not yet. Tonight, the city lights and vacant crumbling buildings, remnants from another time, were badly needed diversions. For a while, the dirty old city helped me forget that I had a body with a genetic flaw and an abusive mind.

The streets were almost empty. At the corner of Cherry and Huron, a small group of Naub street people blocked the walkway in front of an electronics store. The Naubs were a study in uniformity, dressed in the same drab texoplex bodystockings. Their pale, stringy hair and pasty complexions suggested they all belonged to the same genetic family. Their one point of individual joy seemed to be the pride they took in the tooling work on their utility belts. All their life's possessions dangled from these belts, combs, knives, talismans, a cup and skillet.

I stopped for a few minutes and watched the simulated image of Ramjet writhe to his latest kakos hit. The few lyrics I understood meant little to nothing to me. "Ate-your-meat-now-I'm-insane! Fucked-your-clones-into-daisy-chains! Breathe-in-my-rust. Jerk-off-my-lust. Chomp-my-pain, licking-at-my-lips. What's-new? Ratu! Meat-from-the-sun-we're-done-with-you. Irradiating-is-fun-without-the-sun. Vegetables! Vegetables! Vegetables!" Kakos music was android music, but it was extremely popular with bios that liked its adrenaline pumping energy. I could only guess its effect on androids when they plugged their wrists into the kakos source.

One block from the southwest traveltube, at Walnut and Superior, was a bar called the Pink Slipper. A larger-than-life slipper danced across a screen over the door. I walked by this place every time I came into Toledo. Tonight, I went inside because I was cold and wanted a drink before the trip home. It was early evening and the Pink Slipper was almost empty. A couple sat in a rear booth drinking fortified Martian ale and laughing. The woman's breasts jutted out like prehistoric Titan rockets beneath a red texoplex halter-top. Her left hand was busy massaging her companion's genitals through the open fly of his pants. Every so often, the man's head wobbled on his neck and kept landing in the valley between her breasts. Then she would giggle softly.

An ancient Tyrowsian android sat in the rear corner playing an upright piano. He tinkled the keys in a sad, bluesy kind of way and began singing a song about his reprogramming. "Got-the-process-down, then-I-swallow-my-pill. Makes-no-difference, 'cause-I-lost-my-will. Got-the-lowdown, lowdown, past-live-blues." The place had the atmosphere I needed, the android singing songs from another century about when he was new, the drunks, and the bartender with a paunch, who looked more real than anyone I had seen in a decade. I wanted to stop, at least for a while, and wallow in the comfort of this particular Pink Slipper.

"Evenin', what'll it be?" asked the bartender.

"Got any Pavlovian wine?" I wondered aloud.

"Sure, right next to the Dom P'erignon."

"Well what do you have that won't make me sick?"

"The usual, beer, some nice pink Chablis for the ladies. Got some pretty good Venunition distilled for the hardcore."

"I'm in the mood for something different, something aged with a bit of forethought."

He paused before speaking. "What the Hell! A sweet young face, such as yours, always brings out my generous side." He didn't even attempt to sound sincere, merely enthusiastic. "I think I may have what you are searching for, but it'll cost you—50 credits a drink." I winced but agreed to pay the price. I needed an instant cure, a painkiller; and wanted to believe in something, be it meager or vapid as alcoholic spirits. From under the bar, he retrieved a bottle whose label was sepia with age. "Bushmill's Irish whiskey, it's hard to get nowadays. Probably not even a thousand bottles exist anywhere in the Spur. Guaranteed; my personal stock."

He poured the liquor into a small whiskey glass as if it were a sacrament. When I tasted it, the heat from the amber resin trickled down my throat warming all the way to my belly. Irish whiskey was a taste from ancient times when Ireland was as remote as the Andromeda Galaxy. I took another sip and the spirit of the Irish whiskey seemed to move into my head. The old Tyrowsian android began singing a sad song about a lost life as a taxicab driver on the planet Calypso. Then I began to wonder, something I had been doing a lot of late. Then suddenly, I was ordering another Bushmill's Irish whiskey.

Around ten o'clock, the business at the Pink Slipper picked up, mostly singles straggled in, searching for other singles. The desperation was thick in the air as the couples quickly paired-off and exited into the dark, February night. By then, I was floating along on the golden vapors of Irish whiskey and spent a third of my month's salary on getting as drunk as possible. I felt remote from everything, as if I was a thin whiff of smoke hovering near the ceiling. Then the spicy scent of tartan ratu wafted over my left shoulder and interrupted my private party. Tartan ratu is a sticky, curry-colored powder that users most often dab under the nose for a quick fix. Ratu is illegal in many places, which makes it all the more desirable for those who want it. I tried it a few times, back when I was a regular at the clubs. The drug doesn't last long; but it makes anyone who is convenient look sexually attractive for about twenty minutes.

Le odour de tartan ratu grew stronger as someone touched my back and then leaned over my shoulder. "Buy me dink, sugaree?" asked the pleasure prince. This pleasure prince was a long way from home, speaking in the patois of Old Ulsha Bramanth of the Kulupan System. Its sharp little nose made it appear birdlike and its cosmetically modified ears protruded like convenient little handles and made me wonder about possibilities. Its long, waist length hair was tightly plaited and pulled into a ponytail-type arrangement like Tyrowsian females favored, but this pleasure prince was no Tyrowsian female. It was impossible to tell the race of humanoids it belonged to because of the extensive body modifications. It tossed its hair from side to side making sure the hair touched my cheek. Two ritualistic chevron scars dominated its left cheek advertising that it could swing both ways. "Buy me dinkee, we pigeonhole all nightee?" it pouted.

I longed to say something caustic and nasty, something clever, but I froze in fascination. The pleasure prince leaned against my back and the scent of ratu grew overwhelming. "Please go away," I said feeling like a complete fool. Vines of neediness crawled up my neck and I was on the verge of going down a path I knew I would regret.

"Don't be nasty," it cooed. "Make Human mama happy. Tres grand, fill you up!"

The bartender interrupted with, "Piss off or I'll call the streetguards." The threat of streetguards made the pleasure prince vanish without another word. "Sorry," said the bartender and he paid careful attention to the way he cleaned the bar in front of me. "We get a lot of prostitutes and itinerants in this area 'cause we're so close to the traveltube."

"I need to get going," I said. "What's the damage?"

"Stick around, the evening is young. Anyone annoys you again; you give me a holler. Name's Bryan. Have another drink, this one's on me. Around 11:00 o'clock, the fortuneteller usually drops in and makes her rounds. You definitely don't want to miss Bell." I stayed and he poured me my fourth. I did not want to go out on the street alone, not until I got the smell of tartan ratu out of my nostrils.

Tonight the fortuneteller was early, arriving just before 11:00 o'clock. "Over here," Bryan yelled as she visited the tables and booths looking for business. "I have a customer that needs your guidance. What's your name?"

Bryan asked for the first time.

Besotted, I felt brave. "Hibernia; my name is Hibernia."

"Well, Hibernia, I'd like you to meet Bell. She's a real Trinity witch and a fortuneteller extraordinaire." Bell was a Gathosian from one of the nine hundred planets making up the Island Worlds of Gathos System. Her hands were three-fingered with opposing thumbs and her eyes were blue-black with golden shafts intersecting through her irises. Everything about her was dark and swishy, from the rustle of her green skirts to the tinkle of the crystal beads adorning her raven hair.

"I've resigned from the Trinity order," said Bell. "But I retain the psychic gift and I can interpret The Cards."

I asked, "How much?"

She held up two fingers on one of her four-fingered hands and told me, "Twenty credits."

As my financial nest egg took another hit, I thought, this better be good.

"Let's go to the rear where we won't be disturbed," she suggested and we ended up sitting in the same booth the passionate drunks occupied earlier. Bell cleansed the energy around the table by crossing her graceful hands with a dramatic sweeping motion. She laid down a red silk scarf where she placed the cards. In a half-drunken whimsy, I had a quirky notion that it would be sufficiently odd if she read my fortune with only a portion of the deck. "Are you going to asked me to cut the cards?" I asked.

"At the proper time," she replied and she continued shuffling the cards better with eight fingers than Gertie did with ten. Bell finally handed me the cards and instructed me to arrange them into three separate piles.

I laid down one pile then handed Bell the remaining cards. "Forget about these cards. Read the cards on the table."

"Are you a witch?" she asked.

I laughed and said, "Sure, I'm a bitch of a witch."

"It's my duty to point out that you are limiting your options before you know what they are."

"Sounds like life to me."

"Fine, we'll do it your way." The deck was the ancient Trinity tarot, the deck Trinity witches claim emanates from The Source of All Knowing, the New Delphi Crystal. As Belle began to turn over the first few cards, she made little sucking sounds between her teeth and lips. "This spread is difficult. Do you see what you've pulled—all Major Arcana cards? How did you accomplish such a trick?"

"Maybe you simply did a lousy job shuffling the deck."

"Not so!" She thumped her breast. "I'm an experienced card handler. So be it! I bow to the wisdom of the New Delphi Crystal. Listen to me carefully, my child. With only Major Arcana cards in this layout, the cards wish to relate their message in the strongest possible terms. See the card in the center, the High Priestess. This card is your destiny; the path of the High Priestess rules your life. One who draws the High Priestess knows innately how to draw divine light and strength. Gifts from the High Priestess include psychic powers, creativity, and finally great wisdom. You are blessed and destined to be the handmaiden of the Essential Heart."

Whatever the Essential Heart was, I doubted that it took Casuals for handmaidens. I did not ask Bell for details because details would have set free the devils of doubt in my mind. The amber waves of my Irish whiskey intoxication softened all her words until they disappeared in the sand.

She pointed to a card with a red-lacquered fingernail. "This card is The Tower, which represents your past. The Tower brings ruin and destruction and in your case, a curse. Look at it this way. Your Tower has fallen and you stand unshielded, perhaps for the first time in your life. Do not despair because The High Priestess tells me that you have the divine energy to recreate your life in any way you want." Bell picked up another card, the Wheel of Fortune, and her voice assumed an exclamatory air. "Your future awaits! It will lift you up; take you with it. Wherever you end up, I cannot predict but I do see you taking a long trip to a faraway place. Yes! I see it clearly now in your Wheel of Fortune. You will go farther than any Human has ever gone before."

"Fortunetellers are always predicting someone is going to take a trip, but your prediction is quite a stretch."

"You are the one who selected the cards," she reasoned without humor. She moved to the next cards and said, "These three cards are convergence cards which indicate the archetypal influences that are the parameters of your present challenge. You drew Angel of Aesculapius, Daedalus of Wings, and The Empress. Aesculapius is the symbol of healing and rebirth, a card of both passion and compassion. The energy of Aesculapius circulates around ancient souls and gives them the knowledge to sooth the most abject sufferers. The Daedalus card is a younger card, a card of the mind. Daedalus attracts curious souls, endowing them with ingenuity and skill. The third card is The Empress, a symbol of fertility, bounty, compassion, an enriching symbol of The Mother. Is motherhood a role you aspire to?"

My face flushed hot but I said not one word. Sober or drunk, talking about reproduction depressed me.

"Your final card is The Hierophant, which indicates the probable outcome from the proper assimilation of the archetypal convergent cards. The Hierophant is the masculine form of The Empress and sits on a throne between two spiritual beings, which are of course, The Angel of Aesculapius and Daedalus of Wings. Notice the two crossed keys before The Hierophant. This is pure blessing, grace in its highest form, the gift to expound ancient Mysteries. If you follow this path, you will learn to interpret sacred texts and understand esoteric principles."

"What does that mean?"

"It means you have a great deal of free will at your disposal."

"Free will, that's the best joke I've heard in a month of Sundays." What was the use of free will if I did not know what to do with it?

With that, the efficient Bell collected her cards. She carried a small scanner in her handbag and promptly subtracted twenty credit points from my account. She winked at me and said, "I gave you a huge discount. In time, you'll realize how much you owe me." Then she got up and left me there with my free will and the rest of my life to live.

I returned to the bar to settle my bill and Bryan appeared friendly and eager. "What did she predict?" he asked.

"The usual, I'm going to take a long journey. The only thing she didn't promise was I'd get rich anytime soon."

The trip home went fast. A thick fog of Bushmill's swaddled my brain. It was past 2:00 a.m. when I curled up in my chilly bed. The strangeness of the day puzzled me as the bed warmed and I drifted off toward sleep. I experienced a short snippet of a dream where I saw another person pretending to be me. *Who are you? I demanded.*

I'm Hibernia and I'm back, said the stranger.

Good, I told her. Your fortune has to be better than mine is.

****

The February tempest howled and groaned. I snuggled deeper under the bedcovers, but could not get back to sleep. My eyes were dry and it was impossible to focus as my head reeled with a hangover. Slowly and gingerly, I crawled out of bed and prepared to face the consequences. I brewed a cup of tea and took it with me to the multidex. The multidex sensed me near and chirped, "Top of the mornin'," in an Irish brogue that I programmed into the system months earlier.

"Access, Atlas Map," I replied.

"Password?" it asked in its merry Irish lilt. I sat down and typed in, "AzimuthOSP3467."

"Have a nice day, Jane," flashed on the screen in crescendo nonsense, getting larger and larger until it filled the screen. I watched the flashing, "JANE, JANE, JANE," and felt like vomiting. That's when I remembered the dream and suddenly reality flipped me and I felt as if I was standing on my head. Jane's memories were there; but Jane, the tenacious little trooper was gone. I sat my teacup down and stared at my hands on the multidex keys. Unknown fingers extended from my arms. I waited for them to do their job, but nothing happened. Jane was no longer there to do the work and I felt disoriented and unsure. Hibernia spoke up inside me suggesting a change of scenery would be nice. *You have six weeks of vacation coming that you can take anytime you want,* she reminded me.

But I'm supposed to give two months' notice if I want to take it.

Silly girl, she giggled. *Write a memo to Wantanabi. Tell him you need to take time off for your health.*

While Jane was busy questioning her integrity, Hibernia was composing a letter to Mr. Wantanabi, explaining the situation. Hibernia even promised a letter of confirmation, forthcoming from the Sandusky Clinic, a decision that seemed risky to methodical Jane. After Hibernia wrote the lie in black and white, Jane entered the number code for Mr. Wantanabi and Hibernia sent the letter. *This is easy,* Hibernia declared and she kept pushing. She brazenly called up United Spaceways to check for flights leaving Toledo in the next forty-eight hours. The screen confirmed there were two, one for Mars, and one for Earth's moon. *Please advise about interconnecting tours between Moon and Wonder World,* she typed with lightning speed.

A window for Tricomet Tours flashed open. As Hibernia pressed the forward key, the multidex delivered its pellets of gratification. Wonder World, in flash-freeze frames, sold itself. The cheerful male voice behind the pictures proclaimed, "Yes indeed! Why not join us at Wonder World, the planet of continual pleasure for the young at heart? We have package tours to suit everyone's budget." Hibernia soared. This was all so easy for her. Within seconds, she determined that plenty of seats were available on the Moon shuttle and a few seats left on the Wonder World Tour.

I leaned back in my seat and switched to voice command. "Confirm," I said, helping Hibernia in her madness. I gave Tricomet my number code and within thirty seconds, I had my escape route planned.

Confirmed for flight 558, February 29, depart Chicago, Earth—14:10 CST—arrive Earth Moon, 5:00 MT—onward bound, flight 01 for Aeternus Space Station—onward bound, flight 45—932.593 cycles—arrival Wonder World 16:10 WWST. Account for J.SmithOSP3467 debited 3000 Earth credits.

Not prepared to take full responsibility for my behavior, I nevertheless, packed two suitcases with clothing, trusting something I scarcely considered. I switched off the multidex for the first time in ten years. When the multidex was black and lifeless, the pod seemed stagnant with old reminders from the past. I was anxious to go now as if a window had opened just for a moment and I had to go before the reminders pulled me back into the stagnation. I was afraid to tell Gertie what I was doing. She would try to talk me out of this madness. Still, I couldn't leave without a word and I found myself crossing the wind-blown courtyard and knocking on her door. "Where have you been since yesterday afternoon? And what's that?" she asked, pointing to my suitcase.

"I've decided to go away for a few days."

Her expression changed to a look of concern, her bottom lip dropping slightly into its typical way and her shoulders rounding forward. "What did your doctor say?"

"He said I needed a vacation so I'm taking a few days off. I took care of everything with Atlas. Here's my keycard in case you need to get into my pod."

"Like for what?"

"I don't know; something might go wrong."

"With you?"

"No, not with me, something might go wrong here—water pipes might burst from the cold or the roof might blow off in this windstorm that seems to be gaining in strength."

"Oh, I see! I guess I'm supposed to stay here and handle your crisis while you go off somewhere having fun on a holiday."

"On second thought, forget about it Gertie. If the water pipes burst, let the water flow. I don't give a damn if the entire pod park floats out into the middle of Lake Erie." I backed off her porch. Gertie and I glared at each other for another defiant moment. "Okay, you have my number if you need to talk to me. I'll see you—when I get back." I could have handled it better, but I was sure Gertie would not understand Hibernia. Hibernia was like Buddy, footloose. Hibernia kept urging me forward, advising me to escape while I was still alive.

****

The next few hours, I felt like an escaped convict. Taking the express traveltube into Chicago's O'Hare Spaceport, I waited for two hours to board the Moon shuttle. I wore dark glasses thinking someone I knew might see me and send me home in disgrace. Of course, this was ridiculous; but my heart was racing with the thrill of escape.

When I boarded the moon shuttle, my spirit soared. Inside my head, choirs of angels sang in exaltation, "HALLELUJAH, HALLELUJAH, EN EXCELSIA HIBERNIA." Today was the twenty-ninth day of February, leap day, and I had taken the biggest leap of my life, right off the planet Earth. Everything felt new and exciting and I peered out the little porthole next to my seat as I left Earth behind. I could see the same winter storm from space that awoke me that morning at the Erie Pod Park.

Up the shuttle went through the towering cumulus clouds and I lost sight of Earth. An instant came of breaking through and a sudden dose of golden sunlight burned through the clouds and cured my chronic depression. Up we continued through the gradually thinning layers of translucent blue toward the darkness. In those timeless moments, the sacred sky was mine. After several minutes, the contour of Earth was visible and the crusty, craggy beauty of the topography unfolded. Earth had suffered so much through the centuries and yet from the exosphere, she still appeared primeval. The greater my perspective, the more Earth crystallized until she turned translucent like a cabochon floating on the black throat of God.

I knew then that my life could be more than my snaillike crawling over the flat, prosaic surface of the American Midwest. The trajectory of the shuttle arced and I lost sight of Earth for the first time. My umbilicus severed, all I could see was deep space. A wave of vertigo washed over me and I was stunned and awed by the depth of the blackness beyond. SPACE IS, said a voice in a cosmic announcement. No words, pictures, or holograms can capture the essence of that moment of separation, that casting-off toward cosmic freedom. I was riding in a mechanical contraption flying at the speed of 21,000 nautical miles per hour while I sat inside in perfect comfort and witnessed the grandeur of our universe. I deemed myself blessed by this opportunity to witness and experience more than my conscious mind could ever grasp or understand. My heart never stopped pounding the entire way to Earth's moon.

****

Tranquility City, Moon was a sprawling network of thousands of connecting structures nestled in the mouse-gray regolith of the surface. Gagarin Spaceport was the largest single complex in the Solar System. The center of the fifty-story-high, five-kilometer-wide structure was a dome that alternately opened and closed like a camera lens. Every few minutes the dome lens would wink open and swallow dozens of spacecraft waiting for clearance. Landing was different without gravity. We floated down into the belly of Gagarin and the ceiling resealed with our shuttle inside.

"Welcome to Gargarin," said the feminine voice simulator. Suddenly, I felt the different gravity of being on Earth's moon. "Please stay in your seats, until Gargarin gravity control is complete." Then, a light flashed yellow—then red along with the announcement, "gravitational adjustment complete."

I made it! Something like enlightenment, like being born, like an orgasm rushed up my spine and I felt more alive than I had in years. I knew something I had not known before. I had spent boring years of my life clinically mapping featureless craters, seas of nothingness I thought was Earth's moon. I never knew the moon, not until my five senses experienced the moon for themselves.

It was 4:00 a.m. moon time. I had one hour to locate Tricomet Tours and make my connection for Aeternus Space Station. I yearned to go to the observation deck and gaze back toward Earth, but did not have enough time. My life was accelerating on fast-forward and I was a traveler on my way to somewhere else. It was not exactly smooth sailing at Tricomet. I soon discovered the shuttle to Aeternus left thirty-two minutes before I arrived on the moon. The droid behind the Tricomet nametag said, "The multidex made an error in your reservation. You still have plenty of options. Option one; you can stay on the moon and Tricomet will book you into the Dark Side Hilton, which we now are offering at special discount rates. Option two; you can return to Earth and Tricomet will refund the tour portion of your trip. Option three; Tricomet will arrange for a space taxi to take you to a rendezvous point where the Morpheus shuttle can pick you up."

"What about option four?"

"There is no option four," said the droid.

"Damn! What do people do at the Dark Side Hilton?"

"Observe the stars. If you need time to decide, please step aside so I can assist someone else." Four people standing in line behind me were fidgeting in impatience.

"Wait a minute. I guess; let me see; okay, I'll take—option three."

At first, the space taxi sounded like an okay idea. Then I stepped into a vehicle that appeared about as sturdy as a flying egg. Inside, the three-meter enclosure, a very basic console sat between two banquettes on either side. When I realized no other living soul would be aboard but me, I wondered if I should have taken option number one, the Dark Side Hilton. The Tricomet personnel assured me that they used space taxis all the time and I would be perfectly safe. When they eventually convinced me that I was, "as safe as if you were sitting in your own home," I settled aboard.

****

The taxi door squeezed shut and the console came alive. A voice simulator informed me, in the most liquid and honey of voices, that my trip would take a little over four hours, at which time I would rendezvous with the Morpheus shuttle. "Please help yourself to snacks, drinks, and accept, with our compliments, a carton of champagne, located in the minifrig drawer below," and it projected a hologram to show me the proper drawer. "Have a splendid trip!"

Gazing out the tiny porthole, I wished I had brought some of my star charts. The star patterns were changing quickly and after a time, it was impossible to determine where I was or where I was going. I opened the gratis carton of pink champagne and turned on some entertainment that was available through the console. The champagne tasted like the Chablis Gertie and I drank on Sunday afternoons, except this wine had bubbles. After a couple of glasses, it tasted like water and the slight bit of inebriation I experienced made the time go faster. I selected a concert that featured an artist named Amtaee Htsoiure from the planet Euterpe in Apollo Muse Gathering. Amtaee played these fantastic BIG DRUMS, the kind that make sound echo off the heart. The sounds and rhythms of his music reverberated off the walls of the taxi for over an hour. After drinking two-thirds of the carton of champagne, I felt tipsy.

Amtaee began a song called, "Jungle Midnight," and he danced through the air and snaked his way toward me. "At-midnight, a-bweha-stocks-its-prey," he sang. He came so close to me that I could see every detail of his face and his sinewy, cocoa-colored skin. A dewy sweat glistened across his upper lip from his exertions at the drums. His long lean body moved like an undulating coil as he danced through the air. At one point, he put his lips on mine; but I felt nothing. Still, the visual seemed to testify to his reality. "Come-my-love, hold-me-by-the-fire. We-can-chase-the-night-away." I reached up and put my hand through empty space to convince myself that he was not real. The spool stopped and the room went dark before brightening again with the cabin lights. A few minutes later, I heard a subtle change in the engines and peered out the porthole, but it was impossible to tell if the taxi was moving or standing still. I began to worry about Tricomet's competency and quality control and then I remembered how Tricomet stranded Gertie and me in Mumbai for three days in a marginal hotel. No Morpheus shuttle appeared and I started poking around through the compartments and drawers on the console where I found a plastic knife, an obsolete map of Earth's moon published by the Atlas Map Company, and a pair of woman's black lacy underwear. Under the underwear, I discovered a keychain strung with seven cardkeys. One was labeled, "Emergency access." I waited two hours more before definitely deciding it was time to call for help. The console had seven card slots in the main drawer. One by one, I tried each slot with the emergency access card. The voice simulator responded each time with, "Improper card, try coffee card," then, "Improper card, try waste disposal card."

I eyed the last slot but obstacles continued. The final slot was jammed with another card. I retrieved the plastic knife from the drawer and pried the old card out of the slot. It took a half-hour of careful maneuvering before the slot was clear and would accept the emergency access card. When I inserted the card, something activated and a new row of touchpads lit up inside the drawer. The display consisted of a series of letter codes with no explanation about what any of them meant. My anger flared. "Damn it!" Clenching my teeth, I put my fingertip on the touchpad marked "EA," which I hoped meant "emergency access." Nothing happened. "It didn't work!" I panicked. Then I began pushing every damn touchpad on the screen. I heard or saw nothing that indicated that I had activated anything that made a difference.

Between the seventh and eighth hour of waiting, I alternated between pacing and peering out the porthole and retrying every touchpad on the console. Meanwhile, I was adrift in a frozen world of silence. I felt exhausted; but forced myself to stay awake. Around the sixteenth hour, I realized I truly was lost in the Tricomet shuffle. Perhaps the multidex had dumped my ticket. All I knew was, somewhere down the line, someone would blame someone else until the multidex took the ultimate blame. I pictured myself as a playing card lost under the table. No one was going to pick me up this time. Nobody needed me to play any game of life. That was painfully obvious now. All my bitter cynicism rushed back to claim me and I knew the joke was still on me. At a time when I was determined to break free of my limited mold, something was short-circuiting my escape plan. Was this my curse? Perhaps Bell was right for even the gutsy Hibernia could not figure out how to get me out of this predicament.

A sinister picture of my fate crystallized in my mind. I was supposed to die out here. A meaningless life begets a meaningless death. Was this my punishment for wasting my life, to die alone in space? No one would miss me because no one cared. Perhaps a few neighbors at the Erie Pod Park would ask, "It's odd, why did Jane leave Earth without telling anyone?" It would be a passing curiosity. Nevertheless, I almost won, or rather, Hibernia almost won. Where was Hibernia now? Nobody but my bewildered questioner was awake to wonder what had gone wrong. I pulled the seat cushions off the banquette and plopped them on the floor. Sinking down between the seats, I began to fall asleep. *Let her die as she lived*, said a smug voice which caused my body to jump.

THREE

My eyes opened to the sight of a crystal sphere of light hovering over me. A pulsating, amber wand emerged from the sphere, and came straight for my face. I panicked and thought to scream, but before the scream emerged from my throat, the wand touched me, causing a blissful tingle of energy that exploded inside my chest. The crystal sphere expanded encapsulating me within it, with the sphere's master. "Don't be afraid," said the mesmerizing beautiful face floating over me.

The eyes were bright as sapphires. The face was both handsome and beautiful. The body was slim and muscular and the skin was pale with a pearly glow of health. The long loose hair was nearly white and reminded me of the way moonlight shimmers across Lake Erie on cold winter nights. "Are you an angel?" I asked with some trepidation.

"My name is Doctor Sante," said the angel. "Captain Jana Cle and I operate the rescue ship *Daedalus* for Orion Spur Space Security here in Daleth Sector."

"I'm in Daleth Sector? How did I get way over here?"

"I don't know but we picked up your distress signal about six hours ago and, it seems, we arrived just in time. Oxygen levels were down to roughly twelve percent in here." The mention of the security ships of the OSSS rang a bell. Once I had seen a UG holospool concerning the OSSS rescue ships. In my fuzzy state of mind, I remembered only that these rescue ships had something to do with promoting goodwill among various Orion Spur humanoids.

I continued to babble like an infant. "Then I guess I'm still alive." Tears of relief erupted from my eyes and began meandering down my cheeks.

"You're safe," said Sante with a reassuring smile. "I'm going to deactivate the vitarattha now. Do you think you can stand up?"

"What's a vitarattha?"

"The energetic sphere around us is a vitarattha. Don't worry; hold onto me and I will support you until you can stand upright." Sante touched a medallion affixed to his/her black uniform and the crystal sphere around us vanished. I was standing but crouched in confusion as I dabbed at my teary eyes with a tissue. "What's your name?" asked Sante.

"I'm Jane Hibernia Smith OSP3467 from Earth." I apologized. "I'm sorry for crying. I'm grateful you found me."

"We found each other."

"We did? If I knew I was going to find you, I would have put some effort into how I look."

That perfect androgynous face smiled and said, "Why? You look perfectly beautiful to me." It was a magnanimous statement from someone that extraordinarily handsome. Sante helped dry my tears and said, "From the remote fingertip planets to the inner megalopolis of this galaxy everyone knows that tears wash the soul clean."

Amazed, I saw authentic hope in Sante's eyes and was fascinated and suspended in an ocean of their warmth. It was then that I realized that Sante could not be this perfect and still be real. Part of me started demanding that I define this person's mortality, species, and sexuality, but the more I searched for those distinctions, the more shaded the boundaries became. I put all my itching curiosity on hold because things started happening quickly when Sante spoke into an instrument attached to his/her wrist. "*App-twa taha**," Peering through the porthole of the taxi, I saw an ellipsoid spaceship creeping toward us. Its shiny silver surface emitted light that appeared to be bouncing off the taxi.

"Your ship is beautiful," I said.

Sante looked out the porthole over my shoulder. "Beauty is the sideshow. *Daedalus* is communicating with the taxi, explaining the problem, and advising it to power down. Don't worry; it's merely a precaution." With that, the *Daedalus* closed in on the taxi, opened its bottom mouth, and swallowed us in one neat gulp.

Sante picked up the spacesuit on the floor behind me and I asked, "Did you space walk from your ship to this taxi in that flimsy space suit?"

"Yes I did. As for the space suit, it's lightweight, but not flimsy."

"Open space seems exceptionally precarious to me."

"You have good instincts." The smile deepened. "However, nothing dangerous was involved in this particular rescue. This was a great pleasure, a short dance through a few meters of open space. And look what I found, Jane Hibernia Smith."

*"pick up okay"; language origin, Cuneate

Together

The watch-like instrument on Sante's arm spoke. *"Appa-twa secot*,"* said a remote voice in return. Sante continued to smile, acting as if happiness was a natural state of affairs. The airlock opened but the taxi had no stairs, and the distance to the floor of the *Daedalus* below was at least three meters. Like a graceful feline, this amazing being leapt the three meters with ease. Then I saw the other one, the one Sante called Captain Jana Cle, staring up at me from the floor of the *Daedalus*. The appearance was so much like Sante's that they had to be either twins or clones. Yet, this new one had a sturdier and more muscular appearance. Despite the masculine façade, the general appearance was more elaborate and more effeminate. Hundreds of small aurora-crystal beads entwined through the pale plaits of his/her long hair. It was in that moment that my mind attempted to override my confusion and decided that Sante must be the female and that this quasi twin was the male. The twin and I stared intently at each other for a moment. On his part, it was an intense, probing stare, full of questions and intellect. In the next moment, I witnessed the incredible. In one superman-like bound, the twin jumped from the floor below to a place next to me in the doorway of the taxi. The being greeted me in Cuneate with, *"Qualmerrie."*

"How did you do that?" I pointed to the floor below.

"Reduced gravity. Welcome aboard the *OSSS Daedalus*. I'm Captain Jana Cle. Do you have a number or a name?" This new OSSS rescuer seemed all business and I understood exactly what the question meant. It was a polite way of inquiring if I was a bio or artificial intelligence.

"Jane Hibernia Smith OSP3467 from Earth," I supplied and my mouth went right back to gaping in astonishment. "What planet are you and Sante from?" I managed to ask. Proper etiquette had decided ages ago that it was okay to ask, "Where are you from?" but everyone still considered it impolite to ask, "Are you bio, biodroid, or android?" That's why people used all kinds of euphemisms such as, "Do you have a number or a name?"

"Sante and I are from Aeternus Complex," said Captain Cle.

"You speak Universal like an Earth native."

"Thanks," and he showed me a clever smile and some impressive white teeth. Jana Cle went to the console of the taxi and began fiddling with the touchpads. Within seconds, he had access to the taxi's guidance system.

Pondering these two space jockeys, I thought, *Now I get it!* Everything about them screamed advanced genetic artistry. They certainly were not Casuals, created from genes that dominate the biological stewpot. I began imagining their creator. Standing before me was an eccentric genius, a delicate sensualist, an impossible-to-know recluse, dressed in a flocked shirt

*"pick up secure"; language origin, Cuneate

and baggy pants popular during the Italian Renaissance. Elements of reality fueled my fantasy. For centuries, genetic engineers tinkered with and fine-tuned biological forms until it was possible to create individuals of incredible beauty and talent. Endless biological variations were living proof of what was possible, from the aquatic Manoquads to Bioletic superstars. Unfortunately, genetic engineers never solved the difficulties associated with gradual degradation within the biological body.

The classic cloning experiments conducted by Hammermill and Yates proved genetic drift was an authentic phenomenon. Research showed cloned twins, reared separately, and nurtured within a controlled environment, could not maintain fundamental integrity to each other or to their prototypical form. In as little as thirteen years, genetic drift between two clones produced two distinct individuals. After a lifetime of studying this mystery, Hammermill concluded," the soul maintains the integrity of the body, not genetic composition." When I stared at the twins, Sante and Jana Cle, I wondered if, at last, genetic engineers had solved the secret to divine mirroring.

Sante and Cle were from the Tyrowsian stronghold of Aeternus Complex. For centuries, Tyrowsians had involved themselves in creating endless exotic varieties of androids and genetically engineered bioforms. Tyrowsians were notorious for creating lifeforms they refused to be responsible for and handled with insensitivity. Tyrowsians were progenitors of half the intractable social ills in the Orion Spur Alliance. I remembered seeing a UG holospool about a rogue ship of escaped androids that attempted to destroy the planet Calypso—another Tyrowsian world—because Calypso was the nerve center of android reprogramming. After a lengthy investigation, the now defunct Galaxy Council uncovered Tyrowsian culpability concerning android and bioform violations. Eventually, the Tyrowsian controlled Artificial Intelligence & Robotics Systems (AIRS) Institute went belly-up under the enormous fines levied upon it. When the OSA Alliance Charter became law in this area of the Spur, the Orion Council penalized Tyrowsian manufactures by instituting a two-hundred-year sanction forbidding them to create or reprogram androids on any Spur world. This decision proved to be the economic coup de grace for the planet Calypso. Calypso's economy has floundered for the past 130 years, depending solely upon its vineyards and fishing industries to sustain its dwindling population of Tyrowsians.

****

Jana Cle continued to play with the touchpads and suddenly the taxi bumped the landing pad below. "I can't park it," Jana Cle announced. "There's a scramble in the landing program." Glancing over a perfect square shoulder Jana Cle grinned at me with a confident space-jockey expression. At that moment, the projected demeanor seemed so masculine that I endorsed my assumptions. Jana Cle was male. "I bet you can't wait to get out of this piece of junk? You better sit down and hold tight for a few seconds more." I sat down and then the taxi fell again, bumping and swinging to one side. I abruptly slid off the seat and fell on my backside to the floor. I wasn't hurt, only embarrassed and Jana Cle jumped up and said, "Sorry, let me help you up." I picked myself up and straightened my clothing before peering out the open door of the taxi. It still was a long way to the deck below; but we were closer now, perhaps within two meters.

Sante stood on the deck of the *Daedalus* and reached up and grabbed my ankles, then my waist, and eased me to the floor. I was keenly aware that Sante's hands stayed around my waist a moment longer than needed and when she made a welcoming gesture and said, "Welcome aboard," I noticed her hands were beautiful like a woman's hands that did fine, meticulous work. Endorsing my own assumptions I told myself again, Sante must be female. Yet something was off and I knew it. A part of me still wanted to demand that these two creatures explain and define themselves, but I knew most of Earth's planetary neighbors considered Humans intrusive and too direct. If these two beings were from Aeternus that meant Tyrowsian Culture inundated their lives. In particular, Tyrowsians considered it impolite when Humans quizzed them about the personal details of their lives.

Jana Cle gracefully sprang down beside us. "I'd better run a diagnostic on this piece of space junk," he said.

"Aye," agreed Sante. They did a strange, little handshake entwining their fingers together. Sante took me firmly by one arm. "Let's go to my clinic. I'll need to check your travel documents." We stepped onto an elevated platform. She touched a panel marked with Tyrowsian Cuneate symbols and, without the sensation of movement, moments later, a door opened that led to the ship's clinic. She showed me around, pointing out an examination cubical, a laboratory, and a dozen or so empty hospital rooms.

"I didn't expect your ship to be so large."

"Sometimes it's not large enough. We just transferred fifty-five patients to the Medical Center on Tnamis Space Station. It was a circus in here for a few hours." The androgynous voice shifted gears, going soft and intimate. "I realize you're exhausted after your ordeal; but I need to make sure your documentation is in order and find out what happened so I can file a report. Then I'll let you get some rest."

I told Sante the whole story from the time I left Earth's moon until they picked me up. I left out the morose details about my thoughts of death. She was sympathetic and promised to assist me with a claim against Tricomet Tours. "Could I see your documentation, health certificates, immunization records etc.?"

"I left Earth rather suddenly and forgot to bring hardcopies of my records."

"No problem; I can access your documents through the multidex. What's your number code again? Oh, that's right! You already told me, J.SmithOSP346."

"That's right." I thought about my Casual status and certainly did not want this perfect creature to know my shameful truth. I apologized. "I hope I haven't inconvenience you and Captain Jana Cle or exposed you to any Earth contagions."

"I'm not worried about contagion; I'm merely thinking about the ease of your journey." She put an arm around my shoulder again. I did not resist her touch or the warmth of her hand against my neck. In those split seconds, between our words, I wondered how her beautiful hands might feel touching my bare flesh. "Get some sleep and when you awake refreshed we will talk about your documentation. If you need immunizations, I can provide them right here on the *Daedalus*. Quarantine time will be—let me see—approximately ten cycles."

"Ten cycles! That's a long time."

She smiled again and I was certain that I saw delight in her eyes. At this rate, would I ever get to Wonder World? I put off my questions because all I wanted to do was sleep. My luggage was still in the taxi so Sante gave me a clean white gown. She left and I undressed and climbed into bed. After a moment, I heard a soft knock on the door. It was Sante again. The tender concern on that angelic face reminded me my grandma Lilly. "Would you like me to stay with you until you fall asleep?" Sante asked.

No one had asked me that since I was five years old. Under normal circumstances, the thought of someone watching me while I was attempting to fall asleep would prevent me from doing just that; but Sante had eyes that inspired trust and I found myself saying, "Yes, I would like that." She tucked me in and stroked my hair with a gentle touch as my mind floated closer and closer to the edge of sleep. "Are you always this nice to your patients?" I think I asked.

"I try to be; but I do admit you are special to me."

You're special to me too, I thought. As I drifted off, I knew I mattered to someone for the first time.

****

When I awoke one of my first thoughts was Sante's last words; "You are special to me." No sounds filtered in from beyond my room. Eventually, my hungry-Human-in-search-of-food part roused me and I took a shower in the adjacent bathroom. My suitcase sat next to the bed and when I opened it, I grabbed the yellow wrap-dress Gertie had talked me into buying but never wore. Beyond my room, the clinic was empty so I took the lift to the bridge level where I discovered Jana Cle standing in front of the bridge console staring out into space.

The bridge was small and hot, but it had an authentic space window in the floor. The walls and ceiling were jammed with hundreds of brightly colored screens. Some screens trembled with waiting information and a few twinkled while emitting soft bleeps. "Hi," I said. "Is it alright for me to come on your bridge?"

He turned toward me and smiled and I felt a strange nervous quiver between my knees. "*Qualmerrie*," he said. "Come ahead." Black shorts and a black sleeveless shirt hugged his body in all the right places. Through the shirt, I could see he had the hard-sculpted chest of a man. Evidence was growing that Jana Cle was male despite his smooth, hairless face. A gold armlet, stamped with Mescale* rilets, snaked its way around the defined muscles of his upper arm.

"Good morning," I returned.

Jana Cle laughed in a flippant way. "That's a funny thought, a good morning in space."

"Sorry, should I have said *qualmerrie* instead, Captain Cle?"

He stopped and focused on me, appraising me up and down, and his confidence further enhanced his masculinity. "First, you may call me Cle. Jana is my family name. Second, morning has the connotation of new beginnings and you look fresh as a Delta Urbanian butterfly in that yellow dress. So, perhaps, you and me, right here and now, this is the closest we're ever going to get to a good morning in space." He nodded. "Good morning, Hibernia." Cle glanced toward the space window and went back to tapping the touchpads on the ceiling. "By the way, *qualmerrie* doesn't really mean hello or good morning as most people assume even though it's used as a greeting. Tyrowsians use *qualmerrie* only the first time they meet another person and never after two people know each other well. When one says *qualmerrie*, it connotes that I accept you based only upon what transpires from this moment onward."

"That sounds like Tyrowsian philosophy."

"In what way?"

"I guess Tyrowsian refusal to acknowledge the past."

Cle raised perfectly arched eyebrows. "I see your point but *qualmerrie* can also be interpreted as an offer of acceptance and perhaps even a willingness to trust in what the future will bring."

"Whatever you say, after all, you obviously know more about Tyrowsians and their language than I do."

Something outside in space held Cle's concentration. "Sante and I grew up on Aeternus so we are steeped in Tyrowsian ways of thinking." Cle settled more firmly into his masculinity and he turned to the left and played

* the major language from the Island Worlds of Gathos

with some separate touchpads, appearing to be completely ambidextrous. Despite his masculine façade, his fingers were long, delicate, and feminine just like Sante's hands. His fingers moved with lightning speed over those screens that filled with Tyrowsian Cuneate that was unintelligible to me.

Cle might have felt like a Tyrowsian; but he certainly did not resemble any Tyrowsian I ever saw. Tyrowsian evolutionary development was analogous to Human development and as far as the ability to jump three meters high, it was more likely geneticists could modify a Human to perform that feat than a Tyrowsian. Milksop Tyrowsians, with their stringy little arms and legs, were the physical weaklings of the Spur.

I stepped back from Cle because being physically close to him made me feel slightly short of breath. He was exceptionally handsome and I was becoming increasingly conscious of my Casual status. He had a sharp critical eye and I knew it would be impossible to deceive him; but I longed for him to see me in my best light. Lusty thoughts drifted through my mind that I was struggling to suppress. At the same time, I was annoyed for feeling as I did, but rationalized my attraction for these two by blaming their creator—believing that hypothetical da Vinci had created these two androgynous angels as sexual lures. Old insecurities, my Janeness, continued to prod me. I wished for one thing about myself that I could point to with pride. I wanted to tell Cle that Jane Hibernia Smith matters in the greater scheme, but I identified only with my inadequacies. I was Eliot's Prufrock, "an attendant lord, one that will do to swell progress, start a scene or two …deferential, glad to be of use …full of high sentence, but a bit obtuse." I was neither beautiful nor wise, but I knew my "ethereal mermaids" had arrived and I was unprepared.

Taking a deep breath, I attempted to pace myself. "Where's Sante?" I asked.

Cle motioned toward the floor portal. "Space side." I looked where he indicated; squinted, yet saw nothing. "About twenty degrees right of the center," he explained.

Then I heard Sante's voice in breathy Cuneate coming from a speaker above my head. "Appa-twa taha, susu hyperbaric neipa*."

"Excuse me," said Cle, "I need to activate the hyperbaric chamber in the clinic. Wait here. It might be unsafe for you up there." Watching out the floor window for signs of life, after a couple of minutes, three connected, space-suited figures emerge into view. I heard the groan of a hydraulic space door open somewhere on *Daedalus* and then close. A few minutes later, Cle reappeared on the bridge. He ignored me and began to activate some new controls. I sensed we were moving in relationship to some, small

---

*"pickup okay, activate hyperbaric chamber"; language origin, Cuneate

meteors off the starboard side of the ship. A silver satellite glinted in the distance and grew larger as we flew into range. The object appeared similar to my house at the Erie Pod Park. Indeed, it was an authentic space pod. Meteor clusters had destroyed the rear, giving it the strange appearance of a theatrical set. "Space junk!" declared Cle. "I hate space junk." Then we quickly made space between the pod and our ship. A flash of light left the *Daedalus* and in an instant, Cle had incinerated the pod into oblivion. "That's one less hazard." He turned and gazed at me with another smile. "That's was a good morning's work—don't you think?"

"Yes I do. Who'd you bring aboard?"

"They say they are Tyrowsian mystics."

"Isn't Tyrowsian and mystic a contradiction in terms?"

Jana Cle laughed and it definitely was feminine, almost girlish and I was amazed that his masculinity could vanish so quickly. "You might be surprised to learn that some Tyrowsians are opening up to the universe and outside influences. We encounter them all the time, sometimes in groups and sometimes alone. They allow their pods to drift through space unprotected as they search for their own particular brand of higher cosmic consciousness. They refuse to maintain forcefields around their pods, claiming it interferes with their ability to commune with the universal forces. Unfortunately, in their search, some don't survive."

"Are the people you rescued okay?"

"The female is in critical condition. By the time we reached them, they had been floating around in open space for several hours, waiting and hoping for a miracle." A painful faraway expression took control of Cle's soulful blue eyes for a moment. "Miracles in the morning," she whispered half to herself. "I haven't experienced any of those in quite a while." Then, this incredible sexual changeling turned toward me and put her hand on my shoulder as if she had done it a thousand times before, as though she thought she had a right to do it. What power did these two creatures exercise over people and specifically over me? Cle closed her eyes and said. "I feel it too." Was she reading my mind? "I'm glad we are both alive at the same time." Cle's mood changed and then he/she was neither male nor female but completely androgynous again. I was fascinated with Cle's ability to be whatever he/she wanted at the drop of a hat. "Are you hungry?" Cle asked.

Cle made me forget I was hungry. "Yes," I nodded.

"Then let's eat." We went down to their personal quarters and stepped into a wide, tall circular space. The room was a symphony of simple beauty. A large convex window domed the ceiling, through which the stars shown sharp and bright. Off to one side was a sitting area with huge, lounging chairs and an entertainment center. A library of discs, spools, books and other mementoes adorned one wall. A medium sized whirlpool and sauna set off to one side. By all appearances, they lived well here in space. "There's an exercise space around the corner if you would care to indulge." Their private space included a real kitchen, something I did not even have on Earth, which Cle explained, "When we have time, we cook instead of using the food replicator."

They ate and needed exercise. Proof positive! I decided. They are biological. I suddenly hoped they were as biological as they seemed to be. Cle indicated their bedroom sat behind some closed, louvered doors. Did they even sleep? The fact that they needed sleep was even more promising. We went into the kitchen area and despite Cle's intentions to cook breakfast, a masculine dominance began overshadowing his femininity. He made me a cup of, what he called, "tea." It was frothy and grass green in color. He took out a pan and rubbed his beautiful feminine hands together asking, "Do you like scrambled *jerves*?"

"I never heard of scrambled *jerves*."

"You'll love it, especially the way I make it with a hint of garlic."

"Will Sante come down for breakfast?"

"Sante won't leave the clinic until the patients are out of danger."

"Sante seems like a dedicated doctor."

Cle's expression plunged into feminine tenderness when she said, "Sante is— the best!"

I threw out some verbal dice. "Yesterday, Sante said something intriguing to me as I was falling asleep."

Cle gave me an interested look. "Sante said I was special to her or should I say him? I bet there is not a thought or emotion within the walls of this ship that slips past you. What do you think Sante meant by that statement?" I guess Hibernia was running this conversation.

An expression of intellectual amusement emerged on Cle's face and he was clearly a man at that moment. He was so clearly a man that I ridiculed my previous doubts that he was. "Are all Earth women as direct as you?" he asked

"I don't know. Are all Aeternus creatures as elusive as you?"

His perfect eyebrows arched more dramatically. "How am I elusive?"

"By answering my question with another question."

He focused more intently in my direction. "My dear Hibernia, I am many things; but no one has ever claimed I am elusive. Sante usually tells me that I'm as subtle as a supernova." He laughed openly and, incredibly, the laugh came out as a hearty masculine baritone. "Now I get it! This is a game—isn't it?"

"I don't know. The only thing I'm ready to admit is your smile is distracting."

"A smile is the universal symbol of good will, at least among Humans. Do you object to my smile or my good will?" He leaned across the counter and devoured me with his smile as he handed me a plate of *steaming* jerves. His face was so close to mine I felt the heat of his breath against my face.

"You still did not answer my question," I said as I accepted the offered plate.

I could see he was thinking about it. "Okay, Sante always speaks truth and if Sante said you are special, then you are." Suddenly, he seemed relentless and his masculinity peaked. "I must admit you are a shining lure. Do you want me to bite, Hibernia? Would you like to go beyond *qualmerrie* with me?"

"I don't know. It all depends on whether you are a he or a she and what your relationship is to Sante."

"If you spoke Mescale we could settle your confusion with a few simple words."

"I don't speak Mescale."

"Too bad. Sante and I can't define ourselves in Universal dualities." Cle hesitated and I could see she was forcibly putting on the brakes. "Eat your *jerves* before it gets cold," she said sounding like my mother from long ago.

Jerves tasted like a cross between corn and rice. Cle had put cheese on it, so it tasted familiar and rather good. Cle picked up another fork and proceeded to taste my food off my plate. "Surprise! Surprise! It tastes good!" he said like a man who thinks he is a gourmet chief after he cooks his first scrambled egg. "Among all my other unexplored talents, I'm an excellent cook." Cle hesitated with the food halfway to his lovely feminine mouth the second time. "You don't mind sharing—do you?"

"I love sharing with you; help yourself."

Cle kept slipping in and out of his masculinity as easily as a woman slips in and out of a slinky dress. "While we are waiting for Sante to join us, let's definitely talk about you," Cle suggested.

"What do you want to know?"

Cle pumped up his masculinity even more. "I want to know everything; tell me all your secrets."

My heart fluttered. "You're too intense," I said looking away.

"I don't think so," he said and he gently touched my wrist. "All my instincts tell me you need some intense attention." I dropped my fork on my plate and the noise clattered like a gong.

"Would you be shocked if I told you I am a Casual Human?"

He softened and took both my hands. "I knew it! Tell me more, wildflower."

I revealed some noncommittal minutiae about myself and he continued to probe until he had me exactly where he wanted me. Somewhere near the end of my rambling story, he interrupted. "So, as a cartographer you had mapped out your life, blueprinting the future only to find that in the end you had lost your direction and purpose?" Amazingly, Cle summed up my life in one sentence. I knew nothing. I was a newborn—a toddler embarking on the great unknown. I felt liberated as I considered this new insight. Suddenly, I knew that I wanted Cle to know the real me and I began opening like a flower that had finally found the light. Old knots and constrictions fell away as I realized my truth was stronger than the rickety illusions I had built around my life for protection.

When I finished talking, he said. "I was on the planet Sutcay Tay in its final days. It was beyond terrible on Sutcay Tay, the most horrible—" His eyes clouded and his expression turned so vulnerable and feminine that he reminded me of the weeping Virgin Mother.

Behind his words, I sensed an avalanche of pain. "What is it? You can tell me."

"Not yet. At this moment, something else is more important that I want to share with you. Sante and I try not to speak for each other. That's why I hesitated before when you asked me why Sante said you are special. You see in many ways we already lead lives where the line between us is somewhat muted; but this I can tell you firsthand. Five cycles ago, we were on Wonder World. While there, we visited the Future World Pavilion. It doesn't contain any new inventions or prototypes for the future as we naively assumed. Future World is headquarters for future-gazers and Trinity witches. The place probably gives shelter to every charlatan in the Galaxy." Cle laughed uneasily this time. "We were on holiday and searching for innocent fun so we decided to visit one of the Trinity witches and have our Tarot read. On a whim, we told her to read our cards as if Sante and I were one person. She protested at first but when she relented and read our cards, her demeanor changed."

"This sounds all too familiar. Did all your cards fall within the Major Arcana?"

"How did you know?"

"Because a few days ago a Trinity witch read my Tarot, after I insisted she read only a third of the deck, she turned up cards only from the Major Arcana."

Cle delicately touched her fingers to her lips. "Were Sante and I revealed in your cards?"

"At the time, it was a joke, a whim, the same as you."

"What did the witch look like?"

"She was a typical Gathosian female, dark hair, and those piercing rutilated eyes. She was dressed in Trinity witch green."

"By any chance, was her name Bell?"

"Yes—her name was Bell.

"Surely, this is not happenstance. Bell told us that within five cycles we would encounter a special woman that could chart a course that would change our lives."

"Are you certain she used the words, 'chart a course?'"

"Positive! I have an exceptional memory."

"That's an interesting choice of words considering I earn my living as a cartographer." I struggled to remember what Bell said that evening but mostly I remembered my drunken haze. "I can't remember the details of what she said to me," I admitted. "I was drinking alcohol."

"I remember every word she said. At the time, I didn't believe her, but it was clear that Sante did. When we found you, needless to say, it was exactly five cycles."

"Haugh!" I laughed a little too loudly. "I'm flattered but I can't be the one she meant. I certainly am not—let's put it this way—if you knew me longer, you would discover—I'm extremely average."

Cle was serious. "Why do you make such a self-deprecating statement about yourself? Perfection finds residence in everything that exists. Besides, I sense that you are extremely passionate and that tells me you have great energy."

My face felt hot again. "What makes you think I'm passionate?"

"Some truths are self-evident, especially to me. Beyond that, Sante believes you have a great capacity for love and I trust Sante unconditionally."

"You trust Sante unconditionally?"

"Unconditionally," he said again with more emphasis.

"Please, don't tease me," I begged. "It's not fair. You know everything about me and I still know so little about you and Sante."

Cle came closer and his masculinity turned steamy hot. "Oh, but I want to tease you—can't you see that yet?" he purred like a feline. I could not think with him so close. The space between us was on fire with sexual tension.

"Please stop," I begged.

Cle glanced away and his masculinity vanished like a mask. Playing the androgyn, he/she took the empty plate away from in front of me. I got up and helped tidy the area, grateful for something practical to do. Once or twice, our hands touched as we cleared the dishes. For me, each touch felt alive with electric sparks. We finished and Cle declared, "I'm going to the clinic to see what's keeping Sante." The statement was decisive and masculine and he did go. After he was gone, the room seemed cold and lifeless and I immediately wanted him to return. When he peaked around a corner, a few seconds later, I again felt as if she was reading my mind.

"I hope I haven't come on too strong," she said. It seemed like the statement from a powerful woman that knew she was powerful but did not want to lose her feminine self. "I want you to understand that Sante believes you are special and now that I've met you, I agree. Please believe me when I say, I never would toy with your emotions."

"Okay," I said weakly. My okay collapsed like beach sand under the ocean of Cle's intensity. "We are finished with *qualmerrie*," he declared and I knew exactly what he meant. Minutes later, Cle returned from the clinic with my suitcase. "You will need to remain here until we reach Aeternus. Sante tells me the Tyrowsians have no immunizations records either so there is no use exposing you to unnecessary risk. Please make yourself comfortable and feel free to use our sleeproom if you feel tired. I need to return to the clinic and assist Sante in a temporary tissue transplant."

"You assist Sante in surgery too?"

"Yeah, sometimes Sante calls me Captain Jack of all Trades."

Cle was gone for over an hour the second time. I had some private fun, playing their music spools and using their whirlpool and sauna. My mind never left the unanswered questions swirling around inside me. My planned trip to Wonder World—"the planet of continual pleasure for the young at heart"—was beginning to seem rather mundane compared to my present situation and I had to admit the truth. I was looking forward to a ten-cycle stay on the *Daedalus*. The more I thought about the notion, the more the idea appealed to me; but the decision to remain opened up a new set of questions for which I had no answers. Evidently, Sante and Cle were inseparable. What was my part in all this aside from the obvious?

****

I stepped out of the sauna with a big towel wrapped around my middle and noticed that Sante was sitting across the room on one of the sofas. She looked wet as though she had been in a sauna too. Her long pale hair was hanging in clumps over her shoulders. "Would you sit with me?" she asked.

"How long have you been out here?"

Her eyes fluttered. "I'm not sure. I think I fell asleep for a few minutes." She patted the seat cushion and I obediently sat down next to her. The protracted silence between us lasted for almost two minutes and I knew something was building. "I'm sorry; I'm tired; I feel completely used up right now," she admitted and she put her head back and stared out the space dome over our heads. I studied her profile against the light and that's when I noticed that she had a scruffy beard on her cheeks and chin. I blinked my eyes and she was a woman. I blinked my eyes again and he was a man. My own exhausted need to define had to admit that I was thoroughly confused.

"Could I get you a glass of water?" I asked.

"No thank you. I would like you to sit here, with me, for a few minutes and then I will try to speak."

I desperately wanted to touch this astounding creature. I wanted to reach out and attempt to soothe in the same feminine way Sante had soothed me when she found me in the space taxi, but I did not know how to begin. As I sat there, I realized my feminine capacity for nurturing was

42

clumsy, an unexplored part within me. Whatever Sante was, he or she was a feminine genius. Then quite naturally, as though we were old lovers, Sante rolled toward me and gently laid her beautiful head in my lap. Her beauty at that moment was so fragile and transparent I wanted to weep. In my entire life, I never saw eyes able to hold so much compassion and love. Silent tears began to glaze those tired midnight blue eyes. I wondered if she realized what she was doing. Would she suddenly put on a brave face and move away from me, tell me it was nothing, a weak moment? At last, venturing to touch her damp hair, I said, "I'm listening, Sante."

"One of the Tyrowsian mystics we found was pregnant with her first child. I couldn't save her or the child." Sante began to weep and I felt her despair. She amazed me. Where did she find the courage to exercise her empathy and compassion to such a degree and still survive? I had never gone to this place, not even when my own mother died. Now my insecurities stoked my fears of seeming inappropriate. I felt trapped inside an inadequate part of myself. My mind kept making judgments, suggesting my every response was trivial and unfelt. What should I say? I'm sure you did everything you could do, or merely, I'm sorry. Then I remembered Sante's words when she found me in the taxi and I told her, "Someone I met recently told me that tears wash the soul clean."

Sante touched my cheek as tears trickled freely down her cheeks. "I feel your living breath on my fingertips," she said. "Cle and I need you in so many ways." Sante pulled me down until our foreheads touched. I wanted to kiss her then for she aroused every dormant, sexual feeling within me. Aching desire echoed between my heart and groin. "Please stay."

"I'll stay," slipped out of my mouth. My feelings finally surged and cascaded over my mind and I honestly did not want to question what I had just committed to doing. My feelings began to dance and I added, "Not even the great magnet at Petris could drag me away." Then in a series of beautiful movements, like the opening of a flower, Sante barely touched my lips with her fingertips. It was a strange, unearthly gesture, almost like the ritualistic dance of an exotic mating bird. I was transfixed. Her bare arm came up and that's when I noticed that her arm was too muscular for a woman. She was wearing an armlet exactly like the one on Cle's arm. It was common knowledge that Tyrowsians exchanged wedding bracelets instead of finger rings. Were they married?

"We probably should get underway to Aeternus," Cle said as he walked into the space. Startled, I literally jumped.

Sante made no move to get up from my lap; instead, she snuggled her head against my stomach. "Hibernia has promised to stay with us," she announced. "Didn't I tell you, Cle? It's going to be just as I predicted, only better."

Cle sat down next to me and said, "Welcome to our confusing life,

Wildflower." Sante smiled at us both from that upside-down position on my lap, looking clever as a feline. Cle leaned over and gently stroked Sante's hair, twirling the tiny damp wisps into ringlets. "Are you feeling better?" he asked.

Sante's eyes went dreamy. "Perhaps, if you tell me what I am longing to hear I'll feel better."

"Okay," replied Cle. "You were right."

"And as usual, you've healed my wounded heart," replied Sante. "A love gesture would make me even happier."

Cle responded and he caught me lightly by the chin and turned my head until we were face to face. "Like this?" he asked. In a slow motion, he performed the same ritualistic gesture, touching my lips with his fingertips.

I wanted to respond to them both. I even searched my memory for some beautiful gesture that might equal their simple yet beautiful act of touching someone's lips with the fingertips. What in the Human repertoire of love could be new enough to convey the unique feelings these two creatures initiated in me? I wanted to feel instinctive but felt daunted by their obvious beauty and wit. I was the insipid Christian compared to Cyrano in expressions of love. "I want to touch your heart," I started to tell them.

"You already have," whispered Sante. She took my hand and placed it on the left side of her chest. Her chest was flat and hard like the chest of a man. "Do you feel it?" he asked with a great deal of authority. "My heart beats in the same rhythm as yours." I knew then that whatever they were, they were alive and that was something more than I had been in a long time. I also knew that whatever lay ahead, it would be unlike anything I ever experienced before.

FOUR

An alarm went off inside the *Daedalus*—an incessant, blaring, BLEEP, BLEEP, BLEEP shocked us out of our reverie. A split-second later, Sante and Jana Cle were up from that sofa and on the move. I dressed and followed them to the bridge a few minutes later. When I arrived, Cle's hands were flying over the console. "It's coming in—weak signal—looks like binary light code—breaking-up—coming in from—cadix point 594.06."

"That's Hawking Space Station," said Sante.

"Signal still breaking-up. Got it! Hawking has lost gravity control. Signal's dead again."

"What's the time to Hawking?" asked Sante.

Cle played with some separate controls. "0.102 cycles. It's your call." The captain of the *Daedalus* waited for the doctor to decide.

"Any other nearby vessels?"

"Three Martian phalanx cruisers are at cadix point 748.9. That would put them—wait a sec—approximately 0.8 cycles from Hawking."

"What's the population at Hawking?"

"Thirty to forty Humans—mostly Earthlings, and a few Hattonians."

Sante turned on his masculinity and it matched Cle's in every way. Suddenly he was moving like a man and his voice deepened. "Okay, let's do it!" he decided. "Let me know when we're in range. I'll be in the clinic."

Cle attempted to raise a signal from Hawking and all we heard was dead space. Twenty minutes later I asked, "Why is it taking so long to get there? I thought you said we were only 0.102 cycles distance."

"We use Aeternus time and our space hours are forty minutes longer than Earth hours. Hawking should be coming within range in about ten space minutes. You're a cartographer so you must know how to operate an

Electronic Telescopic Viewer (ETV)."

"You've have an ETV aboard?"

"Yeah! Want to lend a hand?"

"I'd love to." I could not believe I was going to have an opportunity to use the bridge equipment. This was expensive electronic apparatus and an important piece of instrumentation for cartographers working in space.

"Thank you, Wildflower. As you can see, I can use an extra hand." Cle gave me a thirty-second tutorial on this particular ETV and then he watched as I set the cadix point for Hawking Space Station. "Increase magnification by twenty percent," he instructed. He glanced over my shoulder at the ETV screen. "There's Hawking! Interesting, not a sign of life anywhere." Cle turned toward the ship's intercom. "Sante, please come to the bridge. Hawking appears dead in space."

****

When Sante returned to the bridge, scanners were indicating that a constellation of magnetic radiation clouds had just moved through the area. "Any reply yet?" asked Sante

"Negative," said Cle. "I'm going to execute a fly by." Hawking Station came into sharp focus as we came into visual range. "This is the *OSSS Daedalus* calling Hawking Space Station," Cle said several times. We listened and Cle stared at the jumping light squiggles on the console screens for signs of life.

Then out of the silence, we heard a weak, "Hello? Is anybody there? This is Doctor Bjorn Gotenberg, chief engineer at Hawking—"

Cle sighed with relief. "Doctor Gotenberg, this is Captain Jana Cle of the *OSSS Daedalus*. We're within range and prepared to assist. What's the nature of your problem?"

"Two hours ago we began getting bombarded with high concentrations of magnetic radiation. Our ionization chambers went crazy and our gravity control is kaput. We're running on emergency backup and time is running out."

"What's the status of your shuttles?"

"Can't access shuttles—airlocks doors are jammed—inoperable."

"I'm landing," Cle decided. Hawking had a large grid-marked landing platform on which the *Daedalus* just fit. "I'll go this time," Cle offered and he left the bridge. Five minutes later, I saw Cle through the floor portal as a white figure against an endless sea of star-studded black.

"Doctor Gotenberg, this is Doctor Jana Sante aboard the *Daedalus*. Captain Jana is in route to assist you." I noticed immediately that Sante said his name was Jana. Maybe they were married. What were their proper names? "Cle, be careful. Bridge scanners indicate that pressure is rising in all the Hawking airlocks."

"I understand," returned Cle.

"Controls on all four airlocks are jammed," said Gotenberg

"They're not jammed," said Cle. "They're fried." It was silent for almost twenty seconds while the truth sank in with everyone. "Proceeding with magnetic de-scrambler; maybe I can realign the internal lock bars enough to get the door partially open. Doctor Gotenberg, please keep me informed of any internal changes that might affect my efforts out here. By the way, *talar du Svenska?*"

"Sorry, only Universal," replied Gotenberg.

"Too bad, I could have used the practice."

Sante glanced my way and whispered, "Cle is trying to keep them calm." Sante leaned closer to the console, as if the gesture shortened his distance to Cle. "You have twenty minutes—do you hear me, Cle?"

"Is there anything else we can do from in here?" asked Dr. Gotenberg.

"Yes," said Sante. "You have to get one of those inner doors open."

Doctor Gotenberg was losing his cool. "We can't breach the integrity of both doors at once," he shouted in frustration. "That would be suicide."

Sante let go a tiny sigh. "Listen to me; seal your personnel in the safe core of the station. Then put someone into a spacesuit and get that person to cut open the inner door. You'll be out a lot faster if we work from both sides."

"We can't do that. We don't have enough energy to close down internal chambers."

"Surely you have manual door controls," said Sante.

"Doctor, you must realize they haven't put manual controls on internal doors for twenty years."

Frustration showed on Sante's face. "Did you hear the bad news, Cle? I'm ready for one of your bright ideas."

"Door still jammed," said Cle a short time later.

Sante covered the headset speaker in front of his mouth. "Seven minutes," he announced to me.

"I'm going to try something," said Cle. "I'm going to puncture the door with a rephazer. Maybe that will release some of the pressure."

Sante's lips suddenly trembled. "Cle, that's too dangerous."

"Got any better ideas, let 'em fly. I'm running out of time."

Sante stared down at the console and watched the seconds vanish. When he looked up, he said, "Okay, go for it! Doctor Gotenberg, maybe you should suit up just in case. Be assured that if this doesn't work, we are not going to abandon you."

A second later, Cle's words were lost. The last thing I heard him say was, "the air—" The exterior door of Hawking Space Station silently exploded outward and hit Cle in the chest. It happened so instantaneously, Cle simply disappeared from sight. A moment later, I saw the end of his tether drifting in space.

The color drained from Sante's face and yet his voice remained controlled. "Cle, answer me?" Silence loomed. Sante put his face against the space portal in the floor and peered into the black beyond. "Keep 'em busy," he said and he did not wait for my answer.

Sante definitely was made of tougher stuff than I was. I was trembling with shock and fear. "Doctor Gotenberg? There's been—an accident," I stammered.

"What's going on?" Gotenberg asked.

"I'm not sure." My heart hammered against my chest. "Please stand by," I said, knowing it sounded stupid. Then I wondered how I became involved in this life and death drama. A few days before, my life revolved around a multidex screen in the Toledo suburbs. Now I was standing on the bridge of a sophisticated spaceship, acting as if I knew what I was doing.

I heard Sante's voice outside the *Daedalus*. "Hibernia, please listen to me carefully. I'm not wearing all the equipment I should be wearing out here. I left my remote for the airlock inside—serious mistake. Look on the right side of the console and you will see a timer. Do you see it? It's the one thing illuminated in amber."

"I see it!"

"How much time do we have?"

"It says, 4.2 minutes."

"Good. Below the timer, to the right, are a series of touch screens. Count them—the third from the left. That's the control for airlock one. Close it." My hand trembled as I touched the screen. Hearing a door close on the *Daedalus*, I hoped that it was the right door.

"Do you see Cle?"

"Time?" demanded Sante.

"3.6 minutes."

Protracted seconds of silence followed until I heard Sante say, "Hibernia? Keep telling me the time and at thirty seconds, reopen the airlock."

I read off the elapsing time and touched the appropriate screen as Sante asked me to do. "Thirty seconds!" I said. "Is anyone there? Twenty-five seconds—Sante?"

"Close it. Tell Gotenberg we'll get back to him; then get down to airlock one as quickly as you can." I raced down to airlock one in the clinic, not quite sure even how to get there, I took several dead-end turns on my way. When I found Sante and Cle, they were inside the open airlock and Sante was stripping off their whitesuits. He picked up Cle, who was unconscious and limp as a rag, and brought him fully inside the ship. "Close airlock," Sante shouted at the door and it slid shut. Cle's face was white and I thought he was dead.

"Keep your distance!" Sante told me sternly. Sante returned seconds later with an armload of equipment and tossed me a heavy smock and gloves. "Put them on," he ordered. He ran a mediscan over Cle's chest. The scanner hummed; it did not beep and I feared the worst. Sante ripped open the front of Cle's shirt and the strength, speed, and intensity of purpose never wavered. "Aminoply," Sante said, as if aminoply meant something to me. He injected the drug into Cle's chest in the area of the heart.

"Help me get Cle's clothing off," said Sante, tossing me a pair of scissors. Together we cut off most of Cle's clothing. My scissors were poised and Sante said, "You can leave the undershorts." From what I could see, Cle's flawless body looked like the body of a young man. His chest was muscular and flat and his hips narrow. He had no hair on his chest and very little on his legs. Sante ran the amber-lighted scanner over the length of Cle's body a second time and this time I heard a steady beep. "Cle is going to be okay." Sante said. Between us, we dragged Cle to a nearby shower jet for what Sante called a, "general decontamination procedure." Just when I hoped to see more of Cle's hidden sexuality, Sante said, "Go pick up all those clothes and put them in that disposal bag that I left on the floor." At that point, I forgot about Cle's sexuality and began to worry about my exposure to magnetic radiation. Was my flesh going to turn black—boil off? Would all my teeth drop out in a week's time?

When I returned, Cle was semiconscious and Sante had Cle wrapped in a large towel. Sante ran the scanner down the length of Cle again. "It's those damn beads in Cle's hair!" declared Sante. "They're emitting radiation. We need to get 'em out—pronto!"

"You cut my hair off and I'll never forgive either of you," mumbled Cle, who was coming around.

"If you have a hammer, maybe we could smash the beads," I suggested.

Sante jumped up and ran down the hall and when he returned, he had a hammer and a vacuum cleaner. "I'll smash them and you suck up the glass," he said. Afterward he said, "Let's get our clothes off too and evacuate the area. I'll seal it off. Let the Aeternus robots clean up the mess. Cle, do you think you can stand?"

"I think so; although I feel as if a space freighter hit me in the chest."

We quickly discarded our clothing and changed into sterile smocks. I helped Sante get Cle to the bedroom in their personal quarters. It was the first time I had been in there and I noticed the room contained only one large bed. The ceiling was the same translucent material as the ceiling in the main area, allowing them to lounge in bed and gaze at the stars.

"Would you get Cle another towel from out by the whirlpool," Sante asked me. When I returned, Sante was hovering over Cle like a mother hen—their faces almost touching. Sante's masculine side vanished again and she was almost weeping as their fingertips touched each other's lips. They said something to each other in a language I did not understand.

"I'm so glad you are still alive," I told Cle.

"I'm nearly indestructible," Cle claimed. "Besides, you don't think I'd die before I get a chance to make love to you—do you?"

Sante gasped. "Cle, as usual, you're going a tad too fast for the rest of us."

"Which one of us would you choose first," teased Cle.

I was not going to lie—not anymore—not to them and certainly not to myself. "I'm attracted to you both," I said.

We all three looked at each other with an expression of complete honesty. No reason existed to lie or pretend. We all wanted the same thing. Sante sighed and said, "It really can't be any other way." I knew already that Sante and Cle were hand in glove. They were essential to each other as air was to the support of Human life; but there were many questions yet unanswered and as the moments slipped by, they were weaving me inextricably into the tapestry of their lives.

****

"I still have to deal with Gotenberg and his staff," Sante gave me a conspiratorial nod. "Why don't you come to the bridge with me and we'll allow Cle to get some rest."

On the bridge, Sante contacted Doctor Gotenberg who asked, "How is your Captain?"

"He claims to be nearly indestructible," said Sante. "What's going on down there?" I still was listening intently for clues and a red alarm went off in my head when I realized Sante had referred to Cle in the masculine. I was itching to ask.

"We have outside access through airlock three now; but the shuttle is still inoperable," said Doctor Gotenberg,

"Please listen carefully," said Sante. "Your personnel must suit up if they haven't done that already. How many people do you have at Hawking?"

"Forty-sixty in total."

"We'll use airlocks two, three, and four on the *Daedalus*, which access the clinic directly. I'm sending you a schematic—prepare to receive. I'm going to leave a window of three minutes. I know it is not much time, but I am trying to limit your exposure to the high radiation in this area. Please understand that this is not an arbitrary decision on my part. We have proven protocols in place for these types of emergencies and you will be fine if you follow my instruction to the letter. So are you onboard with the plan?"

"Definitely," said Gotenberg.

"Once your personnel are in the closed airlocks, you will have another sixty-second window. Inside the airlock, you must discard all your clothing. Leave it inside the locks. Bring nothing inside this ship except your physical bodies—do you understand?"

"I read you loud and clear," said Gotenberg.

"As soon as everyone is safe inside the airlock, discard all your clothing and put them in the hazardous waste bags you will find in the dispenser on the wall. When you've done that, I will open the inner door and you will proceed directly to the showers. Wash yourselves thoroughly including your hair with the special soap provided. After you've showered, give me a call and I'll come to the clinic and examine your personnel. And please, don't go wandering around my clinic. Another patient is close-by and he already is in critical condition. Do you have any questions?"

"I think we can handle that." It took 20 additional minutes for the residents of Hawking Space Station to prepare. Finally, Gotenberg said, "We're ready," and we watched forty-six individuals scramble across the platform toward the *Daedalus*. "We're all inside the airlocks!" shouted Gotenberg. "Shut the outer door!"

"Do we have to leave all our clothes in the airlock?" I heard someone cry.

Gotenberg roared, "Yes, everything dammit!"

Seconds later, several voices shouted, "Open the inner airlocks."

Sante tapped a control on the console. "Everybody is inside and accounted for," said Gotenberg.

Sante sighed in relief and touched the appropriate screen that closed the airlocks. "Let me know when you're ready for me to come down. Afterward, he sat down on an empty spot of the floor and perspiration ran down his angelic face. He looked at me and smiled. "Sorry," I didn't mean to subject you to a baptism by fire so soon."

I could hold back no longer and I asked, "Sante, are you a man or a woman?"

Sante laughed dryly. "Me? I'm a little of both."

"I'm serious, Sante. Why did you call Cle a 'he' when talking to Doctor Gotenberg?"

"We were speaking Universal and no pronouns exist in Universal to describe Cle's sexuality. Consequently, I can jump around and take my pick."

"I need to know more about you and Cle before—"

"I completely understand. You are much more patient than I would be. All we need is some uninterrupted time and Cle and I will tell you everything. Right now, let me finish with Gotenberg."

****

Bjorn Gotenberg called and said his personnel had finished showering. "Do you want to go to the clinic with me?" Sante asked me. "I guarantee it will be as amusing as a day at the nudist colonies on Point Hope."

We went down to the clinic together and it was in chaos. The crew of Hawking Space Station had managed to find enough towels and sheets to cover themselves. They looked like the bedraggled remnants of a college toga party. "I'm Doctor Jana Sante and this is my colleague Jana Hibernia," said Sante and I gave him a pointed stare, wondering when I was promoted and to what.

Bjorn Gotenberg came to the front of the fold. He was tall with white on white hair and steely-blue Swedish eyes. In his sheet, he looked quite erudite. All he needed was a crown of laurel to complete the look. "I can't thank you enough," he said trying to shake first Sante's hand and then mine. "You Amalgams are incredible."

Sante suddenly turned stiff when he heard that word, "If you don't mind, the term Amalgam is rather distasteful to us. People don't usually use that term—at least not to our face. It's the equivalent of me calling you a Nordic barbarian, if you get my gist."

"Oh! I'm so sorry; I didn't mean to offend." Gotenberg clearly was embarrassed.

Sante took my arm as we walked a short distance away from the group before saying, "Maybe you should go check on Cle."

I left Sante with the Hawking Space Station crowd while the mystery deepened in my mind. Amalgams? My curiosity was driving me crazy. Furthermore, I knew I was falling in love with these Amalgams. I amazed myself because I could not cobble together a logical sequence of events that led to the blossoming of these feelings in me. My blind acceptance of Sante and Cle and my situation confounded me. As I imagined, were Sante and Cle the product of some modern-day da Vinci, or was Gotenberg suggesting something more sinister? What did I know for sure about Sante and Cle when it was obvious that I knew so little? Who were they beyond their obvious beauty and brains? Clearly, they were willing to risk their lives for strangers so what might they do for love?

Going down to their personal quarters, I peered into the bedroom. Cle was sleeping so serenely, he looked like an innocent child. His face gave off a pearly radiance in the dim light. I tiptoed into the bedroom and laid down on edge of the bed, afraid to move closer. After a few minutes, my neck and shoulders hurt with the tension and the sheer effort I was exerting to hold myself still. Yet Cle was so close I could feel the heat coming off his body and could smell his damp hair. He stirred, moved closer, and when he realized someone was there, he wrapped his arms around me. He did it as though he expected someone always to be there. Did he think I was Sante? My heart beat so loudly I wondered if the sound might awaken him. "It's Hibernia, not Sante," I whispered.

"I know," he whispered in return. "You smell all feminine and sweet like a peach I recently ate." Then Cle held me as he fell back to sleep. Gradually my heart stopped hammering against my chest and I began to enjoy the stillness within the room and the feeling of Cle's arms around me and the warmth of his body against mine. A wonderful peace settled over me and sleep took me away too.

Slight movement on the edge of the bed awoke me. "Sorry I disturbed you," said Sante. I turned and touched his arm but he whispered, "I can't. It's been nine cycles since I've slept."

How was that possible? How could any biological being go without sleep for nine cycles? As I prepared to ask, I felt his warm sweet breath against my neck and knew he was already asleep. I lay there laughing to myself. I'm sleeping with two beautiful creatures and we've never made love. It was beyond strange; for me, it was unprecedented. Yet here I was, warm and safe as an innocent kitten curled up with its littermates. After a while, I drifted off to sleep too, dreaming that my life was real, vibrant, and alive with possibility.

FIVE

Awaking without effort, I witnessed dappled stars playing touch-tag with their lights across outer space. A moment before, in an old dream, I had wandered empty halls, narrow corridors, searching for a home. Yet here, in these precious moments of first awakening, I found myself in a sacred harbor of new possibilities. Closing my eyes, my mind reached out to the stars of our universe and they told me, all life asks is that we experience it. A voice interrupted my dreamy reverie with the Cuneate words, "*Ra tukcah.*" I opened my eyes and Sante was standing over me appearing rather masculine. Perhaps it was because he held a hypodermic syringe in one hand. "It means, good morning," he said. "Cle told me you liked to say good morning." He sat down next to me on the bed.

I pointed to the syringe. "What's that for?"

"A special soup I've concocted for you. It contains immunizations against Gathosian Ring Fever, Ganat Mind Disease, and the Hattonian Seven-Day Virus—also a small dose of B.T.C. to counteract any radiation you might have absorbed. Give me your arm or your hip—your choice."

"Are all these preventions going to give me an incurable disease?"

He smiled. "I took care in formulating this particular concoction. Don't worry, Hibernia, my plan is to protect your heart. I'm a doctor and I have dreams of healing everyone. Now give me some part of your body before this solution drips and stains these expensive sheets Cle insisted we needed."

I extended an arm. "Ouch!" I said. "That burns. Your technique is not as smooth as a robotic phlebotomist."

"I'm working on my technique. You will need a booster in ten cycles. Between now and then, consider doing some aerobic exercise. Exercise will help boost your immune system. And, thanks for stepping in and helping us with Hawking. You're wonderful Hibernia, more than I ever expected. Your hammer solution, to the crystal bead dilemma, was inspired. We are fussy about our hair. Cutting it off is sort of like pulling our fingernails out by the roots. Cle lost a few hairs, but those will grow back in time."

"Your hair is beautiful," I said. "May I touch it?" Sante leaned into me and offered up her hair showing me her smooth nape. I took liberties with Sante's hair, running my fingers through it. The hair felt alive to me.

"I like that," she admitted. "Too bad we have to nip this foreplay in the bud. We'll be docking on Aeternus in about twenty space minutes. When we get there, Cle and I will need to check in with Flight Command. It will take a few hours because we have to file a report on the Hawking incident. I've been thinking about the Trinity witch Bell and her predictions. In particular, her prediction of you charting a future for us—do you have any clues yet about what she might have meant?"

"Not really."

Sante put arms around me then and pulled me close. "When we meet again, we will not leave that space until we know each other without barriers. I've willed this private time for us and it will happen, I promise."

"Tell me something—please? I need a few words of assurance until we reach this private time."

"Whatever I tell you in the next two minutes will only elicit more questions." He hesitated before saying, "We all are bigger than a few words. Cle and I are Janaforma. Our genetic model does not fit conventional molds. We are genetically—different. Nothing in your Earth languages can adequately explain us. Ménage à trois comes close because our family units are triads but the Latin word *una* 'in one together' comes closer." Sante stopped talking. "I'm sorry, I'm definitely rambling. Do you see what I mean? We need uninterrupted time."

"I accept that this will be a three-way relationship." Sante smiled and I felt happy merely because he smiled at me.

"You do? Great! From the first moment I saw you, on the floor of the taxi, my future-vision widened. On top of that, you are physically beautiful. I love your pale skin, your eyes are amazing, and your lips are perfect. You are going to be very easy to love for the rest of my life. Personally, I'm sure I loved you before in another life. Do you have any memory of me?"

Cle's voice interrupted coming from the intercom. "Secure for landing in five."

"Ah! We've here. I do need to get back to the clinic," and he kissed me on each cheek. He plunged into his femininity as if diving into water and said, "*au revoir*."

****

I went to the bridge to say *au revoir* to Cle too. Out the bridge portal, Aeternus loomed large like a galaxy across space. Its magnificent Catherine

Wheel structure, in imitation of the Milky Way Galaxy, blazed with light. "It's one of the most beautiful sights I've ever seen," I told Cle.

Cle came close and gazed out the portal with me. "It's more than engineering," he said. "Aeternus is a synergy of its collective elements. Sante says that Aeternus is mortal art imitating God." Aeternus control said something I did not understand and Cle replied, "*Secot, OSSS Daedalus, Fehtau* Cle, *ohti t ot**." I felt a slight vibration as the *Daedalus* made contact with the landing platform and then a transparent lens closed over the ship.

"*Veth-puna, secot. Bhti-eene t ot***," said Aeternus control.

"All official communication is in Cuneate on Aeternus," explained Cle.

"You and Sante seem to speak so many languages. How many languages do you speak?"

"Unfortunately, all of them."

"Nobody speaks all languages."

"Perhaps you're right. How many languages do you speak?"

"I'm beginning to think I don't speak any. Although, Sante just taught me a new word."

"What's that?"

"*Una.*"

"Yes! In one together." The ship's systems were shutting down and the console lights dimmed to stand-by mode. After a bit, all I could hear was the hushed sound of the ventilation system. Cle leaned against the edge of the console and stared at me. His eyes were intense, clear blue with an unfaltering gaze. "*Una!*" he mused. "In time, I'm sure we will have some intensive dialogues on the topic of *una*. Together, we will test the validity of *una*—are you game to see it though?"

"You definitely have me intrigued." Caught up in merely gazing at him, I thought Cle could seduce anyone.

"Did Sante mention that we need to be away for a short time?"

"Yes, Sante explained."

"We've arranged for Nova to take you to our apartment where you can wait."

"Who's Nova?"

"Nova is the only person, other than Sante, who has my unconditional trust." Cle smiled with a private joke. "Watch out for Nova and those big blue eyes and golden hair and you'll be okay. Sante and I need to go through a debriefing on Hawking, but I expect no problems to arise. Everyone got out alive. By the way, I plan to register a complaint against

---

*"secure, *OSSS Daedalus*, Captain Cle, over and out"; language origin, Cuneate

**"landing gasket secure, over and out"; language origin, Cuneate

Tricomet Tours with the Space Safety Commission. If you could get a statement together in the next few cycles, it would help substantiate my complaint."

"I'll do that."

We lingered. "You will wait—won't you?"

"Of course."

"Before we part, may I touch you in some special way? While we are apart we could remember the special touch until we are together again."

"How do you want to touch me?" came out as a gasp.

"In any way you will let me." Cle closed the few remaining steps between us, brushing my face with her fingertips, allowing a hand to touch my breast. I trembled as hands wandered where lust willed it. "How do you love?" she whispered in my ear.

"From my heart," I said and I felt I had said something that meant something real to me.

"*Qualmerrie*," said a new voice.

"Nova! Those new terminal droidbots are getting super quick at attaching those walkways." Cle partially released me, but kept contact by putting an arm around my waist.

Nova smiled. "They've knocked three minutes off the old time. I guess I arrived three minutes too early." Nova certainly was a Janaforma. He/she was similar in appearance to Sante and Cle. Nova's eyes were a deep endless blue. His/her hair color was different though, the hair reminding me of polished gold. "How's your section of Daleth Sector holding up?" Nova asked.

"As you can see, it's yielding some unbelievable benefits." As Nova and I prepared to depart, Cle said, "Take care of her. Bell says she is going to chart a course for our future. You never know, Nova. She might be able to chart your course too." Cle turned to me and assured me, "You're in safe hands with Nova." Cle kissed me then; he kissed me with committed passion. This was the token Cle left until he returned. Cle was my hero and, perhaps, I was his worshipping maiden. The only difference was this hero might have been the maiden too. Whatever our roles, our kiss was a promise. "Until completely," my hero/maiden whispered in my ear.

Nova and I sped across Aeternus in a private ground shuttle. Since Aeternus was not a natural world, the sky was black beyond the translucent crystaglass shield. I could still see stars, but they did not shine with the immediacy they did from open space. Aeternus was big, bright, and flashy. Suburbs were well planned and spacious, and not until we reached the inner core of Aeternus did the jumble of sentient species reveal their haphazard structures. Nova stared out the window of the ground shuttle and told me, "Aeternus is in competition with the natural universe. In a few thousand years, our kind will consider living on natural worlds an unnecessary risk."

"So I've heard but my biological senses would feel deprived without organic stimulation."

Nova appeared quizzical. "You're not what I expected; you are much more."

"I could say the same thing about you. You look enough like Sante to be—are you siblings."

Nova smiled before speaking just as Sante and Cle did. "We are related. We have the same grandparents."

"I'm not asking to pry, but ever since I met Sante and Cle, I've felt unsteady and I'm trying to find my way."

"I do understand. You can ask me anything you want. I'm not a Tyrowsian worried about protecting my personal history. I do believe in the past and I even have hope for the future. Actually, my life is rather mundane, Hibernian. I work for OSSS exactly as every other Janaforma here on Aeternus does. Have you seen a Class 3 Explorer yet?"

"I've seen a hologram of a Class 3 Explorer. They seem huge for a space cruiser."

"They are, about twice the size of the *Daedalus*. I'm captain of the *Cygnus*. We carry a crew of six, which makes life easier, although our space-time is double that of the *Daedalus*. We should get together, that is if our duty rosters don't clash. I would like you to meet my mates." Nova stopped talking and eyed me with scrutiny again. "Sante told me about Bell and her predictions. At first, I had my doubts."

"Despite her predictions, I'm still insecure."

"I can see that, but your insecurity is a waste of valuable energy. You're very pretty. It's obvious you already won Cle over."

"What about Sante?"

"You want everything at once? Sante is cautious, the results of being burned one too many times."

"What do you know about that?"

"Frankly, too much. Sante and I were young and psychically simpatico. We already suspected the truth when we approached the genetic consultants for clearance to form a triad so it came as no surprise when they told us that genetically we were too close. The very thing that made us psychic allies prevented us from producing viable offspring. We went our separate ways." Nova looked up abruptly. "I'm sorry; I honestly did not mean to meander into so many details. Perhaps I am beginning to sound like a gossip. Anyway, Sante and Cle should be the ones telling you what you need to know."

"On the contrary; I'm interested in everything you have to say."

"Okay, but this the last bit you will pull from me. Cle is famous here on Aeternus."

"How so?"

"The Janaforma are starting to call Cle, 'Our Number One Janaforma.'"

"Why is that?"

Nova stopped talking again. "I definitely think I'm monopolizing this conversation. Now that we established that it's okay to ask what one does—what do you do? You're not a media reporter—are you?"

Nova made me laugh. "No way; I work as a cartographer for the Atlas Map Company on Earth."

"We use Atlas star charts in the fleet. I bet I've seen your name on the copyright screens."

"I didn't do any original work—that's why I quit."

"You quit? Does that mean you are searching for new employment?" Nova pressed a button on the ceiling and the shuttle came to a stop. The door sliced open and we stepped out and into the lobby of a building. We walked across a fancy tiled floor and Nova gave the android at the front desk an access code. "By the way, I'm pals with Clidmore and Kinsey," Nova mentioned. "They're here on Aeternus, even as we speak. They're planning a long-term mission and are desperately searching for qualified cartographers. I'm thinking about signing up myself."

"You know Clidmore and Kinsey?"

"Yes; would you like to meet them?"

"Would I ever! Do you know anything about the mission?"

"They want to map the vast region Humans refer to as 'the Square of Pegasus.'"

"Wow!" I said. "Is this one of those generational expeditions?"

"The commitment is definitely for a lifetime. It's a lot to consider. The decision to go should not be made without serious consideration." Nova hesitated, then leaned down and kissed me on the cheek. My heart did a little loopty-loop when he did that. He oozed the same sexual magnetism, the same powerful energy as Sante and Cle.

****

Sante and Cle's quarters, on the twenty-second floor, consisted of a large sitting area, a kitchen, two huge bedrooms, three baths—complete with a whirlpool and a sauna in one—and a small room with nothing but pillows. Bedrooms were equipped with gravity regulators. Sleepers could free float if they so desired. The master bedroom and sitting area ran along an outside wall of windows overlooking Aeternus. It was a magnificent view, with the lights of the city and the dramatic stars of space beyond. I could not help exclaiming, "wow!" several times, as I strolled from room to room and took in the ambience and spectacular view. If I owned a place such as this, I would never leave. The rooms were all decorated in creams and beiges as though the interior designer had unlimited money to waste. This place put my pricey old relic of a space pod to shame. I consoled myself with the thought that Earth space was at a premium and space-space could be as expansive as the imagination might decide. I found myself asking—why would I sign up for a trip to map the square of Pegasus when I could stay here on Aeternus and fall in love with Cle and Sante and, perhaps, live in this beautiful apartment?

Ordering food from room service, I went to bed early and watched a few of the holospools stacked on top of the bedroom multidex. One called, "Ipanema Beach" caught my eye, and a sweet memory of Gertie made me smile. It was a sleepy tropical morning in Rio de Janiero, before the dew had lifted, and Gertie was up and moving around our hotel room. "Get up," she called to me from the bathroom. "We only have today and tomorrow here in Rio and one of the things I've promised myself is that I'm going to see Ipanema Beach."

Slipping the holospool in the player, Ipanema Beach came into focus in gold and orange splendor. Three people moved into camera range, Sante, Cle, and a woman (I decided she was female because of her authentic looking breasts, which were covered by one of those skimpy Brazilian bikinis). I was experiencing difficulties distinguishing Janaforma sexuality but had no problem identifying who was Janaforma and who was not. This particular female was gorgeous. Long black hair tumbled over sensuous shoulders as she came closer to the camera and flirted with me through another dimension. Laughing a laugh of the truly happy, she said something in Mescale I did not understand. All three waved and ran into the surf. There was more; but I felt spooked by seeing Sante and Cle with a beautiful female and I felt guilty as if I had pried. Afterward, I lay in bed thinking about Sante and Cle with that nameless Janaforma beauty. When I awoke several hours later, I made a resolution. I am going to be the best I can be. I will be beautiful, generous, and understanding. I will nurture this opportunity for love and I will be happy forever.

As Sante suggested, I decided to get some aerobic activity into my life and I made an appointment at the resident health spa for starters. When I arrived the female Tyrowsian at the spa desk was incompatible with my assumptions. She sported muscles. Most Tyrowsians favored the slender, pasty look. Her well-developed physique clashed with her long, snowy-white hair and red eyes. She spoke Universal with a thick breathy Tyrowsian accent. "I can set up a special exercise program for you," she offered. "We can program a Coach to play on any level of sherechi, tennis, racquetball, and orbitball."

"No games involving balls," I pleaded. "I always get hit in the nose."

"We have aerobic classes or I could set a Coach to lead you through our track program?"

"My doctor told me that I need to do some aerobic exercise. Recently, I was exposed to radiation."

"We have lots of people with that problem here on Aeternus. Running is a great aerobic exercise as long as your knees are okay." I agreed to give running a try. She waved a little black box in front of my face and asked, "Do you have any genetic problems I should take into consideration?"

"Not one" I replied.

She waved the box in front of my face a second time. "Besides running, the Coach recommends elevated variables if you ever want to give it a try."

She attached the Coach to my left arm. "Press this button when you are ready to start. It will blink yellow to let you know it is in standby mode. When the light turns red, begin your routine. The Coach will monitor everything and make proper suggestions at appropriate intervals."

I went down to the track and turned on my Coach and a holographic jock appeared dressed in tight white shorts and a top that said, "Eat fit, Be Fit." In yellow mode the Coach told me, "Lie down on the floor and begin to stretch your hamstrings. This is level one so I'm not going to work you too hard," it continued with sporty enthusiasm. "Stick with me and soon you'll be running alongside me."

"Where are your legs?" I asked.

"I've heard that joke many times before," said the Coach. "Ha-ha, very funny. Now let's walk a bit and get the feel for the track. Okay, a little faster—you're holding your arms too high. Okay, we're ready to pick up the pace." The Coach blinked red. "On your mark, get set, run. Remember, you have nothing to prove. The important thing is we get your heart rate up to the proper conditioning level and maintain it for twenty minutes." A short time later, it advised, "slow down." It was quiet for almost thirty seconds and then broke the silence with, "Watch you posture! Good job! You're doing great!"

I felt tired well before the twenty minutes elapsed. My inner voice was beginning to compete for attention with the voice of the Coach by telling me, That's enough for the first day.

"Don't quit; you're already three-quarters through the routine," countered the Coach. The program continued with its sticks and carrots and somehow I managed to hang in until the end. "You're on your way to victory!" it cheered. "Be proud of what you have accomplished. You deserve a massage." The Coach turned green and disappeared.

Wrapped in a towel, I waited in the sauna and breathed in the smell of eucalyptus and pine needles while I waited for my massage. Fifteen minutes later, a Tyrowsian masseur collected me. He took me to his cubicle and I lay on a mat on the floor. When he knelt beside me, he began testing one area of my body after another and told me, "You have tension in your neck and shoulders." I spent another hour of pampering under his strong, smooth, capable hands. The sounds of simulated rain put me into a twilight sleep and afterward, I felt soft, like butter. When I was dressing, I peered in the mirror and saw my best self. I'm Hibernia and I'm never going to be Plain

Jane again.

I was under orders from Doctor Sante to be happy, so I decided to get my hair done. At the Scarlet Curl Salon, next to the health spa, I had a beauty consultation with a Tyrowsian hairdresser named Piper, who was a colorful exotic among the pale Tyrowsians. Her knee-length hair was dyed blood red and matched the red adhesion lenses she wore over her eyes. She told me, "Your hair dates you; it's too short and your eyebrows should be completely removed and given a more graceful shape. She also offered to put a temporary stain in my eyes, turning them my choice of solar red, sunset amber, vitril, or rainbow. This final option was the only one that tempted me, but my new burst of internal honesty decided against doing anything overtly artificial. I already had endured sessions with Earth's cosmetic surgeons in attempts to hide my Casual status and this time I held firm. This was me, for better or worse. Cle and Sante chose this me above all others, so why would I change? I allowed piper to wash and trim my hair. She was an expert at running her long fingers through hair to relax her clients. When my hair was perfect, I looked as good as I was going to look with the face I was wearing; although, I do wonder what it might be like to have long purple hair and violet eyes for an evening. As I left the salon, she handed me a complimentary supply of hair encourager. "Try it. It will make your hair as beautiful as any Janaforma."

****

The pampering left me feeling light, airy, and about three kilos thinner. When I opened the door to Cle and Sante's apartment a short time later, strains of music drifted from the bedroom. "Is someone here?" I called. Cle ducked her head around the bedroom door and the thought *very feminine* popped into my mind. She was wearing an unbuttoned white shirt with a triangular OSSS logo on the pocket. "You're back?" I gasped. *This is it!*

Cle immediately dropped into male mode. "I was motivated to rush," he said in a low, sexy voice.

Dressed in only a towel, Sante stepped around the corner of the door a moment later. Beads of water lay across his sculpted chest like liquid jewels. My jaw dropped as I experienced an energy rush. "I want you," slipped out of my mouth.

"Show us," Cle immediately challenged.

Time thawed before melting away, leaving me in the perfect sunshine of eternal joy. Released, my feelings swelled and bloomed with pent up desire and the perfume of direct experience lured me into its fold. I took another step forward and the three of us plunged into a pool of mutual desire. Our fingertips met first and entwined in their own ballet. We covered one another in an endless rush of eloquently expressed touches. My dauntless love was nimbly prepared to embrace whatever it found in my new lovers. In naked honesty, there were sexual surprises, but every surprise was

62

beautiful, accommodating, and ready for love. As I surrendered to the current, I knew my critical mind was wrong about them both. The more feminine Sante was masculine, complete with all the normal equipment and the more masculine Cle was a hermaphrodite. Yet time would reveal that even these overt designations could not define them.

Cle reached beyond me and kissed Sante. "*Ejesay epay**," Cle whispered. This kiss ignited Sante's passion and it was like a lit match thrown into fuel. Love trapped me in the middle of this fire between them. On my part, there was no room for reticence so I threw away my last shredded rags of Puritanism and jumped across a gap within myself to become my complete self. I was thirsty. I had survived time's desert where loneliness had desiccated my feelings. Now, here, I bathed in an oasis of sensual pleasure and submitted to everything I ever wanted. When Cle put his hands under me, drew me up like water from a deep well, we flowed together like two merging streamlets. Every part of me drank in the experience as we kissed long, deep, wet kisses. I had never known passion like this, never knew my mortal body could move with so much fluidity. Cle whispered and his voice was deep and even husky against my ear when he said, "*ejesay epay*."

Sante breathed little feminine kisses against my neck as Cle returned me to his lover. "Touch me," she begged. "Make desire my total reality." I could wait no longer and she caught her breath and sighed when we merged. She lifted me so high that we seemed to be floating off the bed. Our first movements together were small, tentative, and intense as though we might lose each other. And then Sante whispered, "Let's fly."

I assumed the obvious but truly did not know what Sante meant. Even before my assumption subsided, we were on our way to somewhere else. We were flying through a dimension where only Sante and I existed. It was as though everything save us was an illusion. We were together in one passion: one perfect, living, evolving love. She moved in me; but I moved through the feminine part of Sante too. Yet all the time this physical being, Sante, pressed hard inside me keying responses within my secret self.

This is our eternal refuge, said Sante within my mind. This place is ours. Cle's lips kissed the nape of my neck and her hands cupped my breasts as I fell asleep. For a while, I do not know how long, we stayed wrapped in silent bliss, just the three of us outside the demands of time. Just as Cle started to stir the passion again, the multidex extension on the bedside table bleeped. Sante reached over Cle and shut it off. For a long time, no reality existed except the one reality we were creating together. Sante said, "Truly, we are in one together." I felt the truth of those words. Love fused hours

*"my love will be fulfilled only in you," language origin, Mescale, personal tense into timelessness until we slept from exhaustion. No dreams came because I was complete. When I awoke, I knew many new things. I knew I could not define Sante and Cle as either male or female; and yet, their maleness and femaleness were intensely alive and incredibly active. Beyond that, I knew I wanted to spend every moment of my life filled with their love.

For hours that stretched into the following cycle, my sacred androgyns and I stayed intimate. Our talk was play filled with the most extravagant promises of love we could conger. When we awoke the third time, no one quite knew or even cared how much time had passed. Cle filled the giant tub in the bathroom with perfumed water. The bath felt deliciously warm and caressing as we floated in silence together. Then Cle said something that began their confessions, those secrets they initially feared to confess. "You never asked us about birth control," Cle began.

"I know. I'm fitted with an internal protector. I can't get pregnant," I assured them.

"We have a redundancy of birth control devices in this room," Sante said and he pressed my finger against a spot on his groin. A small nodule protruded where a subcutaneous, birth-control device lay. Sante smiled his feminine smile. She showered me with compliments and words of love. "You are so special—so perfect for us. We need to return to the *Daedalus* in a few days and we want you to come too."

"Will you come and live and work with us—sleep with us through the dark hours in space," pleaded Cle. "I promise, you'll find that you can't live without us."

I laughed and told them, "I already know I can't live without you. But I do have a few fears—a feeling that all Smiths carry the curse of loneliness. Yet you both make togetherness seem so—natural."

"It is," they assured me. We got out of the tub and went into what I still called the "bedroom" and what they called the "sleeproom."

"Lay with us," said Sante. Our bodies were still hot and damp from the tub. The bedclothes smelled of our sweat and sex juices and I gratefully wallowed in us. I was soaking in a sexual freedom that was brand new to me.

Cle pulled me close and asked, "Do you feel how naturally we fit together?" I tried to pretend everything was natural—hoping that in time, I would convince myself that I was as free as I was acting. I was surprised when Cle said, "We were unfair to you. We made love before we told you the whole truth. I take full responsibility for seducing you the moment you walked in the door." He giggled and it was feminine.

Sante added, "Now that she loves us she will forgive us for this rush."

My confusion was still a mountain higher that Mount Everest. Nevertheless, I was certain the da Vinci, who created them, had discovered a method to divide what we normally consider male into two separate individuals. I had not yet seen a female Janaforma, but it was obvious their creator had split the male into two bodies and the type like Cle possessed both male and female anatomy. "Please, tell me who and what you are?" I asked.

"On the surface, it's simple," said Cle. "Orion Spur Space Security had a desperate need for biological beings that could handle the rigors of space, so AIRS commissioned the creation of the Janaforma."

"Are you referring to the Artificial Intelligence & Robotics Systems on the planet Calypso?" I asked.

Cle was looking direct in a male kind of way. I knew they were not Casuals; but knowing AIRS on Calypso was involved hinted that laws probably were broken. "AIRS didn't have the technology to create us but they knew two scientists that did. AIRS acted as the go-between in the deal. Simon Forma and Jana Revba created the Janaforma. Forma and Revba created us for long-term space life. Our DNA is Human. We're told that Forma and Revba selected Human genetic material because of its potential for intelligence and superior strength. Aeternus Tyrowsians still are withholding much of our genetic information so the in-depth particulars of our inception remain hidden even as we speak. All Janaforma are struggling to piece together a picture of our history. What we know for sure is Jana and Forma discovered a new method to speed up evolution through gene sifting. From a cross-sampling of millions of Human individuals, they selected genes to create a Human more adaptable for space."

"So that's why Dr. Gotenberg called you Amalgams."

"I guess we are Amalgams," admitted Cle. "We are random bits of genetic material plucked and cloned from millions of Humans. It's the connotations surrounding the word Amalgam that make it a slur."

Sante looked a bit uncomfortable for the first time. "That brings us to a few particulars that might be difficult for you to accept. Human and Janaforma women are genetically similar. Both possess 46 chromosomes and during meiosis or sex cell division, both donate 23 chromosomes to create a new individual."

"I do feel as if I'm missing the point," I said.

"No you're not," said Sante. "Because I'm just reaching the point. Janaforma need three sexes to procreate, a consort, a lifegiver, and lifebearer. Cle is a consort and has 46 chromosomes. During meiosis, he donates 23 chromosomes to the reaction. However, Cle's 'starting material,' contains only 23 chromosomes and has no life. That's where a Janaforma such as me comes in handy. I'm a lifegiver. My job is to bring Cle's sperm to life."

I guess my mouth was hanging open in amazement because Cle said, "It's easier to understand if you realize that we all carry recessive genes down through generations. Those genes remain silent, perhaps not expressing themselves for generations. In the Janaforma consort, all genes for reproduction are present, but the life-giving gene is recessive."

"Wow!" I said in amazement. "Your genetics sound complex. Do you know how they created you?"

"As far as we know, no Janaforma holds the key to our formula," said Cle. "However Forma and Revba created us, it genetically separated the Janaforma from other Humans. Our love bonds are triadic unions."

"Why would Forma and Jana want to isolate the Janaforma from the Human race?"

"There's plenty of speculation among us," said Sante. "But the truth remains that all our reasons are rationalization we've developed after the fact. Some believe it's because space teams always were teams of three consisting of a pilot, engineer, and doctor. Others believe Forma and Jana did it to prevent a Janaforma population explosion. A male can impregnate hundreds of females while a female can usually have only one child at a time. The Janaforma need a consort and a lifegiver to impregnate one lifebearer, so it slows us down even more.

"As usual, the social implications were never considered until after the fact," said Cle. "We Janaforma are indoctrinated with beliefs in our 3C programming."

"What's involved in your 3C programming?"

"Our 3C programming can't be explained in a few words either, but our programming makes the Janaforma a tight group."

"There's more," said Sante. "Problems exist for Janaforma and Humans when they attempt to procreate. Perhaps in the future, someone will discover the key to overcoming these problems. The Janaforma are only fifty years old and we have not logged in enough time to sort out our genetic peculiarities—at least not without help from the AIRS Institute."

"Do you want to have children?" I asked.

"Someone's ability to produce children has never been a prerequisite for winning my love," said Cle. "However, if we decided to have children in the future, I would expect to embrace the role with full attention and my best efforts. The key word here is future. You don't know this yet, Hibernia, but I have a lot on my plate at this particular time. The Janaforma people need a champion here on Aeternus and I am beginning to assume that role."

"What are you championing?"

"The Janaforma have made space travel safer in the Orion Spur at a high personal cost. We believe it's time for the Aeternus government to give us equal rights as citizens and access to our genetic records."

"Is it because you are taking on this role as champion that the Janaforma have begun calling you the Number One Janaforma?"

"Where did you hear that?"

"Nova told me."

"That business about Number One Janaforma is nonsense," said Cle.

"You're my Number One Janaforma," said Sante.

"Phooey!" said Cle. "I'm not special and Nova knows it. I just happen to be in the right place at the right time with the courage to speak up. Don't worry about the Number-One-Janaforma-business. I'm just an average Janaforma consort in love and that makes me a little bit over the top."

"My feelings are new," I told them. "All my life I dreamt about—fervently wished for someone I could love and who would love me in return." I looked at Sante and stopped short. A sad expression surfaced on his face. "What's wrong?"

"I have a personal need that's difficult to describe," said Sante. "I'm not sure you will understand; but I have a deep driving urge to bring things to life. Only a Janaforma lifegiver understands this particular impulse. That's probably why so many of us become doctors." Tears filled the corners of her eyes.

I covered Sante's face with kisses and told her that I had the same feelings as a Human woman, but had suppressed my desire for children because of my Casual status. "If a time ever comes to have your child and I knew it would be free of my genetic defect, I would welcome it," I told them. This time my words stunned me. Did I mean what I said? My genetic defect was merely the face of my imperfections. I had scars on my soul.

Cle said, "You don't need to make promises. You don't need to do that with us." I stopped Cle's words with a kiss. We began to make love again and I remembered the Mescale words and spoke them to my sacred lovers. "*Ejesay epay.*"

SIX

Urgent messages were accumulating on Sante and Cle's multidex and two needed immediate replies. One was from a Commander Vertain at Space Security saying, "The *Daedalus* is clean and ready to fly." Cle called Space Security and a reserved a launch slot in 92.3 space hours, or about 4 Earth days.

Meanwhile, Sante was sitting on an ottoman in the corner talking to Nova on a remote microdex. They were speaking Mescale, but every time Sante glanced my way, the language instantly shifted to Universal. "Sounds wonderful; wait a second and I'll check with Cle and Hi. Nova has extra tickets for a show at the Earth Pavilion. Guess who's appearing, Cle—Ariana!"

Cle's face lit up. "Marvelous! Going to the Pavilion would be a fabulous way to celebrate."

"Who's Ariana?" I asked.

"The greatest jazz singer alive," Cle said without hesitation. Then Cle turned into both my girlfriend and father. "You'll definitely need something dazzling to wear. Go down to the boutique in the lobby and get something new to wear and don't skimp. See if you can find something clingy in a sapphire blue. Sapphire blue is definitely your color. Just remember Sante's eyes and you'll hit the mark."

"Do you want to go with me?"

"I'd love to but I have a long list of things I must do." Cle handed me a silver-colored credit card and said, "Remember, don't skimp."

****

At La Carrefore Boutique, I met Yurgie, its oh-so-dapper Tyrowsian owner. Yurgie showed me his Exquisite Line calling the creations, "art for the body." Fabrics were bejeweled with tiny seed pearls and crystals. The satins draped like liquid gold and the velvets looked as deep as the vistas of space. I touched a gown of Naiven Silk, a silk lighter in weight than any Earth silk I had ever seen. Hand-embroidered threads of gold looped around the collar and hung down like a golden mane over diaphanous layers of golden silk. "Wearing this is like going nude," said Yurgie with a flirty wink.

"It's beautiful but the wrong color. I'm looking for something in a sapphire blue."

"Is that dark blue?"

"It's a clear deep blue, like the blue in a Janaforma eye."

"Oh! I see," said Yurgie with a knowing giggle. "You've had the pleasure—I see. The Janaforma are quite exquisite—all those heroic ideals wrapped up in a gorgeous package. By the way, sweetie, are you a size six?"

"I'm a size four on Earth."

"You look like a six to me. Well, we'll see." Yurgie started pulling out dresses for my inspection. "This is vintage, an original Stuartana. The fabric is composed of micro-thin fiber-optic filaments. The colors bleed from blue to violet to white and then blue again. So with this dress you will be wearing blue at least part of the time." The dress was 12,000 credits, which was more than my yearly salary at Atlas Map. I examined about fifty dresses, tried on twenty, before a spectacular creation caught my eye. When I saw the dress draped over the back of a chair, I knew it was going to be mine.

"Oh that!" said Yurgie. "That's brand new and reasonably priced too. We just got it in—from some new designer on Thalia." I tried the dress on and the heat from my body caused the dress to shrink and expand in all the right spots. "It always fits perfectly," said Yurgie, "so you don't have to worry if you are a four or a six."

I looked in the mirror and said, "I never thought I could look this good.

****

I returned to the apartment and found a small box on the bed with a note. "Wildflower, we've gone downstairs to the health club to exercise—pick you up at 18:00. This is for you. Hope it doesn't clash with your new dress. *Jesay*, Sante and Cle."

I opened the box and gasped. It was a necklace of what appeared to be Venunition sapphires. I examined the necklace under a stronger light and the stones glittered with authentic sparkle, especially the large one in the center that was resting inside a circle of diamonds. "How rich are they? No one can afford Venunition sapphires on a salary from Space Security."

They were punctual and returned at 18:00 on the dot. Sante was tall, straight, and handsome. He was dressed in a short, black kimono and black pants. A golden clip secured his hair at the nape of his neck and something about the outfit reminded me of an ancient, Spanish matador that I had seen in the holographic chambers. Sante had called himself a lifegiver and everything about his appearance testified to the vitality of his life-giving powers. I could see an aura glowing around him or perhaps it was merely emotion collecting in my eyes. I did not know which of my new lovers to feast my eyes upon first. Cle was dressed in midnight blue, which deepened the eternity behind her eyes. Her long hair glistened in the lights of the room and the crystal beads were back in her hair. "You're not wearing the necklace," Cle noticed immediately.

I took the necklace out of box again and admired it. "It's gorgeous, but what does it mean?"

"It means you are important to us," said Cle. "Say you'll accept this small token of our love." Then he lifted my hair and Sante fastened the necklace around my neck.

Sante nodded in approval and added, "Perfect." I did not ask about their abundance of credit, at least not that particular evening.

We met Nova and his mates at the Earth Pavilion. Nova introduced us to Patra and Liart and they bypassed the handshaking and went straight for enthusiastic hugs and kisses, kissing me on either side of the forehead. Patra was beautiful with flaming red hair and violet-blue eyes the shade of periwinkles. Her skin was reminiscent of freshly poured cream. Liart was a new kind of Janaforma lifegiver with such an exquisite profile that I could see it stamped on a gold coin. Sante was delighted to see Patra, who was pregnant. He kept his arms around her unnecessarily long, patting her cheeks and touching her belly. If Sante was envious that Nova was having a child, no word or gesture betrayed him. But the attention Sante lavished upon Patra was both deferential and tender and it didn't take me long to realize that I was jealous that Patra was having a child and I could not.

We celebrated. Everyone was relaxed except me. "Would you like wine?" Cle asked me. "We usually don't drink because our system can't handle it, but if you would care to have something we could order."

It was a novel idea that I might enjoy myself without liquor. I was tired of forgetting the details of my life so I said, "No, I want to remember this evening forever."

Moments later, Patra asked me, "You want to do the powder room routine with me before the show starts?" On the way, she told me, "I have to pee all the time now," as she rubbed her baby bump.

"When is your baby due?"

"In a few weeks." As she fussed over her hair in the ladies' room mirror, she told me, "I'm so happy Sante and Cle found you in that space taxi. It must have been frightening. Space taxis are tin cans equipped with simple magnetic power packs. They should be outlawed." She swatted the topic away with her hand and said, "Sorry, I didn't mean to get on my soapbox. Nova said you are a cartographer and toying with the idea of joining the Kinsey and Clidmore Expedition. I said to Nova that you should consider joining Space Security instead. Sante and Cle are skilled veterans, two of Space Security's best; however, I still think Commander Vertain is wrong in letting Sante and Cle run the *Daedalus* a crewmember short. If you joined Space Security, you could round out the *Daedalus* crew and then the rest of us could relax."

"You Janaforma are so accepting of everyone." Did Patra believe me capable of becoming a space jockey?

"That's true; we love everyone. It's innate, put into us by our 3C Janaforma genetics. We believe Jana and Forma enriched compassion in our genes so we could serve without prejudice. Whatever the case, I sense that you are special to Sante and Cle. Perhaps it's simply because I see how happy you make them." She kissed me on both cheeks. "Welcome to our family."

I sensed the love of which she spoke. Sante and Cle had invited me into their lives, but their lives encompassed a network of Janaforma love that was opening its heart to me. For the first time in my life, I had so much love that I could afford to spread it around.

****

We returned to our table where everyone was in high spirits. Sante and Cle exchanged stories with Nova and Liart, talking about recent incidents in space. As we ordered and ate a delicious dinner, Cle talked about Hawking Space Station. "Whose bright idea was it to puncture the door?" asked Liart.

"I take full responsibility for that crazy idea," admitted Cle.

"I went along with it," insisted Sante. "Commander Vertain was not happy about the mess we left inside the *Daedalus* airlocks. She said we should have checked with the three Martian phalanx cruisers to see if they had a robotic arm even though they were four hours away."

If we waited, everyone would have died," said Cle. "And I knew I couldn't die because Sante would follow me to Hell."

"Damn right," said Sante. "Get back to life and work."

Everyone laughed. "It's easy for Vertain to sit behind the desk at central command and second guess our decisions out in space," said Liart.

"Give her a break," said Patra. "She has our backs with the Tyrowsians. That's a fulltime job. Besides, you must admit, Cle, you are always there on the edge of the cliff, spitting into the wind."

"I abhor taking chances!" replied Cle. "I merely keep finding myself in situations where I have few options."

Liart laughed. "The last time I talked to Vertain she referred to you as the Sutcay Tay daredevil." Cle's face dropped into a dramatic frown. Sante was suddenly uncomfortable and squirmed in his chair. "I'm sorry," said Liart. "You know I'm always on your side."

Cle cleared her throat and abruptly changed the subject. "Patra, are you still space-walking?"

"No way; I haven't been space-side in sixty cycles—can't even fit in a whitesuit. Maybe your Vitarattha R & D Empire could work on developing an egg-shaped whitesuit for pregnant lifebearers."

Cle laughed. "I'll mention it at the next board meeting."

The room lights dimmed and multicolored beams of light freckled from the ceiling. A Human man in dark glasses walked onto the small stage. "It's my great pleasure to introduce this year's winner of the Euterpe Jazz Competition, the fabulous and incomparable songbird—Ariana!" People jumped to their feet with loud applause. The room was dark and everyone's attention was on the stage. I'm glad because I'm sure that I looked stupid with my mouth hanging open in amazement. Ariana was a literal songbird. Ariana was a little yellow bird about a quarter of a meter long that flew across the stage and landed on a perch attached to the top of the piano. Without singing a note, she already had blown my mind.

"Thank you," she said in perfect Universal.

"Is that bird real?" I asked Sante.

"As real as anyone can be in show business," Sante replied.

The piano went into a long jazzy introduction. "The Orion Spur knows the best music is Earth music," crooned Ariana. Several whistles came from a table of Humans I spotted earlier. "Now Euterpe knows it too!" The applause was deafening this time. "Thank you. I'd like to sing a few old favorites this evening." The backstage lights came up. A man with a saxophone stepped forward while blowing a series of bluesy combinations. With that, Ariana broke into, "Summertime—and-the-living-is-easy. Fish-are-jumping-and-the-cotton-is-high." The saxophone slid into the song and Ariana's voice lingered almost like a hum, yet her hum was crystalline and soulful. Ariana was a musical gymnast—Olympic class. She sang, "with-daddy-and-mammy," and "standing" seemed to echo on forever, as she explored the nuances around the melody.

The piano went into another introduction. "Good evening all you beautiful people!" she shouted. "We got Sammy Quickstep's fingers on the piano, Josephine Amaryllis' mouth on the saxophone and Jimmy Zilyon's big callused fingers on the bass and of course—fantastique moi! I'm Ariana and I'm here to sing a few songs. I can see we are lucky enough to have several of those good-looking Janaforma consorts in the audience this evening. I'd like to get myself one of those love machines and sing a few songs to each of them personally." She purred like a feline and then caught her breath and the audience laughed. With that, she flew into the audience and proceeded to look around. Finding exactly the Janaforma consort that she wanted, she landed on Nova's shoulder.

"Hi!" she cooed. "You are so pretty," and she rubbed her yellow feathers against Nova's cheek. Nova was embarrassed and blushed. "Play it,

Sammy." Sammy Quickstep did a few dangerous, heart-rending runs down the keys and Ariana sang, "It-took-me-some-time-to-recognize-the-feeling; but-I-know-tonight-I-don't-need-no-clues. Cause-you're-on-my-mind-from-morning-through-till-evening. Nobody-does-me-like-you-do.'" Ariana put an open wing against Nova's cheek and pretended to whisper while Josephine Amaryllis went into a jazzy excursion around the melody. Some of us at our table were having a difficult time stifling our laughter at the sight of Ariana sitting on Nova's shoulder and singing her heart out. "I-chased-after-dreams-that-never-came-to-nothing. I'd-tried-being-free-but-the-nights-were-so-blue. It's-easy-to-see-that-I'm-lost-without-your-loving. Nobody-does-me—nobody-loves-me, sugar——like-you-do*." Even after seeing Ariana up close, I still could not tell if she was a real bird, a genetic arrangement, or an android. Maybe Sante was right. Who is to say what is real and what is not real anymore? The music never stopped and neither did the enthusiastic applause as Ariana flew back to the stage.

Ariana took an upright position on her perch and sang softly, scatting around a melody before singing, "Fools say, Dulce-has-moved on, gone-to-the-greater-Delphi-in-the-sky. But-every-lover-knows-he can't go home, not until he discovers his true love." She started to sing one of Dulcerary Cœur's ballads then, taking it into realms of sound that might have amazed even the composer. The song started out simply enough, but within a few bars, moved into the most fantastic range I ever heard. Her voice made chills run up and down my spine. She ended on a note that was unreachable by any Human voice. "Thank you," she warbled. "I'll be back in an hour if you want to hang around." She flew down and landed on Nova's shoulder again. "Thanks for being such a good sport," she said in the voice of a young woman. A photographer came over and took Ariana's picture perched on Nova's shoulder and she presented the picture to Patra with good wishes and flew backstage.

"Here," said Patra handing the picture to Cle. "You're the one who is crazy about Ariana."

"Thank you," said Cle. "I'll treasure it forever." Cle propped the picture against the candle so we could all admire it.

"Cle, can you interpret the lyrics to that Dulcerary Cœur ballad?" asked Nova.

"Classic Mescale?" asked Cle. "I wouldn't insult Ariana or The Divine One by attempting an imitation."

"Come on, Cle," begged Patra. "You're the only one here who can speak classical Mescale."

*"Nobody Does Me Like You Do," by Rod Temperton, Human species, planet Earth

"Let me see," said Cle. "I guess it goes something like—'Let-us-join-then-you-and-I, when-green-Eno-kisses-the-sea. Splay-your-wings-upon-the-air—fly-with-me. We-build-a-nest-of–fertile-green-among-pink-blossoms-so-rare. The-cadence-of-our-song-mounts-my-joy-with-sweet-lovedew-making-me-the-anointed-in-one-with-you.'"

"Whew!" squealed Patra and she fanned herself. "I don't want any closer translation. That's hot enough for me. That's some sexy bird song!"

"She sure is the sexiest bird I've ever seen," groaned Cle.

"Do you have a weakness for yellow feathers?" asked Nova.

"I did until I realized Ariana likes you better. 'Cause-no-one-does-me-like-you-do,'" Cle sang, imitating Ariana's voice at last. Uncannily, Cle sounded like Ariana.

"How did you do that?" I asked.

"You didn't know that Cle is incredibly talented?" asked Patra.

"It's a useless talent," Cle insisted. "Sometimes it comes in handy at boring parties."

"Do my voice," begged Patra.

"No, I don't feel like it," insisted Cle.

"Come on," said Liart. "Do somebody and we'll guess who it is."

Cle changed his voice into someone else. "If you don't stop taking so many chances out in space, I'm going to dock your pay a thousand credits."

"Commander Vertain!" everyone said at once.

On stage, a small band began playing and dancers began to move onto the floor. It was easy to spot the Janaforma; they were dancing as trios. I could not help but smile because the sight appeared slightly odd to me. Then Sante and Cle asked me to dance and I said, "I don't know how."

"It's easy, we'll show you how," Cle insisted. At first, my self-consciousness made me awkward. I was one of those people I considered slightly odd minutes before. When I noticed no one paying attention to us, my self-consciousness subsided. Of course, Sante and Cle were good dancers. After a while, I was having fun, which is something I had forgotten how to do. The dance movements were soothing, very much the precursor to lovemaking that I knew would follow. Aside from the passion, I got a taste of what life would be like living in a triadic relationship. I was not always the center of my lover's attention. Sometimes their arms reached beyond me to each other. I was important but not the exclusive focus.

We stayed for Ariana's second show and danced some more. No one wanted to leave. Everyone was happy, including me. Every few minutes somebody broke into the song, "Nobody-does-me-like-you-do," which caused everyone else to erupt in fits of laughter.

Patra called it a night saying, "I hate to be the one to end this delightful party; but we need to be on duty by 14:00 this cycle. Baby and I need to get a few hours of sleep first."

Nova took me aside, as we were preparing to leave. I had noticed during the evening that something about Nova was more dominant than either Sante or Cle and now Nova's dominance peaked. He put his hands around my waist. The Janaforma were a touchy-feely bunch, finding all sorts of reasons to touch everyone; but when they were with each other, it seemed the touching never stopped. I looked into Nova's sparkling, turquoise eyes and tried to concentrate on what he was saying instead of his hands embracing my waist. "What about the Kinsey and Clidmore Expedition?" he asked.

"I'm no longer interested in Kinsey and Clidmore."

"Then you definitely are teaming up with Sante and Cle?"

"I'm not sure what you mean by teaming up. I'm in love with Sante and Cle."

"Love is all you need, the rest you can figure out with Sante and Cle's help."

Sante joined us and I noticed that Sante's femininity became more conspicuous every time Nova was around. "She's teaming up with us, not you," said Sante and she gently poked Nova in the ribs. "Nova thinks he's a sex god since Ariana has proclaimed her admiration."

Nova embraced Sante. "Before we part, give me one of your special hugs." Nova pulled Sante forward and into an embrace. The embrace went way beyond hugging. Was this merely more Janaforma touchy-feely stuff or something more? Nova kept his arms around Sante hips as they talked, quite literally, leaning his genitals against my new lover. I glanced around, waiting for Cle, Liart, or Patra to notice and yet nobody acted as if what Nova and Sante were doing was the least bit odd. "I'll see you in two months and celebrate the birth of my first born." They were eye to eye and Sante kissed Nova, on the lips. "Through *hataeasta*."

"Through *hataeasta*," returned Sante.

****

"What's *hataeasta*?" I asked as we walked away.

"Where did you hear that?" asked Cle.

"Sante just said 'through *hataeasta*,' to Nova."

Sante and Cle exchanged stares. "I'm tired and don't feel like jumping into the murky waters of *hataeasta*," said Cle.

Then Sante changed the subject and asked, "What did you think of our extended family?"

"Nova is godly handsome. I think his name should be Apollo. Liart is attractive and the patrician profile is easy on the eyes. I loved Patra; she is beautiful although she said something odd when we went to the powder room."

"I hope she didn't bore you with the subject of Devina," said Cle.

"Who's Devina?"

"Whoops!" said Sante. "You stepped right into that one Cle."

"Patra thought I should sign up with Space Security because you two are running *Daedalus* a crewmember short." Their expressions changed. "Why do you both look so guilty?"

"We are running a crewmember short," Cle admitted.

"Do you honestly believe I could round out your crew?"

"Why not?" Cle asked.

I exploded. "Are you crazy? I know nothing about spaceships or medicine."

"You can learn," Sante shrugged.

"Impossible. Are you forgetting that I'm a Casual?"

"So what!" said Sante. "Greatness is not a formula instilled through genetic engineering. No one can predict where genius might strike or the Janaforma would be demigods by now."

"Listen to me," said Cle. "I've served with some incredibly noble and brilliant people at Space Security. Not all of them were Janaforma and not all of them had The Genetic Edge or were even experienced veterans. Some were rookies right out of the space academies. Besides, I always know who is going to make it at Space Security and who isn't. You're going to make it; but you're not going to make it if you don't try."

"You might believe that now; but what is going to happen when you find out I am a slow learner?"

"You will need to trust us until you learn to trust yourself," said Sante.

Everything was simple for them. Could they ever understand how difficult learning was for me—and what if I fell short? If I disappointed them, would they stop loving me?

"I guess this is a good time to tell you about Devina," said Sante. "It's bound to come up sooner or later. When Cle and I served on *Aeternus One*, we fell in love and made a commitment to each other. When we pulled the *Kirtland* assignment, we teamed with Devina and attempted to establish a personal relationship. I'm not going to lie and say that we didn't love her. We did."

"To be fair," said Cle. "Sante loved her more than I did."

Sante grimaced. "How can you say such a ridiculous thing?"

"It's true. You loved her more."

It's not a problem," I assured them.

Sante felt that she needed to explain. "I was committed to making it work until I understood that it could never work."

"What happened to the relationship?" I asked.

"We broke up," said Cle. "It wasn't exactly a friendly parting either."

"I'm glad she is out of the picture and you were free to find me."

"There was Devina and—and a few others, especially for me, before I met Cle," Sante admitted. "But when I saw you, it was like the first time I saw Cle and he came into my surgery with an injured knee. I just knew."

I just knew too. My internal chemistry had worked its alchemy upon me. My heart was free and now this miraculous love-thing had happened to me. However, trust—the faith to take it as it comes and believe that it will work out—was an attitude that did not come easily for me. With or without the Smith curse, a million unconscious ways existed for me to sabotage this relationship. I still was walking on eggshells.

****

The following cycle we went to Space Security headquarters and they introduced me to Commander Vertain. Cle's imitation of her voice, the previous cycle, was eerily accurate. She was the first older Janaforma I met and her maturity had a powerful and confident air. While perhaps Patra seemed more feminine because she was pregnant, Captain Vertain seemed more masculine than either Sante or Cle. Yet, I knew she was a Janaforma lifebearer (it was the breast thing again). Her uniform was tight in all the right spots to show-off her perfect feminine figure.

Cle, acting very masculine and serious, told Commander Vertain, "As captain of the *Daedalus*, I want J. Hibernia Smith on my space team."

Vertain immediately began to examine me. "How are you trained?" she asked me.

I told her my Earth number code OSP3467 and she sent for my resume and records. "I have an undergraduate degree in mathematical arts and geometry," I offered. "My Ph.D. is in quantum graphics modeling. My research focused on charting the historical and genetic, ethnographic migration patterns of Humans; but my funding evaporated, so I did additional post-graduate work in a slightly different area of computer graphics."

"And you now work for the Atlas Map Company as a cartographer?" asked Vertain, perusing my records as they flashed on the screen in front of her.

I felt an internal wince of embarrassment. "Yes, I do refinement and editing work on charts prepared by space teams."

"Well let's hope you have a more rewarding experience working for Space Security," she said with a smile.

"Does that mean you want me?"

"We definitely want you. Space Security is desperate for cartographers. Let me explain a little about our organization and our method of operation. We give an apprentice test every ninety cycles. Learning takes as much or as little time as you need to function as a full-fledged officer. I'm not saying training should take the rest of your life, but neither is training-time a race. Apprentices must have a serious commitment to their teammates and strive to qualify as soon as possible. Because the pressure is so great on senior officers, while you are an apprentice, their word is law while in space. If at any time they want to disqualify you as a candidate, it is their option. When you and your team believe you are ready, you can petition Space Security for your officer's degree. We want new people at Space Security; but one must be superior in order to qualify and it's not easy to quality even if one is Janaforma. My suggestion is to go out with Sante and Cle and get a hands-on-feel for what we do. Space Security is important to the Janaforma and we pour our beliefs, energy, and sometimes our lives into this vehicle of service." Commander Vertain pointed to a vitarattha device on the lapel of her uniform and explained the etched symbols on its triangular surface. "Loyalty, altruism, self-sacrifice," she said. "The symbol in the center stands for Community. Simon Forma, our creator, instilled these virtues in the Janaforma through the 3C gene. As a result, we feel these virtues most profoundly. You are Human and will not have the same genetic compulsions that drive the Janaforma; however, you must find a way to ignite these virtues within yourself to succeed. Good luck, as you Humans say and thank you in advance for your service."

Afterward Sante and Cle cheered and Cle exclaimed, "Great! I'm surprised she gave you such a small salary though. They usually give newbees at least 15,000 credits a quarter."

Vertain was paying me 12,000 credits a quarter and I thought it a fortune. "I could have bought that Naiven silk dress from Yurgie," I said.

"As long as this triad is simpatico, we will be the strongest structure in this universe," said Cle.

I felt as if I was playing solitaire again with half a deck of cards. "What do I need to learn to qualify?" I asked.

"Let's play this the Tyrowsian way," suggested Sante. "You don't need to know everything immediately."

"I'll never be able to do this," I moaned a little later.

"Okay. I'll allow you to say that one more time," cautioned Cle. "Go ahead. Get it out of your system."

"I don't want you to ruin your reputations with Space Security," I tried to explain.

"Okay," said Sante. "That's it. You've used up your last opportunity to belittle yourself."

"You can't stop me from thinking these thoughts," I argued.

Sante turned around and tapped me in the middle of forehead with his index finger. "Your fear can be reduced in stages if you stop reaffirming your worthlessness."

"Stop that!" I squawked. "You remind me of a woodpecker tapping my forehead as if I'm a tree."

"Sorry!" He made a gesture that meant, "Hands off."

Cle snickered. "Listen to Sante Woodpecker. Take the first step and say, I can poke a hole in this problem."

About fifty replies ripped through my mind, all of which led to my sabotaging the future in some critical way. "Okay," I said instead. "I'm going to do this!"

"Hooray!" they cheered.

We went down to the supply store and I received six black uniforms and a whitesuit. "You don't need to wear these uniforms unless you want to," said Cle. "Uniforms are optional aboard the *Daedalus*."

When we arrived back at the apartment, Cle and Sante gave me another gift. Sante presented me with a gold armlet that matched theirs. Engraved in fancy script along the length were the Mescale rilets that stood for self-sacrifice, loyalty, and altruism. "Welcome to the Janaforma Community," said Sante. Then Cle fitted the bracelet on my arm above my elbow with a bit of ceremony.

SEVEN

Flight plans for the *Daedalus* appeared on the multidex the following cycle. Two hours before launch, we went down to the hangar to do the prep-up. I was concerned over my decision to attempt this challenge. I wanted to face my future as the gutsy Hibernia but still felt like an imposter pretending I was someone else.

Cle ran a loving hand over the sterile, white belly of the *Daedalus* while explaining to me, "This ship is our mother, our life-support in space. We always make sure she's meticulous before taking her out. We tune in to her—listen to how she runs. We let our intuition lead us on an inspection of the hull and working systems."

Sante was running a program with a gismo called a thermoionizer, looking for any lingering radiation inside the airlocks. "It's clean," he reported with a salute toward our captain.

Cle was full of instructor's zeal asking me, "Do you understand how a thermoionizer works?" He started talking about a thermoionizer in an abstract, technical lingo he slipped into from time to time. Then he looked up, noticed my confusion, and said, "You probably should concentrate on navigation first."

There they were—all those words standing between me and understanding—radical departure point, limited range, lapse momentum, and Proteus' imaginary line. What Sante and Cle did and understood was way beyond difficult; it was baffling. "The first thing you need to learn is the Tyrowsian language," said Cle. "You can't rely on a translator. Sorry, it's picayune but Space Security takes it seriously. Don't worry! Cuneate is easy. You can learn conversational Cuneate in a few weeks." That was coming from a genetically engineered creature that claimed to speak all languages. Language lessons began immediately. Everywhere onship, objects appeared wearing Cuneate nametags. I began taking copious notes on a microdex that I wore on my belt. I was the awkward freshman again, only this time, I knew how awkward I was.

"What are you doing?" Cle asked me.

"Taking notes—why?"

"Don't take notes. You can't listen properly when you take notes. Besides, life is not a rehearsal for a performance given later. Pay total attention the first time—be in the moment and you will remember everything you need to know." Cle was going to be a tough teacher; but that was all right; my life was full of tough teachers.

"Wait a second. I don't have a genetically engineered brain. You have to allow me my little crutch, the written word." I continued to take notes, but more discreetly.

Cle changed topics yet again. "This is a *ditcitra*." A *ditcitra* was a stubby little pen-type device used for writing Cuneate. Cle began making marks on a piece of paper. "You don't need to learn to write Cuneate by hand; but it might be interesting to know how to do it." Twenty-eight symbols appeared on the paper. "I love you, is *aber gut*," Cle said showing me how it looked. The *ditcitra* barely touched the page as it slid along. The beautiful picture of those words, like master portraits of thought, revealed a well-practiced hand.

"As you can see, it depends on which way you shade the dot that indicates whether you have ha, ea, oo or ta sound, which are somewhat like English vowels. Adjectives follow nouns—verbs prefix pronouns. So I love, is *aber gut* and you love, is teaber gut, etc. Look at me. Touch my lips and feel the words as they emerge from my mouth." Cle said something in Cuneate. "Do you feel the strange breathlessness in the words? Cuneate words are formed on the breath as an exhale." Cle was right about the strangeness. The Tyrowsian language had a gasping quality with pauses for gulps of air. "Cuneate has no future or past tense. That's what makes the language easy to learn. If you are around Tyrowsians, or the Janaforma, you'll hear the word *hataeasta* all the time."

"*Hataeasta* is the word Sante and Nova used. They said, 'through *hataeasta*' when we left the Earth Pavilion. "Tell me, Cle; what does it mean?"

"Literally translated into Universal, *hataeasta* means, 'only now.' The true meaning of *hataeasta* lies in the transcendental or, a striving for experience beyond ordinary reality to expand the various frameworks of realities and blend them into a cohesive whole, or Now."

"What?"

"Don't worry; I'll give you some reading material that will help you understand the subtleties of *hataeasta*. It's important because I don't want you to get the wrong idea. Seekers who flirt with *hataeasta* often come out fundamentalists. They believe all they need to do is deny yesterday and ignore tomorrow and voila, they are home free, which only goes to prove—

no matter how brilliant a philosophy, someone can dumb it down to its lowest common denominator. Anyway, two other expressions you might hear are, *keirtoyyan hataeasta*, which literally translated as, 'now gone by' and rattha *hataeasta*,' translates as, 'now yet to happen.'"

"That doesn't make any sense."

"It does in Tyrowsian," Cle assured me.

"So how do Tyrowsians state the present?"

"*Hataeasta*. Tyrowsians believe time is a third dimensional construct, so neither the past nor the future really exits for them." I took the microdex off my belt and attempted to write a few notes about what Cle was saying. "See!" Cle exclaimed triumphantly. "I told you. You'll need to approach learning in a new way."

Cle swept the *ditcitra* across the paper creating something like a sideways V. "There is a simple device used in writing Cuneate. This symbol" — > — "indicates future reference while this symbol," — < — "indicates past reference. Notice when Tyrowsians speak, their minds will shift to the future or the past and—whether they admit it or not—they will unconsciously make this symbol with their fingers." After three cycles, Cle insisted that I refer to objects on the ship by their Cuneate names. I relied heavily on the phonetic Universal, inconspicuously filling it in under each word.

Along with books written in Universal about the Tyrowsian philosophy of *hataeasta*, Cle gave me a book of fairytales written in Tyrowsian that I was supposed to translate. The first story was entitled, The Cerribeame Guard. It certainly was a strange introduction to this new language. It was obvious from the first page that Tyrowsians lived in fear and were passing that fear on to their children. The Cerribeame were creatures who, "march like zombies in phalanx formation through the night, their skin like suid." The closest Universal equivalent to suid was tomentose, meaning, "covered with short, densely-matted, wooly hair." The Cerribeame dressed in identical, heavy, gray clothing and were able to spy on a sleeper's dreams. Then, if they did not like what they saw, they would steal your soul and use the body to their own ends.

I complained to Cle, "These are not fairytales; these are horror stories."

Cle shrugged. "Tyrowsian children tease each other with the fear of the Cerribeame. It's legend among them."

Sante suddenly became involved and said, "It's also a mind-control game for those who know how to play. When I was five bio-years old, I had a few Tyrowsian playmates and they told me about the Cerribeame Guard. It scared the Holy Presence right out of me."

I felt as if I was getting deeper and deeper into the muck of bewilderment. "And what's the Holy Presence?" I dared to ask.

"It's a Tyrowsian expression that sometimes is used as an exclamation," said Cle. "A moment happens, you notice it, everything shuffles, and then you realize reality is a bit more complicated than you suspected. You shake off your old vision of reality and now you are within the sphere of the Holy Presence where you are able to gain a greater perspective of reality."

"Where did you two learn all this stuff?"

"Sante is gifted and talks to spirits in other dimensions," said Cle. "I'm lucky. I had a great education. My parents were original Janaforma, bred in Simon Forma's nativity vats. They were brilliant and my lifebearer parent had incredible ingenuity. I was their only child and they gave me everything they could. My mind was hungry and absorbed knowledge like a high-density spool. One of my degrees is in linguistic studies. I don't use it much anymore, but language still fascinates me and with you, I can feel my old enthusiasm for the subject returning."

"Poor Hibernia!" Sante joked. "To be on the crest of Cle's enthusiasm for a new passion can be exhausting."

"It might be interesting for Hi and me to explore word origins and what drives changes in languages—for example, the word Cerribeame. In the present, ask anyone what Cerribeame means and they will tell you, Cerribeame is a Cuneate word that refers to, 'fearful Ganat females.' However, Cerribeame began as a J'hop or Ganat word that referred to a tribe of Ganat females that originally came from the mountainous regions of Calypso. Tyrowsians called their rifter ships 'bogeys,' which meant 'an odd jump."

Sante added, "The odd jump was the ability of those rifters to breach hyperspace."

"Rifters were crewed with young Cerribeame females," said Cle. "When Humans heard about the bogey rifters, they thought it was a joke and that Tyrowsians meant, 'boogie' as in 'boogieman.' Tyrowsians quickly dropped the bogey reference and simply called their ships Cerribeame rifters."

"It sounds like six of one or half dozen of the other to me," I told them. "Cerribeame and boogieman are both the manifestation of open-ended fear—of the unknown."

My efforts at the end of the third cycle left me exhausted. In the ambient light of the sleeproom, my teacher sat next to me on the bed and fondled my hair. "Cuneate is okay for ship's communication; but a language without a past or future tense, can never explain how much you mean to me," said Cle.

"Does the Cuneate language have any suitable pronouns for lifegivers or consorts?" I asked. "Or do I have to spend the rest of my life referring to you as he/she?"

Cle laughed. "Afraid not. Cuneate is more limited than Universal." Cle pulled me into an embrace. Cle's accent changed to a soft, romantic foreign lilt; but the words were perfectly clear. "How about I teach you Mescale too? Not only does Mescale have twelve thousand variations on the infinitive, 'to love,' but Mescale has pronouns for the consort and lifegiver."

"Please tell me what they are Cle?"

"A lifegiver such as Sante is *le*, *lim*, and *lis* and a consort such as me is *ce*, *cim*, and *cis*." The actual pronunciation of *ce* and *le*, *cim* and *lim*, and *cis* and *lis* were almost identical and only a slight inflection in the voice indicated the difference. I needed to learn Cuneate, but I embraced the Mescale language with enthusiasm. Learning and using those Mescale pronouns liberated me, and I began to use them more and more. I no longer had to stuff Sante and Cle into Universal dualities and they were free to be their unique selves.

****

During the following cycles, I became increasingly aware that Sante and Cle functioned on very little sleep. My internal time clock was utterly confused and I was sleeping more. I lazed in bed with my awareness tuned to the inner workings of the *Daedalus*. A peaceful sound, perhaps like water pouring into a crystal glass, came from somewhere in the ship and gently lulled me back to sleep. I awoke later and the bed next to me was still cold. The emptiness aroused me and I became determined to find my lovers and discover what they were doing. When I found them, they were sitting by a window staring out into space. "Sit down and meditate with us," Sante said.

"I don't know how."

Sante's hands extended to me. "We can show you the way in, however it is up to you what you do, once you get there." I sat and waited with Sante and Cle in the darkness, not knowing what to expect. At first, I discovered my yearning to know was intense and my meditations turned into a great adventure where lively arabesques of colors and patterns leapt up before me in dances of symbolic suggestion. My inner loneliness slowly dwindled as I began to peek inside my greater consciousness. I realized that it was bigger and more elaborate with knowledge than I could comprehend. Consciousness was not limited to my body; consciousness traveled out and could join with the far removed Tyrowsian mystics afloat in their space pods. Consciousness weaved a network of peaceful minds together across space and demonstrated to me that I was not alone.

****

The next cycle, Sante casually suggested that it was time for me to step out into space and my palms immediately turned sweaty. "I've never been weightless except for the few seconds when the moon shuttle landed and then with you inside the vitarattha when you rescued me."

"We'll take care of that," said Cle. Straightway, we went to the buffer zone that separated the inner and outer hulls. This area doubled as a running track; but today it was my testing ground. Cle flipped a C-shaped lever on the wall, which reduced gravity in small increments. After a couple of minutes, my stomach seemed to be floating up inside my throat. They stared at me, waiting to see if I could pass this first, crucial test and not get sick.

"Don't fight it. Make peace with your nausea," called Sante.

The freedom of movement is what intrigued me and suddenly I honestly began to enjoy myself by turning somersaults. "You're a miracle!" Cle exclaimed and *ce* blew me a kiss. "Soon we shall experience Zero-G together and in the grip of passion, make red hot love."

I barely had an opportunity to savor my truce with microgravity when Cle began showing me how the vitarattha worked. "Literally, vitarattha means 'future life protector,'" *ce* explained.

Technically, I wasn't sure what a vitarattha was and hesitated even to ask. If I asked, Cle would explain in detail. Then *ce* would expect me to remember everything and ask all appropriate questions until I understood how the gadget worked. No confusion existed about the critical importance of the vitarattha. The vitarattha was the ultimate gadget that had the ability to generate a protective shield around the physical body in open space. "Critically important!" emphasized Sante. "If your vitarattha isn't working, don't step off into space. By the way, Cle's parents invented the vitarattha and that's why Cle is filthy rich."

Sante's charge got a rise out of Cle. "My wealth is not filthy!" said Cle and *ce* pointed a finger at Sante. "Did you learn that expression from Humans or Tyrowsians?"

Sante winked at me and said, "I don't remember."

"Don't listen to *lim*," said Cle. "My parents earned their wealth through ingenuity and hard work."

"I apologize," said Sante. "Cle is right," and *le* attached the vitarattha device to the left side of my shirt, near my heart. "Always wear your vitarattha in this exact spot so you instinctively know where it is inside the whitesuit. When you activate it, you will feel a split second tingle around you to let you know it is prepared to activate a forcefield around you." Sante embraced me and said, "Go ahead, initiate function one." I touched the center of the pin and a second later, heard the vitarattha make its characteristic whooshing sound. Sante and I were inside the vitarattha together and I immediately loved the feeling of intimate safety with *lim*.

****

A short time later, the alarms went off inside the *Daedalus*. It was our first mission with me as a crewmember. The ship's multidex had locked in the exact coordinates of the incoming call, but Cle insisted I learn how to figure out coordinates from the ship's sensors. Without too much trouble, I calculated the correct coordinates in about two minutes time; but by then, we were already on our way. Cle told me, "You'll never beat the multidex. The important thing is you understand how the multidex calculates the coordinates in case the multidex fails."

"Multidex redirect to Universal Translator (UT)," said Cle to the multidex. "This part is easy," *ce* explained. "All you need to do is redirect the signal into the UT function. Every known language and code is in there. Here it comes—multidex telemetry is confirming the signal is coming from cadix 4.008." Cle began sending a message in standard star code.

"Wouldn't it be quicker to verbally confirm the message?" I asked.

"It might be a bit faster, but this method is definitely superior. I can choose the appropriate code with a simple touch, attach it to the original signal we intercepted, and simultaneously transmit it in several different codes to different locations. See, I just did it. Now Central Command, along with every other Space Security ship in Daleth Sector, knows we are on our way to cadix 4.008 and why."

"Are the messages we get always in star code?"

"No. Hawking Space Station used a binary light signal. A message can be in a hundred different forms. Sometimes we are not smart enough to know what we are receiving, but the multidex usually knows."

"I'm getting more now," said Sante. "It's a small Euterpean cruiser, called the Hesperian. It's on route to the Festival of Auroras on New Delphi. They're asking if we have a doctor aboard. Sounds made to order for me. Let's go, Hi. Your maiden spacewalk waits." Thank goodness, Sante did not expect me to do anything except accompany *lim*. We worked fast, Sante talking all the while as we suited-up, reminding me of a million things I needed to remember. In ninety seconds, we were inside the airlock where all I heard was the sound of my ragged breath, inside my whitesuit helmet. I heard a click and glanced down to see that Sante had hooked our belts together. "Take a few deep breaths," said Sante. "Cle said you are respiring too fast."

"I'll be okay," I said in a shaky voice. The exterior doors flashed opened and we stepped outside into the black nothingness. I was scared and could barely breathe. It was an old nightmare of stepping off into an endless abyss; but, "Oh my god!" This time the dream was real! Absolutely nothing stood between eternity and me except that thin, mortal-made vitarattha. Glancing backward, toward the *Daedalus*, I saw my growing distance from safe haven and my fear nearly turned into panic. Yet, I did not give into my fear. I had the good sense to remember what Sante told me earlier. "Look beyond, into the heavens." I looked off, into the faraway, looking farther than I ever believed possible. The magenta and blue Trifid Nebula seemed close enough to embrace. I reached out toward its nursery of stars and a moment of awe consumed me. I don't know if it was a moment of Holy Presence, but for a few seconds, I was stunned with awe. The universe was alive, a moving and evolving spectacle, and I was in it and moving and evolving with it. Beyond that, I knew that I had transcended even my wildest dreams of what I was capable of doing. I was a Casual Human, but I was capable of walking in open space and seeing the Trifid Nebula with my naked eyes.

We moved toward the Hesperian. Finally, the outer airlock door flashed open, and I scrambled inside first. "*Secot appa-twa*," Sante relayed to Cle in Cuneate, meaning the *Hesperian* picked us up and we were secure inside its airlock.

The inner airlock door opened and a Gathosian, named Syroon, met us in an antechamber, and introduced himself as captain of the Hesperian. Syroon was dressed as a Hectarian mystic and wore a voluminous saffron-colored robe. Hectarian mystics are an ancient Gathosian cult seeming to be as old as the beginning of time. For centuries, along with the Trinity witches, they've controlled the New Delphi Crystal on the planet Delphi.

Hectarians claim many things about the Crystal, such as the Crystal is one of the power centers of our galaxy and contact with the Crystal brings the power of enlightenment. Gathosian culture is rich with ancient legends about New Delphi, tales about ill-fated lovers and passion-infused vendettas sometime ending in suicide. Despite the Hectarian and Trinity mythos surrounding New Delphi, each spring, careless youth and inflamed lovers flock to the Crystal to undergo the bonding ceremony that many claim, link them together through eternity.

Like most Gathosians, Syroon's eyes were blue-black with flashing gold rutilated shafts of light intersecting through the irises. He was swarthy, exceptionally handsome and he didn't jibe with my preconceived images of a humble holy man. Sante scanned the air in front of us and indicated that it was okay to lift our helmets and deactivate our vitaratthas. Sante greeted Syroon in Mescale and Syroon led us through a bulkhead door into the interior of the ship.

Hesperian's passenger manifest was made up of Gathosians, Humans, and Tyrowsians, all headed for the New Delphi Crystal. Many passengers were young lovers gearing up to commit to the bonding in the presence of the Crystal. The party atmosphere was heady with the fragrance of tartan ratu and palmaide, which is a potent fruity liquor brewed on New Delphi. Following Syroon, we wound our way through a labyrinth of amber-lighted walkways. When I caught my first whiff of tartan ratu, my heart began to flutter. The temperature aboard the *Hesperian* was too hot. They were running in nightmode and many of the cabin doors stood open along the passageways, exposing the intimate activity of private lives. Visual feats of scantily clad bodies, freeze-framed silhouettes of entwined legs and arms, winked in and out of my line of vision.

We traced Syroon's steps, going deeper and deeper into the heart of the ship. The combination of ratu and visual stimulation was beginning to affect me so Sante said, "Use your vitarattha. Keep the settings low, just enough to give you some light protection."

I glanced down to adjust my vitarattha and just then, out of the corner of my eye, I spied someone walk up behind me and then quickly veer off and slip down an adjacent hallway. She was dressed in the green habit of the Trinity witches with a dark hood pulled up over her head. I turned and called after her. "Excuse me; don't I know you?"

"Who was it?" asked Sante.

"I think it was Bell."

Syroon ushered us into a room with a strange stone table in the center where the temperature was just above freezing. "Is this some kind of walk-in refrigerator or your morgue?" Sante asked.

"We're in the ship's galley," said Syroon. "It's cold in here because we're having problems with the air exchangers." In the center of the stone table lay a man of indeterminate age. He was soaking wet and covered in tartan ratu dust. His lips were pale blue and he seemed to be unconscious or perhaps even dead. Sante activated *lis* own vitarattha before proceeding with the physical examination. Running the mediscan the length of the patient's body *le* said, "He's alive but suffering from hypothermia and an enormous overdose of raw tartan ratu." Sante turned to Syroon and asked, "What went on here?"

"I have no idea," replied Syroon. "All parties on this ship are private affairs and how this particular one ended up in the galley, I don't care to know. All I can say is some individuals attempt to take on more than they can handle."

"Why did you leave this man in this freezing room?" asked Sante.

Syroon shrugged. "I couldn't get anyone to touch him because he is covered in raw ratu."

The man stirred from the tingling effects of the mediscan. His eyelids sprang open and his body went stiff with a spasm. That's when I noticed that he had five-fingered hands like a Human, but Gathosian eyes. These Gathosian eyes appeared tortured and the rutilates fractured. Some personal terror, beyond the room, held his attention. Sante leaned over the man telling him, "I'm Dr. Jana Sante of Orion Spur Space Security. You're going to be okay." I pulled a thermal sheet out of our medical kit and wrapped the sheet tightly around our patient. "Call Cle and transmit his vitals." Sante touched the patient in several specific places—neck, chest, and wrist. "I'll be right back. I'm going back to the *Daedalus* and fetch the mini-shuttle. We'll transport him that way so you can practice that aspect of an actual rescue."

I plugged the mediscan into a port on my utility belt. "Cle," I called through my communicator. "Get ready to receive the patient's vitals,"

"The bioform have a number code or name?" asked Cle.

I was so sure the man was a bio that I leaned over him and asked, "Can you tell me your name?" His cold blue lips moved but no sound came out.

Then he mumbled forcing me to lean closer to hear what he was struggling to say. The ratu was so concentrated that I thought I could smell it through my vitarattha. "I think he said his name is Dulce," I said to Cle.

"Dulce? Like in the Divine Dulce?" questioned Cle.

"I don't know. He says his name is Dulce though."

"We are bound forever together," choked the man who called himself Dulce. He struggled to lift his head from the stone table. Some imagined terror seized him and he attempted to claw my arm; but my vitarattha gently repelled his hand. "You don't understand. Don't help me. Let me go." His voice broke through the dryness in his throat. "No more Trinity witch tricks—I beg you." When Sante returned *le* pasted two sound tranquilizers on either side of Dulce's temple and he screamed, "Take them off! Get that cacophony away from my ears!" Spittle dribbled from the corners of his mouth washing the dusty ocher of tartan ratu down his chin before he passed out.

Sante showed me the proper way to move a patient and continued giving me bits of advice. "Know the proper procedure, but don't get locked into it. It's more important to follow your instincts."

"Why didn't we go by mini-shuttle in the first place?" I asked, still remembering my fear of open space.

"It's easier to maneuver in a whitesuit with a jetpack strapped to your back than to get the mini-shuttle in and out of tight places. Besides, many ships are incompatible and we like to protect the shuttle until we know what's unfolding. If something happens to the *Daedalus*, our mini-shuttle might be our only means of escape. Remember, not all fellow travelers have honorable intentions. Even if the situation seems innocuous, when beings are in crisis, they can become unpredictable. That's why you should always be super-alert when entering strange spaceships."

"Don't we get to carry any kind of weapon?"

"We don't need weapons; we have Shardasko defense."

With a questioning stare, I asked, "Shardasko defense?"

"Yes! Shardasko defense," *le* repeated. '—the ability to anticipate the unfolding hub of time, the advantage of being able to see something happen right before it occurs. I, personally, consider it my insurance of free will. Don't worry, Hibernia. You can learn Shardasko too; and until you do, I will protect you. Remember, in ninety-nine percent of the cases, the dangers are not from people, but from space and the situation. However," *le* grinned, "I wouldn't want to be caught without my Shardasko and my vitarattha, at least not in this universe."

Inside the mini-shuttle, we locked the gurney to the floor and Sante flew the few hundred meters back to the *Daedalus* where the mini-shuttle clicked into its template on the belly of the *Daedalus*. When Cle opened the double-airlock, *ce* asked, "What's the story on this one? Hi said his name is Dulce."

"Whatever his name, he's another victim of raw tartan ratu. I'm going to have to bathe him before I treat him." Sante's voice sounded as if ratu overdoses were as common as mosquito bites. I asked *lim* about it and *le* admitted, "It's not unusual, especially between Euterpe and Delphi."

No sooner did Sante take Dulce off to the clinic than another communication came from the Hesperian. Someone, who identified herself as Dulce's granddaughter, was requesting to come aboard the *Daedalus* so she could talk to, "Doctor Jana Sante." The *Hesperian* engines pulsed until it snuggled up closer to the *Daedalus* and this time the *Daedalus* was able to extend a vacuum walkway between the two ships. The woman who walked through the *Daedalus* airlock was the same individual I saw a few minutes before in the hallway of the *Hesperian*. With her hood down, I now could see that it was Bell from the Pink Slipper and probably many ports in between.

"We meet again," said Cle and *ce* took a deliberate step backward.

"It is you!" I said in amazement.

"Yes," she said with a throaty growl.

"Sante?" Cle called through the intercom. "Please get down here—pronto! You'll never guess who just stepped aboard." Cle stared at the woman intently. "This is not serendipity—is it?"

"Certainly not," Bell agreed. "However, I did not plan this rendezvous—did you?" Her voice sounded different—foreign, mysterious although she appeared the same as she did that night in the Pink Slipper. "Perhaps, this time, your vanity called me here."

Cle peered at her with that questioning and potent stare of *cis* that always made me want to squirm. "What are you suggesting? We barely know each other. We've met one time before."

"Technically, that's true. Wonder World was our first physical encounter, but we've been circling each other for centuries. I was present the evening Simon Forma began collecting the DNA blood samples that made you possible." Cle's eyes demanded—prove it, but Bell was undaunted. "You might say I knew Simon Forma intimately for a while. You, the 3C Janaforma, were the manifestation of his most sacred vision. I know Jana Revba tried to reap much of the public credit; but he merely was a smart technician that became a slick businessman. Simon Forma was the authentic genius behind the project." Bell hesitated for a moment. She looked Cle over carefully and asked, "Are you ready?"

Cle was acutely suspicious. "Ready for what?"

"To suspend your weak presumptions and become what Simon Forma intended. Or perhaps, I should put it into terms your Tyrowsian educators instilled in you. Are you alert to your Holy Presence?" Cle opened *cis* eyes a little wider. Bell began to play with Cle in a dangerous way and I was surprised she possessed the temerity to do it. "You are like Simon in so many ways. Clearly, you have his inquisitive mind. Do you possess his passion too? Aaah! Yes! There it is," she said peering into Cle's eyes. "But there is so much pain hiding behind your passion. Tell me; was your lust your undoing or was it merely your ego this time around? When did you make the jump? Was it on Sutcay Tay where truth shattered your glorious illusions?"

Color drained from Cle's face until *ce* was pale as any Tyrowsian. "You appear too young to have known Simon Forma," *ce* said.

"Please excuse me. My genetic memory sometimes is overwhelming. I have little personal life—perhaps a few stolen moments—a bit of pleasure now and then from ratu. My life is a whisper compared to the blaring noise of the past. I am a kite-tail to my mother's life and her mother's life, and her mother's life before. Karmic accretion determines the direction of my every word. I endure the mocking residue of those lives as my present reality in recompense for my ancestors missing their mark. That's why I say, I knew Simon Forma well. Through the window of genetic memory, I picture past centuries as clearly as today. The predicament that now holds us began a long time ago on the planet Euterpe at a late-summer party. That night, at the estate of El Cantar, Pavlovian wine flowed like water." Bell's excitement increased. "Voluptuous bare-breasted Terpsichorean dancers lured young virgins to our tents in droves. Nubile boys and girls stood two and three deep waiting for our attentions. You look like Lyfe, a young whore we used that evening although your brain is far superior to his. He was anxious to unload his virginity. We gave him satisfaction and he gave us his genetic material and said, 'you are welcome to it." Lyfe's beauty so impressed Forma that he built the entire premier generation of Janaforma on the genetic matrix of a beautiful young Human male. Much happened that night! We were high and believed we were changing the future for the better. How were we to know that our own madness would spiral around and attempt to devour us?"

Sante walked into the light of the area. "I knew it!" *le* said in astonishment. "The sight of you suggests manipulation is brewing."

"Doctor Jana?" said Bell and she brought her full attention to bear upon Sante. "I will not mince my words, not with you. I am here on my grandfather's behalf. Be his savior and end his suffering and mine."

"You grandfather is safe and he will live. No harm will come to him while aboard the *Daedalus*."

"You misunderstand. I'm not asking you to save his life; I'm asking you to become grandfather's escort into death. Take off your mask of stupidity and use the talents Simon Forma put into you." Sante took a step backward as Cle had done earlier. "You have barely scratched the surface of your innate talents and yet you already are notorious among your Janaforma peers. They tell me you have the ability to fly blind anywhere in the Orion

Spur and never get lost. That means Simon Forma built pathways in you that no other Janaforma has. You know the way through the fourth dimension to the other side. You can help Grandfather get safely through. He is weak and needs an experienced escort such as you."

Sante appeared baffled, but Bell turned bolder. "Listen carefully; I haven't much time. Long ago, Dulce was involved in a fundamental shift in this universe. The New Delphi Crystal fell in love with him and changed its allegiance. After that, the message of the Crystal was unintelligible to the Order of Trinity Witches."

"I've heard this legend," claimed Cle. "Are you suggesting that the Dulce up in our clinic really is the divine Dulcerary Cœur, the great composer and musician who they say somehow cracked the musical code of the New Delphi Crystal?"

"One in the same," said Bell. "The Trinity witches did everything they could to regain their influence over the Crystal, but to no avail. Dulce used the sacred music as the framework of his Panansha Symphony and released it to the universe. The Trinity Order lost most of their psychic power when this happened. Their remaining power they used to curse Dulce, his family and progeny. My Trinity witch grandmother adored Dulce and felt trapped between her loyalty to him and the Trinity Order. The Crystal now prevents Dulce from dying while the Trinity curse torments him night and day. Understand my dilemma; in this curse, I too pay."

Sante took another step backward. "I've sworn allegiance within my profession to do no harm."

"Grandfather wishes to die. Ask him yourself." Sante glanced away. "Damn you! Listen! Open your mind. My intervention helped you find Hibernia." Bell looked toward me. "Believe me; I am your only champion at this crossroad. Beg your angelic Sante for this saintly favor. I gave you a fair and accurate tarot reading. You were quite drunk that evening and would not have known the difference if I faked it. Out of feelings of mercy, I planted a seed of change in you before you earned the privilege. You're lucky. Charity came late in my development. I learned compassion the hard way. Now I know true kindness and I know death is the kinder choice for Grandfather." Tears began washing down her cheeks and she fell down on her knees. Through great sobs, she pleaded, "I beseech you; in the name of charity, good Doctor Jana, help my grandfather through the fourth dimension. He is weak and without help, a chance exists that the powers of the Fourth Dimension could extricate the music from him. Make Sante listen to me Hibernia. Dulce is your great-grandmother's soul mate. You and I could be sisters."

"What? Is this true?" I asked in astonishment.

She spread her arms before clasping her elegant four-fingered hands to her breast. "It's true, sister. This curse sets you aside from love as much as it does me. Only when Dulce dies will the Trinity witches cease tormenting us. I should know; I once was one of them."

Bell picked herself off the floor with no help from us. At that moment, she seemed beaten down by disappointment and loss. She turned to Sante again and looked up into *his* blue eyes with her black rutilated Gathosian eyes. She softened when she spoke to *him* just as everyone did. "I know it is difficult for you to understand, but you were chosen by Dulce's oversoul to do this deed. Many souls along the timeline have told me of your distain for involvement. Your reputation is legendary in that regard too; however, I stand here, before you, and see the complete you. The holiness and compassion behind your eyes is real—use it. You can be Grandfather's bridge of light into his next incarnation and be the answer to all our salvation at the same time."

"I'm sorry for your dilemma. I realize now that Dulce's problems are more complicated than a dose of tartan ratu, but his problems are surmountable. He can be healed."

"If you know anything about the legend, you will remember that Dulce's death can come only through the purity of one such as you. Besides, do not think of the act as mercy killing. Think of it as freeing his tortured spirit. You owe me, doctor. My generosity is not free."

"If you are referring to Hi, I acknowledge that you helped us find her; but you never mentioned the cost would be so high."

"I don't believe you fully understand. While I am kindly asking you to do this deed, your only option is to do as I ask. In other words, you need to make this jump—right here—right now—this very minute! Reality is doing you a favor by throwing you a curveball, showing you that nothing works the way you assumed it did. Don't you understand? You are in the Holy Presence. Make the jump before the window closes."

"No thank you," said Sante. Sante's no carried a tone of finality.

Bell was astonished. "I cannot believe it. Of all creatures in this universe, I thought you would understand. Don't you realize evil laughs up its sleeve at us—amused with our predicament?" She covered her eyes with her four-fingered hands as if unwilling to witness what she was seeing. "Oh!" she moaned. "Holy inevitability! Here it comes! Even now, I see your purity veering toward the obscene. My dear angelic Janaforma fools, you will find that even your Shardasko defense will not be able to protect you."

"Enough of this nonsense," said Cle, coming down hard with a voice of grounded authority. "I don't believe in curses."

"Nonsense?" Bell glared. "Now I see the flaws in the Janaforma. Your perfection sets you aside from honest compassion. You hold yourselves above mortal suffering. You cannot go forward without us, fools! You are double-damned by your own gullibility." Bell backed away from us toward the airlock. She spread her lacquered fingertips, pointing at us one by one.

"*Hataeasta* already is disintegrating before you for your rigidity of thought. Our progeny already are doomed to endless circles of illusion—tortured memories, while half-truths will distort their thinking."

"Vague doom and gloom!" said Cle. "Bottom line, your logic is circuitous."

"I have a question," I piped up. "That night at the Pink Slipper, you told me I possessed free will. Which is it, Bell? Do I have free will or am I cursed?"

Bell was indignant. "You mock my words. You are a fool suffering from bad attitude and that seems unlikely to change. My advice to you is—die quickly and hope for better genetics the next time around."

"Don't you dare speak to Hibernia like that," countered Cle and then *ce* opened the airlock and forced Bell to return to the Hesperian. The airlock snapped shut and Cle paced up and down and said yet again, "I don't believe in curses." The quiet turned monumental as Cle waited for us to agree. I was no longer sure; maybe free will and curses could coexist. One thing for sure, I never knew happiness until Bell ignited my internal fire. Until I met Cle and Sante, I knew the curse of loneliness.

"Do you think she tried to kill Dulce herself?" asked Cle.

"No," Sante said. "He told me that he tried to do it himself. He has a severe case of FSP. Suicide always is a possibility when someone is in that much pain. Something else too—recently, he suffered sexual abuse. He refuses to give names or even discuss it."

Sante contacted the *Hesperian* and talked to Captain Syroon in hushed tones. "Under the circumstances, I've decided to keep Dulce aboard the *Daedalus*. I want to take him to Aeternus and have him checked out." We prepared to depart and a moment later, the *Hesperian* was lost from view.

Within two hours, Dulce was awake, but still weak. Sante attached three sound tranquilizers to Dulce's forehead. The tiny yellow lights in the center of each tab played in rhythm across his forehead. He propped himself up on one of his elbows and stared at me intently as I approached the edge of his bed. The rutiles of his eyes appeared fractured and dull. Despite his eyes, he was an exceptionally handsome man. When he talked, everything he said came out as poetry.

"You are a holy vision!" he said, when he first saw me. "—the image of her!" He reached out and took my hand.

"How are we connected?" I asked.

"This universe is stranger than either of us can imagine."

"Are you really the Divine Dulce Cœur?"

He sneered. "I'm about as divine as dirt."

"Your granddaughter Bell told me that you were my great-grandmother's soul mate."

The corners of Dulce's tortured eyes filled with tears. "Beautiful Mellé!

Her eyes were my inspiration."

"The only thing I knew about her was that she spent eighty-one years in space alone. Is that true?"

"Yes, it's true. She took to space to get away from me. Mellé had an incredible mind, a beautiful face, and a purity of spirit that left me in awe. She was the only person I ever met that could clone herself and the clone remained an angel. If I cloned myself, the clone would be a fire-breathing dragon. On top of that, she was a committed player, not like me. I never asked to be the chosen one. The Crystal snatched me and saturated my being with new song." He looked painfully wistful. "Some gifts are most reluctantly accepted, my dear." He attempted to pick himself up again and clutched at my arm. "What was I to do, set the great gift adrift?" His eyelids squeezed tears. "I had to use what was inside my head. That it was sacred made it all the more compelling." Dulce seemed desperate to explain. "I did what I had to do, what the Crystal begged me to do. I—" Dulce hammered his chest with his fist and his face contorted in pain "—allowed this universe to brand me thief while I gave it transcendent sound. Do you have any notion how important sound is? Certain sound combinations know how to get inside the brain and coax it to evolve. I coded the sacred music into the Panansha—" He screamed in pain despite the sound tranquilizers on his forehead. "—I opened the possibility of enlightenment to everyone."

I called Sante immediately. While I held Dulce's hand, Sante gave Dulce a stronger sedative. He continued to mumble as he fell asleep but it was garbled and impossible to understand.

****

I was exhausted. I fell into bed only to hear Cle say in plain Universal, "Space proficiency is the most important part of the test. You need as much space exposure as possible so you can handle any situation."

From Sante, I learned that part of the qualifying test was a solo space rescue where I would be responsible for making all decisions. I still wondered how-in-the-universe I would get through such an ordeal. I fell asleep and dreamt of Dulce. He wore a long scarlet and purple robe like those of the Tyrowsian aristocracy. On some bizarre and gothic altar, he offered the first words of the Panansha Symphony. "Beea birtha, nei michi en Panansha," he chanted, as nubile altar boys swung fumigators of tartan ratu over us all.

I awoke with a start. I remembered the smell of ratu from my dream and desperately needed to make love. I located Cle and Sante in the buffer zone. Sante had not slept since we left Aeternus and now Cle was not sleeping either, yet they still possessed enough energy to think about exercise. They were performing their once a cycle routine—running. I watched for a while as their sleek, sweaty bodies swept around the inside perimeter of the ship. "Come and join us," shouted Cle on one of *cis* laps, so I began running too.

****

Cycles rolled eternally on and the fact that Sante and Cle slept less and less amazed me. I wanted to sleep for a week; but instead I plodded to the bridge with my copious notes to review what I learned so far. I had settled myself at the multidex when a coded message started flashing across the screen. Bone tired, I certainly did not want to go for a spacewalk. Still, I did what I knew I had to do.

Cle appeared on the bridge seconds later and asked, "What do you have so far?"

"The message is coming in from somewhere near Tnamis Space Station."

"That must be the *Cygnus*."

"Isn't that Nova's ship?"

"Yes, sometimes we need to act as backup if something major occurs."

The coded message read, "*OSSS Cygnus* to OSSS *Daedalus*—need assistance—cadix 0.522 by 0.23—Liart."

Cle switched to Cuneate and sent a message to Aeternus Command. The reply returned immediately. "Aeternus command doesn't know what's happening. We've got provisional clearance to assist if we can get someone to cover our space."

"Maybe Patra is having the baby."

Sante suddenly appeared on the bridge and said, "I don't think so."

"I'm checking with the *Seevaj* in Tzaddic Sector to see if they can cover for us," said Cle. Suddenly the *Daedalus* alarm went off and Cle did not even feed the message into the translator. Incredibly, *ce* merely looked at the light code flashing over the screen and translated the message. "It's a Martian freighter, called *Gemstone*—about fifteen minutes from here. Their engines are down."

"So where do we go first?" I asked.

"We're required to cover our own territory first," said Sante.

Cle started doing several things at once. "*Seevaj* is in rescue mode—can't take the freighter," *ce* reported. "Let me check with *Cygnus* and see if they can wait." There was a moment's hesitation and then the message returned from the *Cygnus* saying, "Will hold. Come when you can."

"Come here, Hi," said Sante. "You can answer the freighter because they are communicating in Universal. Do you remember what to say?"

"I tell them we've picked up their call, confirm their position, and give them a rendezvous time?"

"Tell them 12.4 minutes until rendezvous," said Cle. As I sent the message to the *Gemstone*, Cle turned to Sante and said, "I'll go. A problem with engines I can probably handle."

"I'll go too," I volunteered.

"Okay, let's be quick," Cle said. Within three minutes, we were suited and inside the airlock. "Don't worry, I'm not going to let anything happen to you," Cle promised and *ce* blew me a kiss from inside *cis* vitarattha. "Let me tell you a secret. The first time I went out in space, I got sick. I knew if I vomited, I would be dead." We pulled down the helmets on our whitesuits. "My whole life was geared toward space and yet I almost washed out my first time. Believe me, it was not easy going out the second time."

Sante's voice spoke to me from inside my helmet. "Receiving you," *ce* said from the bridge.

"Tell Hibernia about your first time in space," said Cle. "Maybe it will inspire her."

"Not yet!" insisted Sante. *Lis* voice turned intimate. "I want to tell you personally. Not this way, not through ship's communication."

Cle either sensed or understood my fear better than Sante and *ce* stayed close by my side until we reached the *Gemstone* airlock. *Ce* surprised me when he said, "I'm going to let you take charge of the initial approach so we can identify your strengths and weaknesses." *Ce* handed me the scanner. "You're going to be great. Just be your sweet charming self, identify us, and we'll wing it from there."

"Orion Spur Space Security in position at airlock four," I said. "Request permission to come aboard?" The outer door flashed open and we stepped inside the airlock. We waited in the small, dark chamber as it filled with air. The inner door opened and we stepped inside the freighter. I could see through my visor that the captain was a Human woman. We raised our helmets and I said, "This is Captain Jana Cle of the *OSSS Daedalus* and I am Jana Hibernia. How can we be of assistance?"

Suddenly I heard a blast of kakos music rage from an adjacent area and Cle suddenly warned, "Maintain your vitarattha."

"I'm sorry," said the Captain and her eyes darted away. I sensed something furtive. Her swollen lips struggled to speak, but fear muffled her words. Then four men appeared out of nowhere. They were strange, threatening-looking beasts in Human form. Everything about them boasted danger and intimidation from their tattooed faces to the bandoleer of chain maille rings the apparent leader wore across his chest. Hostility was in their posture, anger was in their eyes and intimidation was in the careless way they intruded into our personal space.

Cle slowly took off *cis* gloves, one finger at a time, concentrating on *cis* hands. *Cis* voice was deep with casual authority when *ce* asked, "What's the problem here?" It was ludicrous to believe that Cle was unaware of what I felt so strongly and yet he seemed guileless at that moment.

A makeshift gun appeared in the hand of the leader. The tip of the gun glowed red near its release. I thought of Bell and her predictions as evil hovered over the scene like a virulent virus eager to infect. A powerful consensus of my senses affirmed—the next few seconds would determine our fates.

The four men closed in on Cle, but could not touch *cim* through the vitarattha. "Now aren't you a pretty boy," mocked the leader. "Drop your protection or I'll incinerate the captain to carbon ash." Amazingly, Cle reached inside *cis* open whitesuit and deactivated *cis* vitarattha. One of the monsters tore the communicator from Cle's head and stomped it to smithereens while the one with hands like iron claws, snatched Cle from behind and held *cim* by the jaw.

"I fancy your ass and that Tyrowsian shuttle you just cruised in on," sneered the leader. He stuck out his ecru-coated tongue and licked along Cle's face leaving a long, snail-like trail of saliva across the angelic cheek of my lover.

"There is no need for hostility," said Cle. "Orion Space Security is in space to help everyone. Just tell me where you need to go and I'll take you there. No charge."

"Well isn't that neighborly," mocked the leader. He laughed a leaden, humorless laugh. His voice was as cruel as his face. "Take your clothes off or I'll take them off for you."

Cle looked uncomfortable for the first time. "Can't we at least get to know each other first?" Cle raised the open palms of *cis* hands in surrender.

"Take off those whitesuits—NOW!" I jumped as his sharp voice pricked the air like needles and my vitarattha reacted, crackling with the tension I was giving off.

"Tell em, Porkcur!" said another of his men.

Fear locked me in place. "You need some help, sweetheart?" asked Porkcur leering in my general direction.

"Go ahead, take off your whitesuit," said Cle stepping out of *cis*. "Do everything they say." I still did not move and I could not believe Cle was going along with what they demanded.

"Help her out," ordered Porkcur. One of the monsters tried to touch me; but he was unable to penetrate the forcefield of my vitarattha.

Everyone was staring at me and then Cle reactivated *cis* vitarattha. Porkcur went spastic with rage when he saw what was happening, and then, the situation exploded in violence. In less than ten seconds, the clash that would change all our lives was finished; but I witnessed events in the slowest of motions, as adrenaline pumped through my veins. Cle disappeared inside *cis* vitarattha and when *ce* appeared a split second later, *cis* body was spinning like a top. An ear-piercing howl came from *cim* and the vitarattha energy fell away in a peculiar way, gathering around *cis* feet as golden sparkles. In perfect efficiency of motion, Cle emerged and for a second, *cis* left hand touched the floor while *cis* right foot spun forward, kicking the gun from Porkcur's hand. Cle's foot continued around, catching the side of Porkcur's head, which moved at a sharp right angle to his neck.

The sound of breaking bones would forever haunt me. The gun hit the ceiling and then a wall. When one of Porkcur's companions attempted to move toward the weapon, Cle flexed *cis* elbow toward the man's jaw and he fell like a severed tree. One last time, Cle jumped, this time *cis* foot above *cis* head when *ce* delivered a spin-back kick to another of those amazed beasts. As the last timid one quickly glanced down at his three fallen companions, Cle grabbed his hair and pulled his head down into *cis* knee—smash. The last monster crumpled to the floor like a bag of bones.

"Are there anymore?" asked Cle, looking at the *Gemstone* captain. Suddenly, *ce* was all Janaforma reason again.

"All dead, all dead but me," cried the captain. The story spilled out of her. "They overtook us in a Space Security shuttle—"

"Where's your crew?" asked Cle.

"Dead. Tom, Coco, and Mike—all dead." Her voice dropped and her lips quivered with emotion.

Cle swept her body with the mediscan and told her, "You're safe and you are going to be okay." Cle looked at the smashed communicator on the floor and told me, "Call Sante. Tell *lim* what happened and that we have a Human female suffering from multiple trauma shock—" Cle leaned down to scan the four bodies sprawling across the floor like throw rugs. "Human male number one has head and internal injuries; Human male number two has a broken jaw and minor head injuries; and Humans three and four—are dead."

"Did I hear you right? You say, they are dead?"

"You heard right. Two are dead."

Opening a frequency to the *Daedalus*, I called, "Sante?" but *le* did not answer. "Sante, please, come in?" More silence. I began to shake—violently. I felt as if I was falling backward through time and nothing could stop me. "Sante, please answer me."

"I'm here," Sante finally said. "There's another problem; but it can wait." *Lis* words were emotionless, *lis* tone almost dull. Was it Sante or was I experiencing the after-shock of what just happened? "Let me talk to Cle," Sante said. I handed Cle my wrist communicator and Sante said something in a language I did not understand. It was not Mescale and it was not Tyrowsian or Universal. I was sure the language shift was intentional so they to speak to each other in private.

When Cle glanced up, *ce* had softened and *cis* eyes were glassy with tears. "Acknowledge," *ce* said. Cle turned to the captain of the *Gemstone* and *cis* voice was at first unsteady. "Can you tell me your name?" *ce* asked.

The captain thought about it as if searching for an appropriate answer to Cle's simple question. "My name is Ruth—Ruth Gordon," she finally told us.

"Wildflower, help Ruth into a whitesuit and get her over to the

Daedalus." Cle patted Captain Gordon on the hand and said, "You're safe. These savages will never harm you again." Cle told me, "I will stay here and do what's necessary. Signal me as soon as you are safe inside *Daedalus.*" Cle's face took on a strange expression. "Can I count on you, Hibernia?" *ce* asked with great emphasis.

"Absolutely, you can count on me." I helped Captain Gordon into her whitesuit. She had more experience in open space than me; but she was certainly not in any condition to cheer me on in this solo endeavor. I was a tad better this time knowing I needed to be the responsible party and without too much trouble, I took Captain Gordon to airlock two on the *Daedalus.* Sante was waiting and immediately opened the airlocks and helped us. *Lis* eyes were red from crying. I remembered how upset *le* was about losing the pregnant Tyrowsian woman; but all my instincts told me this was something much bigger. I took off my whitesuit and Sante scanned us both.

"How is Cle?" Sante demanded.

"Cle is upset, but doing what *ce* needs to do."

Sante had a faraway look in *lis* eyes. "Bell was right. *Hataeasta* is beginning to disintegrate and it's my fault. It's already too late to rectify the situation."

"What do you mean?"

"Nova is—" Sante caught *lis* breath. "Nova is dead."

The word "dead" felt like a lead weight had fallen on me. "How?"

"I don't know the details yet. I need to get this patient up to the clinic. Go to the bridge, open a link to Cle, and monitor everything coming in through the bridge. I already called the *Seevaj* again and they will be here shortly. Call me when they arrive." Sante put *lis* masculine arm around Captain Gordon with the tenderness of a loving woman. "Let me take care of you," *le* said. I remembered that it was one of the first things *le* ever said to me. They started to walk away; then Sante turned and said to me, "Hi, we can't make any more mistakes. We have no margin left for error."

Beautiful Nova was dead. Nova was incredibly alive—how could that be? And Patra—what about her? I went to the bridge and called Cle on the *Gemstone.* *Ce* answered immediately and assured me that *ce* was okay."

"Nova," *ce* said and then *ce* went silent.

"Sante just told me."

When Cle spoke the next time, *cis* voice was different, more efficient. I listened as *ce* talked to Sante in the clinic. "His respiration is shallow," said Cle.

"Make sure his throat is clear," cautioned Sante.

"I've done that."

"Then administer Septation V?"

A call from the *Seevaj* interrupted our three-way link. Sante came to the bridge and took charge as the *Seevaj* attached a vacuum walkway between our two ships. Two Janaforma came aboard without putting on whitesuits. They were wearing activated vitaratthas. They scanned us and quickly dropped all their shields. The blonde, a lifebearer, was Captain Avooth and the other one was Commander Maxis. "*Qualmerrie*," they both offered. They switched to Universal when they realized my Cuneate was limited.

Sante, Avooth, and Maxis conferred and Sante and Maxis decided to board the *Gemstone* so they could examine the two surviving hijackers. Captain Avooth and I went to the *Daedalus* bridge to assist in any way we could. Sante spacewalked over to the *Gemstone* and reported to us shortly later, that the third hijacker had died and the fourth was in critical condition.

Then the bottom airlock on the *Gemstone* opened and out moved a mini-shuttle that came straight for the *Daedalus*. Then I saw it, a large, triangular symbol emblazoned the side of shuttle's white hull. Directly under the Orion Spur Space Security logo was the silhouette of a swan—the *Cygnus*. I knew the truth without the details; I knew the truth as if Bell had turned over the cards, one by one, and explained each one in detail to me. Some strange curse held us all in the palm of its hand. Closing its fingers, this curse had destroyed Nova.

Captain Avooth and I waited at the hangar airlock. In a moment, the door opened on the *Cygnus* mini-shuttle and Maxis, Sante, and Cle jumped out. When everyone was aboard the *Daedalus*, consensus decided that the *Seevaj* would take charge of the one survivor and we would take the bodies back to Aeternus. "I'm sorry we can't take the bodies for you," Captain Avooth apologized. "But we are not scheduled to return to Aeternus for ten cycles."

"It's all right," said Cle. "This is the second time we've had to return early. We're getting used to it."

"I'm so sorry about Nova," said Captain Avooth. "I served with Nova and I have tremendous respect for *lim*." Sante had nothing to say. Captain Avooth kissed Sante on the forehead; but *le* did not respond. "If you need us again, let us know," she said.

The *Seevaj* crew departed, the walkway telescoped in and closed behind the airlocks. We were alone again. The *Daedalus* was somehow different—quieter, perhaps more tomb-like. We left the three bodies of the dead *Gemstone* crewmembers and the three dead hijackers inside the mini-shuttle in the belly of the ship.

On the bridge, two old messages waited on the multidex. The first one read, "*Cygnus* to *Daedalus*—rendezvous Aeternus ASAP." The second was a message from Orion Space Security. "Be on the lookout for four convicts who have escaped from Herzayzen Prison. They are armed and dangerous. Last seen in the area of Tnamis Space Station." It was a little late for that message. Cle immediately called Space Security on Aeternus and told them the details of what happened.

After that, silence fell over the *Daedalus*. We ran in nightmode, but no one slept. Sante spent all *lis* time in the clinic with Dulce and Captain Gordon. I slept on the floor of the bridge while Cle sat in front of the controls. I did not want to be alone. It took us ten hours to reach homeport.

****

Daunting all neighboring stars, Aeternus was waiting in all her glory. Her billions of lights gleamed through the black of space. When Aeternus came into range, Sante came to the bridge. "How can they call it Aeternus?" *le* asked bitterly. "Nothing lasts forever. Sometimes I wish I were a child again, back before I realized there was such a thing as time. Of all the paradoxes about time, the strangest paradox of all is as soon as you discover its value, you begin to lose it." *Le* put *lis* arms around me and kissed me on the neck. "Do you know how fearful Tyrowsians are of time?" *le* asked.

"Take it easy," said Cle.

"I'll never be able to take it easy again," replied Sante. "Besides, Hibernia has a right to know about the insecurities we inherited from our Tyrowsians mentors. Humans might have insecurities about sex, but Tyrowsians have insecurities concerning time. Tyrowsians hope that by ignoring time death will go away. Here is another Tyrowsian fairytale for you. It's similar to Earth's Adam and Eve myth. You will eventually read it in that book of fairytales Cle gave you. 'In the beginning, Vian and Ertil dwelt in Paradise until they drank from the River of Time.'" Tears streamed freely down Sante's cheeks and *le* bit *lis* upper-lip, tasting *lis* own tears, feeding from *lis* own misery. "Not to be left out of this mortal dilemma, the Janaforma have a myth that we were created in our maker's image—an image of perfection that is now twisted by time, death, and desire." Sante's tears fell like rain and *le* refused consolation from both Cle and me.

Aeternus loomed large before us and Sante focused and gained a measure of control as we landed. *Le* wiped *lis* eyes and started communicating with Space Security Headquarters in an attempt to assist Cle. It was a joyless landing. The beauty of Aeternus mocked us with its sparkling spires. A picture laid on the console, beyond Cle's dancing fingers, a picture of Nova and Ariana taken at the Earth Pavilion on that fabulous evening of celebration. I picked it up and stared at it. For someone I knew for such a short time, Nova's loss certainly left a large hole in my heart.

A base crew arrived and removed the six dead bodies and the *Cygnus* mini-shuttle. I went to the clinic to say goodbye to Dulce and Ruth Gordon, but they were already gone.

At Space Security Headquarters, we waited to see Commander Vertain. First, she called in Cle and then Sante. I waited alone, outside her office, for two hours and then Sante came out and said, "She is allowing us to be present during your interview. Just tell the truth," and *ce* patted me on the shoulder.

What was the truth? I wasn't sure.

Commander Vertain looked as sober as Sante and Cle. "I'm sorry that your maiden voyage was so traumatic," she said. "I would like to get a perspective about what occurred from your point of view. Could you please tell me what happened once you boarded the *Gemstone*?" I explained the best I could how events rocketed forward. "Did you know Nova was dead before you boarded the freighter?"

That question threw me. "We knew something was wrong aboard the *Cygnus*. I thought perhaps Patra was having her baby."

"When did you find out Nova was dead?"

"When I returned to the *Daedalus* with Captain Gordon."

"Do you know exactly when Cle discovered Nova was dead?"

"I'm not sure." I explained about the broken communicator, but did not mention that while I was still on the *Gemstone* Sante had spoken to Cle in a strange language that I did not understand. I was sure Sante had told Cle about Nova in that foreign tongue but I had not yet asked them about it.

Vertain turned to Cle. "Why didn't you use the backup communicator on your wrist?"

"I wasn't wearing one. I never found a wrist communicator of much value since you can't use it until you take off the whitesuit and I hate wearing anything on my wrist that I can't use."

"Do you know why they waited to tell you about Nova?" Vertain asked me.

"I told you why we didn't tell her," interjected Cle.

Vertain stared at Cle and calmly said, "You either keep quiet or you're out—understand?"

"What's going on?" I asked looking to each person in the room for a clue. Sante and Cle stared at the floor.

"Did Cle's attitude change once *ce* finished speaking to Sante?" asked Vertain more forcefully.

I had a gut feeling this was a particularly important question. "We were concerned with the survivors. Cle said, 'We needed to do our duty.'"

"What did Cle mean by that?"

"Cle could see that I was upset about what just happened and *ce* was reminding me to maintain my composure until the job was finished."

"How many perpetrators were still alive when you left the freighter?"

"Two."

"Did you examine them personally?"

"No."

"Why not?"

"Cle took charge when events spiraled out of control. *Ce* told me to take

Captain Gordon back to the *Daedalus* and that is exactly what I did."

"When did you discover the third man was dead?"

"About ten minutes after Sante and Maxis boarded the *Gemstone.*"

"One last question. In your opinion did Cle use unnecessary force in subduing these men?"

"I'm sure they would have killed us if Cle hadn't stopped them."

"That's all for now; but I'm sorry, you all are grounded until we get this matter cleared up. I'll need to talk to the *Seevaj* crew and get their perspective. I must say this, Cle. I warned you previously about your tendency to play fast and loose so I hope you are leveling with me concerning this incident."

We left her office. "What is Commander Vertain trying to imply?" I asked.

Cle frowned. "Vertain thinks someone might accuse me of killing the hijackers in revenge for them killing Nova."

"That's absurd! You didn't even know Nova was dead until much later."

"My decision to kill them had nothing to do with revenge."

"What do you mean—your decision to kill them? Wasn't it an accident?"

"Nothing is ever an accident, especially in Shardasko defense."

"You don't mean that," I insisted.

"Yes, I do. I am not as pure as Sante."

"Tell me, how did Nova die?" I demanded.

The expression on Sante's face suggested *le* was witnessing what happened firsthand. "The *Cygnus* shuttle was making a routine transfer of patients from the hospital at Tnamis Space Station. They couldn't get the walkway gasket to seal between the station and the shuttle. Nova was in open space checking out the problem when those brutes moved in and attacked. Patra was on duty on the bridge and saw it happen. Death was instantaneous." Sante swallowed hard. "I understand that it was a large gun and nothing was left to recover."

****

Neither Sante nor Cle had slept more than an hour or two in the last five cycles so we headed straight back to the apartment at the Hilton to get some rest. It felt like a crime to return to those beautiful rooms with our sadness. As soon as we arrived, Sante fell across the bed, face down, and did not move.

"Let *lim* sleep," said Cle. "Tomorrow will be difficult." I covered Sante with a blanket and Cle and I went to the kitchen and made steaming cups of tea. While we drank the tea, Cle said, "It's still not too late for you to change your mind. Believe me, this is not what I had in mind for our collective futures."

"How can you say such an absurd thing?"

"Don't look so shocked." Cle's face filled with pain. *Ce* tried to hold something back but the little confessions broke through the surface. "My dear Hibernia, don't you understand what's happening? I've postponed facing my inadequacies; but now my punishment is inevitable. Sante and I promised each other that we would protect you; but we were fools to think we could. We control nothing. No level of commitment or amount of expertise can protect any of us from the madness loose upon this universe."

"I never asked you to protect me."

"I know; but it was something Sante and I promised each other."

Sante appeared in the doorway. *Le* was exhausted. "I can't sleep if you aren't there." We all went to bed for Sante's sake. Within a few seconds, my lovers were fast asleep in each other's arms, the sound of their steady breathing played like a soothing mantra.

I lingered on the edge of inner twilight and then abruptly—I was facing a sea of dark water set against a darker sky. A storm was approaching. The energy within the storm was creating lightening that erupted into jagged ropes that trailed down into the sea. Then the storm came upon me and I saw a thousand ropes of possibility dancing and frolicking around me. The only question was—which one should I use? I paced myself. I ducked among them as if I'm about to jump rope. I reached out and put my foot on one that trailed along the ground and looked like a promising possibility. When I grab the rope firmly with both hands, I realize only then that the rope was sentient and objected that I wanted to use it as transportation. My job was to tame it. My struggle turned into an arduous hand over hand battle—the ropes twisting round my wrists, entangling me in confusion. I burned with sensations of physical pain but refused to quit. I glanced back, toward safety, to where I've been, but was looking at a past I barely remember. Where was I going? I can't remember. I'm lost at sea between yesterday and tomorrow and I awake in a land called life for the next rope out.

I must have stirred in my sleep because Sante whispered, "You're okay," and *le* wrapped *lis* arms around me for protection. *Le* went back to sleep almost immediately. I stayed awake for a long time staring into the darkness and waiting for the rope to return.

EIGHT

The instant Patra saw Sante she burst into tears. "Why didn't you stop them? There had to be a warning, a shadow—I know you saw something?" The expression on Sante's face suggested horror. Then *lis* eyes moved closer together as if *le* were staring at a single spot before *lis* eyes.

"I didn't understand in time—I swear," *le* told her.

"She doesn't know what she's saying," interrupted Liart. "She hasn't slept since—since it happened." Sante put arms around Patra and held her until she stopped sobbing. "I keep seeing Nova die," she moaned. "I'm so sorry, Sante. This tragedy is destroying your honeymoon of joy."

"We are here for you and Liart," Sante said firmly. "This is our tragedy too."

"Is there something you can give her so she can get some sleep?" asked Liart.

"I don't want anything," Patra insisted. "I want to feel this pain. It's all I have left."

Sante knelt before Patra and placed a hand on each of her shoulders. "Listen to me, Patra. You have Liart and a child coming. Concentrate on *hataeasta*."

Through swollen red eyes, Patra stared down at Sante with veritable contempt. "I don't want to hear anymore Tyrowsian garbage, especially right now. I'm finished with *hataeasta*. From now on, I will live in the past."

Sante snatched her under the chin. "Nova is *hataeasta*. Something shifted in Sante and *lis* voice slid deeper into the pool of femininity. At that moment, there was no doubt in my mind that Sante's essential soul was feminine. *Lis* words were silver-tongued alchemy from the depths of the eternal waters. "There is no life except *hataeasta*. Say it with me, Patra." *Le* tapped Patra's lips with delicate fingertips and after a moment, Patra began to say *hataeasta* with Sante. "You want to sleep now and feel refreshed." Patra's eyelids fluttered once or twice. Her appearance turned trance-like and then she fell asleep. "When you awake you will take great comfort in being with Liart who will guide and complete you." Patra was still and Sante touched a spot between her eyes, on the side of her neck and the palms of her hands as if taking her pulse. It was the same way *le* calmed Dulce. Sante motioned to Liart and *le* picked Patra up and carried her into their sleeproom.

"Thank you," said Liart upon returning. "Nova always swore you were the finest doctor in the fleet. Nova often waxed poetic when *ce* talked about your hypnotic powers too."

"Patra is going to have the baby soon," said Sante, "probably within the next dozen cycles."

"Would you help us when the time comes?" asked Liart. "We both want you there and under the circumstance, I believe Nova would want you too."

Sante appeared surprised and glanced toward Cle. "I don't think I should."

Cle immediately went to Sante and they embraced until they were face to face. Cle meant *cis* words for Sante alone, but I heard their exchange. "Do it," said Cle.

"Maybe," replied Sante.

We stayed with Liart for the next few hours. *Le* was exhausted, but refused to go to bed. "It will be difficult to sleep in the bed we shared," *le* confided. Sante took two sound tranquilizers and pasted them on either side of Liart's temples. For several minutes *le* sat blinking, fighting the effects of the tranquilizers.

Sante finally told Cle and me to, "Go home; I'll stay here until Liart falls asleep." The statement was so typically Sante that Cle and I both knew Sante would be quite a while.

****

Cle and I sat side by side inside a traveltube car as it sped across Aeternus. "Do you think Sante will accept Patra's offer to be present for the birth?" I asked.

"I want the lifegiver in Sante to be satisfied so if this will do it for *lim*, then I'm all for it. The only problem is being with Liart and Patra during the birthing will bind Sante closer to Nova's spirit."

"What's your take on the relationship between Nova and Sante?"

"Nova is Sante's soul mate and they have a strong telepathic link."

"Does that bother you?"

"Sante gives me *lis* complete love. What more can I ask for?"

At the apartment, I went into the sauna and let the dry heat penetrate to my bones. When I emerged, Cle was lying on the bed. "I was remembering the first time I saw you," *ce* said staring at me in *cis* typical studied way. I sat down next to *cim* and *ce* brushed back my hair with *cis* fingertips. "You know, I didn't believe Bell's prophecy when we met her on Wonder World. I scoffed at Sante's faith; although, as you can see, Sante's psychic abilities tower way above mine. When I first saw you, you changed me. Suddenly, I felt alive, optimist, and I was ready to give this life another try."

"Even though I'm cursed?"

Cle let go a little ironic laugh. "Curses are mere distractions in this life, like the buzz of an annoying mosquito." Cle seemed so melancholy, as if *ce* had resigned *cim*self to whatever would be.

A purr-ring at our door brought our attention to the moment. "Sante probably forgot *lis* key," I said. "I'll go let *lim* in." I threw on a robe. It was not Sante. It was a beautiful, brunette lifebearer. Then I recognized her. She was the lifebearer I saw in the Ipanema Beach holospool with Cle and Sante. Her appearance had changed only slightly. Her short, dark hair curled around her ears and she wore the pastel silks of the Tyrowsian elite.

"Is Sante here?" she asked in Cuneate.

"I don't speak Cuneate very well," I replied in Cuneate.

"I need to speak to Sante," she said in Universal as she peered over my shoulder.

"Sante is not here but Cle is. Would you like to come in?"

She stepped inside. "Tell Cle that Devina has come to offer her condolences." It took me a few seconds to connect the name to the already familiar face.

I went into the bedroom and Cle raised *cis* head off the bed. "Devina is here to offer her condolences."

"You must be kidding."

"I'll keep her company while you get dressed." I returned to the main room and offered Devina something to drink. Cle walked into the room about thirty seconds later and Devina got up from her chair and kissed Cle on the forehead in the Janaforma manner. Cle submitted to it, keeping *cis* hands jammed in the pockets of *cis* robe. Pangs of jealousy shot through my heart because Devina was incredibly beautiful and I knew they once were lovers. I could not see her expression because she faced away from me; but I could sense the intensity between them in that Cle could not look at her for more than a second or two at any one time.

"You look good—considering," said Devina.

Cle stepped backward. There was something familiar about Cle's gesture of stepping back. It was a revival of that moment on the *Gemstone* right before *ce* struck like a pit viper. The movement definitely had something to do with Shardasko defense and this worried me. "What happened to your hair?" asked Cle.

"I cut it," she said, her fingers abruptly went up to touch her shorn locks. "I think it's cute—don't you?"

"Very cute!" *ce* exclaimed. Cle's tone was so sharp it could have cut glass. "So what do you want beside the opportunity to offer your condolences and show us your new hairdo?"

"Would you like to sit down," I quickly suggested.

"I need to speak to you in private," said Devina, ignoring my invitation to sit.

"I'm not interested in speaking to you in either private or in public," said Cle.

"I don't mind," I offered.

"I do!" snapped Cle and my bottom immediately plopped down on a nearby ottoman. Actually, I did not want to miss a second of what would follow. Cle was so annoyed *ce* appeared capable of shooting thunderbolts out the ends of *cis* fingertips.

"I have something to say and it is for your ears only," Devina still insisted.

"Hibernia stays. Besides, do you think you are the only one privy to gossip? I've heard what you want from at least a dozen different people. I will tell you what I told them. Your timing has always been poor but you have balls made of stainless steel."

Devina laughed and her tone held a mocking quality. "My balls have absolutely no interest in you. Sante is the treasure, not our castrated Number One Janaforma. You're zilch without Sante."

"Condescending insults directed at consort sexuality have no effect on me. The facts are these: Sante adores Hibernia and Sante and I are one. Case closed."

Devina spoke to me as if she were casually commenting on the weather. "You,"—and she pointed her index finger at me—"will never be able to qualify for a position in Space Security. If you think you can, they are lying to you or you are fooling yourself."

Cle's eyes riveted on this person I was beginning to hate. "I see now that your poison is growing. Go away. Believe me, nobody here is interested in your flimsy opinions."

"You can't qualify and you will destroy Sante in the process," she continued. Her words cut with the precision of an experienced butcher. She was as bitter as I had been with Gertie on that Sunday afternoon when I criticized her love for Buddy. I could see that now. I wondered if Devina's life was empty as mine had been.

"You better leave before—" Cle stopped short with a threat poised on *cis* lips.

Devina obviously liked playing with fire. "Before what? I've heard about your new penchant for violence. Suits your Sutcay Tay daredevil image you've been honing for years. Let Sante go, Cle. *Le* will need my help when Space Security dumps your ass. Lots of bullshit has gone down between us in the past; but this is fact and we both know it is true. The word is out on you from the Aeternus Council of Three—all the way down the ranks of Space Security. Your wealth and connections cannot save your career. Do something unselfish for once in your miserable self-centered life and free Sante of *lis* love commitment to you."

The front door opened and closed. This time it definitely was Sante. The tension was thick when *le* entered the room. "How's Patra?" I asked.

"Still sleeping," Sante said, but *lis* attention was riveted upon Devina.

"I'm so sorry about Nova," she said. "I know *ce* meant a great deal to you." She rushed toward Sante, but stopped short of embracing *lim*. I knew she was waiting for any small sign of encouragement.

"Nova meant more than a great deal to me," said Sante and *le* stepped backward but this time it was to hang up *lis* coat in the hall closet. When *le* returned *le* asked, "Devina, why are you here?" *Lis* tone was too relaxed for the occasion and I was still afraid. I was beginning to identify this casual stance along with the stepping backward gesture as something that predicted trouble was imminent.

"Nova's death shocked me," she said. "It forced me to put many things into perspective—"

"You're a liar," Cle said much too calmly. "You barely knew Nova."

Devina gulped. "Hear me out, Sante. I've come here to tell you that I've spent a lot of time thinking about what went down between us because of Cle. I can't save Cle, but I can still save you. Walk away from this ugly mess, come back to me, and I'll keep my mouth shut about everything." Sante's eyes darted around the room in confusion. The death of Nova was painfully difficult for *lim*; but Devina was the proverbial straw about to break the camel's back. Then she played her last card and she did not allow any cards to slide under the table the way I had. "This time I'm prepared to give you a child if that's what you still want."

Sante swallowed hard before glancing my way. "I assume Cle introduced you to Hibernia. She is our new lifebearer."

"This creature is not a Janaforma lifebearer," Devina said and she put her hand over her heart. "How can you expect a Human entrenched in duality thinking to embrace the complexity of our Janaforma life? She can't bear you the child I know you desperately want." Then she turned intimate with Sante and I hated her for her self-confidence. "I know you so well. I remember how you like it."

My mouth was hanging open over her audacity and then she turned on me again. "Don't you realize everyone in Space Security is gossiping about you? You are a Human Casual. You certainly are not good enough for the perfection of a 3C Janaforma lifegiver. Sante is several light years ahead of you in evolution."

I could barely speak. After a moment, from somewhere deep inside me, came a voice. Devina kindled the spark that fired my long lost dignity and I got up off my ottoman and pointed my finger at her. "I do not consider being a Casual a handicap. You see, Casuals are not programmable and therefore we are quite unpredictable. That's an advantage you'll never have or understand."

"I absolutely love it!" shouted Cle. "Hibernia is twice the lifebearer you could ever hope to be."

The now speechless Sante sank into a chair and gazed off into empty space. "This is insane," *le* groaned. "Everything is falling apart. Nova is dead. Don't any of you comprehend what that means or how much we've lost?"

"Come on Sante," said Cle. "Be strong for a change. This is important too. Tell Devina how you really feel."

"I thought I just did. What else to you want from me, Cle? Besides, why do you always expect me to be the strong one in our relationship?"

Cle clearly was amazed. "You believe you are the strong one in our relationship? Listen to me, my only lifegiver. Devina doesn't want me. She never has. She's here to stake a claim on you and you know damn well, I can't answer for you." The silence that followed was an ocean carrying us away from one another. Sante's face fell into *lis* hands and after a moment, Cle got up, knelt before Sante, and put *cis* head on *lis* lap. Cle was submissive but direct. *Ce* looked up into Sante's eyes. "I mean it," said Cle with greater emphasis. "Sante, I worship you, but I can't endure a life with Devina. I put up with her once because of you, but never again."

"You put up with Devina because of me? You have memory problems." Sante got up from the chair and Cle fell backward on the floor. I could not believe Sante would treat Cle so carelessly when Cle was asking for so little. "I'm surrounded with crazy people," said Sante. "Please leave me alone for just one small hour. Do you all hear me? I'm exhausted." Then *le* went into the sleeproom and slammed the door with a loud bang. The undaunted Devina followed a second later.

Devastated, I stood in the middle of the room in stunned silence. Neither Cle nor I moved for thirty seconds. "I don't believe this," Cle said and *ce* picked *cimself* up from the floor. "This is absurd. I'm going in there."

"Leave them alone," I said. "You're right. Sante needs to decide."

"Maybe so, but if Sante wants to be with that bitch it is not going to happen here." Cle started for the sleeproom again; then changed *cis* mind a second time. "You're right. Sante has to decide."

"Do you smell that?" I asked.

"Yes, I do." At last, Cle and I found our excuse to interfere. We smelled tartan ratu.

Cle and I went to the sleeproom door. It was standing ajar and we peeked inside. Sante was lying face down on the bed and Devina was leaning over *lim*. The spicy smell of tartan ratu was definitely in the air.

Furious, I burst into the room and screamed, "You underhanded, conniving, bitch! Take your hands off my lifegiver. You may be a Janaforma, but my father was a Tiffin Marine and he taught me how to fight."

Sante glanced up and giggled in an inappropriate manner. A small curry-colored spot stained *lis* upper lip and *lis* disposition had undergone a radical change. "Your father was a Tiffin Marine? I thought you told me you didn't know who your father was." Then *le* sat up and said, "I feel sick; I think I'm going to vomit."

"That's it!" shouted Cle. "Get your ass off my bed and your body out of my home."

Sante immediately jumped up from the bed and ran toward the bathroom. "Wait," called Devina.

Sante peered around the corner of the bathroom door and giggled as if everything that just happened was the biggest joke on Aeternus. Water dripped off *lis* chin from where *le* rinsed the ratu off *lis* face. *Le* shrugged like an animated clown a couple of times before saying, "I am totally committed to Cle and Hibernia and there is no room for you in this equation. Besides, if you think I'd desert the magnificent Cle—who is the best thing that ever happen to me—then you are the most insane person in this room. Furthermore, whom Cle and I choose to take as our mate is absolutely none of your business." Then *le* laughed. *Le* tried to stifle it by putting a hand over *lis* mouth, but then *le* started to cry. Finally, *le* shut *lim*self in the bathroom and refused to come out.

"Thank you!" said Cle, with an expression of satisfaction.

"You worm!" seethed Devina. She strode over to Cle and this time she did not stop short. I was amazed. She attempted to slap Cle across the face but *ce* merely stepped backward and her blow fell short.

Cle stared at Devina with one of *cis* I-can-see-right-through-you looks. "I'm feeling a little ballsy right now," *ce* said. *Cis* mocking tone made her even angrier and she tried again to strike *cim*, this time with the back of her hand. Cle moved right, then left, and ended up blocking her by grabbing her forearms. When Cle released her, it was with a hands-off gesture.

They both stepped back from each other and the gesture almost seemed ritualistic. She nodded toward him and said, "I hope you go bald."

Cle laughed for about five seconds before saying, "I suggest you leave before I report your actions to Commander Vertain as I should have done three years ago."

Devina turned and ran for the door leaving a trail of tear-soaked tissues behind on the carpet. In another moment, we heard the front door close and Cle turned to me and asked, "What's this about your father being a Tiffin Marine?"

"I just made that up to scare Devina. Do you think it worked?"

"I don't know but you sure scared me—a Tiffin Marine, I wouldn't want to run into one of those in the swamp at night." Cle went to the bathroom door and knocked on it. "Sante, are you okay?"

"Is she gone?" Sante called through the door.

"Yes. You may come out."

Sante opened the door slowly. "Don't you dare say one word to me," le said and le still was smiling. "I hate feeling this way when I am dying inside."

"I wasn't going to say anything," shrugged Cle. "Feel free to be as befuddled for as long as you need to be."

"I'm sorry, but I can't help it," said Sante clasping lis lips with lis fingers, still trying to stifle a smile. Le fell backward on the bed and snickered about something private. "Hibernia?" le said to the ceiling. "I've been thinking about our relationship and we definitely need to have a serious talk about the future."

"Why don't you sober up first," suggested Cle.

Sante ignored Cle and began talking to the ceiling again. "Something is missing. Our love is not enough. I need more."

I still was wound up from my confrontation with Devina so I put up my shield and prepared to spit fire. "What do you mean our love is not enough?"

"Pay no any attention to lim," said Cle. "Sante can get high on fresh air." Cle touched cis own temple and made a knowing gesture. "Sante, take a nap. You're exhausted, and high on tartan ratu."

"Let lim talk. I want to hear why our love is not enough."

"I'm sure Sante didn't mean it in the way you think," said Cle.

Sante giggled and picked limself up on one elbow. "You both are so silly," le said, "and neither of you are high on tartan ratu, like me." Le looked inebriated and I could not understand how anyone could get so high on one dot of ratu.

"I want to say something to you both," I lectured. "My whole life has been an apology and I have had enough. I am not going to be ashamed anymore. I'm a Casual. It's true—I cannot give you a child. If that is what you need to make you happy, then straightaway, go to Devina. Please understand this: if you do not want me, I certainly do not want you." My heart was breaking at the thought of losing them, but I truly did not want Sante and Cle if they were not one-hundred percent in love with me.

Sante was still giggling. "I guess I'm not making much sense. I wanted this to be more romantic. I was going to say it is not enough, because I want the three of us to make a deeper commitment. I want to commit to you. That is if Cle is ready to commit too."

"Hibernia knows how I feel," said Cle.

"Then you asked her already?"

"Well, I was going to ask her and then Devina burst in and attempted to burn the apartment down."

"Will you bond with us?" asked Sante.

I was suspicious. "What do you mean—bond with you?"

Sante's emotions swung like a pendulum and *le* started to cry again. "Please understand, Hibernia. I do not want to have a child unless it is with you and Cle. I cannot believe either of you would doubt my love. It must be my fault. Am I aloof?"

"You sure are sensitive to the effects of ratu," I said.

"I'm sorry," and more tears rolled down *lis* cheeks. "But I mean every word. Come here Cle." Cle climbed into bed, next to Sante, and *le* began dancing *lis* fingertips over Cle's lips in what I knew now, was another way to say I love you. "Let's recreate some love," whispered Sante, looking longingly into Cle's eyes. "I need you. Excite me with your love as only you can do." It took several hours for Sante's tartan ratu trip to wear off, but we all enjoyed the ride while it lasted.

****

The next cycle was the memorial service for Nova. The event took place at Space Security Headquarters and it was a heart-wrenching affair. We sat three rows behind Devina. She wore large dark glasses and never glanced our way.

Orion Spur Space Security bestowed full honors on Nova. When the service was complete, we went to Patra and Liart's apartment for the *hataeasta keirtoyyan**, which is what the Janaforma called a "death gathering" or wake. About twenty-five people were present—mostly Janaforma, but a few Tyrowsians too. Thank goodness, Devina was not present. People milled around crying on each other's shoulders until Cle said in Cuneate, "Please sit down." I put my translator in my ear hoping it would help me understand what was happening. Liart helped Patra to sit down between *lis* legs. *Le* gently rocked her back and forth, trying to comfort her, but her mind was somewhere else and she barely looked at anyone in the room. Cle looked down at the floor and did not speak, allowing the silence to accumulate for several minutes, as a sign of respect for Nova. Cle finally began with, "We are here to indulge our sorrow in *hataeasta keirtoyyan* and remember our loved one, Jana Nova. For those of you who never did this before we follow only a couple of rules. Please respect the grief of those suffering. If this is difficult for you, you need say nothing and you may get up and leave whenever you wish. When someone leaves, please fill in the empty spot in the circle."

*"now gone by"; language origin, Cuneate

Cle walked to the middle of our circle, placed a holospool device in the center, and activated the play function. A life-like image of Nova, as beautiful as ever, took shape in the middle of the circle. When the image was complete, Nova turned slowly, *cis* long golden hair fanning out like a million fiber-optic strands. When *ce* stopped turning, *ce* appeared to be staring directly at Sante. It was uncanny. "My precious family," *ce* said. "If you are watching this, I am the topic of a *keirtoyyan hataeasta*. Please forgive my indulgence, but as they say, 'It's my party.' Perhaps my loving parents correctly named me when they chose Nova, for, as you know, a nova increases greatly in brilliance and then gradually grows fainter with time. This is a perfect metaphor for my life. Although nova is a Universal word, I feel it should be Cuneate because the nova lives for a moment and never saves itself for *hataeasta rattha**. This is how we Janaforma live and die with the jobs we are destined to do. We give ourselves to each moment of life. As you watch this shadow of me, let me go peacefully, without regrets, into my *rattha* and we will meet again in *hataeasta*. So think of me as a Tyrowsian, remember me as a Human, but love me tenderly as a Janaforma consort. For the people I love best, death will not destroy my connection to you." Nova turned around as if looking at us all for a final time. Tears filled every eye in the circle.

Everyone was weeping as the holospool slid into a line and disappeared. Cle got up, turned it off, and after a short pause began to speak. "Many words of praise I could heap upon Nova. But the virtue that owned Nova was *cis* ability to offer unconditional love to so many people. The last time I saw *cim* a group of us went to the Earth Pavilion to see the Great Ariana sing. Out of the hundreds of people in the audience, Ariana picked Nova as her prop. She flew over, sat on *cis* shoulder, and began singing this sexy song in *cis* ear. Part of the lyric went, 'I chased after dreams that never came to nothing,' —and when she sang the line, 'It's easy to see, that I'm lost without your loving,' we all knew what she meant. Ariana had nailed Nova in a song. Everybody that knew Nova eventually fell in love with *cim*. Whatever Nova was, *ce* was as a lover first, a lover with great respect for the journey of life. Nova came closer than most of us to the Janaforma ideal. Beyond *cis* loyalty, altruism, and now *cis* tragic self-sacrifice, *ce* was creative, humble before the unknown, and totally unflappable in a crisis."

The first time I met Patra she said the Janaforma ability to love was a trait brought forward in their genes, so they could serve all without prejudice. I was beginning to understand the boundless love within the Janaforma community. It was here, here in this circle as they poured out their love for Nova. The *keirtoyyan* slowly moved around the circle and

---

*"now not yet happened"; language origin, Cuneate

when my turn came, I mentioned how willing Nova was to accept me, and how *ce* volunteered to introduce me to Clidmore and Kinsey. "Nova was the kind of person who quickly breaks down the formal barriers that keep people acquaintances instead of making them friends." After I made that statement, I remembered that Cle told me the Janaforma consider a consort as a metaphorical bridge between the lifegiver and lifebearer. I could see now that Cle was right. Nova had that ability and *ce* used it everywhere *ce* could.

Liart talked about a few incidents they shared in space and about a time when Nova saved *lis* life. It sounded like a replay of Sante and Cle's relationship. It was easy to see how much Liart loved Nova. Almost everyone spoke except Patra and Sante, but no one got up to break the circle.

When Sante finally decided to speak, *le* began in an undertone so hushed I had to strain to hear. "Nova always will be—" *le* began. *Lis* voice broke and *le* fell silent. Everyone waited for *lim* to gather *lis* composure and the silence that followed seemed overwhelmingly long. "I need to talk about Nova," *le* said a little louder the second time. "But the subject is so overwhelming I find it difficult to know where to begin. No words composed by me could possibly explain our connection. But this I do know: Before I knew time existed, I knew Nova. *Ce* is my energy source to the infinite and *ce* taught me that love is the only thing that makes *hataeasta* possible. On a strictly one-lifetime basis, I agree with all your observations. Nova was wise and determined. Nothing disturbed *cis* focus and composure in the fray. We spent our carefree childhood together and at school, *ce* was the sibling I never had. I was so innocent that even before I noticed the differences between our sexes, I was in love with Nova. Over the years, life proved with its damnable logic that we were not destined to be together as mates, so we parted. Though separate, our connection remains strong." Sante again fell silent. *Le* struggled to say, "Your message is clear to me, Nova. I think of you as Tyrowsian, remember you as Human, and love you as a Janaforma consort." There was nothing left for anyone to say beyond that, so the *keirtoyyan* circle slowly dissolved.

During the following sleep cycle, Sante awoke with a nightmare. *Le* refused to discuss the dream; but I heard *lim* mumble Nova's name several times before *le* sat up in bed. I was sure Cle heard it too.

NINE

Our lives were uncertain as we waited for the crew of the *Seevaj* to make their formal statements and for Patra to go into labor. The day after Nova's *keirtoyyan*, Patra added her voice to Liart's, asking Sante to help in the delivery of their child. After a few hours of soul searching, Sante agreed to help Liart and Patra during the birthing process. Four cycles later, Liart sent us an urgent message that Patra's labor had begun. When we tiptoed into her sleeproom, she was sitting on a black-padded, birthing chair, and putting up a fine display of confidence. Of course, Liart was by her side.

"I'm excited," she told me. "The child is a lifebearer. Nova wanted a lifebearer—you know."

"Have you decided on a name yet?" asked Cle.

"We've decided to name her Nova," Liart said.

Patra reached out and held my hands. "Nova taught me about love too. I don't want to separate you from Sante and Cle in any way. I understand about painful separations. Please say that you and Cle will stay too and share this experience with us." She winced with an emerging contraction.

"We'll stay," said Cle with more enthusiasm than I felt. Unsure, I kept my reservations to myself. We took turns offering Patra words of encouragement. Every so often, Sante would place *lis* fingertips on her forehead as though *le* were cueing her in a particular way. Whatever *le* was doing lulled her into a deeper state of tranquility despite her strengthening contractions.

Cle explained the process to me as, "a type of hypnosis based on the concept that pain can be reframed. Once pain is reframed, it can be put into perspective." Whatever Sante was doing, it seemed to be working, because Patra was way beyond brave; she was relaxed.

When baby Nova emerged from the womb, and opened her eyes to life, she made a few bleating sounds and some gurgles. "She's strong, healthy, and looks like Patra," announced Sante and *le* handed the infant to Liart. Liart brought the child to Patra and Sante offered them a scalpel. Patra took the scalpel and said, "I give this vessel to the soul that has blessed it with life. Go forth in love my child." Then Patra cut the umbilical cord. Sante helped and tied the knot near the navel."

"Make sure you do that right," said Patra. "I don't want her to have an ugly navel."

"It will be perfect," promised Sante and *le* smiled.

When Cle had said, "We'll stay," I felt a wee bit uncomfortable, but what happened broke through my discomfort and melted my heart. I was a puddle of emotion because I knew I had witnessed the true thread of evolution, the birth of a child. Any infant, but most especially this infant, was a symbol of hope for the Janaforma.

Baby Nova was all wrinkly beautiful. "She's a miracle," proclaimed Liart, beaming at their new creation. Liart instinctively cradled the infant, lowering her tiny body into a warm, ceremonial bath. The baby lay against *lis* arm for support and protection.

When Liart removed the newborn creation from the bath, Sante asked, "May I hold her?" Liart wrapped Nova in a blanket and handed her to Sante. Cle and I watched carefully as Sante took the newborn in *lis* arms. *Le* said nothing, but it was as obvious as daylight that this child had captured *lis* heart.

The look of awe on Sante's face sent me into a tailspin and I began thinking about having a child again. The notion fairly ran wild in my mind, stampeding every logical promise I made to myself about not reproducing. An imagined collage of happy events unfurled in my hypothetical progeny's life—from birth to graduation day. Later, on the way back to our apartment, Cle broke the silence by saying, "I'm thinking about petitioning the Tyrowsians on Calypso for the Janaforma genetic records at the AIRS Institute."

"The Janaforma certainly deserve direct access to their genetic records," I agreed.

"If we could get those records, perhaps their contents would reveal the miracle we need."

My heart went out to Cle and our ridiculous situation. "It's not you—it's me! It's the responsibility of Casuals not to reproduce. You know that."

"Human propaganda! Sante checked you out from head to toe and nothing is wrong with you."

"Statistically, something could happen to my heart—you know that."

"Statistics also predict that the chances of Sante or I dying in the next five years is rather high, yet we accept the risk because we face it with our eyes wide open. If the three of us want to have a child, we should assess the risk and decide together if we should do it or not. It is no one else's business."

"A short time ago you were ambivalent about having children. What's changed?"

"You've changed me. Don't get me wrong; meeting you is one of the most important things ever to happen to me. But the dynamics between Sante and me are different now. You've changed Sante too; *le* wants the complete family package. Didn't you see the expression on *lis* face when *le* held baby Nova? If we could get those genetic records then maybe it could happen for us too." Later, when Cle told Sante what *ce* was thinking, Sante was overwhelmed with delight as if the undertaking was already *a fait accompli*.

****

The same cycle, the multidex bleeped with a message from Commander Vertain. The crew of the *Seevaj* had made their statements, so we went down to Space Security Headquarters to see where we stood.

"*Qualmerrie*," said Commander Vertain. She motioned us toward seats. She was all spit and polish dressed in her black uniform. Someone in Space Security had died in another accident and she said, "I like to wear my formal attire to a *keirtoyyan hataeasta*." She sat down behind her desk and tinkered with her multidex. "If you could bear with me," she said zipping through dozens of screens. "Here it is! The crew of the *Seevaj* endorsed your version of events. Captain Avooth in particular added the statement, 'These Herzayzen convicts were evil incarnate.' I agree. We now have a clear picture of the path of destruction they created across space. The four were complete bios who had been mindstripped many times. Their names were Yarrow T. Box, Ronald Porkcur, Hector Limpet, and Petre Saunders. In their escape from Herzayzen Prison, they killed three sentient androids; made their way to Tnamis where they killed Commander Nova and stole an Explorer 3 shuttle worth five million credits. The picture gets a little fuzzy here, but they ended up aboard the *Gemstone* where they sexually molested Captain Gordon and killed her three crewmembers. By the way, Captain Gordon is still in hospital and I'm sure she would appreciate a visit from you."

Vertain glanced up from her multidex. "Our outstanding problem is the one surviving convict." Vertain looked down at the multidex again. "That's Yarrow T. Box. Mr. Box claims that only Ronald Porkcur possessed a weapon and that Hector Limpet, Petre Saunders, and himself, were unarmed. The physical evidence found on the bridge of the *Gemstone* and your statements concur. Only one weapon was involved. Mr. Box also alleges that he and Hector Limpet were denied adequate medical attention, once they were down."

Cle was halfway to furious. "That's totally untrue!"

"They'll never be able to make that claim stick," added Sante. "I was in constant contact with Cle and I documented everything minute by minute."

"That's good news," said Vertain. "Now let's deal with these issues one at a time. The first problem we have is they are accusing you of something Box's lawyer is referring to as, 'Space Security brutality.'"

"Ronald Porkcur's rephazer was glowing red, set to kill and pointed at Captain Gordon who was standing there with blood all over her uniform. It was just me, along with Hibernia, a trainee, out on her second mission, facing four mind-stripped escaped convicts looking for any excuse to murder us. What would you have done?"

"If this had happened to anyone but you, I could understand. But it always happens to you. You seem to walk blindly into life-threatening situations and then resort to gross heroics to escape by the skin of your teeth. I know I asked you before, but tell me again—why did you have to kill them?"

Cle slumped backward in *cis* chair and *cis* head drooped to one side. "Shardasko is not an exact science."

Vertain's expression turned edgy and she was almost gritting her teeth. "True, but we can't cover up the fact that you are a master of Shardasko Defense. If the Aeternus Council of Three needs to use it, they will."

Cle was shocked. "It's gone that far?"

"I'm not sure, but if it happens the Aeternus Council of Three will examine your life with a magnifying glass. I'm worried. Box's attorney, Liacann has already asked for copies of your official service records."

"Not, good, news," admitted Cle.

"That's why I need to know everything. Tell me the truth, Cle. Was revenge for Nova's death any part of the equation?"

Sante jumped to *lis* feet. "How could you accuse Cle of something that hideous? We didn't know they murdered Nova until we found the *Cygnus* shuttle in the freighter's hold."

Vertain turned to Sante. "You don't understand either—do you? The Aeternus Council of Three not only knows about Shardasko Defense but they know about the psychic powers of the Janaforma too."

"She's absolutely right," agreed Cle. "When Captain Gordon said hijackers overtook them in a shuttle, I knew it was an OSSS shuttle. I also knew a Janaforma crew would never give up a shuttle without a fight. Moments afterward, I found out Nova was dead. It was simple deduction. When I saw the *Cygnus* mini-shuttle in the freighter hold, I put in the last piece in the puzzle and the picture was complete."

"What about you, Sante? Did you experience any psychic flare-ups?"

Sante glared at Vertain. "I'm under no obligation to make periodic reports on my psychic insights."

"Why don't you make an exception this time," said Vertain.

"It's a big responsibility—knowing too much. My urge to interfere is constant so I don't need more pressure from you."

Sante knew! I realized in astonishment. *Le* had to know because even my puny suspicions had tormented me for acceptance.

"Is there anything else you can add to this Miss Smith?" asked Vertain.

My face flushed hot. "I agree with Sante and Cle completely."

"You are under no suspicions. If anything, you did an exemplary job under the circumstances. Do you think you are brave enough to face interrogation by the Aeternus Council of Three and still support Cle's statement?"

"Of course," I said. Vertain did not really know me. I would have done anything to protect Cle. I would even lie.

"I'm glad you think so, because the council has a reputation for being tough."

"They won't be able to use her—will they?" asked Sante.

Vertain thought about it. "As it stands, she is merely your teammate. You are not legally bonded. Frankly, Miss Smith—I'm impressed with your credentials and your willingness to learn. The OSSS is desperate for individuals such as you, individuals that can make a difference in space. With the right mentors, you will make a fine navigator. If you allow me to team you with another crew, I can almost certainly—"

"No thank you; I'm in this only for Sante and Cle."

"Certainly, it's your choice." Vertain returned to Cle. "Go and see Rebecca Dykestra, as soon as possible. She's our legal liaison with the Aeternus Council of Three. She can prep you if they decide to subpoena you."

Sante was subdued as we left Vertain's office. The minute we were outside, *ce* grabbed my hand and said, "Wait. I saw things—visions I ignored. I swear on my Janaforma soul that I will never withhold my insights from either of you again. If I see the smallest shadow, you will know about it."

Cle laughed at Sante, telling *lim* it was too late to change anything. "Don't you understand, Sante? All the cards are dealt. The only thing we can do is play out the cards we hold."

****

Later that cycle we went to see Rebecca Dykestra. She was a Human born on the planet Hattonia. She was tall, lean, and looked like a long distance runner. Her hair was short and conventional compared to the hair of any Janaforma. Her record of accomplishments, of doing battle with the Tyrowsian government on Aeternus, was long and impressive and she had built her career upon presenting cases before the Orion Spur Council. Her no-nonsense manner and polish suggested she was a good attorney and knew her way around the tricky Tyrowsian legal system.

Rebecca Dykestra gave us the bad news. Through her connections, she heard that the attorney for Yarrow T. Box had petitioned the Aeternus Council of Three for a hearing and they promptly granted it. She expected to receive official notification the following cycle. "You must understand that you might be under tremendous pressure to verify Cle's version of what happened," she told me. "One of the biggest problems we'll be facing is that in the fifty year history of Space Security, this is the first time a Janaforma has taken any life, let alone three lives. Every Janaforma knows that any Shardasko master could easily step around the situation, but you chose not to do that." We all appeared worried so Rebecca added, "You do have an excellent reputation in the Janaforma Community and I expect everyone will rally round you when the time comes."

Dykestra explained our present dilemma as a three-handed game of Zeppelin. "Sitting in for this hand we have the Orion Spur Council acting as the dealer, the Aeternus Council of Three, and Space Security. Cle may be a star in the Janaforma Community, but *ce* is of no consequence in this particular game to either the Council of Three or the Orion Spur Council. Space Security is a showcase supported by Tyrowsian business interests here on Aeternus. Believe me; they will want this incident to end quickly and as quietly as possible. They don't want this case going to the OSC for review. If the matter goes to the OSC, negative publicity surely will follow. No matter how odious these convicts were or how self-sacrificing the Janaforma are, those who can profit from exploiting this incident will spin the publicity to fit their agenda. Never forget, Tyrowsians are under an injunction from the Orion Spur Alliance, which prohibits them from creating or recreating lifeforms. Tyrowsians want those markets back. Others, within the Alliance, are bound and determined to keep that injunction in place. Cle will be caught in the middle."

I asked, "Why is the Council of Three conducting a hearing if they want to bury the matter?"

"One of the problems is Liacann, who is handling Box's case. Liacann is an elusive Tyrowsian who knows how to cover his tracks; so thankfully, we don't need to look far to see his motivation. Liacann's mate is Bit Tipple, CEO of the private equity firm, Bit Tipple, Pronghorn, and Reed."

"I remember something about Bit Tipple," Cle said. "A few weeks before my parents died, Bit Tipple approached them and wanted to buy Vitarattha Research and Development."

"Bingo!" exclaimed Rebecca. "They're after Vitarattha R and D. For sure, Liacann lost no time in petitioning the Council of Three for a hearing. He also managed to get Box put into protective custody in—can you believe it— a Space Security facility? It's become a matter of public record so it's impossible for the Tyrowsians to whisk Box away. The Council of Three has no choice but to respond. The one safe response is to purge

Space Security of Cle."

"I will have the support of the Janaforma Community," Cle assured her.

"Is that right? Where is it? The Janaforma are a minority and you have no formal organization other than Space Security. You don't even have a grassroots movement for social justice. Think about it, Cle. Who among the Janaforma is equipped to take on the Tyrowsian government of Aeternus, which is backed by the Orion Spur Alliance?" Rebecca smiled a nasty smile. "Consider ancient history, if you will. That subject makes Tyrowsians squirm. Remember what Tyrowsians did on Calypso. Calypso Ganats were tribal and took little interest in the notion of central government. When Tyrowsians moved in, under the auspices of administrative control, it didn't take long to obliterate the fragile Ganat ecosystem along with Ganat culture. Tyrowsians have twisted history with their denial resulting in most Tyrowsians still believing their ancestors were liberators on Calypso rather than invaders. As George Orwell once wrote—and he must have known a few Tyrowsians— 'who controls the past …controls the future: Who controls the present controls the past.'"

"Then you believe Tyrowsians use *hataeasta* as a manipulative device?" asked Sante.

"I most certainly do," said Rebecca. "*Hataeasta* is an interesting philosophical idea; however philosophical ideals are continually snatched by the power hungry and used to rationalize their goals. Tyrants always hide under philosophy and religion. Tyrants use philosophy and religion as tools to inflame the hearts of idealists so they will lay down their lives for a cause. The idealists die while the tyrant feeds off their energy to build his kingdom of power."

Skepticism marked Sante's expression. "You believe Aeternus harbors tyrants of this radical nature?"

Rebecca patted Sante's hand as if *le* were a naïve child. "Aeternus Tyrowsians make your average tyrant look like a softy. These tyrants are not your average ne'er-do-well tyrants that managed to grab power in a coup; these tyrants are congenital tyrants, bred and hardened to rule. Wake up! The education you received from your Tyrowsian parents is full of revisionist history."

Cle raised *cis* eyebrows. "I received a first class education."

"How many of your teachers were Tyrowsian?" questioned Rebecca.

"Most of them," Cle admitted.

Rebecca frowned. "Case closed. You received an education strictly from the Tyrowsian perspective, an education of half-truths with a creative spin. Tyrowsian lies permeate the Orion Spur wherever you go, but here on Aeternus where Tyrowsians rule, you live in a dream world of half-truths. As I said earlier, I am on your side. If the Janaforma are not smart enough to enjoy full political rights, I don't know who is. It will be a great day for

Aeternus when the last Tyrowsian-appointed governor picks up the hem of his skirts and runs for his life. But before that happens, the Janaforma will need to move a few mountains and you can bet your vitarattha that I am here on Aeternus to help move them. Every small victory, such as yours, helps. If we work together, keep our eyes on the big picture, we can win."

"You can count on me," Cle said immediately.

"Wait a minute," said Sante. "How did we get from clearing our reputations in this incident all the way to gaining social justice for the Janaforma?"

"Don't you see?" asked Cle. "This is an opportunity to make our fight bigger than simply saving my career."

"Let me remind you that we have much to be grateful for here on Aeternus," said Sante. "We are not prisoners here. Any Janaforma has the freedom to walk away from this life."

"Yeah, it's almost funny," said Rebecca. "I think Simon Forma threw a spanner in the Tyrowsian works when he created you two. Maybe it was his way of saying 'fuck you' to the Tyrowsians."

"You may not approve of our education but Tyrowsians have never restricted our flow of information," said Sante. "Why should we attempt to overthrow a government that's done so much for us? Everyone, including governments, shade truth to put themselves in the best light possible."

"You mean like a government that withholds our genetic records?" asked Cle.

"Cle is right," said Dykestra. "That's one of the bigger battles. I'm not going to pull any punches. I'm looking for warriors." She sighed. "I must admit, my motivation goes back generations. Have any of you ever heard of an Earthling named Crysto Weaver?"

"My grandmother's maiden name was Weaver," I offered.

Rebecca brightened. "Was her name Lilly?"

"Yes! How did you know?"

"Because Lilly Weaver was the daughter of Crysto Weaver and Mellé Cœur."

"Wow! We're related. We have the same great-grandparents. What do you know about their lives?"

"I know that in Crysto Weaver's lifetime, he worked on Calypso as a diplomat. His mission there was to persuade Tyrowsians to join the now defunct Galaxy Council. He was never successful and after seven years, he left in disgust and returned to Earth. On his trip home, his spaceship developed a rampant Xeytinic mold. When everyone aboard believed they were lost, a ship of android jumpers rescued them. Back then, Tyrowsians were sending out tracer ships called bogeys. Bogey tracers sought out android jumper ships, essentially electrocuting all life aboard. Then a Cerribeame crew flew in, salvaged the ships, and took the androids back to

Calypso for reprogramming. While Crysto Weaver was on that jumper ship, he dedicated himself to the cause of android rights. I continue his fight and gladly widen it, to include all species and all planets under Tyrowsian dominance."

"What do Tyrowsians really want here in the Orion Spur?" I asked Rebecca.

"Nothing tyrants haven't always wanted from the beginning of time— power, domination, and wealth. However, I think we have the ammunition to win this battle, but I would like to know the three of you are committed to a legitimate outcome."

Sante was still upset with the idea of a Janaforma insurgency and *le* said, "Miss Dykestra, I don't like several of the words you use. Perhaps it's the harshness of Universal with all its metaphoric references to battle, war and ammunition—"

"First, you may call me Rebecca. Second, I think all our worlds are past the point when we are going to get a rephazer and do hand-to-hand combat with a bunch of milksop Tyrowsians. The notion is amusing, but ludicrous. Change, and especially social change, needs to happen within the legal precepts of the Orion Spur Alliance; but no change will take place unless we make a concerted effort to bring injustice into the light. Have you ever heard of a planet call Pybatium?" Cle and Sante had heard of Pybatium, but not me. Rebecca explained. "Pybatium is the Tyrowsian planet of origin. They destroyed it in a nuclear accident and now Tyrowsians have no planet to call home. That means we are stuck with Tyrowsians and their way of thinking and doing." She sighed and looked at each one of us asking, "Can I count on you?"

Cle again said, "yes." I told her yes, not because I believed in a positive outcome but for Cle's sake. Sante was also reluctant and I had the impression that Sante also said yes to appease Cle.

"Good," she said. "We have thirty cycles to prepare a defense. Right now, I'm working on another case, but expect to be finished in about seven cycles. Let's meet again in twelve cycles. That will give us eighteen cycles to prepare a defense. If you have business, you need to take care of, between now and then, do it, so your mind is free to concentrate. Wait a minute—" she said scratching her head. "What's the personal status among you three?"

"We're committed but not yet bonded," said Cle. "We Janaforma intentionally ignore legal marriage. No offense, but we see legal entanglements as a profit making enterprise for lawyers into an area of our lives that we consider sacred."

"No offense taken," said Rebecca. "You are entitled to your beliefs, but sometimes people ask the law to intervene and we can't do that unless a legal commitment exists. My personal belief is if you love someone enough then you should be proud of your love and make a public commitment."

"Do you have a problem with our relationship with Hibernia?" asked Sante.

"No! Of course not," said Rebecca. "What bothers me is the Tyrowsian Council might try to call Hibernia as a hostile witness and she might have to testify if she is not legally married to you. The fact that she is a Human Earthling and a Casual is bound to get the media's attention. I'm trying to anticipate any negative publicity that might rear its ugly head. It would help our cause, and your case, if we could leak something positive about your personal lives to the media."

"No!" said Sante and *le* put up a hand that meant stop. "Cle and I don't want Hibernia to be subjected to any invasive scrutiny because of us."

"I give up," said Cle. "Let's get married and then Hibernia will not have to testify against me since Earth law governs her. We could even use her as a collaborative witness to the events inside the *Gemstone* and the Council of Three will not be able to do anything about it."

Rebecca offered, "I could obtain all the legal papers through the multidex. We could do it right now. By the time of the hearing, it certainly would be legal."

"This is backwards," said Sante. "The psychic bonding should come first."

Cle got up from *lis* chair and leaned over Sante, kissing *lim* on the cheek. "All right," *ce* said. "Prepare the papers."

"Wait a second," I said. "Neither of you asked me if I want to get married?"

"I'm so sorry," said Cle. "Will you marry us?"

"I'd love to." So by the time we left Rebecca Dykestra's office, we were legally married but the paper had no real impact on our lives.

****

I returned to the apartment alone and Sante and Cle went to the hospital to visit Ruth Gordon. When they arrived home, something new was bothering Sante. "We saw Captain Gordon only briefly," *le* said. "She's still subdued. Apparently, she talks little and trusts no one. I'm going to see if I can get her transferred to a Janaforma facility where she can get better treatment. Something else happened, which I need to confess. I saw Dulce too. We talked again and I decided to give him what he wanted. I stayed with him until he was gone. It didn't take long, about twenty minutes and he was cold. If I had done that in the first place, none of these terrible events would have happened."

"That's nonsense," Cle still maintained. "None of this is your fault."

"What made you change your mind?" I asked.

Sante appeared resolute. "Dulce told me that he wanted to go home to mingle with his true loves, where he would be complete. It seemed like such a simple request. I can understand his yearning. Sometimes I feel as if I want to go home too."

"You were so adamant before."

"His suffering was still intense. I didn't realize how intense until I saw him. Nova died because I refused to help Dulce. The two things might seem unrelated to you, but they are linked."

"Is this one of your psychic things?" I asked.

Sante grimaced. "A connection is strengthening between Nova and Dulce." Sante shook *lis* head as if trying to pull something into better focus. "It's still vague; but I see Dulce extending a hand, like a consort, waiting for Nova."

"How did you do it? Was it an overdose of medisleep?"

Sante shrugged. "No drugs were involved. I merely showed him the right door. He opened it and went through. As I said, I waited twenty minutes and he did not return. Still, it was a difficult decision. Physically, nothing was wrong with him. It was the depth of his anguish that swayed me."

"What do you mean by the right door?"

"I mean the door between this dimension and the next."

After that, a melancholy hung over us all. First Nova was dead and now Dulce. Two beings I met briefly had caused major waves in my life. Was the causal connection Sante saw in the situation the impetus or the result? Perhaps the whole damn thing was a loop and I would never find a beginning or an end.

A short time later, Cle said, "I think it would be good if we got off Aeternus for a few cycles."

We talked about a few different places to go. "What about Wonder World?" I suggested.

"Too frantic!" said Sante.

"What about Earth?" Cle asked. "I would like to take a closer look at some historical records that are independent of Tyrowsian databanks. What do you think, Hi? How deep do you think the Tyrowsians have put their fingers into the Earth pie?"

"I don't know if you can get a fresh perspective from Earth; but I did leave a few loose ends that I need to tie up. I have a few belongings still important to me; I could sell my house; and there is someone I'd like to see." We decided within the hour that we would travel to Earth. Six hours later, we were aboard a commercial ship and headed toward Earth's moon.

****

Sante and Cle were antsy at being passengers on a commercial space transport, although neither complained about the situation. Eighty-two hours later, we were aboard an Earth shuttle headed for Chicago, Illinois. The three of us crowded onto the double bed in our quarters and watched the shimmering blue and white orb grow larger as we approached. "Earth is always so beautiful," said Sante.

Remembering the holospool of them with Devina on Ipanema Beach, I felt secure enough to confess, "I played the holospool on top of the sleeproom multidex, the one marked Ipanema Beach. I was jealous when I saw it because Devina was so beautiful and once was your lover."

"Devina is a toad compared to you," said Cle. "We were on Earth, with Devina, about three Earth years ago. We did this tour of the largest cities on Earth. We visited, Mexico City, Rio de Janeiro, Hong Kong, and Mumbai—"

"You're kidding? Gertie Martinez and I took that same trip—just about three years ago! Wouldn't it be crazy if we were on the same trip?"

"Totally crazy!" said Cle. "Maybe we whisked past each other in Hong Kong. I did see a Human female in the airport there. Her hair was blonde and she wore a yellow dress. Was it you, Hibernia? Perhaps you arrived early to show me the lifebearer I was with was a toad."

Sante asked, "Whose Gertie Martinez?"

"A good friend, I guess my only friend, until I met you and Sante."

"Is Gertie a former lover?" asked Cle.

I laughed. "We're girlfriends and neighbors and we both were associate cartographers at Atlas Map."

"You can admit it if you were madly in love with Gertie. We aren't jealous," said Sante.

"I am," Cle snickered suggestively.

I laughed too. "Gertie and I weren't sexually intimate. We're friends. How can you believe I would be involved with another woman after I've been with you?"

Cle and Sante stared at each other and shrugged their shoulders. "It happens," said Cle.

"Not to me!" I snapped.

"Underneath, everybody is bisexual," insisted Sante.

"You're crazy!"

"And you're being awfully defensive about your fundamentalist beliefs," said Cle.

"If you think I'm a sexual fundamentalist, then you must agree with Sante. Do you believe everybody is bisexual underneath too?"

"I absolutely agree with Sante," said Cle.

Sante glanced at Cle and talked about me as if I wasn't there. "I think she's falling back into her Human denial because were getting so close to Earth. Have you ever known a Human who didn't have a problem with sexuality? This is a great opportunity. We can help her realize her full loving potential."

Cle laughed and winked at me. "We assumed you had the capacity to love everyone, no matter what sex they were because you accepted us so easily."

"I never thought of the situation exactly like that."

"If you're afraid to admit your true nature because of negative social connotations, Cle and I understand. We know all about social stigma."

"Tell me something, has anyone ever accused you and Cle of being bisexual?"

"Humans throw the term at us all the time," said Cle. "Of course they don't know what they are talking about. I'm not bisexual, I'm trisexual!" Cle raised *cis* eyebrows dramatically. "I'm aware that some Humans think the Janaforma are a Human perversion, but I've never let that stop me from being my wonderful, consort, trisexual self."

"The Orion Spur is a big place," I said. "It contains some spectacular creatures and some unusual sex habits. I cannot believe Humans would give a second thought to the Janaforma. Are you sure you aren't being too sensitive?"

Cle smirked. "Humans ignore the sex habits of other species; but the Janaforma are a little too Human for Human comfort."

The conversation turned to Nova. "When Nova and I were lovers—" Sante began.

"Wait a second," I said. "I realized you loved Nova deeply. I didn't realize you two were sexual partners."

A small laugh slipped between Sante's lips. "I'm beginning to think you nurture your naiveté. Nova and I were intimate lovers. What else could we be with all that passion between us?"

"Okay! You got me. I figured you and Nova were lovers that evening at the Earth Pavilion. *Ce* had *cis* dick pressed up against you, kissed you on the lips. Since everybody else acted as if what you were doing was normal, I thought maybe I was overreacting. I guess this is a good time to ask. Is there anything else you want to tell me?" I was struggling to sound open-minded, but the harder I tried, the more narrow-minded I sounded.

"What do you want to know about Nova and me?" asked Sante. "I'll tell you anything you want to know."

"It's none of my business what you did before I arrived."

"Certainly, it's your business," insisted Sante. "You joined this triad. To conceal the truth about Nova would make you less a partner in our relationship. Would you like to know the details? I love to talk about Nova." I did feel curious, but my Human curiosity still embarrassed me. Sante had observed that Humans still had inhibitions about sex and I was proving *lim* right. I squirmed with the bonds of my own limitations and felt the discomfort.

Cle was sympathetic. "Do you remember when we landed on Aeternus and we were waiting for Nova to arrive? I took you in my arms and asked you, 'How do you love?' You told me 'I love completely' but I knew how difficult it would be for you to accept the details of our sexuality. I was afraid that if you found out too much, too soon, we would lose you, so I held back. Sante was steadfast though. *Le* believed in you and your capacity for love and it didn't take me long to realize Sante was right."

I felt so brave with them and I did not hide my feelings or thoughts. "Love came so quickly between us that I never considered differences," I admitted. "I know now that we are different; we come from different cultures that, more often than not, are at odds. I know Earth culture influences me in subtle ways and I'm mostly oblivious to my own behavior when I think, act, and react. Still, I would not change one thing about either of you or myself or the way we met. You have brought home the importance of love to me and I never will let that go. And if I need to become a space jockey to make this relationship work, I'll do it. All I want is to be with you both for the rest of my life."

****

We landed at Chicago's O'Hare Spaceport. It was April 15. We took an express traveltube and forty minutes later, we were in downtown Toledo. It was twilight when we arrived. A warm breeze from the southwest gently stirred the crimson blossoms on the trees that lined Cherry Street. Springtime magic perfumed the air. The crumbling antiquity of Toledo's infrastructure managed to appear romantic in the hopeful light of spring and I felt a resurgence of love for natural Earth. We took off our jackets to enjoy the feel of the soft spring breeze blowing against our naked arms and faces. "I've missed the earthiness," I happened to say.

"What's earthiness?" asked Sante.

Cle smiled like a happy professor. "The way Hi explained it to me is earthiness is a connection to the soil, a sensuous feeling, and using the senses to enjoy life."

"That's a pretty good description," I said; "but a description of earthiness won't suffice. You must breathe it in until you feel it in your heart."

Sante laughed and said, "Okay, let's inhale the springtime drug." Sante knew what *le* was talking about because springtime was a drug ten times more potent than tartan ratu.

"I'm feeling this Toledo scene," said Cle. "It's quaint. I often wondered what it would be like to live on a planet with natural light and organic atmosphere. It's probably a lot to deal with—all the seasonal transitions. I've noticed that people that live on organic planets seems overly concerned about their weather. Even when the weather is mild, the topic of weather is so pervasive that when I talk to friends on Delphi, Delta Urbana, and Urania, they give me weather reports right after saying hello. They seem to use weather as seques to getting around to saying what they want to say.

They always keep me guessing. If the weather is stormy on Urania—does that mean my friend Roget is about to tell me bad news? Are you a weather aficionado, Hi?"

"Probably. I remember mornings, getting up, and going directly to the window of my space pod to check the weather. It's rather a depressing exercise in the winter. The weather can be cold and wet with snowfalls up-to-your-ass."

"Sometimes the light during the middle of the day bothers me when I'm on an organic planet," Sante admitted. "It's too bright for my space-accustomed eyes. From a purely taste perspective, a blue sky can be beautiful, but seems almost too garish on a cycle-to-cycle basis, or I guess I should say, day-to-day basis. When I look out a window, I want to see the comfort of a black expanse dusted with stars."

Now it was my turn to laugh. "A sky should be black? You definitely have been in space too long." The local traveltube was ahead and then I saw the Pink Slipper dancing across its rectangular sign. "Look! That's where I met Bell."

Cle decided, "We have to check out this place."

It was strange walking into the Pink Slipper again. It was early evening exactly as it was the first time. And just like the first time, the place was empty except for Bryan the bartender and the piano player. It was déjà vu and yet now, my life was very different.

"Hi, do you remember me? I asked Bryan. Cle and Sante pulled up stools on either side of me. "I was in here about six weeks ago. You sold me some Irish whiskey."

Bryan scratched his chin. He had grown a goatee since the last time I saw him. "Yeah, I remember you."

"Does the Trinity witch, Bell, still come in here?"

"The last time I saw her was the night you were here. Guess it was time for her to move on. We get drifters, who sort of come and go—'cause we're so close to the tube and all. Hey, I still got some Irish whiskey left and it is still 50 credits a shot."

"I'd like to taste it," said Sante.

"You don't drink," I said. If one dot of tartan ratu could send Sante over the edge, what would a shot of Irish whiskey do?

"Can't see any harm," said Sante. I want to see what's so potent about Irish whiskey that it changed your life."

Bryan laughed and said, "Irish whiskey certainly can change your life. It will turn you inside-out."

"Metaphorically speaking, I'd love to be inside-out," said Cle. "Pour one for each of us."

Bryan took the bottle from under the counter and poured the amber-colored liquor into three shot glasses. The bottle was almost empty and I thought, not much magic left.

"What's it they say when they drink these?" asked Cle. "Bottoms up or something like that?"

"*Sláinte*," said Bryan. "It means, 'to your health.'"

"*Sláinte*," said Cle and *ce* tossed the shot down *cis* throat. *Ce* inhaled sharply as if stunned and when *ce* exhaled, *cis* face flushed red.

"You okay?" asked Bryan.

Cle nodded yes. "It's a tad hot."

"You're supposed to sip it, not gulp it," lectured Bryan. "This is expensive stuff."

Forewarned, Sante tasted a bit from the shot glass in *lis* hand. "Gee," *le* said. "It tastes like the antiseptic cleaner I use on my hands before surgery."

"Where'd you get these two?" asked Bryan.

"They're not used to drinking spirits," I explained.

"I hate wasting good liquor on amateurs. Can't a pretty girl like you find better drinking companions than these two lightweights?"

I drank my drink down in one gulp and slammed it down on the bar. My eyes blinked in unison with the heat of it. "They're not lightweights," I insisted. "These two are the most heavyweight characters I've ever met."

"What's your name?" asked Bryan. "I can't remember."

"It's Hibernia and these are—my mates, Cle and Sante."

"Right! Now I remember. Hibernia—Irish whiskey and Irish name. Well, Hibernia, I bet you twenty credits that your heavyweight friends here cannot take another drink of Irish whiskey and say fast—and I mean really fast, 'Peter Piper picked a peck of pickled peppers. If Peter Piper picked a peck of pickled peppers, how many pickled peppers did Peter Piper pick?'"

"That's easy!" said Cle "I can do that. I'll have you know that I have a photographic memory and I'm a linguistic expert. I speak over six hundred languages and I'll take your bet." I couldn't believe it. Cle's ego was displaying all the classic symptoms of intoxication on one drink.

"I'll cover that bet," said Sante slapping *lis* credit card down on the bar. I was astounded. My angel was gambling.

"You may be a linguistic expert, but you are a featherweight in the drinking department," challenged Bryan.

"I can do it, I really can," said Cle trying to convince us all. *Cis* words sounded forced.

"First the drink," said Bryan, pouring Cle another. Cle downed the second drink in one gulp. *Ce* did not enjoy it anymore this time, but *ce* showed no negative reactions. "Would you like me to repeat it once more?" asked Bryan.

"That won't be necessary," said Cle looking rather unsteady.

"I know—you have a photographic memory. Well let's hear it Professor Linguistics!"

Cle cleared *cis* throat. "Peter Piper picked a peck of pickled peppers. If Peter Piper picked a peck of pickled peppers, how many peppers did Peter Piper pick?" Cle reeled off without a hitch. Not only did *ce* say it perfectly; *ce* used Bryan's voice.

"Bravo!" I shouted. Bryan was disappointed. Like many other people, he did not recognize the sound of his voice coming back at him.

"You ready to up the ante?" asked Cle. "How about I recite it backwards this time?"

"Nope!" said Bryan. "Can't afford to hear you recite it backward."

Despite Cle's bravado, *ce* was wobbly. "How many peppers do you think Peter Piper picked?" *ce* posed. "I guess it would depend on what kind they were and what their average size was—don't you think?"

"Who cares?" asked Bryan.

"Well that's the best I can do if you won't give me any more information. Pay up!"

"Want another drink instead?" asked Bryan.

"Let's call it a draw," suggested Cle. "You keep the drink and your credits and you call me the winner. You were right; I am an amateur drinker."

"Well, I owe you," said Bryan. "The next time you pass by the Pink Slipper, come on in. Drinks are on me." Bryan nodded toward Cle. "And you, I'll serve you a glass of fresh squeezed orange juice."

****

I managed to get my two lightweights out of the bar. Cle kept acting silly and Sante was urging the silliness on. Cle began singing and wanted me to dance down the street with *cim*. The three of us stopped to embrace and Sante turned me around and around until I was dizzy. The few people we passed seemed amused by our spectacle; but I felt self-conscious. People in Toledo never acted crazy, at least not on Cherry Street on a weeknight.

"How could you two possibly get drunk so fast?" I asked.

"We're just having fun although Irish whiskey does seem like an unstable high," said Sante.

All the way to the Erie Pod Park, all they wanted to do was fool around. We sat down in the last car on the traveltube and Cle dangled an arm over my shoulder and nibbled my ear. Sante sat down next to Cle and massaged *cis* thigh and the hand kept getting closer and closer to Cle's crotch. When Sante and Cle started kissing, an elderly Tyrowsian man across the aisle strained to look straight ahead. I never thought of Sante or Cle as having inhibitions; but they had a few that Irish whiskey unceremoniously whisked away.

"Stop it," I said. "You're embarrassing me."

"Gee. What a stuffy place where you can't *zlit** in public.

A Human woman, two seats down, peered over her newssheets, and raised her eyebrows. "I agree," she said. "We hide our love while murder is on public display." Then she went back to reading the news.

It was dark by the time we reached the Erie Pod Park. The pumpkin-colored moon was full and near the horizon. The optical illusion that it lay just beyond the trees, further suspended reality. I breathed deeply and the sweet April air filled me with spring fever. The soft buffeting breeze was still blowing and I spread my arms wide and dreamed I could fly.

Sante and Cle had sobered a bit and as we walked down the moonlit platform, I could see the wheels turning in Cle's head and knew *ce* was making plans. "It's dark enough. Let's do it here," *le* whispered in a sexy breathless way.

"Wait, my place is not far," I said.

"Why wait. We can have a quick *zlit* here and a couple more when we reach your place. As long as Sante keeps me stoked, I can go all night." I was beginning to understand more about our three-way relationship and the way it worked. Sante often waited for Cle to initiate sex. And Cle could work both side of the equation, getting Sante excited on one side and me on the other. Of course, once Sante was "stoked," fireworks ensued.

Cle backed me into a darker shadow and pressed *lis* groin into the softness of my belly. I unzipped *cis* pants and glanced nervously up and down the platform. It was deserted. *Ce* leaned closer—cis eyelids fluttering in anticipation. *Cis* lower lip trembled as *cis* ready sex filled my hands. *Ce* moaned softly when I lowered my head and began to fellate cim. "Your hands are so cold and I'm so hot," *ce* said.

Sante put *cis* hands on the back of my head and I looked up at *lim*. Light played over *lis* long pale hair and off one shoulder. *Le* looked like fluid moonlight and I almost had a vicarious orgasm from the expression on *lis* face. Then I heard the click, click, click of footsteps. "Someone's coming," *le* said.

"I wish it was me," said Cle.

"Heads up!" said Sante. "A person is walking this way."

I wiped my mouth and got up off my knees. "Good lord!" It was Gertie.

"Janey!" she cried. "Is that really you?" Cle was standing slightly behind me. In a second, I heard the unmistakable sound of *cim* zipping *cis* pants.

"Greetings Earthling," Cle snickered.

Sante came out from behind me and put *lis* arm around my shoulder in a nonchalant but possessive way. Gertie shifted her eyes from Cle to Sante and then back to me. "What are you doing here this time of night?" she questioned.

---

* *"zlit"* meaning, "link," current slang usage, "fuck"; language origin, Cuneate

"I came home to clear up some details."

"Details like all the hot water you're in with Mr. Wantanabi? He knows nothing was wrong with you. Why did you leave and allow everyone to believe you were sick?"

"I told you I was okay and not to worry. If you give me a chance, I will explain everything. First, I would like you to meet Jana Sante and Jana Cle."

"Hello," she said, finally acknowledging their presence.

"I have some great news. I'm married."

"You're married? Who'd you marry?" Gertie glanced from Cle to Sante and brightened some, but her expression was marked with suspicion.

"I married them both." I waited for her reaction.

"Huh? You say both like in a three-way?"

"Why don't we start walking," suggested Cle, "and I will explain as we go. May I take your arm, Gertie?" Cle didn't wait for Gertie to say yes because Cle was used to getting what *ce* wanted. "Have you ever heard of the Janaforma?" By the time we reached the courtyard, Cle had given Gertie a general description of the Janaforma.

As I strolled ahead with Sante, I could hear Gertie saying to Cle, "I told her a long time ago that she needed a real man. By the way, are either of you real men?"

"I have a dick but no balls," said Cle and I shook my head in disbelief. "Sante keeps me stoked and I've never heard any complaints that I ever left any lover unsatisfied."

"No kidding," said Gertie. "I'd love to hear how you Janaforma—do it."

"We could probably demonstrate, but I doubt Hi would go along with the idea."

"You're right. I wouldn't," I said.

We hesitated as we approached my front door. Sante yawned and said, "I'm tired; it was a long trip and I'm looking forward to a good night's sleep."

"I suppose," agreed Gertie. "Travel is so exhausting nowadays. I still have your keycard, Jane. You want to come and get it?" I followed Gertie across the courtyard to her pod. While she searched for my keycard in her junk drawer, Poppy came out of the bedroom and padded over to say hello. I gave him a scratch between the ears. "You look happy," Gertie said. "Where in creation did you find two lovers that handsome? I can't wait to hear all the details. Tell me one thing—give me something to dream about tonight. Are they as good in bed as I imagine them to be?"

"I'll leave it at yes."

"Oh my god!" said Gertie. "Point to the exact spot on the star chart where your taxi went kaput and I'll go there, sabotage the engines, and wait for two gorgeous Janaforma to rescue me."

Crossing the courtyard again, I found Sante and Cle involved in foreplay on my front porch. "What took you so long?" asked Cle.

I fumbled with the keycard in the dark shadows of the porch and told them, "Gertie wanted to know if you are as good in bed as she imagines you to be."

"What did you say?" asked Sante.

"I said you were everything I've ever wanted."

"Is that true?"

"You know it is."

Cle cleared *cis* throat. "You two might feel like standing here on the porch all night and flirting with each other, but I want to make some down-and-dirty love and I am going to do it either here or inside. So if it happens here, I guarantee, Gertie is going to get an education in Janaforma sexuality. If it's okay with you then it's okay with me. I enjoy an audience."

"That's because you're a showoff," said Sante and *le* snatched the keycard from my hand and said, "Let me help. I'm good in the dark."

As soon as we stepped inside, Sante started looking around like a curious feline. "Where's your sleeproom?" *le* asked. I pointed in the general direction.

Cle started unbuttoning *cis* shirt and said, "Sante, say something inspirational to keep me going."

"How about I love you?" asked Sante.

"Forget it," said Cle. "Let's open some windows and get some fresh air in here. Maybe it will help my mood." The three of us ran around the rooms opening windows while Cle shouted, "*Carpe noctem!*" We settled in and showered and by that time, they seemed almost sober. Cle slugged down a huge glass of water before telling me, "Tonight is special."

"I know; you've both been alluding to something for hours. What's going to happen tonight that hasn't already happened?"

"Right here, where this place holds so many special memories of you, Sante and I will bond with you through the way of Una."

"And how do we do that?"

"Come, your lifegiver and consort will show you," said Sante. They took my hands and led me toward the bedroom. The bedroom was cooler now. The mauve-colored curtains gently undulated with the breeze and made me feel dreamy. Desire had chipped away at me for hours, eroding my reserve, and passion quickly came to a head. I thought we were edging toward the bed, but Sante said, "Let's make love in my vitarattha. You game, Hi?" *Le* showed me the hardware in the palm of *lis* hand and before I could say yes, Sante activated the forcefield. A split second later, the three of us were free-floating inside a Zero-G bubble, in the middle of my bedroom. I started laughing because the notion that I was inside a vitarattha, here in my little space pod on the southern bank of Lake Erie, with these two fabulous creatures was almost more than I could get my mind around. I suddenly felt giddy as Ebenezer Scrooge running down the street on Christmas morning because just like Ebenezer, I knew things I never contemplated before. I saw a Trinity witch ritually cleansing the table and laying out her full deck of cards for me. She told me clearly, with no mumbo-jumbo involved, *Your fate intertwines eternally with these two beings. You began this game in prehistoric caves and were destined, through* hataeasta, *to play out your passion in endless ways.*

"I want much more from you tonight," Cle told me.

"Anything you want," I said. Cle moved my legs to a wider position to make a place for *cim*self. Moonlight, the color of daylight, streamed through the window illuminating the side of *cis* face. *Ce* came forward; *cis* long hair sliding like silk over my shoulder where the cool crystal beads tickled my breast. I shivered with delight. *Ce* was being deliberately tender, moving slowly and carefully. *Ce* traced my lips with *cis* tongue. "I need to be with Sante inside you," *ce* told me.

"I love you completely," I said helplessly. "But I don't think I can do what you want. What I mean to say is I don't think I can physically accommodate you both at once."

"The Way of *Una* is not a physical feat but a metaphysical quest through the window of sex," said Cle. "You and Sante have created a special place between you. Sante took you there the first cycle we made love. I am asking you to allow me into that space tonight."

I caught my breath. "Oh!" One of the first impressions I ever had of Cle was that it would be impossible to deceive *cim*. Of course, *ce* knew about the phenomenon that occurred when Sante and I made love. How could *ce* not? When it happened, we shut Cle out, but it was never intentional on my part. The wave of Cle's need washed over me as *ce* felt the extraordinary length of my silence. "I have no life but through my lifegiver," *ce* remind me.

"I am hesitating not because I have any doubts about you. I am hesitating because I have no control over what happens."

Sante embraced Cle and said, "Our triad is complete and it is going to happen, tonight, right now. All you need is little bit more of me in you."

Cle was eager and *ce* surrendered to Sante who took Cle with *lis* love. Cle wanted me to watch until their mutual fire peaked. Watching, I felt like winged Icarus against their heat. The Trinity Witch laid down another card, The Lovers. By full moonlight as bright as day, suspended in the illumination of love, I remembered them fully. Once I called them different names, strange names, even unpronounceable, inhuman names across meadows of unknown worlds. I had suckled them and been suckled in kind. Once we were birds. Cle had showed me the perfection of a wingover and we mated as the thermals kept us aloft. I loved Cle best in that lifetime. Fleeting images of alien bodies—talons—tentacles—arms and compound eyes—all beautiful, luminescent silver scales—seal-skinned—gliding though gelatinous liquids and wings of finest feathers—we had done it all! We lived eternities enfolded in love's promises, died in a thousand lives. This new dimension split us into a trinity of souls. But we were Una, in one together. Lovemaking was the reenactment of Una, our mortal groping for unity. This time we had grown fleshy appendages, new sensations to test for the curiosity of the divine Una. My lovers sighed with fulfillment as we fell asleep in that sacred space that we created with our love.

TEN

Bevies of songbirds cheep and chatter in the hedgerows snaking through the old part of the Erie Pod Park. Beyond, fallow meadows of grasses, orchards of blooming fruit trees release their scented pollens and wait for the bees to arrive. My senses awaken in the Now and I'm aware of two bodies and the way we fit together. I feel their warmth and their smell comforts me. Suspended on the brink of a new day, my natural state is trust. A dappled radiance dances around the room as light threads through my eyelashes. I open my eyes and see through the *vitarattha* to the glass paperweight sitting on the dresser by the window and think, *I must not forget to take it. Mom said it belonged to Great-Grandma Mellé.* I close my eyes again, unable to leave the suspended comfort of the *vitarattha.* I feel life surround me. I feel its nectar pouring out and into the creation of me.

****

Sante stirred and said, "It's too bright in here."

By now, beacons of white-light twinkled off the dresser mirror. Earth's stark daylight began to reclaim us and the romantic night gave way to wrinkled clothing below on the bedroom floor. Cle awoke and shielded *cis* space-accustomed eyes with *cis* hands and started searching for the vitarattha remote. "Help me find it," *ce* said. "I have to pee."

"I have it," said Sante and *le* took us down to the floor and deactivated the forcefield. As soon as we landed, I went to the window and pulled the gauze-thin curtains closed. It was then that I realized my throat felt dry and raspy. My perennial spring allergies were making their seasonal comeback. I had forgotten about them but my allergic response remembered. Sante let go a soft little groan. "I have a headache," *le* said.

"Earthlings call it a hangover," said Cle.

"Is that because you end up with your head hanging over a toilet?" A moment later, *le* jumped up, ran into the bathroom, and vomited.

At the Orbit Diner, two blocks away, we helped ourselves to the day's special, a stack of West Virginia corncakes swimming in butter and artificially flavored high-fructose corn syrup. I watched in amazement as Sante and Cle wolfed down several leaden corncakes. "My mouth feels greasy," Sante said afterward and we lumbered out of the Orbit Cafeteria.

"Well I feel as if I just ate a rock," Cle said.

They had drunk liquor and now they were eating corncakes soaked in artificial blueberry syrup. Was it moon madness, Irish whiskey, or the emergence of spring affecting us? I sneezed and I knew the Yin/Yang of Earth's push/pull was beginning to play tug of war with us all. After breakfast, Cle was organized and specific. *Ce* wanted to follow through on Rebecca's suggestions. "We need to get access to historical information from a Human perspective that is not contaminated by Tyrowsian bias," *ce* explained.

"I subscribe to the Universal Geographic," I offered. "Universal Geographic maintains a huge database of historical information on Earth. Once, they even had an article on the Janaforma—said you were heroic people. I guess they were right about that."

Back at my pod, Sante and Cle went to the Universal Geographic site on my multidex while I contacted a moving company and they promised to come in two days to pack my belongings. I spent the morning poking through my clutter and the treasures given to me by my mother. The few items truly important to me, the cobalt blue calla lily paperweight that belonged to my great-grandmother Mellé, my mother's English tea set covered in pink rosebuds that she insisted was available only in England, and, of course, my collection of Universal Geographic holospools fit into three small boxes. Twenty-four hours earlier, I was sure I left a huge treasure trove of valuable possessions behind on Earth. But now that I saw what I rushed home to save, my assets were few. My Earthly life always had felt like a preparation for leaving and now I knew why. I had never imagined anything as grand as Cle and Sante could happen to me, but here they were and I was going to embrace them and my new life with all the gusto I could muster.

The Universal Geographic contained several thousand files on Earth history and several hundred cross-reference files on Tyrowsian Culture. Cle and Sante took turns speed-reading through the information to see if it was pertinent to their case. By early afternoon, a stack of copied spools sat next to the multidex. "Listen to this quote from a book entitled, The Tyrowsian Mind," said Cle. "'The philosophical origins of *hataeasta* originated with a Tyrowsian religious sect on the planet Herzayzen during its fifth millennium. Tyrowsians adapted and popularized *hataeasta* on every planet in the Orion Spur. On Earth it was introduced in 2230 as the NEW VISION movement—'"

"Let me see that," I insisted. According to the Universal Geographic article, Tyrowsians had influence over Earth politics as early as 2487. That was thirty-eight years before NEW VISION became an overnight phenomenon on Earth. An idea crystallized in my mind. I remembered my history—about how NEW VISION crushed thousands of years of Earth tradition in a stampede for radical change. That vague off-planet influence, that historical truth-eater of Earth's culture disguised as NEW VISION started with Tyrowsians. I began hating Tyrowsians and blaming them for everything that ever went wrong on Earth.

"Do you find Universal Geographic generally reliable?" asked Cle.

"I would trust the Universal Geographic over my own mother," I swore. "It's Earth-Human based and hundreds of years old. It's funded by its subscribers."

"I was hoping to hear that," said Cle.

"What do you plan to do with this information?"

"I'm unsure yet; but if the truth is liberating, it's bound to help somewhere. For Tyrowsians to pervert the meaning of *hataeasta*, to serve their political misconduct is unforgivable."

I wondered how Tyrowsians, who denied the existence of the past, would recognize truth. In a labyrinth of lost pasts and infinite futures, had any recognizable truths survived? "What if nobody on Aeternus recognizes your truth?" I asked.

"I'm willing to take that chance," said Cle. "Tyrowsians are striving to sanitize their image—promoting the idea of freedom and cooperation. This will give them a chance to live up to their new image."

"Does anyone care about the real meaning of *hataeasta* or where it came from?" I asked.

"I do," said Cle.

That evening, in the prolonged twilight of springtime, Gertie crossed the courtyard to my pod for the last time. To see her standing at my door holding a box-o-wine, it seemed no time had passed. She mentioned something earlier that day about teaching Cle and Sante how to play Zeppelin and now she was as good as her word. The four of us took opposing seats at the table while Gertie shuffled the cards. I opened what I hoped was my last box of Pink Chablis and poured us each a glass. The number one topic of conversation, at least between Cle and Sante, was how Tyrowsians were obfuscating the political scene on Aeternus. While we played cards, conversation turned heated.

Cle peered over the sunglasses *ce* had worn most of the day and squinted. *Ce* appeared agitated, as though *ce* had consumed a pot of theobromine Colombian café. "In a world where the past is systematically contorted, the truth is always blurred," *ce* said. Then *ce* drummed *cis* fingernails on the tabletop waiting for Sante to respond.

"The core essence of truth will always be elusive," Sante returned calmly.

"That's why it must be held, gingerly, with an open hand," remarked Cle and *ce* casually laid *cis* cards down on the table. "Look, I've won again!" So far, Cle had won every hand.

Sante ignored Cle's card victory. "That's a nice analogy, but you're playing semantics. You can't hold truth in your hand. Truth must be set free to grow and beckon us forward."

As twilight turned to darkness, the debate raged on. They went on for two hours like that. Gears were shifting and an unpredictable new focus was taking center stage. Something was askew from my perspective. I broke into their debate with my own concerns. "I think we should concentrate on the upcoming hearing and forget about truth and fighting Tyrowsians."

It was as if I dropped a bomb in the middle of the room. Cle sat down *cis* wineglass. "How can we forget about the truth? I didn't ask for this fight; but I can't turn my back on my people."

Sante weighed in too. "I've been thinking about this ever since we've left Aeternus and I've decided to support Cle fully in this endeavor to take on the Tyrowsian government. But we've yet to hear from you on where you stand on this matter."

"Then you're on Cle's side?"

"I'm always on Cle's side. Beyond that, I personally believe we need to take a stand on important issues. I'm just not sure we need to overthrow the Aeternus government to get what we want."

"What are you planning to do?" I asked.

Cle stood up, walked around the table to where I sat, and put *cis* hands on my shoulders. "Nothing radical—at least at first. If Rebecca agrees, we'll see this information gets into the right hands. If we get Janaforma backing, we can petition the Orion Spur Alliance directly to get a representative voice on Aeternus. Perhaps we could get legal control of Space Security, but that's my dream, a real stretch to say the least."

"That's going to take financial capital," said Gertie.

"I have capital," said Cle.

"No, I mean major capital, sweetie."

"Whatever it takes; I've got it. I'm all in," Cle assured her.

"If you have that kind of power then I say—go for it!"

"Nobody asked your opinion," I said. "They don't need more encouragement."

"A major part of gaining our rights," said Sante, "is gaining control of Space Security. And as long as we are creating our personal wish lists, I think we should demand our genetic records."

Cle was still trying to keep me calm and *ce* massaged my shoulders and finally played little kisses off the nape of my neck. "We're going to give the immovable Tyrowsians another push and see if they move this time," *ce* said with a final kiss.

Gertie had this nimbus of excitement around her as if she was involved in a religious conversion. "I'm with you!" she shouted. "Tyrowsians are scum; they ruined Earth."

That night Sante and Cle fell asleep early. This was different too. The Earth factor was definitely disrupting our equilibrium. At midnight, I was still staring at the Ursa Minor Constellation out through my bedroom window. The next morning I composed a letter to Mr. Wantanabi at Atlas Map officially resigning my position as an associate cartographer. This action felt final. I reflected on what Bell predicted that night in the Pink Slipper. "I see you going farther than any of your Human kind have ever gone before." I was intrigued with my prospects for the future and in these final hours on Earth, I forgave everything and everyone, even my mother. I knew I could no longer nurture myself from the desiccated remnants of this Ohio life. As Cle liked to say, "I'm all in," and I was all in with Sante and Cle.

The following morning, movers came to pack my few belongings and take them away for shipping to Aeternus. Gertie took my small appliances, a black lamp that she had always admired and my glassware. The remainder I sold to Atlas. When my space pod was empty, the only thing left was to say goodbye to Gertie.

Cle and Sante were tearful when they kissed Gertie goodbye, Janaforma style, on both sides of her forehead. She enthusiastically embraced first Cle and then Sante, and promised to come and visit us on Aeternus. I wondered if she would come when she wouldn't even move to Mars with Buddy. Who could predict the cycles and variables that might bring us together again? I felt emotional now and I tried to keep it light as I said goodbye. I patted Poppy on the head and knew that in time I would even miss him. Gertie took me aside for a private moment and confessed, "I should have gone with Buddy. I've decided that I'm going to try to find him and if I do, maybe, just maybe, it's not too late." We cried, embraced, and were closer at that moment than ever before. I thought about Gertie all the way to the spaceport. What an odd relationship ours was. We were like two concentric circles. Something changed and we merged for a moment before veering off from each other, perhaps never to meet again.

As the shuttle left Toledo, we soared though a blue sky painted with cumulus buttermilk clouds. Within minutes, we were in black space. I watched through the window as the Earth ball shrank in my widening perspective. Nighttime was encroaching on the daylight of Eastern Europe. "Adieu Earth," I said. Twenty minutes into space, my allergy condition was no more. Earth faded from view and my focus cleared. Out here, it was easier to believe ultimate truths existed and that we had the power to unravel the endless mysteries of life.

Eighty-two hours later, the glittering spiral of Aeternus lay before us. As soon as we landed, we went straight to our apartment. A multidex message waited from Rebecca Dykestra saying she wanted to see us the following cycle at her apartment.

We spent a few hours in one of Hilton's reorientation chambers, to accustom ourselves to the Aeternus time clock, and then went at the appointed time to meet Rebecca. She greeted us at the door wearing the odd combination of a flower-festooned dressing gown, and a serious smile. As usual, she was in high gear and she hustled us inside and into chairs. She poured cups of steaming tea for us all, which were most appreciated, and offered us fresh pastry while explaining the ground rules for the hearing.

"The hearing will be an informal affair," she explained. "The Aeternus Council of Three will allow each of you to present three character witnesses but since no charges are being filed against Jana Sante and Hibernian Smith we don't need to waste time parading out unneeded witnesses. No public records exist on Aeternus for Hibernia, which also is in our favor. And Sante, I came across information in your records, which I need to clarify." Rebecca scrolled through the screens of her multidex. "Here it is. How old are you Sante?"

"Twenty-seven bio years old—why?"

"Is it true that when you were twenty bio years old, you worked as a sexual surrogate?"

"Yes," admitted Sante.

"How many people know you worked as a sexual surrogate?" asked Rebecca.

"Probably everybody."

"Everybody but me." I bit my tongue.

Rebecca shot me a furtive look. "It wasn't a secret," said Sante. "I was good at it and it helped pay for my education. This life style I now enjoy was unknown to me before I met Cle."

"I'm Human," said Rebecca. "So please forgive my clumsiness regarding these matters; but did anything happen during that time that the Tyrowsians might find and could use against Cle?"

Sante appeared confused. "Like what?"

Rebecca shrugged. " —pornographic holospools or pictures, illegal drugs, blackmail, bizarre sexual practices, disgruntled clients that could surface to embarrass us in front of the Aeternus Council of Three?"

Sante laughed. "Pornography, drugs, and black mail are Human perversions regarding sex. Those interests never held any attraction for me. I'm unsure what you mean by bizarre sexual practices. Certainly, what may be appropriate in one situation may not be appropriate in another. My goal always was to help individuals integrate their sexual self with their creative self. That cannot be achieved through crudity."

"Were any of your clients Tyrowsian males?"

"Most of my clients were Tyrowsian males. Tyrowsian males, in particular, have problems making the jump from their midlife adolescence into their full creative selves."

"Okay; let's hope the other side leaves this alone. I don't think Box's attorney will be able to go anywhere with the accusation that the assailants received inadequate medical attention. No evidence exists to substantiate that claim. You do keep good records Doctor Sante; thank you for that. If no more surprises surface, then I believe the Council of Three will scrutinize Cle's record and pull out anything they think they can use to cast *cim* in a negative light. Their aim will be to establish a pattern of past missteps and attempt to link those missteps to this event."

"What exactly are the charges?" asked Cle.

"Liacann is asking the Aeternus Council of Three to consider the charge of voluntary manslaughter," said Rebecca.

Cle's face fell. "Voluntary manslaughter?"

"We are pleading self-defense," said Rebecca. "The burden of proof will be on Liacann. I spent time doing a thorough background check on you. Your records are exemplary in every way. You were a hero on Sutcay Tay."

"What about Commander Vertain?" Cle asked. "Can she hurt me? She was critical of some of my past judgments."

"Go talk to her," said Rebecca. "Ask her to be character witness for you. See what she says."

"I will do that," said Cle. "I also would like to ask Admiral Vista. *Ce* was my captain when I served on *Aeternus One.*"

"Excellent. Who else? What about your superior officer when you served on the *Kirtland?*"

Cle winced. "That was a lifebearer named Jana Devina. Sante and I were attempting to form a personal relationship with her. It didn't take and she blames me."

Rebecca pushed Cle. "If she's an officer worth her commission, she'll be able to separate your personal and professional lives. Go talk to her, Cle. I don't want any loose cannons going boom during the hearing."

As Sante and I left Rebecca's place, my mind was racing. A ridiculous image of Sante as a pleasure prince was becoming a caricature in my mind. Once we were alone, I thought *le* would mention the subject, offer an explanation about why *le* failed to mention that *le* worked as a sexual surrogate; but Sante said nothing. I finally blurted out, "How could you have sex with people for money? How could the most sensitive creature I've ever encountered work as a pleasure prince?"

Sante laughed but *le* was not amused. "You're still a virginal idealist," *le* accused me. "Grow up!"

BOOM! A wall came down between us. "Are you saying this is my problem?"

"I have no problem with my past."

"I guess I can't understand how you could turn off your feelings and operate as a sexual surrogate when you seem like such a sensitive person."

"What makes you think I turned off my feelings? If anything, it heightened my sensitivity to people."

Frustrated, I said, "I'm surprised—that's all. Tell me, what other surprises are in store for me?"

Sante turned psychic, just as *le* always did when I questioned *lim* about the future. "The future holds nothing but surprises, especially right now. I'll see you later; I'm going to see Ruth Gordon at the hospital. Meet me back at the apartment in a couple of hours."

ELEVEN

Two hours before the scheduled hearing, Cle stood before the full-length mirror in our sleeproom attempting to adjust the lapels on *cis* formal, black uniform. Tension orbited *cim* like electricity and it seemed the ambidextrous Janaforma consort suddenly was all thumbs. "I can't even braid my hair!" *ce* claimed. I picked up a brush and pulled it through *cis* long hair. "Make it tight, I don't want any loose strands coming out during the hearing."

A part of me wondered why Cle did it. Financially, *ce* wanted for nothing. Over the last few cycles, Rebecca had sent dozens of documents to the apartment for me to sign—access to credit accounts, wills, bonds, and lots of stock. Among Cle's assets, *ce* held fifty-two percent interest in Vitarattha Research & Development. Cle did not need Orion Spur Space Security, yet it was clear, OSSS was *cis* life.

We met Rebecca outside the hearing room, and Cle immediately asked, "Were you able to get a Janaforma placed on the panel?"

Rebecca appeared apologetic. "One, and only as an observer." Further complicating the situation, Devina refused to testify for Cle. Rebecca appeared serious and perhaps a little less enthusiastic every time we saw her. "Cle, I have to ask you an important question," she began. "My sources told me a short time ago that the Council of Three has already decided to nail you. Do you understand what I am suggesting? You can stop this. If you want to resign your commission with Space Security, we can walk in there—and I guarantee, twenty minutes from now, you will walk out free and clear."

"I thought you needed warriors."

"I do," said Rebecca. "I don't want martyrs."

Cle put *cis* hand on Rebecca's arm. "As I said before, I'm all in."

****

We entered the darkened hearing chamber. Near the rear wall sat a heavy lacquered table with three ornate chairs behind. An android clerk was busy adjusting the multidex that sat on the end of the table. Two simple facing tables sat near the front. Liacann, the Tyrowsian lawyer representing Box, was sitting at one and furiously writing something on his multidex. I could not see his face, but from behind, he looked like a typical Tyrowsian attorney with a tight knot of white hair at the nape of his neck. Rebecca and Cle sat down at the opposite table from Liacann and Sante and I sat behind. The atmosphere was heavy as the inside of a monastery and the dim light cast eerie shadows up the high stone walls. "It's cold in here," I complained.

"Put on a jacket," Rebecca said over her shoulder. "We're in the Tyrowsian comfort zone now."

The Council of Three and one Janaforma observer paraded into the chamber to the "itchy" sound of Tyrowsian music. The Janaforma observer was a lifebearer named, Admiral Compass, but I barely noticed her once the Council of Three began their grand entrance into the courtroom. Three Tyrowsian males, dressed in identical voluminous purple robes, sashayed into the room just as the Tyrowsian music faded into silence. With their heads held high and their long white hair teased into fantastic poufs, they stole the show. I started to snicker and put a hand over my mouth. Sante glanced my way, raised an eyebrow, and then glanced away. I leaned closer and whispered in *lis* ear, "They look like three dandelion seed heads."

"The look is supposed to evoke a feeling of stability and compassion, not humor," *le* whispered.

"It's not working for me," I whispered back.

Rebecca leaned toward Cle. "What do you know about Admiral Compass?"

"Not much," Cle admitted. "I never served with her. Space Security promoted her to admiral while I was still an apprentice. She's old, an original, right out of Forma's nativity vats."

As soon as the Council of Three took their seats, I noticed the fancy gold threads on the cuffs of the center Tyrowsian. The three of them conferred in undertones and the one on the right end, the one with beady red eyes, kept fiddling with the multidex in front of him. Suddenly the lights in the room got brighter and I realized the beady-eyed one was even controlling the lights. A moment later, a prison android brought Yarrow T. Box into the chamber. Box was smaller than I remembered. His arms and legs now shackled, he was a scrawny, neglected mess. Box projected a glare of hatred for everyone present.

"What rock did he crawl out from under?" Rebecca whispered over her shoulder. The android helped Box to a seat, then stepped away as the forcefield locked Box inside.

"Is there anyone here who does not speak Universal?" asked the Tyrowsian in the center. He glanced around the room. "My clerk informs me Yarrow T. Box is language illiterate but can communicate in basic Universal. So please, for expediency's sake, let's proceed in Universal?" I took off my translator.

"This hearing is in session," he announced. "Please activate terminals. My name is Gran Ymotano and I am Regent Governor of Aeternus. To my right is Mi Cochon, my vice-regent and an expert in criminal law, and to my left is Le-Le Kork, my Secretary of Space Affairs and may I introduce Admiral Compass, who is sitting in the rear of the courtroom and will be our Janaforma observer during this hearing. Please note the document now appearing on your multidex screens citing my authority to conduct hearings and appoint Tyrowsian individuals that might have expertise in assisting me in reviewing a case. I will conduct proceedings at my discretion, informally, but we will adhere to judicial protocol as established by the Orion Spur Alliance. All testimony will be held in evidence and will be accessible to a court of Orion Spur law. This cycle, the Aeternus Council of Three will review charges brought by Yarrow T. Box against Jana Cle and Orion Spur Space Security. We are here to determine if sufficient evidence demands an indictment against Jana Cle, a class 3C Janaforma, who holds the current rank of commander. Jana Cle was captain and pilot of the *OSSS Daedalus* until 947.36, when *cis* commanding officer, Jana Vertain, officially suspended *cim* from duty pending this hearing. On the space cycle 947.34, the *Daedalus* received a distress call from the Martian freighter, *Gemstone*. At exactly 14.35 space hours, Captain Cle and trainee J. Hibernia Smith boarded the *Gemstone* through airlock four. Within minutes, Ronald Porkcur, Petre Saunders and Hector Limpet were dead. Captain Cle killed these three men. *Ce* freely admits killing them in a signed affidavit addressed to this court. We are here to decide if the threat from these four men warranted Captain Cle's actions or if Captain Cle acted from hidden motives. One word of caution to both attorneys; prosecution and defense will offer testimony to me, not to each other. Are there any questions?"

"Governor Ymotano," said Rebecca. "The defense asks that you seat Admiral Jana Compass as an active member of the council. We need a qualified Janaforma to help us assess the various subtleties involved in this case."

"Your request is noted," said Ymotano. "Multidex pause." Our multidex went fuzzy. "This is not a debatable issue within the context of this hearing. I will make only one judgment concerning this matter and then I expect you to get on with it. Aeternus law dictates that a Janaforma representative may enjoy only peripheral consideration, in this case, because of an obvious conflict of interest." Rebecca did not follow through on this point, but I thought of many things she could have said. It was already too late and

Ymotano was saying, "Multidex, activate. Prosecution, please present your evidence."

****

Liacann stood and faced the Council of Three. He was a typical Tyrowsian, thread thin, white skinned, and pale red eyes although the jacket he wore with the white piping around the collar and sleeves made him look like he shopped at a consignment shop in Lima, Ohio. "I invite the learned Council to freely question Mr. Box about events aboard the *Gemstone*," said Liacann. "I would like to remind the Council that, under Orion Spur law, only the events on the star date 947.34 may be presented at this hearing."

Mi Cochon, Ymotano's vice-regent spoke up. His voice was high-pitched and had a tendency to twitter. He leaned forward and said, "And may we remind you that you have no license to remind the Council of Three of Orion Spur law. This is an informal hearing and neither prosecution nor defendant is Tyrowsian. *Keirtoyyan hataeasta* cannot protect either party. Mr. Box's past motivations may and will be considered."

"I beg the Council's pardon," replied Liacann.

"So far it's even," whispered Rebecca.

"Yeah," mumbled Cle. "Zero to zero."

"Mr. Box," said Ymotano, making a V-shape with his fingers, which he pointed to the right. Ymotano's mind slowly shifted to the past. "Please tell us how you came to be on the *Gemstone* and what happened in your encounter with the Space Security team of Captain Jana Cle and the trainee J. Hibernia Smith." Box began to speak and I knew for the first time what the statement meant, "Everybody speaks some kind of Universal."

"Well, ya 'onor," said Box. "'appened like this. Ronny's crazy notion was-ta cut loose."

"Mr. Box is referring to Ronald Porkcur," interjected Liacann.

"I was a victim, jus' like any 'elpless stray dog. Nobody wanted ta 'urt nobody! Stuff jus 'appened, plain and simple 'appened! Porkcur was strung-out. 'e 'ad a big rep at 'erzayzen with lifers. 'e was Big Papa wit ta ratu. Makin' us all toe-zee-mark—know what I mean?"

"Mr. Box is trying to say Ronald Porkcur was allegedly involved with the drug tartan ratu at Herzayzen Prison," said Liacann.

"Correcto!" said Box. "Ya didn't do what Porkcur decreed, 'ed cut off your ratu or worse—'ed cut you. Ronny wassa bastard ya didn't fool wit. Ronny was inta some pretty rough-ass games—know what I mean?"

"Mr. Box is attempting to explain that Ronald Porkcur was sexually abusing not only Mr. Box, but other inmates at Herzayzen Prison," said Liacann.

"I think we've grasp the point," said Ymotano. "Now may we get on with what happened on the specific space cycle of 947.34?"

"Ronny got ta Petre, fucked with 'is mind—real good. 'ad em believin in some weird shit. Ronny said big guns at 'ersayzen was da Cerribeame and dat none of us were ever gonna git out alive. Petre got scared. 'ad nightmares—dreamt rats was chewing 'is face off and shit like that. Ronny was real good at fucking with zee mind. 'ad Petre psyched—real bad. 'e made 'im bolt for space, so I 'ad ta go too." Yarrow T. Box grimaced with a memory.

Liacann explained again. "Mr. Box is attempting to tell the Council that he and Petre Saunders had a liaison and Mr. Box felt compelled to accompany Saunders in an attempt to protect him."

Ymotano responded. "Are you telling us that because of your feelings for Petre Saunders you felt compelled to join Ronald Porkcur in a killing rampage across space?"

Box became agitated. "Ya still don't get it. None of ya ever gets nothing. Guys like me and Petre are always gettin' blamed for da bad stuff. 'ector and Ronny did the killin'. They took Petre and I along to punish our asses when feeling zee need. Ronny been through the mind retrainin' at 'erzayzen two dozen times. It made em real bad the last time through."

"Let's skip to the encounter with the Space Security team," said Ymotano. "Whose idea was it to put out a distress call on the *Gemstone*?"

"Ronny was runnin' zee show. T'ere was somethin' fucked up with da shuttle we swiped. Full of newfangled junk, made no sense. 'ector 'ad trouble steerin' it. We jus wanted zee space jocks to take us some place safe. Jus wanted to git as far away from 'erzaysian as possible. Ronny's said 'e wasn't goin' 'urt nobody. 'e was just gonna scare em a little so they'd do what 'e said."

"So you killed no one?"

"Nope, not me."

"What part did you play in raping Captain Gordon?" asked Ymotano.

"Dat never 'appened. Dat's in 'er mind. That Janaforma-son-of-a-bitch over there turned freaky, got bent all-outta shape." Box pointed to Cle. "'e wired like a weirdo on Ronny!"

Ymotano turned toward Mi Cochon and said something. "Run the Ruth Gordon holospool," said Mi Cochon into the multidex. A holographic image of Captain Gordon appeared before us. She read her testimony from a small microdex she held in her hands. She still was shaky; but the statement she delivered was intense with impact.

She looked up and you could still see the trauma behind her eyes as if she was on fire inside. "On star cycle, 947.34, the *Gemstone* was overcome and boarded by what appeared to be four Human men. I soon discovered they were evil incarnate. From holographic-identity images presented to me by Bãthe-Be and Shreeher of the Tyrowsian Constabulary, I positively identify my perpetrators as Ronald Porkcur, Hector Limpet, Petre Saunders and Yarrow Box."

"I was set upon by these four beasts—bound, gagged, beaten, and sexually assaulted. As I lay helpless at their feet begging for mercy, their final insult was to urinate on me and kick me with their heavy boots until I lost consciousness. Believe me, unconsciousness was a blessing. Later, I discovered they had tortured and killed my crew. I am not sure why they spared my life because these men—these raging plague-carriers—tried to kill me in every way possible. I was less than an insect under their feet as they laughed, joked, and went about their deadly game. I used to believe the only dangers in space were mechanical and a remote fear of black holes. Now, it's absurd to realize that the real terror in space is from my own kind, from Humanity. On a personal level, my life remains scarred. Men that drag their anger after them, like dead animals through the centuries, have made me their victim. Please excuse me if, at this moment, I am not optimistic about our chances for survival as a species or I believe times are changing for the better. Anger seems as indelible to the Human male as does my present pain. They tell me that time will heal my grief and I will feel like living again, but that is difficult to imagine in my present condition."

"This statement would not be complete without mentioning the Space Security team that came to my rescue. I thank J. Hibernia Smith, Doctor Jana Sante, and most particularly Captain Jana Cle. I'm certain that if it was not for Captain Cle's quick thinking, I would be dead. I thank the Aeternus Council of Three for this opportunity to make this statement and beg the wise Council to consider a full and appropriate punishment for my perpetrator's hideous crimes." The holospool slid into a narrow line and disappeared.

"She's fulla shit," Box practically screamed. "She came on to us. We gave 'er what she wanted. And those Janaforma freaks—well, we were jus trying ta scare em a little, dat's all and it mighta worked if it 'adn't been for dat son-of-a-bitch over there." Box stood up and pointed at Cle again. His finger accidently entered the forcefield and made a sizzle sound and he fell back into his seat and stuck his finger in his mouth.

"Mr. Box begs the Council's pardon," said Liacann trying to subdue his client. "He is unfamiliar with proper courtroom etiquette."

"Counselor Liacann," said Ymotano. "Common sense tells me that Mr. Box has probably spent a lifetime inside the courtrooms of the Orion Spur judicial system. I will not tolerate another outburst. Understood?"

"Nevertheless," said Liacann, "We beg the Council's pardon. Mr. Box has a minimal-functional intelligence base, which makes it difficult for him to control his temper at times. With the Council's indulgence, if I might be permitted to speak for Mr. Box, I think I can cut to the heart of what we are requesting of the court."

Ymotano let out a long stream of air. "Under the circumstances I will allow it or we might be here into *hataeasta*."

"Mr. Box's contention is that he and his comrades were attacked by Captain Cle for no apparent reason. Only Ronald Porkcur was armed when Captain Cle and the trainee boarded the *Gemstone*. Then, within a matter of seconds, without any assessment of the situation, or any attempt at negotiation, Captain Cle killed Ronald Porkcur and Petre Saunders. Hector Limpet died a short time later from his wounds. Captain Cle is a master of Shardasko Defense and it is our contention that Captain Cle knew exactly what *ce* was doing. Captain Cle took responsibility for who lived and who died. *Ce* usurped the Orion Spur Space Security precept of non-aggression, which I would like to remind you every Janaforma working for Space Security has agreed to and signed. We would like the Council to decide if this individual, Captain Jana Cle, is the type of individual we want in space running our philanthropic rescue ships. We only want justice, justice for Mr. Box and his dead companion Petre Saunders."

Ymotano glared at Liacann. "Is this the extent of your request?"

"It is," said Liacann.

"Then, you and your client are excused. Multidex, hold," said Ymotano. "Before you exit this courtroom, Councilor Liacann, I would like to say that I find your personal responsibility in this matter reprehensible. At a time when we are struggling to reestablish the idea of Tyrowsian solidarity in this universe, you bring a lawsuit against Space Security. This council questions your motives."

Liacann responded. "It's a Human idea," he said. "Everyone, no matter how odious, deserves his moment in court."

"Well you and your client have had your moment," glared Ymotano.

"Governor Ymotano," said Rebecca. "Will it be possible to cross-examine Mr. Box before he is excused?"

"To put it succinctly—no," said Ymotano. "This hearing is solely for the Council to collect evidence; therefore, no opportunity for cross-examination is built into the format. Let me say one more thing to you Mr. Box—and you will notice this is still off the record. This Council is aware that you are already under formal indictment for multiple murders. Since this is an informal hearing, I can allow myself leeway in expressing my feelings about you and criminals such as you. If I were to sit on a jury to hear your case, I would recommend that we jettison you out of the Milky Way Galaxy in a self-exploding pod. Perhaps then, we would all be done with your kind. However, I do not have the authority to orchestrate such an action, so I will return you to Herzayzen Prison where you will await the decision of the court on proper mind modifications. We'll take a one-hour recess, at which time we will entertain the defense."

****

Rebecca was jubilant and she declared, "I was wrong. I have a feeling it's going to be a piece of cake from here on out."

"Yeah, pound cake," replied Cle.

"I mean it," Rebecca insisted. "This will over before the end of this cycle. I will meet you here in an hour. I'm going to call Commander Vertain and Admiral Vista because we're going to need their testimony sooner than I thought."

We went to a cafeteria around the corner, but none of us could eat anything. We sat near a large window that looked out at the brilliant spectacle of Aeternus. We sipped at our hot cups of tea trying to warm ourselves from the cold hearing room. "How do you really think it is going?" I asked Cle.

"Evidence doesn't make an iota of difference when the verdict is decided before the hearing."

"I'm more convinced than ever that the root of this can be traced to Vitarattha Research & Development," said Sante.

"Do you have a psychic hunch?" asked Cle.

"This is more like I've been around long enough and know how people game the system. Liacann's motivation is greed, as simple as seeing an opportunity to get control of Vitarattha R & D and throwing the dice."

"But Rebecca has experience with the Council of Three," I said. "She believes everything is going to be okay."

"Oh I believe everything will be okay," said Cle, winking at me, "but it won't be OSSS okay, if-you-know-what-I mean," *ce* said imitating Yarrow Box. This particular imitation gave me the chills.

When we returned to the hearing room, Rebecca and Commander Vertain and Admiral Vista were waiting. "*Fra** Vista," said Cle. Vista put *cis* arms around Cle and kissed *cim* on both sides of the forehead. Admiral Vista was almost a head taller than Cle. It was difficult to tell how old *ce* was; but something in *cim* spoke of age and, perhaps, wisdom. "I think you know everyone here except Hibernia," said Cle.

"Despite the circumstances, it's a pleasure to meet you," said Vista and *ce* kissed me on the forehead too. The dim light in the room sparkled off the silver beads in *cis* hair. *Ce* was a consort that tipped toward the masculine so *ce* was more handsome than pretty. "So you are the Human that Cle is head over heels in love with. I suppose all this Tyrowsian nonsense seems strange to you."

"A lot of things on Aeternus still seem strange to me, but this type of Tyrowsian nonsense is common on Earth too."

Vista smiled and said, "I like you; you are cynical and funny."

The Council of Three filed in with the Janaforma observer, Admiral Compass, tagging behind. I wondered what good it was doing Cle to have

*"consort parent"; language origin, Mescale

Admiral Compass there. So far, she had said nothing. "Activate multidex," said Mi Cochon. "Defense, present your case."

"I would like to read the service records of Jana Sante and Jana Cle into the records and make a statement concerning J. Hibernia Smith," said Rebecca.

Ymotano informed us only then, "The Council will not need the service records of Doctor Jana Sante or the trainee, J. Hibernia Smith since their actions are not under scrutiny here."

"But if the Council will be using statements from them, it is only fair that we establish their credibility," countered Rebecca.

"And if you were listening to me you would understand that we will not need their statements. However, if we change our minds, I will allow Mi Cochon to read their service records into the file. Of course, I will allow an opening statement concerning Captain Cle and welcome a presentation of appropriate character witnesses."

Rebecca tabbed send on the multidex in front of her. "Please read this document along with me."

"Jana Cle was born on Aeternus cycle 834.56 to the Janaforma triad Dyne, Kerisa and Reyneldi. An organization unique to the Janaforma, called the Educational Gathering, recognized Cle as a prodigy when *ce* was three bio-years old. During Cle's short twenty-eight bio-years among us, *ce* has earned four advanced degrees. At fifteen, United University of Worlds on Hattonia accepted Cle on full scholarship and *ce* simultaneously studied for and received advanced degrees in linguistic studies and space ethics. Cle graduated, with honors, in five years and matriculated to the prestigious Hawking Institute on Urania where, in three years, *ce* earned a Ph.D. in astrophysics and propulsion engineering. For the last five years, Jana Cle has served in many roles with Orion Spur Space Security including First officer to Captain Jana Vista during the Sutcay Tay evacuation. Presently, Commander Cle is captain of the OSSS *Daedalus* and runs the *Daedalus* with the assistance of only one other individual, Doctor Jana Sante. Jana Cle is also CEO and largest shareholder in Vitarattha Research & Development Corporation, which is the sole manufacturer of the vitarattha device and one of the top five corporations on Aeternus."

"While the accolades, commendations, and achievements accredited to Captain Jana Cle are many, the true character of this outstanding Space Security officer is best defined by those who know *cim* personally. I ask the Council to accept and add to the record of these proceedings the following statement from Admiral Jana Vista who was Jana Cle's commanding officer aboard the starship *Aeternus One*. Admiral Vista, would you please step to the front of this chamber?"

****

Admiral Vista came to the center of the chamber and stood before the

Council of Three where Mi Cochon performed an eye screening to make sure this Vista was the authentic Admiral Vista. Afterward, Ymotano asked, "How long have you known Captain Jana Cle?"

"I've known Cle almost *cis* entire life. I served with *cis* parents, Dyne, Kerisa, and Reyneldi aboard the *OSSS Centaurus*. When Cle was six bio-years, *ce* started coming with *cis* parents to crew briefings. *Ce* impressed me immediately. *Cis* métier for languages, even then, was exceptional. *Ce* possessed an almost sponge-like capacity for learning and thinking in new and clever ways. When *ce* was nine bio-years old, I invited *cim* to several diplomatic sessions to greet members of the alliance in their native tongue. I know these affairs were a bit of trifling, more of an indulgence for me, almost a waste of Cle's talents; but *ce* was the happiest when *ce* felt that *ce* was contributing. Space was *cis* passion, even as a child. At fifteen bio-years, when *ce* left for *cis* formal college training at the United University of Worlds on Hattonia and *cis* parents moved on to another assignment, I lost track of Cle. Still, everyone knew Cle's destiny was space so nobody was surprised when *ce* applied for a position with Space Security seven years later. Space Security received such glowing reports from *cis* instructors and advisors at the Hawking Institute that we felt honored that *ce* wanted to serve with us. For two years, Cle served as my first officer aboard *Aeternus One* and during that time, I cited *cim* eight times for heroic actions in the line of duty. At the end of the second year, I recommended *cis* promotion to Commander. A short time later, *Aeternus One* received orders to coordinate the rescue efforts of the final evacuation of the planet Sutcay Tay. I asked Cle to postpone *cis* promotion to help with this nearly impossible task. *Ce* agreed without hesitation. During rescue efforts, which lasted six months, Cle learned to live without sleep. *Ce* was on duty at all times. Much of the time, *ce* was in harm's way. I found *cis* sense of self-sacrifice extraordinary, even for a Janaforma. That's when the crew began calling Cle The Number One Janaforma. When the crisis abated, I recommended Cle for a triple star and a commission as Captain, which would give *cim* the opportunity to command a starship. I must admit that I was surprised when Cle told me that *ce* was going to ask for a transfer to one of the fleet's six-crew pulsars. I personally felt Cle was destined for greatness and was capable of a much bigger role in Space Security. When I pressed *cim* about *cis* reasons for requesting a transfer to a smaller ship, *ce* said *ce* wanted to be where *ce* could do the most good, doing what Simon Forma created the Janaforma to do— saving people in space. I accepted *cis* reasons because space rescue is our fundamental destiny. That concludes my formal statement, but I am happy to answer any questions you may have relating to Commander Jana Cle."

"How long has it been since you served with Captain Cle?" asked Ymotano.

"Approximately 2400 cycles," said Vista.

"Have you had occasion to remain in contact with Captain Cle after *cis* transfer to the *Kirtland*?"

"Yes. We both make an effort to stay in touch. Especially since the death of *cis* parents, we have been especially close."

"Did *ce* ever mention a problem to you about Captain Jana Devina?"

"Objection!" said Rebecca. "Even if he had, it would be hearsay evidence."

Cle looked as if *ce* wanted to say something, but changed *cis* mind. "Overruled," said Ymotano. "Answer the question, Admiral Vista. Did Captain Cle ever mention a problem to you about Jana Devina?"

"About 200 cycles into *cis* assignment on the *Kirtland*, Cle asked my advice about lodging an official complaint against Captain Devina. Cle suggested that they were having personal problems and she carried an argument into open space and was playing dangerous games."

"Can you elaborate on dangerous games?" asked Ymotano.

"Objection!" said Rebecca. "This is hearsay."

"Sustained," said Ymotano with a tone of impatience. "However if Captain Cle would be so kind as to elaborate to the Council on the nature of this problem, then the information would no longer be hearsay. Suppose you tell us, what kind of dangerous games were being played on the *Kirtland*, Captain Cle?"

Cle looked worried but managed to say, "At the moment I don't remember any particular incident that I might regard as a dangerous game."

"Are you asking us to believe that you were prepared to lodge a formal complaint against Captain Devina and yet now you can't remember why?"

"I admit our personalities clashed," said Cle. "We had different ways of operating. I asked Admiral Vista's advice about what to do and then I decided that the simplest solution was to ask for a transfer."

"Why would an officer of your caliber believe that *ce* could lodge an official complaint against *cis* captain and have the basis for that claim be, 'our personalities clashed?' Wasn't there something about Captain Devina you intended to expose?"

Cle stood up and leaned over the table and Rebecca put a hand on *cis* arm as a reminder. Cle had that look again, that casual, predatory look that *ce* used on Devina and Yarrow Box. "Look!" said Cle. "I never registered a complaint against Captain Devina because she never did anything wrong. I was unhappy at the time and my unhappiness clouded my judgment. Nothing was ever amiss on the operational details of the *Kirtland*. We ran a tight ship."

I was surprised. Why was Cle protecting Devina after the way she had treated *cim* at the apartment? I knew Cle was lying, but I wasn't sure about what or why. I loved *cim*. I wanted to believe *cim* and yet I didn't.

Ymotano stood up too and extended his arm toward Cle. Quite

deliberately, his thumb came up and touched his extended index finger and then he seemed to let something go between them. "Wasn't Captain Devina addicted to tartan ratu?" asked Ymotano. The sound of his breathing out was like a sudden evil wind. Tension snapped around the room in an undercurrent of comments.

Cle sat down as if Ymotano's statement had knocked *cim* backward and *ce* turned to Rebecca and said, "Help me—please?"

"Multidex on hold," said Rebecca to the Council. "Tell me, what happened?" she whispered to Cle.

"I gave Devina my solemn word not to expose her," whispered Cle.

"Why?"

"Because it was my fault that she was addicted. I used ratu on Sutcay Tay and she picked up the habit from me. The big problem is she's still addicted."

Rebecca's lips twitched. "Damn Cle! You should have told me." Rebecca quickly gained control of herself. "Okay, let's try to limit the damage. They must know about Devina. You might as well level with them; but please don't tell them you feel responsible."

"It doesn't make any difference," said Cle. "Can't you see? The handwriting is on the wall."

"Please Cle, don't shut down. We can win." Rebecca looked up at the Council. "Activate multidex," she said with a tone of inevitability.

"I would like to elaborate on my statement about Captain Devina," said Cle addressing the Council. "I knew she was addicted to tartan ratu; but decided to cover for her. She continued to perform her duties as captain and I didn't want her career to be ruined."

"Who else knew about her addiction?"

"I was the only one who knew."

"You expect me to believe that on a small ship like the *Kirtland*, no one knew about her drug addiction but you?"

"Let's put it this way," said Cle. "I discussed her problem with no one and no one discussed her problem with me."

"Do you know that Jana Devina is now addicted to tartan ratu again?"

"I saw her a few cycles ago and realized something was wrong."

"Why haven't you ever come forward to report her?" asked Judge Ymotano.

"Devina and I are 3C Janaforma," said Cle.

"And what's that supposed to mean? You sound as if being a 3C Janaforma is some kind of rational explanation."

"For me, it is. Nothing is more important to me than loyalty to my teammates."

A black storm appeared near the horizon. It started to move quickly as bad weather often does. Judge Ymotano began hammering Cle with difficult questions. "That's interesting, Captain Cle. Is loyalty to your teammates more important than your loyalty to Space Security?"

"Yes," said Cle. "It's not even a question in my mind."

Rebecca winced. She put her hand on Cle's arm to steady *cim*; but no way existed for her to stop what began to unravel.

"Captain Cle," said Ymotano, raising his voice an octave. "I find your reasoning somewhat twisted. You hold yourself above Orion Spur law. You ignored a problem and allowed Jana Devina to remain addicted to tartan ratu. Exactly where are your loyalties?"

Cle leaned forward. "All I can say is I am a 3C Janaforma and my loyalties are with the Janaforma."

Judge Ymotano gave a nod toward Mi Cochon and Cochon said, "Let the official record show that after the death of Captain Cle's parents, *cis* first official act as CEO was to appoint the about-to-retire Admiral Vista to COO of Vitarattha Research & Development. I have recommended to Regent Governor Ymotano that another Council of Three be convened to examine the possibility that Admiral Vista was given this prestigious position in exchange for *cis* silence about Captain Jana Devina."

Another wave of muffled comments circled the room and I heard someone behind me whisper, "Ymotano just brought the great Admiral Vista to *cis* knees."

****

Rebecca asked Ymotano for a short recess so she could confer with Cle about the new evidence and Ymotano promptly denied her request. Cle's case took a further nosedive when Mi Cochon started talking again and said new testimony had just arrived that he wanted to put into the official record. Ymotano nodded in agreement and Mi Cochon said, "Multidex, run holograph file, Jana Devina."

Rebecca jumped to her feet. "Objection! Defense has had no chance to examine Jana Devina's statement."

"Overruled," said Ymotano. "It's the Council's right to decide what and when new information will be included in the official record."

"That's Tyrowsian tunnel logic!"

"Sit down or I will have Security remove you from this room and Captain Cle can finish this hearing without representation," said Mi Cochon.

"Let Devina be heard," said Cle to Rebecca and she was stunned at *cis* response. Cle even added, "Devina certainly has a right to be heard since her reputation is being destroyed." Rebecca turned and whispered something in Cle's ear and *ce* told her, "It makes no difference. They won't stop until they get what they want."

"Multidex, run the Jana Devina holograph," said Mi Cochon.

Devina's holograph materialized before us. Just seeing her image sitting there, I wanted to spit in her face. "Jana Cle served as my first officer for 234 cycles during the star year 944. At first, I found *cim* cooperative and was impressed with *cis* enthusiasm; however, after about twenty cycles, I noticed *cis* personality changing. *Ce* was having nightmares about the final days of Sutcay Tay and *ce* became openly hostile and disrespectful to me in front of mutual crewmembers. I continued to work with *cim*; but *ce* became extremely moody and intimidating. *Cis* anger, at times, frightened me. I finally put *cim* on report and recommended that *ce* seek psychological help for *cis* growing personality problems. Please note that a memorandum dated 944.29 exists as part of the medical log of the *Kirtland*, where I annotated the incident. Thankfully, the matter resolved itself when Cle requested a transfer. I believe the problem in our working relationship came from the fact that suddenly there was no audience for *cis* flamboyant style of leadership on the *Kirtland*. *Cis* only challenge was to compete with me for control of the ship. Thank you for allowing me to testify. I am and remain, Admiral Jana Devina, Central Space Security Command."

Sante leaned toward me and whispered. "Now I get it. Devina traded her testimony for a commission to admiral."

"Upon checking the records of the *Kirtland*," said Ymotano. "Let it be noted that only one mention of Commander Cle's mental health problem is found. I submit as evidence an entry by the ship's doctor, Jana Sante, dated, star cycle, 944.29. 'Cle's nightmares continue. Prescribed 5 grains of medisleep and continue therapy.' What is medisleep, Commander Sante?"

Sante didn't answer and Rebecca said, "You said at the outset of this hearing that you would not need any statements from Doctor Sante."

"This is merely general information, not testimony," said Ymotano. "If Doctor Sante's statement should prove pertinent, we will backtrack as I promised and you can present appropriate character witnesses."

"Agreed," said Rebecca. She turned and said, "Okay, Doctor Sante, you may speak but only pertaining to this medical entry."

Sante said, "Medisleep induces sleep by providing electrical impulses to the sleep centers of the brain."

"What kind of therapy was Cle receiving for *cis* nightmares?" Sante again looked toward Rebecca and she nodded her head yes.

"Cle was receiving instruction in guided meditation."

"How is guided meditation interpreted as therapy, Doctor Sante?"

Sante's voice turned sharp. "Guided medication can be beneficial because it clears the mind of distortions."

"Are you telling me that as a trained doctor, you employ meditation as a legitimate treatment? Where did you go to school?"

"My medical degree is from the University of Noble City."

"And is this 'meditation' a course they teach in medical school?"

"Yes, they teach it because they know it works."

Ymotano turned and conferred with Mi Cochon again. Mi Cochon informed us, "What you consider legitimate treatment, the Council of Three still sees as fuzzy science. Tyrowsian scientists have yet to prove the value of meditation and I've seen nothing so far that would lead me to change my mind."

"Perhaps your willful ignorance is just a little too thick to make the jump," replied Sante.

Judge Ymotano grimaced. "Watch your mouth Doctor Sante or you will find yourself in contempt and heading toward a cool Tyrowsian jail cell somewhere."

A rumble went around the room. "Doctor Sante is not on trial here and neither are *lis* methods of treatment," suggested Rebecca.

"No, Doctor Sante is not on trial," returned Ymotano. "But Captain Cle is and if Captain Cle was having psychological problems while on duty we need to know what those problems were and how they were treated. Doctor Sante, I resent your condescending tone toward this Council. Let me remind you that you are a guest in this hearing and I can dismiss you at any time. It's also within my powers to investigate your implications in this matter. In this hearing, we deal with facts. So please, for the sake of expediency, tell me what Captain Cle's mental state was while you were on the *Kirtland*."

When Sante spoke *lis*, voice was as calm as still water. "I am many things," *le* offered. "I am 3C Janaforma, a healer, a committed lifegiver and an Orion Spur Space Security officer. I swore oaths of allegiance to my Community, my profession, my mates and Space Security. I maintain my bond in these relationships through loyalty. Your loyalty is to Orion Spur law and I expect you to respect your loyalty as I respect mine. Check your book of Orion laws and you will see that I, as an Orion Spur physician, am not required to submit to you, any confidential information concerning Captain Cle while *ce* was in my care."

Judge Ymotano turned aside and talked to his vice-regent Mi Cochon who was the supposed expert in Orion Spur law. After a moment, Ymotano said to Rebecca, "Please present your next character witness."

Sante had won the point. I was grateful and I took *lis* hand and whispered, "Good job of kicking ass."

"I would like to present Commander Jana Vertain," said Rebecca.

Commander Vertain came slowly to the front of the room. She was tense and her face was white and strained. "I would like to say, up front, that I am disturbed by what is going on in this chamber. This Council is conducting a witch-hunt. No evidence of misconduct exists here."

"This Council doesn't need a lecture or your opinion," returned Ymotano. "Make your statement of support for Commander Cle or we can skip your comments entirely."

Vertain bit her bottom lip. "All right, if that's the way you want it, you can prosecute us all," she said nodding her head up and down violently. Her long ponytail shook like the tail of an agitated horse. "I knew about Captain Devina's addiction, Admiral Vista knew too, and so did the other crewmembers aboard the *Kirtland*, plus a half-dozen Janaforma at central command."

Ymotano ignored her confession and asked, "Do you have a direct statement to make in Captain Cle's behalf?"

"Yes I do," said Vertain.

"Then get on with it," Ymotano nearly shouted. "I'm bored with this Janaforma drama. My granddaughter has a birthday party this afternoon and I don't want to miss the pony rides." Mi Cochon twittered and Le-Le Kork smiled but it quickly turned into a sour expression that left me feeling as if I had indigestion.

Rebecca was on her feet again and shouting too. "Objection! This is a charade. You've already made up your minds."

"This is your last warning," said Ymotano. "Go ahead and tell us, Commander Vertain—what do you have to say in Captain Cle's defense? We all are waiting with baited breath to hear your impassioned defense."

Rebecca sat down and Commander Vertain turned her back to the Council and addressed Cle directly. "I consider you the finest officer in Space Security," she said.

"Face the Council of Three," demanded Ymotano. Vertain ignored them and continued to say, "You are our Number One Janaforma. You are the creature Simon Forma first envisioned and all he ever hoped that he could create. You proved your worth on Sutcay Tay and never stopped since." Cle showed no emotion over Vertain's words of praise. Then Vertain spun on her heels and faced Judge Ymotano. "Understand, you barbarians. Forma and Jana created the Janaforma from Humanness in its purest form—Community, loyalty, altruism, and self-sacrifice are the basis of our values. Cle is the embodiment of that Janaforma ideal, approaching perfection. The question that baffles me is why you want to destroy *cim*."

"Isn't it true, that you are involved in a sexual liaison with Captain Cle?" asked Le-Le Kork.

Vertain seethed. "This council is comprised of three mad men. You Tyrowsians are unfit to judge any Janaforma."

Ymotano's anger rose like a volcano and his white face blanched whiter. "We Tyrowsians are your judges and as we examine you, you look like an experiment gone bad." Vertain put her hand to her hip, as if searching for a sidearm. Her look was pure defiance. She relaxed like a feline and stepped backward. I held my breath. "If you were so impressed with Captain Cle, why did you put *cim* on report for *cis* handling of the Hawking incident?"

"Because I personally feel self-sacrifice is out of proportion in Cle. *Ce* lives *cis* life as if everyone's life is worth more than *cis*. I wanted *cim* to stop setting *cim*self up in situations as if *ce* is the sacrificial lamb."

"You certainly are dismissed," said Ymotano.

Vertain passed us, then returned, and leaned over Cle's shoulder. "I'm so sorry I lost my temper. I'm afraid I've done you more harm than good."

"It's okay," said Cle. "Thank you for your support."

"Captain Cle," said Ymotano. "Do you have a statement to make about star cycle 947.34 before we decide this matter?"

Cle's reply was automatic and full of resignation. "My written testimony stands."

"Captain Cle has supplied the Council with a physical scenario of the sequence of events aboard the *Gemstone*. Please note that an onboard recorder was operational at the time. After close comparison, we find the two versions virtually identical. We find these facts highly suspicious. Do you realize it is a felony to tamper with flight recorders, Captain Cle?"

"I never had access to the *Gemstone's* flight recorder," said Cle. "I merely have an exceptional memory, what the Education Gathering calls 'total memory recall.'"

"And I say totally impossible!" said Ymotano.

"If I prove it, will you then have faith that it is true?" said Cle using a breathy Tyrowsian accent. Ymotano did not hear that Cle was mocking him.

Cle rose from *cis* chair and slowly walked around the table. *Ce* stood in the middle of the chamber and took *cis* time. *Ce* showed us *cis* palms. "See—no props, no multidex, and no tricks." Cle's voice changed. *Cis* voice was an exact duplicate of Ymotano's breathy voice. "'—let me say this to you, Doctor Sante; I resent your condescending tone toward this Council. Let me remind you that you are a guest in this hearing and I can dismiss you at any time. It is also within my powers to investigate your implications in this matter. So please, for the sake of expediency, tell me what Captain Cle's mental state was while you were on the *Kirtland*.'" Cle fell silent, then added in *cis* own voice, "I suggest you check what you believe is impossible, it might push you to the edge of faith. Meantime, would you like me to go on, or backward, or any other way you might imagine?"

"Incredible!" admitted Ymotano. "Is this talent of yours in the area of what you Janaforma call long or short term memory? I guess what I mean is how long are you able to remember something?"

"As long as I wish and sometimes longer than I wish."

"Then if you have perfect recall, how can you make the statement to this Council that you can't remember your nightmares while on the *Kirtland*?"

"Because it's true. My nightmares are cowards. They only feel safe enough to come out of my unconscious and wreck their havoc while I'm asleep."

Tyrowsians did not believe in the unconscious because if a Tyrowsian couldn't remember something, it never happened. Consequently, Ymotano claimed, "Captain Cle, you are lying again."

"I beg your pardon," said Cle. "You're Tyrowsian; of all people, you must realize that being alive forces one to have selective memory. Take your pick, selective memory, or complete madness. Don't you want to know if I acted rashly or from a hidden motive while on the *Gemstone?*"

"All right, Captain Cle. What were your motives aboard the *Gemstone* on star date 947.34?"

"Thank you," said Cle. "I would like to make a further statement concerning my motives on star date 947.34. Soon after Hibernia and I stepped into the *Gemstone*, I felt as if I had lost control of the situation. I felt as if we stepped onto a platform of death."

"Please be more specific, Captain Cle. Metaphors such as 'platform of death,' are simply more fuzzy concepts."

"I'm sorry. What Tyrowsian words can I use to help you understand? You don't understand loyalty, self-sacrifice, altruism, faith, past, future, and a whole raft of other concepts that dominate my life." Cle said something I did not understand and no one else did either. Maybe *ce* was cursing in one of those six hundred languages *ce* spoke. "I believed we were going to die," *ce* said in Universal.

"Are you a psychic like Doctor Sante?"

"My talents are limited in that area. I make decisions from observation and inductive reasoning."

"What exactly did you know and when did you know it?" asked Ymotano.

"Of course I knew everything was going to happen before it did, but not soon enough to change anything—that's the problem. When the *Cygnus* contacted us, I knew something was wrong. Another Space Security ship does not ask for help unless it's urgent. I knew no space crisis existed because I checked with Aeternus command. Ergo, the *Cygnus* was in urgent trouble. My second clue came when Hibernia and I stepped inside the *Gemstone*. I could smell the odor of death, blood, and raw open wounds. I remembered that smell from Sutcay Tay."

Sante leaned forward and whispered, "Cle? This has gone far enough. You don't have to put yourself through this trial."

Cle ignored everyone. "When Ronald Porkcur stepped from the shadows, I felt his evil. I felt the cold of it slither over me. I remembered how the smell of blood and terror engulfed me on Sutcay Tay. My instincts turned to the one thing I know for protection, Shardasko Defense. I was the wounded bird, with the broken wing. 'Space Security is in space to help everyone,' I said stupidly. It was at that instant that I recognized Ronald

Porkcur. It was at that very second a vision of him molesting the lifeless body of Hibernia consumed me. He excited an image of himself in me and I reacted. I wanted to crush him like a slimy snail just as he wanted to crush me. I knew, at that moment, that I had slipped from grace—that I became a fragment of my true self. I felt ownership of her—Hibernia was mine, only mine; and so, I killed him." Cle fell silent.

"Captain Cle, what do you mean you recognized Ronald Porkcur?"

"I knew him from Sutcay Tay. I encountered him there many times. I fought him, but never won. He is my eternal torment."

"The court has no information that Ronald Porkcur was ever on any planet in The Island Worlds of Gathos."

"That makes no difference," said Cle. "The thing you want me to say and I will say—you are right. I was the judge, the jury, and the executioner, exactly as Liacann claims. Everything I did, I would do again. I would fight until my last breath of air was gone before I'd let a monster like Ronald Porkcur hurt someone I love." Cle bowed *cis* head.

"Very interesting," said Ymotano. "Let the official record show that Commander Jana Cle is a master of Shardasko Defense. Captain Cle, did you kill those men by accident or by design?"

"That's for you to decide," said Cle.

"Captain Cle, would you please answer the question," said Judge Ymotano.

"You have my complete statement. You came here to judge me, now do your duty."

"This is foolish," said Rebecca. "Captain Cle told you the situation and you know the character of these escaped convicts. Why do you persist in attempting to find guilt? Haven't you persecuted Captain Cle enough?"

"Very well," returned Ymotano with a sigh. "Perhaps we do have everything we need."

"I would like to make a statement," said Sante, "mostly for the records, but hopefully for your enlightenment. My psychic abilities are very active. I see shadow of possibilities as clearly as I see your accusatory faces. Certain byways are so blind, so dangerous, so frightening that faith alone can be our sole companion as we attempt to traverse them. Once Cle and Hibernia boarded the *Gemstone*, there was no other decision for Cle except to kill or be killed. Cle and Hibernia cheated death."

"Thank you Commander Sante," said Ymotano with a tone of condescension. "I'm sure the Council will put your psychic visions into proper perspective. I adjourn this hearing. We will notify you of our recommendations through the multidex system. That is all." Ymotano rose along with the two other Tyrowsians and they sashayed out of the room.

****

Admiral Compass, the Janaforma who said nothing throughout the hearing, approached us just as Cle was saying, "Let's get out of here before I puke."

Admiral Compass had the eager look of desperation about her. She grabbed Cle's elbow and stopped *cim* from leaving. "If you lead, every Janaforma will follow—I swear! Aeternus can be our world."

Cle was startled. "I haven't decided what I'm doing next," *ce* returned.

"Let's wait to hear the verdict," advised Rebecca. By the time we reached the Hilton, the decision from the Aeternus Council of Three was waiting on the multidex.

Cle read it to us as *ce* scrolled through the message. "'The Aeternus Council of Three has convened and examined the evidence presented this cycle,' and so on and so on—ah yes! Here it is! 'We find Captain Jana Cle, guilty of misconduct unbefitting an Orion Spur Space Security officer. We here, the undersigned, this cycle, ask for Captain Jana Cle's immediate resignation—' signed, Ymotano. Wait! There's more—an addendum. 'We the Council of Three find no criminal intent within Captain Cle. We recommend all criminal charges be dropped.' Dated and signed this cycle— but I'd bet my vitarattha this document was written weeks ago."

"Never bet your *rattha* on something you don't know for sure," said Sante.

"Case closed," said Cle. "My career is in the toilet so I might as well flush."

"You don't need a career in Space Security," said Sante. "I will resign too. We can go live on Erato or Euterpe in Apollo Muse Gathering. Without all this nonsense we could enjoy our lives."

"I belong here," said Cle. "My life is the Janaforma people and their future in Space Security."

****

Cle sat in front of the multidex with *cis* finger poised on the scroll key. I stood behind and managed to read snippets when *ce* stopped to think about something *ce* just read. A restive mood rumbled through the words on the screen. The news about the hearing was spreading like wildfire among the space teams and the Janaforma community was indignant, urging Cle to step forward, to make a decisive statement and condemn the Aeternus Council of Three. In a long letter that concluded with, "It is your moral duty to defend Janaforma principles," Patra pleaded with Cle to take a public stand. "Do it for Nova," she said. "Don't let *lis* death be for naught."

The Janaforma were pushing hard for change. Admiral Vista sent a letter of complaint to the Orion Spur Alliance on Cle's behalf. Three hundred seventy-six Janaforma signatures endorsed the complaint and threatened to resign their commissions with Space Security if the Aeternus Council of Three did not reinstate Cle. At the same time, Commander Vertain released a general communiqué to all Space Security personnel, which said, "In support of Captain Jana Cle, I ask all teams scheduled for duty time to hold and for space-side teams to return to port ASAP. Commander Jana Vertain."

Rebecca wrote, "CLE, SEIZE THE DAY!"

TWELVE

Artificial twilight lasted but a moment, the light sighing, melting into the greater darkness. Aeternus, the synergistic creation between machine and sentient life shifted into nightmode. Hidden in the sliver between this unholy matrimony was Cle, sitting in deep brooding concentration. The silence in the room lasted a long time. "You need to be prepared," *ce* told me. *Ce* allowed the thought to hang between us before adding. "You need to be strong, even as strong as Sante is now."

I struggled to make my voice sound normal. "What do you mean?"

"Tyrowsians have a way of making people disappear."

My imagination immediately ran wild with fear. I saw a phalanx of Cerribeame monsters marching in machine-like precision, coming for Cle. I could hear the echo of their leaden boots thundering through the bowels of Aeternus. The sound grew inevitably louder and then, one by one, they appeared by the thousands along a horizon, an army of programmed androids. Shield to shield they flooded the crescent line between land and sky. Cle interrupted my unrolling fear telling me, "I need to stay visible for my people. However, staying visible will put me at greater risk of being arrested."

"Why?" I asked for the hundredth time.

Ce sighed. "My little wildflower, I was hoping you would understand." *Ce* looked away, out through the window-walls that overlooked Aeternus. "This is important. I'm the best prepared to help my people make this initial demand. I waste everything I am if I don't act now. For me, it feels like a moral imperative."

"You're not an android and yet you sound programmed."

Cle gazed past me with sad eyes. "Maybe I am programmed. Perhaps Jana Revba and Simon Forma stood shoulder to shoulder in front of their laboratory benches and decided to put a bogey in the Janaforma soup." *Ce* pointed to *cim*self. "This feeling in me is compelling. Please understand, Hibernia. I can be the bridge between the Janaforma and the existing social order here on Aeternus." Sante walked into the room and ignored us both. "Don't get me wrong. I am not a martyr," Cle continued. *Ce* smiled and a small, ironic expression formed around cis mouth. "I love being alive. I love it so much I never want this life to end. I seek the ecstasy only life can bring—sensations, the tactile contact to the physical. All these pleasures constantly call me back to you and Sante."

Sante carefully perused some items on top of the multidex. "Have you weighed it?" *le* asked nonchalantly.

"On The Triangle," replied Cle just as nonchalantly and *ce* formed the Janaforma Triangle between the thumbs and forefingers of the hands.

Sante turned *lis* full attention to Cle. "It's a real question," *le* emphasized.

"There is a logic to my decision," replied Cle.

Sante relaxed into that casual predatory stance again. Until now, I didn't realize they used it on each other. Something new vibrated the air and I knew everything was about to change, yet again. Cle shuddered as *ce* sensed it too. The trembling of *cis* bottom lip gave *cim* away.

"My dear consort, you say there is a logic to it?" questioned Sante. "The word 'a' suggests a parallel logic beside this one." In a quiet ruse of activity, Sante continued sorting through the holospools on top of the multidex. "Perhaps you see only part of the picture. Have you asked yourself if your truth is an ever-widening foundation to support your logic?"

Cle did not answer but *ce* began to squirm. Tension moved toward *cim* like an approaching storm. Sante's words churned through me too and I wondered. How was I supposed to sweep aside the bits of mind fog and avoid all the emotional pitfalls to get to my truth? As a Human, I couldn't even control the ebb and flow of my negative emotions, let alone interpret the motives of other people. I wanted to feel charitable and kind as the Janaforma, but I still felt needy and cynical. I was still more important to me than any ideal of Community. As a Human cartographer, community was a place, a geographical location on a map. To the Janaforma, Community was an active verb, a dynamic interaction among loyalty, altruism, and self-sacrifice.

What was missing in me? Had I, like the blind, lost a vital sense? I wondered about my personal genetics and my history my memory could not recall. What brought me to my current numbness? Had the centuries of Human aggression bred Community out of my spirit? If so, why did Earthlings still congregate in front of musicspool stores in Toledo, Ohio and listen to kakos musicians sing, "so fucking what?" Was it merely a tic left over from when Community meant something real and visceral?

I was a Casual, a reactionary mutation formed from the school of hard knocks. My genes were the genes of Homo Erectus, Genghis Khan, Joan of

Arc, Albert Einstein, and Adolph Hitler. My genes were alive through historical time and historical time had taken its toll on me. I suddenly felt old, a lot more tired, and a little less enthusiastic. I remembered Doctor Patel and his diagnosis that I was in the early stages of FSP. All the symptoms were rearing their ugly heads. The stress from what was happening was pushing me into second stage FSP.

****

Cle moved forward and adjusted *cis* position as *ce* sat in meditation. What was *ce* thinking? How had Jana Revba and Simon Forma sorted the Human gene pool to come up with this exceptional person? Cle was the quintessence of perfection in my eyes. The compassion in *cim* was both obvious and uncompromising. More than loving Cle, I respected Cle and I felt caught between my respect for *cis* compassion and my love for *cim* that wanted to keep *cim* safe. Sante and Cle were nothing like Human men with their testosterone urgings down through the centuries. Neither of them ever waxed poetic about the things that usually interested Human men. At heart, Sante and Cle were female. Cle could handle anything except someone trying to hurt *cis* family and then *ce* turned into a mama bear. When Cle's bear emerged, it became involved in adrenaline-pumping confrontations of the masculine sort. Perhaps not all the gene shifting in creation could rid us of the instinct that compelled us to defend family.

****

Sante walked into the room shaking me out of my doldrums. "Don't worry," *le* said to Cle. "Whatever happens, I am your second. I will be the voice that whispers the truth in your ear when others shout lies. You are the first of many to come and if you do not succeed with the Tyrowsians, others will follow and the others that will follow will begin with me."

Cle was ecstatic. *Ce* went to Sante pulling *cim* into a passionate embrace. "You truly understand!" Cle gushed.

"Tell me," said Sante. "What is your thinking? How should we proceed?"

"It is not within my ability at this present time to know the final logic of what may happen here on Aeternus," said Cle. "I can work only with what I have. I refuse to feel sinful for prior mistakes. I know I'm still learning, but I must make certain decisions in this life. So I weigh equally—mind and soul on the Triangle of Janaforma Love."

I could see that Cle was preparing to sacrifice *cim*self for the Janaforma and I panicked. I imagined life without *cim* and then without Sante. "No!" I cried.

I ran to Sante and *le* asked, "What is it, Hibernia?" and all I could do was sob. *Le* held me in *lis* arms, holding me in a vise-like grip of security; but it was not enough to save my shattering dream of togetherness. "Don't either of you understand? Life is unpredictable! Don't do this to us. I don't want to live if you're not here."

"You need to trust me," said Cle. "Besides, the risk is small."

"That's not exactly true!" Sante challenged immediately. "The risk is enormous and you know it, Cle. Hi has the right to know the truth."

New emotions stirred within the three of us. Cle swallowed hard. "Sante, sometimes you go too far. Why are you frightening her needlessly?"

"She's already frightened. Can't you see that?" Sante turned on Cle and grabbed *cim* by the chin. Sante had us both in *lis* lock and *le* was not going to let go. *Le* whispered, which made us both listen more intently. "If you believe what you're doing is not dangerous, you'd better look again, my consort."

"This is more important than us," Cle insisted. "I understand there will be others; but the others will not be me. This is my time. I can lay a foundation for true progress here on Aeternus and it is worth the risks."

"If you play fast and loose as you have so many times before, you will fail," said Sante.

Cle swore, "I give you both my solemn promise that I will be careful."

I scoffed. What did solemn promises mean to me? I had died a thousand times on broken promises. Solemn promises: another sandcastle built on the illusion of trust. "I refuse to listen a moment more to this nonsense," I heard myself screaming. I poked Cle hard, in the middle of *cis* chest, with my forefinger. "Why are you destroying our lives? We have the perfect love, but it is not enough for you. Ymotano is right about some things. The Janaforma will use you and then forget you, walk over your grave, use it as a shortcut to their next hero, but what will happen to Sante and me without you? Tell me, Cle. How can you feel all this compassion for Community, but can't feel compassion for our relationship?" I turned on Sante. "And you! You're so smug and perfect in your psychic knowing. Why are you suddenly encouraging Cle to do these dangerous things?"

"There's always going to be risks," said Sante. "But Cle still needs our support to make the best decisions possible."

"My God! We're doomed!" I shouted. "Sante's confused and can't see the future. Damn you! Why do you always need to sound so enigmatic, as if you know something we do not? Why can't you simply say that you are not sure what's going to happen and are scared too?"

Sante was annoyed. "That's what I just implied; excuse me for not using the exact words you deem acceptable."

"My decision is logical," Cle still argued.

"Logic has nothing to do with this," I argued louder. "This is all about feelings, your feelings, my feelings and Sante's feelings. My feelings tell me that I do not want you to defend Janaforma rights or any other rights. I don't even understand why you want to be part of a society that is so corrupt. These Tyrowsians are exactly like Humans, like me, not like you.

They operate through the narrow spectrum of fear and need. Neither one of you seems to realize the depth of sentient corruption. You're innocent. The rest of us have existed on the outside and we are tough, primal, and selfish. We had to be to survive. We are totally unpredictable; your higher logic and your grandiose ideals don't work with us."

Cle appeared perplexed. "There is more than logic and grandiose ideals involved if you would allow me to explain."

"Go ahead," I challenged. "Serve it up! Give me something I can sink my teeth into, something I can believe in." I wondered what new insight Cle might reveal that could change my mind for I had heard a million impassioned speeches before in a thousand lifetimes.

Cle opened *cis* arms to me. "May I hold you?" *ce* asked, embracing me before I could say no.

"Are you going to say something about love?" I asked.

"It had occurred to me," *ce* said allowing a smile to creep across *cis* lips. I could not believe it. Cle thought *ce* could smile away my fear. I attempted to listen; but my desperation increased. I tried to play the game of supple woman clinging to a big strong man but it was a joke, just as it always was. A million lifetimes of sublimating my feminine desires to the masculine made the role familiar, but this time I knew it was a lie. "Love and loving you and spreading it around feels right to me," said Cle.

"So what," I said.

"Don't say so what," said Cle. "It's such a flabby expression. I want to explain something important to you, Hibernia. I have to use words, but I can't make you feel the meaning behind my words. You have to find the meaning yourself. I believe the Janaforma have strength in their Community and I believe this strength has the ability to move every one of us to a higher level of consciousness." I heard *cis* heart beating strong and hard against my breast and that was the only thing that was real for me. "Logic suggests that higher consciousness might enhance life's experience. We can begin to make this happen now—right here on Aeternus. I believe in this. This becoming feels right to me."

"I feel only fear for you," I still insisted.

"Take your fear and put it in a jar in the museum where it belongs. Focus in the heartbeat of each moment and realize that life is a journey where our job is to unravel our inner illusions. For example, one should never assume that options are final truths. I made that fateful mistake on the *Gemstone*. I confused an option with an irrefutable truth."

"I'm more confused than ever," I admitted. "I don't think I know what truth is and perhaps I never have. Truth has nothing that describes it to me—no sound, look, or taste—and yet, truth touches everything I love. Show me a good solid truth and I'll build a house on it."

"Your house would sink," said Sante. "Truth sits mostly on quicksand."

Together

"Exactly!" agreed Cle. "Truth is elusive and most especially in the past."

My belief in truth—my last god to fall—collapsed. I once worshipped something I believed was real. A foundational shift occurred in my mind. The idea that I might be on the crest of a final truth, on which I could erect a stable internal credo, always was an illusion. I felt lost without a map for the future. I had better focus in the heartbeat of the moment because the ground around me was quaking with instability.

Life turned difficult and impossible to understand. I was so damn— Human! I still wanted to hold onto things and people I thought of as mine. I still wanted an anchor in life and permanent bliss. Even after three hundred years of Smiths being alone, 1 still longed for the security of a family. I was not self-sufficient. I was needy and still could not see life from any perspective beyond my own. I had solved a few word riddles, but still was stuck in a tangled web of verbal confusion. In this fog, they only word that mattered to me was love.

****

With all the outside prompting, it didn't take Cle long to write a proposal to Ymotano from the Janaforma people. Cle asked Sante and I to proofread it and the only comment I had was, "Use bullets not numbers."

Open Letter to Rimmer Ymotano, Regent Governor of Aeternus Complex:

Time exists; times change; and when a government ceases to move with time that government becomes an archaic burden upon its people. In the light of time's unveiling truth, the Janaforma Community, petitions Regent Governor Ymotano, as the legally appointed governor of Aeternus by the Orion Spur Alliance, to review and endorse the following urgent demands, so together we might align the existing government with the true needs of the people.

•All natural born residents of Aeternus will receive full citizenship rights, guaranteeing them equal representation under Orion Spur law.

•The Orion Spur Space Security Corps will henceforward enjoy freedom of operation in space with an open and public coordinating arm with the Aeternus government.

•Janaforma genetic records, from the Artificial Intelligence and Robotics Systems on the planet Calypso, will be released immediately and in full, unabridged form.

•Private businesses seized by the Aeternus government will be restored to their rightful owners and those owners will have the right to sue for compensatory damages.

Change is upon us and we are prepared to work with you as soon as full rights of citizenship are guaranteed. For the Janaforma Community, Jana Cle.

"Ymotano is going to hate this letter," said Sante. "He is going to call it treason."

"He might not like it but it's not treason," said Cle.

"Send it," said Sante, so Cle did. Fingertips barely touched the multidex and yet the gesture sent The Proposal to 30,000 different multidexes. Within six hours, every Janaforma, whether they were on Aeternus or somewhere out in space returned their overwhelming support. I was beginning to discover the Janaforma were not like Earthlings. On Earth, 74 % of the population never voted and 69 % did not know the name of the elected head of the Earth government. A sincere sense of Community participation existed here. It all happened so fast—and maybe a little too fast, by Earth standards. The Janaforma accepted The Proposal to Governor Ymotano in its entirety. As soon as the last Janaforma had weighed in on The Proposal, Sante, Cle, and I put our fingers together in a symbolic gesture of support and tabbed the "send" button on the multidex. The letter went out to every soul on Aeternus, almost eleven million people. All we had to do was to wait for the letter to do its work. The waiting only highlighted the tension I was feeling. We heard absolutely nothing from Ymotano. The silence gave me a skittish feeling as if I was waiting with the Janaforma lamb as Ymotano released the Cerribeame from their chains.

****

Thousands of people made printouts of the letter and it appeared plastered to the sides of buildings and taped to the fronts of doors. Janaforma were everywhere, many in full-dress uniform, handing out copies to passersby. It was difficult to believe this was happening. In the multidex age, a renaissance of the written word upon paper triumphed and personal interaction was in full swing. Something was stirring the dormant genes of togetherness, awakening the need for physical contact. Excited crowds filled the promenades and squares. The Aeternus streets were as I imagined Earth might have been a few thousand years ago.

People bombarded Cle with requests to make appearances. *Ce* went out in public, giving *cim*self to them so completely that when *ce* returned home, *cis* clothing was dirty from people touching cim. Crowds swarmed and enveloped cim, pressing copies of the letter into *cis* hand, insisting *ce* autograph it.

Cle was definitely the superstar of the hour, albeit *ce* was a cardboard cutout the way the media painted *cim*. Cynicism and prudish judgmental comments tagged media coverage on Aeternus. I was not surprised because Tyrowsians controlled the media while holographic technology made their illusions appear real.

I turned on the multidex in the sleeproom and switched to the news. There we were again and I was sick of seeing our faces everywhere. I played with the controls and made our images jump back and forth between the screen and our holographic projections. I punched in freeze and Cle and my empty form froze in the middle of the room. We were odorless, cold, and quite vacuous. I put my hand through those other selves that levitated in the air and said, "multidex cancel."

The real Cle sat in front of the multidex in the main room answering calls for hours on end. The Janaforma were not shy about expressing their opinions. A tiny red dot blinked endlessly in record mode on the corner of the screen. I was beginning to believe the Janaforma might be a strong, collective force because of their enthusiastic involvement.

Cle received an urgent message from Ymotano. Perhaps he was beginning to realize the strength of the Janaforma, because his tone had changed. He was conciliatory and apologized to Cle for taking so long to return *cis* call. He professed the trouble to be in the time it took for his own advisers to reach a consensus on an offer. The fact that there was going to be any offer, surprised me.

Ymotano was not to be trusted. He was an old-style being, unpredictable, and selfish just like me; but I wanted to believe he was sincere for Cle's sake. My distrust made me listen for those verbal slips that might reveal his true intentions. Ymotano was using words like "cooperation" and "agreement," expressions like "face-to-face" and "sit down together." The words had a smooth feel; but his tone had neither guts nor passion. Whether he simply had a good poker face or was a liar without a moral compass was still a question in my mind. I decided to watch Ymotano for symptoms if I had the chance.

There was an abundance of energy exhausted between Cle and Ymotano through the multidex. Negotiations ran into fourteen cycles. Cle, like a long distance runner, paced *cim*self for what lay ahead.

THIRTEEN

Only Sante and I were aware of the anxiety Cle was suffering. The points of all those incoming messages pained *cim* while a tumultuous battle between self-sacrifice and *cis* ego waged a war for control. The inevitability of what *ce* unleashed and the demands of *cis* closest friends, *ce* felt most acutely. *Ce* stared at the accumulating messages on the multidex screen, got up, and wandered over to the window-wall. "I feel overwhelmed," *ce* confessed. *Ce* brooded there for a long time, lost in the darker shadows of the side curtains.

When Sante put a hand on Cle's shoulder, *ce* jumped. "Please," Sante whispered to Cle. "Let me help you—no filters this time." An endless space minute passed in silence.

"Your words sound like a challenge," Cle finally replied.

Sante sat down cross-legged on the floor in front of Cle, "What you view as a challenge is the posturing of the thing you wish to discard. From here, it looks like an ill-fitting suit, a tyrant over your soul."

Cle moved forward from the darkness and into the glow of the multidex. *Cis* eyes spoke of tortured memories that needed expression yet *ce* told Sante, "You can't help." *Cis* jaw thrust forward and *cis* body slowly wilted toward the floor. Through clenched teeth *ce* struggled to speak and I barely heard *cim* murmur, "Not this time, my love."

Sante still insisted. "Talk to me about Sutcay Tay. Whatever you say, I'm on your side." The words "Sutcay Tay" hung in the eerie silence and seemed to make time go slower.

"You want to hear the dirty details about what still lives inside me?" Cle moaned. "That dying world, that alien jungle of crawling life lives in my memory. Here, without the piss-warm waters of the jungle, it grows gnarled and tougher in its effort to survive."

Together

Sante moved with purpose, arose and took Cle into *lis* arms. "I will hold you until all the pain goes away. I will hold until you feel strong and sure and you can defeat this thing. Together, we can win."

In the dark and silence of our private world, came the child-like sounds of Cle's voice—touching it—always coming back to it—playing with it like a deadly snake. "I'm astonished by my own audacity," *ce* seethed. "I'm such a fool! The Janaforma are as flawed as I am if they think I can lead. I'm clearly stained." Cle stared at Sante. "I killed those three men. I saw them dead before I struck the first blow. The choice was mine."

"I tell you the way was narrow," Sante still insisted.

"Why—because it was revealed in your cosmic cards? Don't you understand, Sante? I saw them dead and they were." Cle dropped *cis* face into *cis* hands. "Where is my genius when I march to all my darkest urges? I feel like an insane addict traveling this universe again, and again, and again doing the same damn thing. I've betrayed my very reason for being and my destruction is as inevitable as Sutcay Tay's destruction. Clearly, I've missed my chance, squandered this life, and now the Janaforma will miss their chance because I've failed. This time, I've fallen too far, lost too much to recover. Space Security was my lifeblood. Sante, if you can heal my misery, don't deny me the cure. Give me your *elixir vitae*! Please, make this avalanche of pain go away. I feel so evil—so dirty."

"Despite your feelings at this moment, you are perfection," said Sante.

Cle abruptly disentangled *cim*self from Sante. "I've never been perfect and I'm sick of hearing it and trying to live up to something that is impossible. I'm done. I will go no further with this particular charade. It's not helping me." Cle leaned forward and kissed Sante. "Tell me you love me," *ce* said.

"I adore you," said Sante. Suddenly some kind of high energy moved through the room. I felt it and shivered. It was as if the threat of the Cerribeame was right outside the door.

Cle moaned. "I told you, Sante; I don't want to do this anymore. Stop!" and *ce* got up and attempted to walk away.

"Don't jettison your vitarattha—not yet!" whispered Sante and *le* stood up too. Then *le* made a wide circle until *le* was standing behind Cle. When Sante reached over Cle's head and gently touched *cim* in the middle of the forehead, Cle fell backward, as if hit by a thunderbolt—right into Sante's arms. "The helix uncoils," said Sante. *Lis* words were so quiet they almost seemed a thought.

Cle's chest heaved and when *ce* spoke, *cis* voice was low and breathless. "I fight, but am helpless. My failure is my guilt. Grief inundates me and I feel my loss. Tell me. Is my destruction scheduled by a cosmic stop clock or is there no plan at all?"

"What else? Touch it."

"It's too ugly to bring into the light." Cle's body went rigid and *cis* back arched upward. A scream came from deep inside *cim* as if the door to hell opened and some unspeakable fear issued forth. "I am infantile lunatic," *ce* raved. "My arrogance makes me sick. Revelation! I'm a freak, an abomination, infertile with my lifebearer without your help. Sante! I want you. I want you to desire me to the exclusion of all others and I want you to fuck me as everyone watches. My pleasures—I feel so heavy now. So weary; stop, please. No more."

Sante stroked Cle's hair and they both collapsed to the floor. "Travel light, my precious consort," Sante whispered and yet it still was not over. Cle saw something before *cis* eyes that existed only for *cim* and *ce* choked, and the choke turned into a horrific scream. The sound of it washed out and over us like The Final Wave. The feeling was so real, the force so solid, it seemed to roll out from Aeternus and take everything in its path. I imagined that somewhere at the end of the universe, a ripple of Cle's psyche touched a distant shore. Bitter tears followed and after a while, the tears turned into absolute silence.

The hum of the multidex brought my attention back into the room and then I glanced up at the screen. By now, I could read enough Tyrowsian to piece together the gist of the message waiting for Cle's eyes. The Tyrowsian board members of Vitarattha R & D were asking for Admiral Vista's resignation. That Liacann penned the letter, in their behalf, surprised me little. Later, when Cle read the message, *ce* showed no reaction.

****

Hours later, I went down the hall to the meditation room. Opening the door a crack, I peered inside. By the light of a single, burned-down candle, I could see Sante sitting cross-legged with Cle's head in *lis* lap. They were perfectly still and completely serene. I stood there watching, feeling their peace fill the room. Then I closed the door and left them alone together.

The multidex continued to accumulate messages. A symbol in the corner of the screen indicated that additional messages waited in an auxiliary file. After Cle read most of the messages, *ce* asked Sante and me, "Will your help me write another letter. This one will be to the Janaforma people. I want to ask them to meet with me, face-to-face, so I can tell them the truth about Sutcay Tay before I take this project one step further."

"Are you sure?" asked Sante.

"Yes," said Cle. "I've found my focus and I choose quite deliberately now. I should have been the Janaforma leader. I know that cannot happen now, but I still can complete this initial task." With our support, which was more moral than literal, Cle composed an open letter to the Janaforma people.

My Janaforma family,

Change now waits at the doors of Aeternus. The Tyrowsians among us fear this change will lead only to destruction and loss, but we Janaforma welcome this change knowing this is an opportunity to live our beliefs and test the truths of loyalty, altruism, and self-sacrifice.

From the thousands of messages I received in the last few cycles, it is evident that many of you expect me to step forward and lead this present groundswell. However, after a descent into my troubled soul, I find myself lacking the necessary virtues to represent the Janaforma. Still, I have one small voice, which I humbly consecrate to our collective need. If you want me to continue negotiating with Governor Ymotano until he meets our demands, I will pursue this goal with all the vigor I can muster. But once we achieve this initial goal, other Janaforma must step forward and be ready to lead. If you choose to use me in this initial capacity, please understand that between my offer and your acceptance, I have much to explain.

Those interested in meeting with me for a more detailed explanation, please meet me at Vitarattha Plaza on 947.64 at 23:00 hours so I may elaborate. In the name of Janaforma love, I hope to see you there. Jana Cle.

****

It was difficult to believe Cle was the same person who went through the depths of hell a few hours earlier. *Ce* looked different—smaller, brighter—as if *ce* had become a concentration of *cim*self. A new certainty modulated *cis* tone when *ce* spoke and I was wondering if *cis* new lightness would last when *ce* felt the pressure of the crowd.

"Free will reaches farther than the wizard's wand," Sante said. *Le* was referring to Bell and her curses. *Lis* statement made me wonder. What hurdles might I need to run in the future? If a time came, a moment, when I needed to confront the ugliness of my ego, how would I fare?

A few hours later, we boarded a traveltube to the Vitarattha R & D complex that was at the opposite end of Aeternus. It was located out near the end of one of the spiral arms and had its own spaceport. The bright lights of the inner core were diffuse near the edge of the forcefield making it easier to see the stars. I appreciated the true immensity of this artificial world because it took us almost an hour to reach our destination. We rode up a crystaglass lift from the station and headed toward Vitarattha Plaza. In the distance, we could hear the buzz and hum of a thousand hyperactive verbal exchanges. As we rounded the corner, a sea of people appeared at the opposite end of the square. "There's a few thousand people here," said Sante.

Several people shouted, "Cle!" and within seconds, the crowd began chanting, "Number One Janaforma," as they moved toward us and swallowed us like a collective hungry mouth. The press of bodies around us was so great, I felt caught as if between two great milling stones. Trapped within the mass, we were moving to a spot I could not yet see.

"Hold my hand," shouted Sante as though we were about to embark on an amusement ride. "Try to stay together."

All eyes were on Cle while Sante and I seemed to be the tail on the kite. What did all these people want? They wanted to wish Cle well, to empathize, encourage *cim*, give *cim* advice, and touch *cim*. "I didn't think there would be so many people," Cle shouted over *cis* shoulder. Then suddenly, the power of the moving throng tore *cim* away from us.

"Let's head over there," said Sante, nodding in the direction of a fence. My eyes searched for familiar faces. It was amazing how much the Janaforma looked alike and dressed alike. Most of them had long beaded hair and all of them were beautiful in one way or another. If they wondered why a casual wildflower was amongst them, they made no indication that I was a weed. Sante and I made our way to the edge of the crowd and climbed on top of a stone bench. From there, I was surprised to see there were also many Tyrowsians among the Janaforma. Whether they were friends or foes, I could not tell. "Look!" said Sante. "There's Rebecca!"

"Rebecca?" I shouted. "Over here!"

She glanced our way, smiled, and began plowing through the crowd. "Isn't this fabulous?" she shouted from a distance. When she reached us, she jumped up next to us on the bench. "I've waited my entire life for something like this to happen," she said.

About thirty meters away, the crowd was lifting Cle up on a platform. The three of us began yelling, "Cle!" and waving our arms. Our voices were lost in the crowd; yet, somehow *ce* spotted us and raised *cis* hands for silence. The crowd hushed immediately. It was amazing—this instant control. Where did it come from? Cle and the people seemed to be hand in glove. "The momentum of the crowd separated me from my loved ones. I need them here, by my side, to speak." Cle pointed in our direction. "Please clear a small path so they could get through." The sea parted only because Cle wished it. Sante helped Rebecca and me down off the stone bench and we snaked our way through the crowd. I felt several people touch my arms and shoulders. Vicariously, I was now important. Cle gave each of us a hand up to a stone platform that surrounded a fountain. "These are my mates, Sante and Hibernia and this is Rebecca Dykestra, the capable attorney that defended me at my recent hearing." Several Janaforma in the crowd kissed the tips of their forefingers and tossed it to us as a sign of goodwill.

"May I speak privately to you for just a moment?" Rebecca asked Cle.

Rebecca and Cle climbed down off the stone platform and formed a conversational huddle. "I don't know if you know this or not, but momentum for our cause is growing," Rebecca whispered. "Fifty-six thousand Tyrowsians have endorsed The Proposal. Tell them, Cle. Let them know we have hope."

"Not yet," said Cle. "I don't want to cause a bandwagon effect." Cle stepped back up on the stone platform and a hush fell over the crowd. "Your enormous outpouring of love gives me strength," *ce* said and the crowd went wild with cheers. Two minutes later, they allowed *cim* to add, "I sense the Janaforma poised on the brink of a new age." A second enormous cheer rose from the crowd and lasted for five minutes until Cle raised *cis* arms over the crowd. Finally, *ce* was able to say, "I give voice to all we know is true. We have the talent; we have the moral clarity; we have the insight, the dedication, and the strength to determine our future. All we need is the authority!"

"Let's take the authority!" shouted voices from the crowd.

"Let's demand it!" shouted Cle and *ce* raised *cis* arms in the air with *cis* palms facing upward. "Together we must decide if we are to go forward as equal partners with the Tyrowsians or if our destiny takes us on a separate path. Too long, we've indulged our corrupt parent—too long, we have allowed the mindless, soulless, willful machine of what was to use us as fodder. It is time for self-determination, it is time for history's truths to be known, for there was a yesterday and through the Janaforma, there will be a greater tomorrow."

The shouts of support rose to a deafening roar. Cle raised arms again, but it took several minutes for the crowd to calm. "My family, separately we will wander for an eternity looking for our way; but together we can create paradise here and now. I ask each one of you to weigh your decision carefully—weigh it on the Janaforma Triangle of altruism, self-sacrifice, and loyalty—for this is not a frivolous commitment. We need to bond with one another as we bond with our family for this purpose of Community."

Cle's voice suddenly changed. It was less grand and archetypal and more like *cis* own. "I know this is a great deal to ask any individual and some of you may even question if I have the right to ask. Most of you think you know me; but I've made errors in judgment in the past." Cle opened *cis* hands showing the crowd the palms of *cis* hands again. It was a well-known Janaforma gesture of peace, coupled with elements of offered surrender. "I am here to surrender my truth to you before the Tyrowsians do."

Cle hesitated. Seconds seemed like hours as the crowd quieted to a dead silence. "All my life, I knew my destiny was Space Security and everything I did—every breath I took—propelled me toward that end. I heard the words—Community, loyalty, altruism, and self-sacrifice—but I never took the meaning of those words into my heart or understood the commitment those words required. My ego dined on praise and raised an internal roar that deafened truth and kept real feelings out. Most of you know I served aboard *Aeternus One* during the lasts days of Sutcay Tay. As I look into all your faces, I see the scarred souls of my friends and family, my community, those who served with me and those gone from us who died in an effort to save an entire civilization. For the sake of those we lost on Sutcay Tay, I tell you that it was on that dying world that I first jumped my 3C genetic programming, my commitment to Community."

Sharp voices arose here and there. Smiles began dropping from the faces in the crowd as Cle took *cis* next irrevocable step forward. "It was in the late stages of the evacuation. Horrendous fires burned everywhere. Flaming asteroids, the size of shuttlecraft pelted the city of Keyvana. I was on my way back to *Aeternus One* from a survey flyover when the third shift bridge commander, Jana Rainy, called me and told me to evacuate 90 individuals at an orphanage, which was located in the Keyvana Valley. My shuttle had an 80 person maximum capacity limit so 90 individuals were no problem. I had learned to ignore capacity limits my second day on Sutcay Tay. When I landed at the orphanage, I found 136 hysterical people waiting with a firewall fast approaching. I called *Aeternus One* for backup but every shuttle was out on another call. Commander Rainy screamed at me with her own frustrations, 'What do you expect me to do? Every situation is as dire as yours is. You're the first officer of this starship, you decide.' I already had experienced so many narrow escapes that my empathy was exhausted. I had no loyalty but to myself—no altruism for the terrified beings that clung to me as their only vitarattha. I lost my vision of self-sacrifice and the meaning of my life in the Keyvana Valley. Instead, something new and hideous took root in me—selfishness and an impatient desire to be rid of all responsibility. No way existed to make orbit with 136 people aboard the shuttle. I told the teachers that I needed ten volunteers to stay behind. It wasn't enough and I eliminated 26 more people. They could not believe my cruelty and verbally tore me apart. We barely made orbit with a hundred and one people aboard. After Sutcay Tay, I served aboard the *Kirtland*. My personal relationships suffered from overwhelming conceit. My behavior was hideous to everyone and, all the while, I was falling deeper and deeper into the pit of my ego. Sante helped me tremendously during this time. Without *lis* support I would not be here now. Despite *lis* love and concern, I never faced the full impact of how far I fell from what Simon Forma intended me to be. These latest circumstances have set about to teach me, in the most painful way possible, what a fool's delusion I've been living. On the star date 947.34, I stepped aboard the Martian freighter, *Gemstone* and faced the brick wall of my ego. I took the lives of three sadistic men." Cle stopped, almost unable to continue. "The Aeternus Council of Three will in time—if they can—use this incident to their advantage. They will tell you I killed those three men on the *Gemstone* with malicious intent. When you hear the Tyrowsians speak of this, remember that I stood here before you and confessed as much of my truth as I understand."

The crowd was deadly quiet now. Cle paused for another moment, almost choking on *cis* words. "I go through this for the Janaforma, as a mutual demonstration, for the truth is clear if you have not veiled it. Most of us here have been through Shardasko training and if you have proceeded to become a Shardasko master, you will know that I saw those men dead before they were. I saw them dead by my hands and acted upon that vision, believing my version of reality was the only path open to me. It was a reenactment of Sutcay Tay. The only difference is on Sutcay Tay my victims were saints and on the *Gemstone*, they were mind-stripped convicts."

There was an astonished gasp from the crowd. Suddenly some voice shouted and the voice was impassioned. "Cle!" it called out. "I lived what you lived. I made that jump too! I'm with you."

"I hear you!" called out another voice. "I've lived what you lived. We are one."

Empathetic understanding began echoing through the crowd, growing, then swelling into cheers of support. Something unprecedented began happening. The Janaforma were evolving and in that evolution, they were gaining momentum and power. Then Cle seemed to lean into the crowd, to spread *cim*self over them like a protective hand. *Ce* gave *cim*self so totally to them at that moment that *ce* seemed to be everyone. "To come to you as I have, to confess my own vanity is the second hardest thing I've ever done," *ce* said. "Facing that vanity was the hardest. Now I tell you plainly, I have made a journey through Janaforma love, through Chaos, back to Janaforma love again. What I am is no longer a gift within me. What I am, I choose logically and willfully with every fiber of my being." The energy between Cle and the crowd swelled into a symbiotic heartbeat. I was not sure who held whom—they were indeed *Una*, in one together. "You decide," said Cle. "Weigh it on The Janaforma Triangle, my talent, my character, and the objectives at hand and tell me if you want me to move forward with the Tyrowsians. Let us now go our separate ways and spread the truth, so others might know our hearts. Let our voices be one and when any one of us speaks, it will be Janaforma truth."

A familiar voice spoke from somewhere deep inside the crowd. It was Admiral Vista. "I believe in you," *ce* called out. "Many of you know Commander Cle personally and know what a courageous and truthful person *ce* is. Those of you who do not know *cim*—know me. Commander Cle was my first officer on *Aeternus One*. I've tested *cis* character and believe in *cim* and I know *ce* is destined to lead the Janaforma toward self-determination."

Admiral Vista's words solidified the crowd even more. There was jubilant shouting again of, "Number One Janaforma! Number One Janaforma!"

****

Later I awoke to the sound of the multidex in the next room. It was almost morning mode, an artificial dawning on a new cycle on Aeternus. The monotony of their unfailing regularity was something I was learning to ignore. Sometimes I missed the powdery morning hues of Earth, the sky-blues and the way the clouds hung over Lake Erie in the winter. Somewhere along the way, reality had flip-flopped and Earth was the treasured memory. I went out into the main room and the multidex screen formed an angelic aura around Cle's body. "What are you doing?" I asked.

"Checking my messages. I have a strong hunch I'll be hearing from Ymotano before too long. About two hours later, a message from Ymotano appeared on the screen.

"What does it say?" I asked excitedly. "All I can read is both your names."

Cle perused the message with a smirk and told me. "He's using the old Imperial Cuneate. No one has used that form in five hundred years. No problem, it's a trivial challenge. The message says, 'The state demands the presence of Jana Cle, class 3C, genetically engineered Human. Posthaste. 3 Lily Pool Lane, Inner Core.' Well! How do you like that? That's Ymotano's official residence." Cle punched in some numbers on the keyboard and the holographic images of Admiral Vista and Rebecca Dykestra appeared side by side. "Ymotano wants to see me at his house in the old Tyrowsian village," said Cle.

"Let him wait," advised Rebecca. "Make him sweat—if it's possible for a Tyrowsian to sweat."

"I'm not in the mood to play a waiting game," said Cle. "I going to see him and see what he has to say."

"Don't back down on any of the demands," advised Rebecca.

"Tell him it's all or nothing," Admiral Vista added.

"Will do," said Cle. "As Tyrowsians like to say, let's parlay."

Cle assumed that *ce* was going to see Ymotano alone, but Sante had something different in mind. "No way are you going alone," *le* said. "I'm going with you and so is Hibernia."

"Sante is right," I said. "So don't argue. I'm going too."

"No problem," said Cle. "You two can be my historical witnesses to what passes between Ymotano and me."

****

It was evening mode when we arrived in the Aeternus Core. This was the oldest, most protected part of Aeternus at the center of the Catherine wheel structure. This was the part the engineers, who played god, put together first—the part the citizens of Aeternus referred to as "the inner glue."

Aeternus' inner glue had no public transportation. We took the A loop to the end and got out at a dark, deserted station. The walkways into the inner core were narrow and the jagged up-and-down unevenness made walking an activity that took full concentration. Housing was a hodgepodge of alien inspired creations, piled high, one upon another, with little to no space between. When we found 3 Lily Pool Lane, it was no more than a tiny walkway off a narrow alley close to the village center. The dim lights of Aeternus reflected off the black water in the middle of a small courtyard. Indeed, there was some kind of pool there, half-hidden in the darkness.

Ymotano's house looked ordinary from the outside. Deep, dark swags of fabric covered the windows in an attempt to keep out the bright flashes of light that sometime emanated from the inner core. Tyrowsian eyes considered the flashes offensive while everyone else joked and said the flashes were Aeternus' attempt to imitate nature's lighting and thunder. We tapped the sensor and Ymotano's flirty little houseboy opened the door and said, "Come on in. "Yommey is expecting you. I'm Louee the new houseboy."

As we entered Ymotano's house, an inescapable feeling of stepping back in time overwhelmed me. The foyer was tall and long and lined with huge sheets of dark gray stone that were utterly depressing to my Human need for color and light. Three unfurled flags hung from the railing of the balcony at the end of the space. The Pybatium banner with one small spotlight concentrated upon it hung between the flags of the Orion Spur Alliance and Aeternus. I shivered, not from the cold, but from the feeling that I had stepped into the house of a feudal lord.

Louee, the houseboy, was leading us somewhere and that's when I noticed we all were tiptoeing—as if stomping might awaken the dragons lurking in the dungeon below. We passed through a dark, narrow passageway. Sante and Cle needed to duck their heads to avoid bumping the low doorframe. We stepped into the final room; this space was wide and tall, the ambiance much the same as the foyer with a predominance of gray marble and stony blue lacquered walls. The one surprise was a great wall of paper books at one end of the room. Were they a holospool illusion created by an interior designer or reality? I couldn't tell without getting closer.

A moment later, Ymotano walked into the room through the same door we entered and said to Louee, "Get out." Ymotano looked smaller up close, just as Yarrow Box did. Without Ymotano's voluminous purple robe and static teased hair, he was just another old Tyrowsian pervert with a houseboy. "I asked to see you alone," Ymotano said, almost laughing through the serious mask he wore as a face. "Why did you bring your family?"

"Ignore them," said Cle "They insisted on accompanying me. You already know my lifegiver Sante but allow me to introduce Hibernia, our wife. I'm sure you remember her from the hearing."

Ymotano's light-deprived arms extended from under the cap sleeves of his black floor duster. His arms looked attenuated as if the slightest bit of pressure could snap them off. He waved them around and said, "Yes, I remember you both. Find a seat and sit."

Sante and I decided to sit on a hard lacquered bench near the wall of books and that's when I realized the books were real. Ymotano sat down on the best chair in the room, a lacquered throne with mother of pearl inlay on the arms. Everything about the room and Ymotano was either black, stony blue, or gray except for the slight yellow discoloration of his white hair. "I asked you to come alone because I wanted to approach this problem on a personal level as one rational person to another," Ymotano said.

"This problem, as you call, it is not between you and me," said Cle. "This problem is between the government of Aeternus and the people of Aeternus."

"You cannot represent the people of Aeternus because you have no authority to do so," said Ymotano.

"The citizens of Aeternus have given me the authority to approach you and to give you a chance to do the right thing."

Ymotano laughed and shook his head in disbelief. "Go home, Cle. You're wasting your time. Even if I decided to give you everything you wanted on your Proposal, the Orion Spur Council would overrule my decision."

"You are the Regent Governor of Aeternus and you do have power. If you joined us, we could present a united front to the Orion Spur Council. I already have the support of every Janaforma on Aeternus and a signed endorsement of 500,000 other elements on Aeternus. That 500,000 was three-quarters Tyrowsian for your information."

"I'm not impressed, merely annoyed," said Ymotano. "We're no longer sitting in the hearing chamber, so I'm under no obligation to coddle you or pretend you have a valid point to make. Here's the truth, upstart. I have lived on many Tyrowsian worlds and have worked my way up through the ranks. I consider this position as Regent Governor of Aeternus Complex my last stepping-stone to a seat on the Orion Spur Council. I will not tolerate disruptive minority elements attempting to ruin the stability of Aeternus or undermine my authority here. Aeternus is a valuable Tyrowsian holding and my job is to make sure that never changes. Listen carefully and understand this: The Janaforma are expendable. Every Janaforma can be recycled right along with androids if I decide to do it and for a few million more credits, I can create a whole army of brainy beings that look exactly like you. To tell you the truth, when this situation started, I thought Liacann was insane and I sympathized with you completely; but you Janaforma are out of control. You are promoting anarchy among other minority elements and The Proposal you authored is dangerous. Before you know it, we'll have androids, biodroids, and half-breeds of every description demanding their rights. For this alone I could order your demise."

Ymotano paused and took a deep breath before continuing. "I tell you,

Cle. Despite your shenanigans, I still like you. Your spark reminds me of my youth and that's the only reason I called you here. I want to give you some sober advice that I might give my own son or daughter. I have lived through this scenario before, on other worlds. I've seen situations play out to no win conclusions on both sides. I've heard the call of freedom from millions, and frankly, it bores me. Words mean little in the real world. You believe you can knock the wheels off an old system but that's not how it works. My advice is to wait. Wait and perhaps in a thousand years, your ideas will make sense to somebody and we'll all give them a whirl. In the meantime, think about your immediate needs. You're extremely wealthy. Laws don't apply to you. Put your high, empty rhetoric to good use and move to Wonder World, where you can write a book about your beloved concept of Community and live a life of ease. Wonder World is where all retired pundits go to chew their cud so you will find others like you there that can pat you on the back and tell you you're right." Ymotano kept glancing my way and eventually asked, "You're not Janaforma are you?"

"I'm Human."

Ymotano jerked an arm my way. "This whole thing is your fault—you know? Human genetics carry all that nonsense about rights, justice, and freedom. All that fuzzy thinking has contaminated the Janaforma."

"Issues around rights, justice, and freedom may not be black and white as you prefer, but they are ideals I am proud the Janaforma adopted," said Sante.

"Don't tell me you believe all this Community nonsense too, Doctor Sante. I thought real Janaforma were smarter than that." Ymotano chortled and his voice assumed a chummy air. "Who do you think thought up those slogans the Janaforma lay down their lives for? Tyrowsians thought up the motto of The Janaforma Triangle so we could have an eye-catching logo to put on the hull of Space Security spaceships. Wise up! You're a public relations project, created to show the Orion Spur that it's a good idea to lift the ban on Tyrowsian corporations that produce androids and bioforms. The only problem is—you've swallowed this fabricated myth, hook, line, and sinker." The smile slipped off Ymotano's face. "You're a trophy fish, Cle. I'd like to keep you; but you're no good to me if I can't get the myth out of you. I care about you and your family only enough to give you the facts. Do you see those books on that far wall? They're not run-of-the-mill Tyrowsian pabulum. They are real history books and I've read them all. They tell me you are never going to get what you want because there are a million more, just like me, making sure you don't. You are worth less than a speck of dust to the Tyrowsian Empire. Persist, and the Tyrowsian state will arrest you and take your mind."

Cle's face revealed no emotion when he spoke. "You presume to be my fatherly council? Would you tell your own child that he or she was worth less than a speck of dust? Why is it that what has come before is the only thing possible for you?"

"I see it now!" exclaimed Ymotano. "You're determined to remain the martyred fool. Mi Cochon was right. You are a bunch of crazy Amalgams."

Cle never blinked when *ce* stood and took a stance. The gesture was intimidating and *ce* appeared so powerful at that moment that *cis* energy fill the room. *Ce* stared down at Ymotano and drew a verbal picture in the air. "I see a cobbled path of threats between us. Threats that were born of mere thoughts are now emerging as realities. It's a nightmare where nothing ever changes until the dialogue begins again. Dialogue is language, a clumsy tool, but used in the right way, it works." Cle leaned closer pushing the intimidation to the hilt. *Cis* voice changed and took on a jagged edge. "Understand this, my genetic ancestor—I know you. I know how you think and operate. Your insults and threats are laughable like static postures impossible to hold. But surly, you must realize that I can play that game too."

"Let me try another approach," said Ymotano. "Let's keep this simple. You and I can solve this dilemma faster and more efficiently; but if we involve the Orion Spur Council, we both will suffer; however, you will suffer more. The most, and I stress the most, I can offer is—if you cease your campaign, I will take some of the pressure off over Vitarattha R & D and allow you to reinstate Admiral Vista as COO."

Cle almost smiled. "That's a start."

Ymotano fell silent. "I'm willing to go as far as allowing the Janaforma some control in future plans for Space Security. Who knows what may happen in time? Things change, but never as fast as any of us want."

"What about access to our genetic records?" Sante asked.

"That's out of the question," said Ymotano. "And since you've finally decided to speak up, I'm curious to know why you tolerate your consort's public histrionics? I thought lifegivers were supposed to be the head of their families."

"You're mistaken," said Sante. "I am not the head of this family. The Janaforma took your corporate myth of The Janaforma Triangle and turned it into a symbol of equality. Consorts, lifebearers, and lifegivers are cornerstones of The Triangle and if you know anything about geometry, you know that a triangle is the strongest structure in the universe. And by the way, I support Cle in this cause and so does every other Janaforma on Aeternus. You are not dealing with just Cle; you are dealing with all of us."

Ymotano sighed. "Okay, you'll get Vitarattha Research and Development back and you can reappoint Vista and I will see Space Security has more autonomy in space. That's it though! You'll get no more from me. Go home, write an apology to the Aeternus Council of Three and I'll keep my end of the bargain. I hope, for your sake, that you comply because if you don't, I will dispatch all three of you with the Cerribeame Guard."

"I no longer believe in Tyrowsian fairytales," said Cle.

"Oh—the Cerribeame are real," said Ymotano. "They're very real and I can send them to your quarters at the Hilton. Yes! I know where you live. They will take you and your pretty mates and carry the three of you away into the darkness of Herzayzen Prison. Picture it! A Cerribeame factory that plucks brains clean of their precious memories. Think of it, an advanced intelligence such as yours, lingering in squalid filth and hopelessness."

"People all over the Spur are beginning to realize what's happening here on Aeternus," said Sante.

"And when the truth gets out to enough people, you will not survive," I quickly added.

"I promise you, if I have to spend every last credit point I have, I will see the truth gets out," Cle promised.

Ymotano laughed. "Go ahead; broadcast your truth about the Cerribeame! Tell everybody! Who cares? If you think you can win by spreading truth, you're more naïve than I realized. Spread your truth and I'll spread my truth, and we will see which truth survives. You may be rich, but your resources cannot match that of the Aeternus government. Right now, you are a superstar. In six months, no one is going to remember you. And do you know why? Because you and your Janaforma siblings are too intense. Intensity quickly becomes boring because we've all seen it before. We listen intently for a bit, but our minds quickly drift back to our holospool concerts and tartan ratu."

Cle leaned closer to Ymotano again and asked, "Do you really know who I am?"

"I know enough about you to know you are a fool on a fool's mission."

"I'm Simon Forma's child, a 3C genetic Amalgam, created from the finest Human genes available. At seven months of age, I had a vocabulary of ten thousand words. By the time I was three, I spoke seven languages."

"So what! I can commission the creation of an android that will be a thousand times smarter than you are. What's your point?"

"My point is words, thought, and meaning—these are my native tools. It's the reason Simon Forma chose me to approach you and why my people call me The Number One Janaforma. While you and your world are drifting back to your holospool concerts and tartan ratu, I will continue to carry the Janaforma message of Community forward. I will speak to people in their own voice—whoever they are and wherever they are. You see, I used to think my ability to imitate another person's voice was a useless trick, but I now realize this gift is my greatest talent." Cle, in an exact duplication of Ymotano's voice, said, "Don't tell me you believe all this Community nonsense. I thought you were smarter than that. Who do you think thought up all those words the Janaforma lay down their lives for?" Cle stepped back from Ymotano and I held my breath until he went over and sat down in the last chair available.

Ymotano was spooked only for a second before his expression returned to one of confidence. "Simon Forma? Now I understand! You are deranged if you believe Simon Forma instilled you with some kind of divine birthright to lead the Janaforma."

Cle's voice changed yet again. It still was not Cle's voice. It was a dangerous voice and I was glad *ce* was sitting. "I could put you out of your current misery. I killed before so surly I can kill you. Tell me Ymotano, why should I spare your life? Debate our difference on this level with me and I promise I will hear you out." Cle leaned forward and *cis* voice took on a confidential tone. "Give me one logical reason why I should spare you or one vestige of your perverted thoughts and I'll let you live."

"You definitely have jumped your programming!" choked Ymotano. "This is over. Get out of my house! Louee! Come quick!"

The dangerous voice vanished and Cle said, "You're scared when I speak to you with your own metaphors, which are threats and time limits. But look beyond my metaphors, and you'll see my threats are real. This is the Janaforma bottom line. You and your Aeternus Council of Three have five cycles—five cycles and your free will to endorse The Proposal in its entirety. If you decide to cooperate, we can begin to create a universal renaissance together. If you decide to deny the Janaforma, we will leave Aeternus and your precious Orion Spur Alliance. We will take our industry, our genius, our lives—all those finer things of your world, our loyalty, our self-sacrifice, our altruism, and our sense of Community. We will leave you. When you find yourselves crying out in loneliness in the middle of your nightmares, you will find you are utterly alone without our virtues. And worst of all, all those answers—all our history will vanish with us."

"You are truly mad!" said Ymotano, his breath spitting through the air. "No one will follow you. Besides, where would you go?"

"Understand this, we will go and be forever dead to you. We will abandon you to the endless stagnation of repeating reality. Now that's a nightmare!" said Cle, looking every bit as mad as Ymotano claimed.

Sante stood up at that point and said, "Let's get out of here."

I stood up and took Cle's arm. "Let's go Cle." I knew Ymotano was never going to change. He wasn't going to hear the right words and turn around and say, mea culpa and hit the reset button. If Cle couldn't find the right words with Ymotano, then no words existed that could move him.

****

It did not take long for one of Ymotano's worst fears to manifest. The Orion Spur media suddenly decided that the Aeternus story had legs. Once Off-World News decided the story was newsworthy, word traveled at light speed and everyone in the Spur knew what was happening on Aeternus—well, sort of.

I turned on the news and switched to holograph on the multidex and a sliver appeared and enlarged into the reality of a reporter standing beside the front gate of Vitarattha Research and Development.

"A disgruntled Orion Spur Space Security officer, Jana Cle, the only child of Jana Dyne, Kerisa, and Reyneldi has become a prominent voice in the Janaforma community, here on Aeternus. Jana Cle is challenging the provincial Tyrowsian government in what may be one of their strongest challenges thus far. Jana Cle who held the rank of commander at Space Security and was captain of the *OSSS Daedalus* was forced to resign because of conduct unbecoming an officer, according to our Tyrowsian sources."

Then the holograph changed and I saw Cle standing before me as *ce* did in front of the Janaforma people making *cis* confession. "I saw them dead by my own hands and I acted upon that vision," *ce* said. Everything was boiled down to that one sound bite. I watched a bit more and pressed analysis as an option on the remote. Two media reporters appeared before me. A title appeared in front of their faces. 947.34 THE *GEMSTONE* INCIDENT. I froze the picture there because I couldn't watch it. The Aeternus Council of Three had released the visual log of the *Gemstone* to the media. The sensationalism of the *Gemstone* was now over-shadowing what was happening on Aeternus. I stared at the holograph of Cle hanging in the air. *Ce* looked as real as my real hand. I stared at the hologram of myself. Who I might be, I still was unsure.

FOURTEEN

The lights-on, light-off regularity of the long Aeternus cycles leaves much to the imagination. Never sure what time it is, I watch the clock more closely nowadays. It was late evening mode. Glancing at my space watch, there were eight identical *ziens* and one lonely *haffa*. The time was precisely 999.999.995. The equivalent time on Earth would have indicated a countdown to a major New Year's celebration; but on Aeternus, time died without a whimper.

Cle startled me and I jumped when *ce* slapped the top of the multidex with *cis* hand. "Well I'll be damned!" *ce* shouted. "Ymotano has agreed to The Proposal in its entirety."

"I don't believe it," Sante said immediately.

"Neither do I," I said. "Ymotano has shown he is incapable of change."

We rushed over to the multidex to read—"Cle, thank you so much for coming to 3 Lily Pool Lane last cycle. It was a pleasure to meet your lifegiver, Doctor Sante—charming—and your new mate, Hibernia Smith—very pretty. I know I've been harsh with you over the last few weeks; but after you left, I realized that I appreciated the thoughtful way you presented the Janaforma demands and your passion for justice. Many of the issues you raised about access to your genetic records and greater control over Space Security and the confiscation of private business on Aeternus make a lot of sense. Full citizenship rights on the other hand will be a tough sell, especially to the Orion Spur Council. Still, the latest survey, which just arrived on my multidex, about an hour ago, informs me that 86% of the citizens of Aeternus are backing the Janaforma Proposal. I am not a despot, no matter what the Janaforma think of me. My sole purpose on Aeternus is to maintain order and facilitate the flow of commerce. I feel that we, you and I, got off to a shaky start and we both chose corners and refused to budge; therefore, I am offering you an olive branch. I will endorse The Proposal on all five points with the Orion Spur Council and we will take it from there. I plan to make a public announcement next cycle and ask that you be present so we can shake hands in public and quell this minor rebellion before it gets out of hand. I will let you know the exact time and place in a few hours," Signed, "Ymotano Rimmer, Regent Governor of Aeternus Complex."

Sante bit *lis* bottom lip and said, "I'm not sure. The words sound sincere but knowing Ymotano—how can they be?"

"Perhaps Ymotano is just another lazy plutocrat," I said. "His primary tactic is to stall until he can't anymore and now that 86% of the population backs The Proposal, Ymotano is suddenly onboard. Give him another month and he'll tell everyone The Proposal was his idea."

"I live with two cynics!" exclaimed Cle. "What possible motive would Ymotano have at this point to tell me he was going to back The Proposal and then not do it? He says that he is willing to go public. It's illogical for me to refuse his offer." Cle leaned back in *cis* chair and I could see the wheels spinning in *cis* head. "Besides, I want to believe Ymotano is sincere because I want to get my life back. If he is lying, we're no worse off. We still have plenty of options to explore especially when we have the backing of 86% percent of the population." Cle stood up, stretched, and glanced around the room. "For now, I'm going to do something selfish, something entirely for myself. I'm going to the health club and get some exercise. Either of you interested in tagging along?"

"I exercised a short time ago," I said.

"Maybe I'll pop over to the Scarlet Curl and get Piper to wash my hair afterward—you interested in a little hedonistic relief, Sante? You know how Piper runs her long Tyrowsian fingers through your hair—helps to clear the mind."

"It's late," said Sante. "I was thinking of getting some sleep."

"I can't sleep; I'm still too keyed up. Let me exercise and get my hair washed and then maybe I can relax." Cle changed into a pair of thin texoplex runners and came back into the main room where Sante and I were watching a Universal Geographic holospool called, The Steppes of Kulupa. "I won't be more than a couple of hours," Cle said and *ce* kissed Sante and then me. Nose to nose, *ce* looked into my eyes and said, "There is going to be an end to this, I promise, Wildflower. We're going to get our lives back. Then it's going to be you, Sante, and me forever. It's just as Sante said. Our love is a triangle, and a triangle is the strongest structure in this universe." Cle picked up *cis* exercise bag and smiled. The smile was sharp, a look of both confidence and authority that had me convinced. "As soon as Ymotano endorses The Proposal, we'll take a real honeymoon—do I hear any takers?"

"Why wait?" asked Sante. "You go exercise and have Piper prime your hair and we'll start the honeymoon as soon as you get back."

Cle's eyelids fluttered in coquettish affectation and *cis* voice oozed with feminine syrup. "I do declare, Doctor Sante; I hear you have the cure for the vapors." *Cis* voice ricocheted back to normal Cle. "Okay, this time I'm really leaving." *Ce* walked to the door and said, "Don't you dare start the honeymoon without me."

****

When the program was over, I took a bath and went to bed. Soon afterward, I felt Sante lie down beside me. We turned to each other in the darkness, sometimes napping, and sometimes kissing, waiting for Cle to return so we could make love.

The reality that Cle was late came slowly to me. I sat up in bed and looked at the clock. It was exactly 100.000.000. A shiver ran through my body when I saw the time. I was just superstitious enough to suspect it meant something important.

It's difficult to describe the mounting agony of waiting for a loved one, the plodding slowness of watched moments. I processed all those mind clichés about forgetfulness and running late. Vague worries about the Cerribeame drifted through my mind and finally Sante threw on some clothes and went to search for Cle. Ten minutes later, *le* returned breathless with beads of sweat dotting *lis* forehead. "The health spa is empty, the Scarlet Curl closed—no sign of Cle." Sante was completely awake now and clearly worried.

"I'll call the concierge," I said and I already was tapping double zero on the remote by the bed.

"This is Dothera," said an image that appeared onscreen. "How may I be of service?" "Let me speak to her," said Sante. "Dothera, Cle is missing. Did *ce* leave the confines of the Hilton in the last three hours?"

"You know I can't give you that kind of information," she said.

"Please," Sante pleaded. "We've known each other for years and you know you can trust me. I need you to make an exception to the rule this one time. Cle's life may depend upon it."

"I hope you're not asking me to jump my programming because making an exception would constitute a breach of my programming etiquette," she said much too cheerfully.

Sante was lost in thought until *le* said, "Trust me 001. I have—0001 clearance. Listen, Dothera. If you could do it, you would do it—wouldn't you 0003?"

Dothera appeared confused for the first time. "I'm not sure what you mean, Sante."

"Listen carefully to me," *le* said, softening *lis* voice. "You want to do the best job you can. Doing the best job you can, will protect you from reprocessing. Doing the best you can, means helping me now. I give you 01 alpha permission and 09 omega authorization to do it."

"Processing—001 trust, 0001 clearance—0003 friend—01 alpha—09 omega," she said. Her eyes turned inward and she was quiet for several seconds. Sante and I were beginning to go crazy as we waited for her Teflon mind to decide. "Continue," she eventually said.

"Good," said Sante. "Check your multidex. See if Cle left the premises."

"Processing," she said. Thirty precious space seconds passed in silence. "I have no record of Cle leaving this building; but *ce* is not now within the confines of the Hilton complex."

"How can that be?"

"Just a minute," she said putting her wristjack down on a circuit and making a central connection. "It's classified. I don't have access."

"Dothera, did you leave the front desk at all during this cycle?"

"I haven't left this desk in 4,784 cycles."

"Then you need a holiday and I think I'm going to give it to you!" Sante turned a lot more personal with Dothera. "Listen, honey, check your personal, visual files. I know you have them. You know, those free memory bits that allow you to observe and react."

Her voice changed. It was stronger and weaker all at the same time. It was the voice of her optional self—her bit of freedom to react that made her appear so real. "I saw Cle leave," she said abruptly.

"Was *ce* alone?" I demanded.

"No."

"Who else was with *cim*?" asked Sante.

"Piper, the hairdresser from the Scarlet Curl?"

"Did anything appear unusual about them or the scene?"

"Something was odd."

"Tell me!" exploded Sante with impatience.

"Neither one of them had any hair. Is that possible, Sante?"

Sante's mouth was hanging open in shock. "Access information on Piper?"

"Classified," Dothera repeated.

"Access your personal files!"

"Piper is always trying to get me to stain my eyes or get rid of my eyebrows. I disliked her."

"Why?" asked Sante.

"She is a bitch," Dothera said sweetly. "Do you need me to repeat any of that information, Sante?"

"No, listen to me. I want you to leave the front desk as soon as we disconnect. Walk outside the hotel. Walk as fast as you can and when you reach a minimal distance of three hundred meters from the outside border of the Hilton, immediately access 0090059, code name—Project Hope.

That number and code will put you in contact with Rebecca Dykestra. She will help you."

"Thank you. Have a lovely cycle!" said Dothera and she abruptly walked out of camera range.

"Something bad has happened," declared Sante.

"Cle said everything was going to be okay."

"Something bad has happened," repeated Sante, "The Tyrowsians are already trying to cover their tracks by deleting the Hilton's entry and exit records." Sante and I went into the main room. We took turns, first calling Vertain, then Vista, then Liart and Patra. No one had heard from Cle.

I called Rebecca and she said, "Vertain, just called. How long has Cle been missing?"

"Almost four hours."

"Damn, *ce* could be halfway across the galaxy by now."

"I'm scared; what should we do?"

"You should sit tight in case *ce* tries to reach you. I'll call the Tyrowsian Constabulary. Better get ready for a lot of commotion in a very short time."

"Rebecca?" said Sante. "I just jumped an android named Dothera. When she calls you, don't let her get away. She was the last one to see Cle."

"Check!" said Rebecca. "I'll handle Dothera personally."

I barely had time to put on clothes before the urgent bleeping at the door began. A pair of Tyrowsian constabularies stood there who introduced themselves as Bãtha-Be and Shreeher. Their names sounded familiar and later Sante reminded me that the two were the agents that had interviewed Captain Gordon. Bãtha-Be and Shreeher were the image of government men—young, intense, tightly braided hair and eager to make a good impression. Bãtha-Be took notes on his portable microdex while Shreeher acted as the mouth. "Was Cle wearing a communicator?" asked Shreeher and he casually adjusted his jacket and I noticed a bulge under his arm and the knurled handle of a rephazer.

"No," said Sante. "Cle hates wearing anything on his wrists."

"Let's go down to the health club and have a look around," suggested Shreeher.

The four of us went down to the lower complex of the Hilton and it was quiet as Toledo on a Tuesday night. Shreeher woke a few of the Naub street-people who were sit-sleeping in the darker corners and asked if they had seen anything suspicious, but they all shook their heads no and went back to sleep.

At the Scarlet Curl, Shreeher opened the locked door with a universal passcard. It was dark inside. Someone found the light and turned it on. Everything appeared to be in perfect order and then we began to take a closer look around. A moment later, Sante froze. *Lis* focus was a black plastic trashcan under the edge of a counter. Something made *lim* stagger—

lis knees caving forward. "What's wrong?" asked Shreeher.

Sante extended a trembling hand into the dark, unknown depths of that hideous can. Then, *le* brought out a tangled nest of braids for us all to see. Familiar jet-colored beads still threaded here and there on their bloody, tangled plaits. The scream that issued forth from Sante took me down into despair. My mind jammed, went rigid with denial, and I refused to accept what was happening. For almost a minute, I struggled to reinvent reality, to superimpose what was happening with something less stark. Instead, the incredible indifference of persistent reality flooded my senses with the smell of death. I looked at the clock, allowing its poisonous time to destroy my hope. My lips moved and I clung to my innocence. "What is it?" I asked.

Sante sank deeper into the floor staring into the mass of woven hair as if it uncurled with its own story. *Lis* head dropped, *lis* face buried in the blood, the beads, and the hair. "*Hataeasta* uncoils," *le* choked.

Bãtha-Be started pelting me with questions. I saw his lips moving but could not string the words together so they made sense. "Is this Jana Cle's hair?" he asked. I would not verify it. I refused to make persistent reality stronger. Meaningless voices began assaulting me with torrents of disconnected words—Shreeher, then Bãtha-Be, and then Shreeher again—pelting questions like driving rain. Over the next few hours, hundreds of faces would come and go in a blizzard of white Tyrowsian hair. My voice uttered questions too—meaningless questions that came from my automatic place, a place that had the ability to make it up because I could no long function.

Sante would speak to no one. *Le* retreated from life and would not utter a word for the next three cycles. Shreeher said they needed the hair as physical evidence and he gently pulled it from Sante's hands and took it away. After the parade of Tyrowsian Constabulary left our home, Sante gathered up all the minute strands of Cle's hair from between *lis* fingers, off *lis* clothes and carpet and carefully put them in a vacubag.

"No matter what's happened to Cle; we are not going to clone *cim*," I said.

Sante said nothing. Only then did *le* go take a shower and wash Cle's blood off.

****

Time faded into hours and days of meaningless waiting. I was awake almost three cycles—hoping for some word that could assuage my pain. I feared sleep. I feared happy dreams and waking only to find Cle still gone. Someone spoke to me and I looked up and recognized Rebecca.

"You look terrible!" she said. "You need to sleep."

"If you think I can't handle this because I'm a Casual—you're wrong! I can be as tough as Sante."

"Go get *lim*," she said. "I've got news." She began opening her portable multidex on the table.

In the meditation room, Sante sat cross-legged and motionless. *Le* had been that way for the last six hours. I touched *lis* shoulder and said, "Rebecca is here; she has news."

Le nodded. "I'll be right there."

When Rebecca saw Sante she kissed *lim* on the forehead and said, "I'm so, so sorry, Sante."

"Thank you. Tell me what you know and skip the flourishes."

"That's exactly what I intend to do," she said sitting down in front of her multidex. She slowly began scrolling through the information as she interpreted it for us. "We have Dothera in a safe-house at Project Hope. She submitted to a personal file analysis. I did it myself and I guarantee she knows nothing beyond what she told you. My underground information concerning The Constabulary says—they are about fifty percent independents. Shreeher is okay, he's an old jumper. I didn't have too much contact with his partner Bãtha-Be. The Constabulary has the hair you found in the trashcan. Forensics completed the DNA matching and—I'm sorry, the hair definitely belonged to Cle. The crime scene investigators found Cle's exercise bag in an alley behind the Hilton—*cis* credit cards and gold armlet were inside so robbery does not seem to be a motive."

"I want that bag and all the items inside that bag returned to me," said Sante.

"I'll see you get Cle's personal effects, but it might take time," said Rebecca. "I talked to Commander Vertain a couple of hours ago and she tells me there are no records that Cle was aboard any public ship leaving Aeternus. *Ce* hasn't used OSSS communication codes or multidex units. We all know this means nothing. Cle could have slipped through a million loopholes. By the way, Shreeher offered me an interesting observation. He said the Scarlet Curl looked as if someone had deliberately sanitized the place. He felt it was too clean, as though someone left the hair intentionally, as, sort of, a Gorgon."

"To scare us off?" I asked.

"More like a challenge to lure us in," said Sante.

"Have you spoken with Admiral Vista?" I asked.

"Admiral Vista is trying to stand in for Cle so we don't lose momentum. You probably haven't had your multidex on or you would realize Ymotano and Mi Cochon have been busy unleashing a blitzkrieg of misinformation to the media. The media is playing right into their hands because the more outrageous their statements become, the more the media replays them. A few hours after Cle went missing, a reporter asked Mi Cochon for a comment and he said, 'The situation here on Aeternus turned too tough for the wealthy Jana Cle and *ce* decided to take a holiday.'" Rebecca hesitated. "One last thing and I'm afraid it is not encouraging. Shreeher told me that he believes the Cerribeame apprehended and processed Cle and that's why there is no trace of *cim* anywhere."

"What did you say?" I asked, pretending to deafness.

"Some people call them the Cerribeame Guard," said Rebecca. "Between sixty and eighty years ago a series of unexplained kidnappings of infant Cerribeame females occurred. Authorities never found the infants and in the last fifty years, clues led to the general conclusion that these kidnapped females became prototypes for Cerribeame killers. The few captured or killed invariably prove to be Ganat Cerribeame clones—small, lightweight, and superfast biological being that can be trained in as little as five years to become efficient killers. At first, the Tyrowsians used them to apprehend wayward androids who jumped programming. Now, Tyrowsians are using them to recycle living beings right alongside androids. Their ships have the ability to jump from this dimension and ride along the timeline and emerge anywhere they want. Ergo, no traces are left behind."

I squandered my last tattered remnants of energy on tears. All I could say was, "I don't understand, Rebecca. Why reprocess people? Why not just kill them?"

"Because Tyrowsians claim they don't believe in murder," said Rebecca. "This recycling, as if Cle were an old suit to be restyled, fits their modus operandi."

"Ymotano threatened to send the Cerribeame after us, but I kept hoping it was just part of their perverse Tyrowsian mythology." I had nothing left but desperation. "Maybe Cle is still alive. We haven't seen any actual evidence that *ce* is dead."

Sante walked away, back to *lis* meditation chamber and away from me. Rebecca began closing her multidex, but I pressed her to give me a lifeline, a thread of hope. "What do you really think, Rebecca?"

"Prepare for the worst," she said.

****

My life became persistent reality with no escape. I stopped looking at clocks. Day and night became the same, especially on Aeternus. Long space cycles accumulated like hours. I was at complete odds with myself, not able to sleep when I went to bed or to concentrate while I was awake. I tried drinking coffee to stay awake and expensive Pavlovian Brandy to go to sleep; but neither drug worked. Sante and I withdrew from each another, our relationship automatic. We could not look at each other because of the pain we saw in each other's eyes and I began to realize that if we continued as we were, I would lose Sante too.

A new part of me wished someone would come and tell us Cle was dead. The tension of not knowing was the ultimate torture. I could not let go of the last thread of hope until I knew for sure. In my mind, to let go of hope without honestly knowing was disloyal. My waking hours were introspections and my mind filled with conversations I would never have. I hated what I felt but could not climb up from my despair. I became the waiting woman, the steadfast Penelope. My tears did not wash my soul clean as Sante once suggested. These tears began to destroy me like acid rain.

My dreams were reoccurring as I wandered through old landfills, junkyards, places where Humans dump their worn out dreams. My mind wandered in despair at all the dark, vague rust and decay of what I could not restore. I awoke with a disconcerting start and resorted to activating the sleeproom gravity block hoping the comfort of Zero-G's would lull me back to sleep. The moment I closed my eyes I was dreaming again. *I climbed over and between walls of wrecked bits of crushed automobiles, rubber tires, and plastic bottles and glass—tearing my shoes to shreds. I leaned down to fix my flapping sole, one, more, time; and there, in a pocket of earth, I saw a morning glory vine twining through the metal spokes of an old bicycle wheel. One perfect purple flower bloomed along the vine. Its inner throat was white satin, its pollen-ripe stamen, a trident tongue capable of speech, "Accept your advantages. Your wild genetics make you free. Exercise your personal will and step beyond predestination." Coiling upward, the morning glory vine captured The Wheel and used it as a support to climb to the light. Immaculate upon the trash heap, the satin petals of the wildflower were triumphant as it lifted its purple head to the healing light.*

When I awoke, I began to ascend from the wretchedness of my despair. Ancient seeds of Human tenacity proved their worth, germinating hope even in the depths of my grief.

****

Cle had been missing now for 47 cycles when the attention signal buzzed at the front door. When I opened it, Rebecca said, "I've been trying to call you for hours. Don't you people ever answer your multidex messages? There's real news." My heart jumped and I immediately wanted to believe. Rebecca looked at Sante and then me. "I think Cle is being held at Herzayzen Prison."

I snatched the golden ring. "We have to get *cim* out."

"This is all through Shreeher and the underground," Rebecca explained. "The Tyrowsians are admitting nothing."

"I don't care. What do we need to do first?"

"Shreeher told me a Janaforma was spotted about 40 cycles ago on a Cerribeame prison freighter headed for Herzayzen Prison."

"It's not Cle," said Sante.

"I want to check it out," I insisted.

"Cle is gone. Accept it."

"You know diddlysquat," I said. "Admit it, Sante. You've been wrong before about a number of things. Why are you destroying my hope? When I first met you, I thought you were an angel. Now you've turned into the coldest bastard on Aeternus."

Sante clenched his teeth. "Don't you understand? That thing in Herzayzen Prison is another Gorgon. Do you honestly want to subject yourself to the brutalized physical remains of a soul we both loved with every fiber of our being?" I hated Sante at that moment. I hated *lim* for stepping on my already trampled hopes and I hated *lim* for *lis* strength.

"Maybe you're right, Sante," said Rebecca. "But what if you are wrong? Even if all that's left is a physical body, we have an obligation to that pattern of flesh that contained Cle. Or worse yet, what if there is some part of Cle still alive and *ce* is suffering?"

I got down on my knees in front of Sante and looked into *lis* sapphire blue eyes for the first time since Cle disappeared. "I need you Sante. I need you to believe with me, to believe Cle is still alive. Remember, Bell said you would meet a woman who would be able to chart a course for you. Well, here I am. I'm prepared to chart our course. My course says that with or without your help, I am going to find out exactly what happened to Cle."

Sante did not answer me; but I had *lis* full attention. *Le* took me by my arms and pulled me forward until we were face to face. He held me there until I could feel the heat in *lis* hands and see the secret depth of *lis* endless eyes. At that instant, I knew *le* was the strongest force in our three-way relationship and I was ready to submit to *lis* truth, ready to admit Cle truly was dead. The words, I surrender, were halfway out of my mouth. "All right, you're playing your ace," said Sante. "You're our cartographer and we will do it your way. However, exactly like Cle, I am the best equipped to execute this task. I will go to Herzayzen Prison and check out this rumor."

"You can't go alone," I said.

"Who could I ask to risk their life in this fool's mission?"

"You could ask me."

Sante continued to surprise me. "Okay, Hibernia, perhaps this is your graduation day. We'll do it together."

Rebecca appeared eager. "Let me help. I know lots of jumpers that can help you—"

"Tell no one; I trust few people nowadays."

"Sante, even you can't do this without help. Isn't it time to start trusting your closest friends, your Community?"

Sante relaxed like a cobra ready to strike. *Lis* eyes turned impenetrable, shutting everyone out; and when *le* spoke incredulity tinged *lis* voice. "You speak of trust? I don't even trust my own perceptions let alone the perceptions of others." *Le* spread *lis* hands out before *lim*. "'Walk across the thin ice of logic for even the face of reason masks the truth.'"

"I not sure what you're talking about," said Rebecca.

"Probably not; you would have to be a Shardasko warrior to understand."

"Listen to me," I said.

"I am listening to you Hibernia. You have my full attention and I've agreed to do your bidding. What else do you want? An apology? I should have listened to you from the start. I was wrong to encourage Cle to take on this project. *Ce* would not have committed to it if we both told *cim* no."

"I never blamed you—ever. I thought I was being selfish because all I wanted to do was keep Cle safe." After Rebecca left, I told Sante, "I don't know if you understand how much I love you, but you are everything to me." I touched *lim* lightly so *le* would not fly away.

"Your love is my star chart," *le* said and *le* managed a weak smile. "Together we will go to Herzayzen Prison and learn the truth." Later I asked Sante to remove the birth control device implanted in me twelve years earlier on Earth. It was a symbolic gesture, a ritual recommitment. It was all I had to give to someone who constantly gave me so much. Afterward, we made love for the first time since losing Cle.

****

The following cycle when I awoke, I heard quiet talking in the main room. I put on some clothes and went to investigate. "*Fra*," I said, as Sante and Cle had taught me to call Vista.

"Good morning Hibernia," *ce* said in Universal.

I smiled, allowing an iota of happiness to enter my soul. "Don't you know there is no morning in space?" I asked.

"So I've heard," *ce* said, "But we might see daylight yet." *Ce* rose from *cis* chair and gave me a hug. "Let me look at you."

"I wish you wouldn't," knowing the Janaforma did not look but examined.

"Sante tells me you are suffering. You are a little white, especially around the eyes." *Ce* touched my cheek with the side of *cis* hand.

"Lack of light. It's just mild FSP. I can handle it, can't I, Sante?"

Sante held up a fist and then opened lis fingers expressively. "Doctor to patient, you need to concentrate upon breathing-in for a while." Sante was annoyed about something, but I decided to let it pass because nothing was worse than the silence between us.

"Sante says there is information about Cle from the underground," said Vista, "And that you've decided to break into Herzayzen Prison and see if Cle is there. I'm all for the idea but—this is nothing personal Hibernia—but why don't you let me go with Sante instead?"

"Thank you for offering," said Sante, "But Hi will be my second on this mission. She has that unpredictable edge that could mean the difference between success and failure. Besides Cle is our consort and it is our responsibility to check this out."

"If that's what you believe then I fully support your decision. Everything I have is yours. How can I help?"

"I need a ship, a small pulsar. Can you get it stripped and veiled?"

"You're going to fly blind?"

"It's the only way I can get off Aeternus without detection. And I have no idea what kinds of security measures surround Herzayzen Prison."

"Sure, I can strip it," said Vista, "What else do you need?"

"We'll need two standard packs, two portable jetpacks, three polymicroflex whitesuits and three BA-type vitaratthas. It would be helpful if you could get us two automatic short-range macro-rephazers. Oh! I also need a thousand meters of electromagnetic rope with braces, and a universal master card. Everything else, I can get myself. How long will it take to prepare the ship and assemble the gear?"

"Everything but the ship is easy. I'll have to ask Vertain for the pulsar and I will need to take it out to Vitarattha R & D for customizing. Not much is going on at Vitarattha Complex since the hearing, so no problem there."

"Telling Vertain means trusting another person," I reminded Sante.

"Why not? She's my second cousin."

"I'll get busy," said Vista. "If everything goes smoothly, expect to hear from me in three cycles. We won't use the multidex. I'll come here in person when everything is prepared."

After Vista left, Sante embraced me with new purpose. I loved *lim* then as never before. Without a doubt, *le* was the most magnificent person I had ever known. *Le* was an emotional genius and when *lis* emotions moved *lim*, *le* could focus like a laser beam and accomplish near miracles. We went into the meditation chamber and sat down on the floor face-to-face. "This will happen if you empty your mind of all presumptions," Sante promised me. "We will move through the mission with our goal in mind and react with our arsenal of options."

"I understand." Through an act of sanctified love, there in the stillness, I gave myself to Sante and the future.

****

Three cycles later, Vista returned and tapped softly on the door. "Everything is ready," *ce* said. The strategy was to leave the Hilton separately. Hiding in the crowds of day mode, we would rendezvous at Vitarattha R & D after dark and leave Aeternus under the protection of night mode. "The pulsar is in hangar 34, level J," said Vista, and *ce* pressed the controller firmly into Sante's palm.

Later, I left the Hilton alone and wandered around the crowded streets for almost an hour. Demonstrations were ongoing with Cle's name on many people's lips. I ducked down an alleyway leading to a seldom-used traveltube entrance, then switched cars three times until I was sure no one was following me. I changed clothing in an underground toilet and pulled my hair up under a hat if the Tyrowsians decided to check their spy eyes that were positioned all over Aeternus. When I emerged from the toilet, the only other person in the station was a Naub vagrant sleeping on a bench. I caught an express car for the sixth spiral arm and kept checking my watch and gauging how much longer it would take to get to Vitarattha Complex. The farther out I traveled, the darker it became. At the last stop, I exited the empty car and waited in the deserted station. Five minutes later, Sante joined me in the shadows.

At first glance, Hangar 34, level J appeared empty. Upon closer examination, a slight blur appeared like a nearsighted distortion near the center of the space. Sante used the remote and an open door appeared suspended approximately three meters off the floor. Sante executed a fantastic leap, catching the edge of the opening, pulling *cim*self up with one, then two hands. Once inside, Sante leaned over the bottom edge of the door and pulled me up to safety.

Floor space inside the Pulsar was small, almost as small as a space taxi. The hundreds of instrument panels spanning the circular walls were black. We had no operable timers, informational screens or cartography. As much as I loved and trusted Sante, the skill to fly a spaceship blind into the black, ever-changing expanses of space seemed an impossible feat to me. We strapped ourselves into chairs as the engines initiated with a quiet purr. Sante opened the first set of space doors and the pulsar slipped inside. *Le* opened the second set of doors and—wham! We shot away into space at the speed of light. In a half a heartbeat, Aeternus vanished and time bent.

****

When Sante said, "There is hell," I knew we had arrived. The engines idled. Our momentum carried us in closer just until Herzayzen's gravitational pull allowed us to teeter on the edge of entry into its polluted atmosphere.

The reality of Herzayzen grew more horrible as we descended. Thousands of millennium ago when Earth sat poised on the edge of its industrial revolution, Herzayzen was declared toxic. The polar caps were black ice. Great chunks of the Northern Hemisphere were missing leaving a festering hole. Subterranean rivers of molten lava, oozing like cancerous sores, scarred and re-scarred the planet's wounded topography. Planetary rings of pebbles and fine debris ringed the equator shutting off light from the distant sun, Hataloben. From space, the planet revealed no signs of life—no blue or green, not even black or brown. Herzayzen belonged to the range of color that had no name, as if a psychotic artist took all the colors in the paint box and mixed them together into one bucket of glop.

I pinned a vitarattha to my clothing and I immediately felt safer. Next, we put on what Space Security called "whitesuits," but these particular whitesuits were more silver than white. The same reflective material that coated the pulsar coated the suits. It made us almost invisible in space, but in the dense Herzayzen atmosphere, it was the perfect cover. Sante put a squarepak on *lis* back with an extra whitesuit. We linked our belts securely together, slipped on our gloves, and pulled down our visors. Suited up as we were, we almost were invisible to each other.

No way existed to camouflage the contrails from our jetpacks that we used as ballast against the downward pull of gravity. No one needed to tell us that what we were doing was dangerous. We would not be confused with birds on this dead and toxic world. We needed to come down in the Southern Hemisphere, some distance from the prison to avoid the sensors that blanketed the area. Downward we descended, not into flat blackness or endless blackness, but into the poisonous blackness of planetary corruption. Through the protection of my vitarattha, I could feel the increasing heat from the ground fires and the oppressive gravity pulling me down.

Smog clogged the air. Great clusters of corrosive, gas-filled clouds hung like gobs of chocolate pudding on all vistas. Here and there over the pockmarked wasteland stood lakes of slimy-green liquid boiling like pots of heated acid. Ten meters above the ground, we turned off our jetpacks. Seconds later, we bounced like rubber balls when our vitaratthas hit the ground.

When we stopped bouncing, we deactivated our vitaratthas and Sante raised *lis* visor slightly and whispered, "It's hotter than I thought. If we cool the whitesuits we won't have enough energy to get back to the pulsar." We quickly decided to discard the whitesuits and hid most of our equipment under a stack of prehistoric rubber tires. We took the electromagnetic rope and braces, a few syringes of aminoply, protective goggles, and breathers; and then Sante handed me a rephazer. "Be careful with this," *le* cautioned. We were a lot cooler and a lot lighter minus the whitesuits, but of course, we were visible. We quickly self-administered shots of aminoply to fortify ourselves for the physical trial ahead.

We wasted no time and began to scale the Everest of trash. The vitarattha was my only protection, but it wasn't enough to block the smell of rot around me. I remembered Ronald Porkcur and Yarrow Box and thought of all the wasted souls yet inside Tyrowsian prisons. How could anyone have any hope of surviving in this place without the benefit of a vitarattha?

The smog obliterated all details ahead. We climbed steadily for over twenty minutes—over tons of broken amber beer bottles, refrigerators, computer boards, broken multidex units, and arms and legs of ancient robots—not able to predict even our next step. Old product names and forgotten logos—words that once meant something to past generations popped up before me on bits of red squished metal and opaque plastic. Ultra Slim•Fast, Texoplex, Frigidaire, and "Coke & Calypso Fits Your Style," and of course, NEW VISION: EVERYWHERE OR NOWHERE.

Sweat poured down my forehead and burned my eyes. We stopped for a moment to administer a second shot of aminoply. When I wiped the salty perspiration away, I glanced down and saw a morning glory flower in perfect bloom and that's when I remembered my dream. The plant had wrapped itself around the spokes of an old rusty wheel. To me, the plant's tenacity was a clear sign of hope that we were going to find Cle and everything was going to be okay.

Suddenly, the smog lifted and I heard a belching noise from somewhere inside the prison. For two or three short seconds, I could see the prison clearly. The walls of Herzayzen rose proudly like the Mont-St-Michel of Hell. Yellow smoke mingled with the toxic air and again shrouded the prison from view. We pushed onward, climbing over a short revetment wall. A few meters inside, the sharp, vertical walls of Herzayzen disappeared in the smog. We would be climbing blind.

Sante cast the first magnetic piton. It disappeared into the gloominess above. We heard a soft click, assuring us the piton caught on the wall. I sent the magnetic rope up through the eye of the snap box and a moment later, we stepped onto the two tiny pedestals on either side of the lift. We nodded in agreement and shot upward only stopping to cast fifteen more pitons.

A meter from the parapet, we stopped. Sante inched *lis* way up the last bit of cable to look around. I waited suspended in the smog, clinging to the woven strands of rope as my lifeline. Instant death surrounded me and waited for its chance to bite. The crest of the parapet was at least three meters wide and spiked with broken glass. We both stared at the obstacle and a speck of doubt edged into the corner of my mind. Sante pointed with a finger showing me a path. "Use your vitarattha," *le* whispered softly in my ear. I primed myself with thoughts of rescuing Cle and the joy of reuniting with *cim*. I took a deep breath and then Sante and I walked across the spiked glass with no problems at all.

Two deserted barbicans stood in the middle of the wall-walk. These dated back to when real people once stood guard here. Beyond, arched double doors stood invitingly open. I guess no reason existed to lock them for I was certain that we were the first to claim the dubious honor of breaking into Herzayzen Prison.

FIFTEEN

My awareness tingled. Like a feline, I was suspicious of open doors. Time pushed me forward—one-step, then another, into the unknown darkness of Herzayzen Prison. My mind projected images of hair-triggered sentinels, bone-crushing traps, and razor snares. I tried to relax, but felt the steeling in my muscles. Slipping the infrared filters down over my goggles, my tentacled-mind probed the darkness—waiting, sensing, then waiting again. Inhaling slowly, the dank odor of fermenting rot choked my nose. My ears anticipated every sound. Somewhere, intermittent water dripped on soft mossy rocks and beady eyes fluttered before scurrying off. Then something living, cold, and hairy tickled my arm and I wanted to scream, but was afraid to breathe. My hands searched the darkness for Sante, my urgency striving for connection. *Le* snatched my wrists—*lis* familiar touch calming and intimate. Little by little, *le* let go as I regained self-control. Then fingertip-to-fingertip, in a tango of trust, we groped our way through a maze of unseen death traps—inching along a rough, stony wall.

Gradually my Earth sense of up and down kicked-in and I realized we were in a long descending corridor. It was cooler now. My shirt, damp-with-sweat, chilled my back while the darkness widened into a larger expanse. Ahead, a faint orange blob of light appeared, then another and another, peppering the darkness like sparklebugs—hundreds of shapes, winking in and out—moving, breathing, streams of light. I fervently prayed that just one of those lights might be Cle. "Kill the infrared," whispered Sante. I flipped up my filters and we were standing on a high battlement overlooking a vast, circular chamber. A steep ramp coiled downward hugging the perimeter wall. I peered over the edge into the wellhole and saw the chamber floor several levels below.

"*Qualmerrie!*" a voice rang out. *Qualmerrie* bounced off the walls seeming to come from everywhere at once. "You can take off your goggles and masks," the voice echoed. "You won't need that equipment in here." We froze, unable to shrink back into the protective gloom. Had we tripped a silent alarm? Would every guard in the prison descend upon us? I sensed Sante relax and step backward and suddenly the lumens increased tenfold until the light climaxed into a stark, artificial daybreak. "Follow the ramp," the voice instructed. "I'm here, below." I peered over the edge of the battlement again and saw a tiny figure standing at the bottom. Struggling to bring the creature into better focus, all I could see was a mere hint of red quivering amid a mass of cloud-like white hair. From a distance, the true nature of the beast was impossible to determine; but whatever it was, it reeked of corruption. It was daylight now and the air cold as a castle in January. We were plainly visible and I could feel the pressing eyes coming from the small openings in the cell doors as we slowly descended the spiral ramp.

"That's right; come on down. I'll get Lawnoia to brew us a pot of hot jasmine tea." The voice was captivating. Patiently, it waited for us to wind our way down into the deepening cold. Around and around we went like predestined fools, past the flag of Pybatium hanging over the railing and slipping past the vigil of silent eyes.

I could see the creature better now. It was wearing finely tailored clothing from another era. Its aristocratic, purple frock coat appeared wrinkled and long unattended. It definitely was a remnant of my da Vinci vision. Slowly and sensually, it began running its slender, delicate fingers through its gossamer hair as if it were pleasuring itself. As we neared, it turned its back, displaying the long, full drape of fantastic white hair. For a moment, I was mesmerized with the rhythmic finger combing. When it turned to face us again, it lifted its angel tresses out at arm's length before allowing the hair to cascade over narrow shoulders. The creature was androgynous, masterful, and consciously seductive. It definitely was Tyrowsian, but I did not know if it was android, biological or some combination of both. "You're finally here!" it said in a breathy Tyrowsian accent.

"Do you have a number or a name?" asked Sante.

It batted its white eyelashes and scolded us. "You're impolite. How would you like it if I welcomed you both by asking if you are an Amalgam and a Casual?" The creature touched its hair near its temple mimicking a weary gesture.

"You presume to know us?" questioned Sante.

"Know you?" The creature pointed in our general direction with a trembling red lacquered fingernail. "I have files on you both that go back lifetimes. You are living proof to me that pain and pleasure die, while irony continues to live on. Whoever would have guessed that Jana Sante, one of

Simon's greatest creations, would find love with a mere Casual Human named—who are you again?"

"Hibernia Smith."

The creature interrupted me with a whistle as if it heard something incredible. "That's right, Jane Hibernia Smith. Now that's a Casual sounding name if I ever heard one! And you're direct too—aren't you? Or are you merely impatient, Hibernia?"

"I prefer to be direct; my impatience is a work in progress."

It tittered with mocking delight. "I haven't met anyone as inexcusably direct and impatient as you since I was on Earth. If memory serves me correctly—which it rarely does anymore—I believe I was somewhere in Indiana. I definitely remember that it was somewhere in the American Midwest." I had seen some strange people in Indiana in my time, but never anything like this bizarre creature. "Anyway, wherever you're from, welcome. Call me Jana Revba and we'll dispense with *qualmerrie*."

Sante's eyes jumped with surprise. "That's an interesting choice of names. Why don't you listen to the sound of my voice, Jana Revba?"

A tiny, breathless, laugh escaped from the creature that called itself Jana Revba. "My lovely 3C genetically-engineered lifegiver, I've got applications in place that prevent me from being jumped. Perhaps you would prefer to listen to the sound of my voice for a change. I'm sure I could teach you a thing or two about jumping androids. I do it all the time." Sante took a step backward. "I know I'm not as pretty as you are, but don't run away. Stay! We'll have a cup of jasmine tea together. What? Is that fear I see in your eyes, my rare beauty?"

"Fear you? I don't think so," said Sante.

"Perhaps fear is too strong a word. Perhaps, I'm sorry I startled you would be less condescending to your fragile Janaforma ego. Forgive me, nowadays I like to paint with a broader stroke. Treat me kindly, especially since I am your father's lover. Show me your deference. Come back to me and I will indulge you like a recalcitrant child. We will sit together and I will anticipate your every thought. I even will entertain your every desire." The arms and hands carved the air in an expressive gesture, beckoning us forward.

I was getting signals from Sante that this thing, whatever it was, was crazy; at the same time a voice in my head was telling me, Say anything! Find Cle and get out of this hellhole as fast as you can. "Are you the caretaker here at Herzayzen?" I asked.

"I guess that would be a fair characterization. I've used Herzayzen since the injunction on Calypso closed me down."

"We're looking for a Janaforma consort that might have been brought here, purely by mistake, about 50 cycles ago."

"Hibernia, you are still too naïve to know better, but your 3C lifegiver realizes what has happened. Didn't you tell her, Sante? My dear Casual Human, you are on a fool's mission. Your Number One Janaforma was recycled and *cis* soul has fled. I hope it finds better residence in its next incarnation."

Confirmation of Cle's death hammered another nail into my hope. Soon I would have to move fully into the fact that Cle was dead. The creature's indifference spurred my anger and I remembered the rephazer on my belt and thought of killing it for the first time. Crowding into its space, I noticed something new. Up close, its eyes were dead and its depravity undeniable. My exasperation swelled and fed my rage. This thing, this abomination, was involved in Cle's demise.

Jana Revba began to titter. It was insidious laughter, like an incessant bell awakening me to my pain. Nursing my rage like a premeditated killer, I wanted to grab it and break it over my knee like kindling to appease my pain. My hand went to the rephazer on my belt. It observed my intentions and puffed, "Humans! You all have the urge to kill. And you are a prime example of Casual Human genetics. You have a tit-for-tat mind replete with a penchant for murder. You entertain a million contradictions—don't you Hibernia Smith? You certainly are not fine and pure like the Janaforma."

"If Hibernia doesn't kill you, I will," said Sante.

Jana Revba abruptly stopped fingering his hair and his expression changed. Like a bad actor playing to the third balcony, he oozed with over-the-top stage presence. "Why my beloved Sante, you truly surprise me. I knew problems existed with some models, but I hoped it was not true of the 3C lifegiver series. If you, the finest example of a Janaforma lifegiver could be this unpredictable—could threaten death to another—I guess the whole line is defective as Ymotano suggested. I hoped that this time it might be different; but I realize now that the Janaforma are merely another failed experiment. Unfortunately, it's my responsibility to recall failed experiments such as you."

"I release you from your responsibility," said Sante.

Jana Revba snickered but it quickly dropped off into sobriety. "If it were only that easy. You are lost in a useless argument."

"You're right," said Sante. "At this moment, I am lost in a useless argument, but guess what? This useless argument will be over in about one minute because my patience is wearing extremely thin. The only reason I haven't already killed you is I'm debating whether the momentary satisfaction would be worth the stain on my soul."

Jana Revba tried to titter again but this time it sounded as if he was choking. "As far as souls are concerned, you and your cheery family of Janaforma were supposed to be living proof to me that the soul was real. Sorry, Simon. I told you so."

I was tired of playing games, tired of treating this insane creature as if he was a rational being. "Listen to me you silly son-of-a-bitch," I said in plain, Midwestern English. "We came here to find Jana Cle. I demand you either direct us to *cim* or get the hell out of our way so we can find *cim*."

Jana Revba smirked and looked truly angry for the first time. "You call me son-of-a-bitch, you daughter-of-a-bitch and daughter-of-a-bitch before her? You are not in any position to make demands. I know all about you, OSP3467, Jane Hibernia Smith, Casual Human. Your crimes are many. You owe me far more than Sante. I've traced your patchwork genes for centuries, ever since your great-grandmother cheated me in a business deal. I was kind to her too. She came whining to me about being lonely. I created a DNA matched android for her—best technology of the time—and she thanked me by stealing an android named Kyoto that I condemned to reprocessing. I do not forget betrayals such as that. You owe me for your great-grandmother's debt. With interest and all my time and trouble—the debt is quite enormous. Understand my Casual Earthling; I am not a sloppy creator. I remember crimes through *hataeasta*."

"I'm not responsible for my ancestor's debts."

"Why not Human, you stand on a platform of their accomplishment? It doesn't make any difference anyway," he said fanning the air in my direction. "Once I enjoyed hating you. When I was in Indiana, I even toyed with the notion of dropping by the Erie Pod Park and murdering you in your sleep. For years, I amused myself with the thought of revenge. Now that you are here, I feel nothing. Anyway, those DNA matched models were obsolete generations ago. Your credit is nothing more than ancient change in my pockets. What gives me pleasure now is seeing you squirm as you stew over your precious Number One Janaforma. Be honest for a change, Hibernia Smith. You are neither clever nor unique; you're a mongrel. What was that marvelously absurd document you prepared for your doctoral thesis? Oh, yes! You called it, The Genetic and Ethnographic Migrations of Humans." You should have studied with me. I could have taught you a great deal about genetic and ethnographic migrations."

Jana Revba perused me carefully from head to toe. "You resemble your great-grandmother. Perhaps you're a bit more refined around the edges. I guess the surgeon's hand has buffed-off the prominent, genetic bump on your nose, has corrected that insipid, Smith chin and mouth, which I have detested for centuries. Your face makes no difference anymore. I see through all your invented faces. Suffice it to say, you are as much a thief as your great-grandmother was. You've seduced my beautiful Janaforma children for your sexual pleasure, contaminating them with your tainted heritage and corrupted their minds. How much easier it would be if you had died in that space taxi."

Something in me then thought I remembered this Tyrowsian shadow—lurking, sulking behind curtains, and whispering doubts in my ear. Was Jana

Revba the curse that followed me, the foot that extended to trip me up every time I reached out for happiness?

Jana Revba raised his hand, brushing the thought of me away and returned to Sante. "My real concern is you." Jana Revba's pale eyes misted over with something like emotion for the first time. "Please try to understand, my beauty. I worshipped Simon. He made me believe in you, made me believe that together we were creating something better than honest, Casual life—something that could sustain its spiritual perfection. Now that I know we failed, it saddens me to see our dream die."

"Do you think I'm going to smile and say 'thank you Father,' then obediently march into your mind-stripping chamber?"

"You can't take life personally. Somewhere down the line, parts of you can be genetically recycled into others. That should give you some comfort."

Sante's tone turned bitter. "Don't take life personally? *Qualmerrie*, for you do not know me at all. You cannot recycle me because you want me to evolve faster. I am who I am—a replica of your imperfections. You and I, we are not different; we are one. Our problem is you believe in nothing and I believe in myself."

"Aaah!" proclaimed Jana Revba. "Words—more programmed words! I know death seems harsh; but I initiated this recall because I must stand behind my creations. It was in the original contract."

Sante took the rephazer from *lis* belt and pointed it at Jana Revba for the first time. "I'm done. How do you want to die?"

"That rephazer is meaningless! You and I—our actions here—make little difference in the larger scheme. Death is inescapable, part of the original contract with us all. The Cerribeame will roam the heavens forever."

"Perhaps death is inescapable; but when my death comes, you will not be there to witness it. Understand, you echo-from-the-past, I am a lifegiver. I have a creative spark you will never know." Sante released the safety on the rephazer.

"Wait!" Jana Revba held up one delicate hand. The blood red enameled talons trembled at the tips for the first time. A new thought danced over Jana Revba's face. His voice gushed with excitement as the thought came spilling out of him. "You are so exquisite, so breathtakingly beautiful. I might spare one. Stay with me and we could explore our mutual digressions. Sleep with me; share my bed and maybe in time we could find a new way to overcome the problems with the 3C gene."

My rage exploded and I reached out and grabbed the inviting cloud of Jana Revba's hair, yanking it wildly. I felt the adrenaline pump through my veins as I released my rage. Jana Revba was shocked. His tiny red eyes darted around the chamber looking for an escape while his hands came up to protect his sensitive Tyrowsian hair. I released him, but my hands held gobs of hair that I tore from his scalp.

Jana Revba tumbled to the stone floor screaming in agony. The screaming ebbed into moans and then whimpers as he wrapped himself into a ball. "How does it feel to really be alive?" asked Sante. For the first time, Jana Revba did not answer. When the body did not move after a minute, Sante warned me, "Stay back." Then *le* carefully approached the creature and bent over it to check for a pulse. "No pulse," *le* reported. Then *le* pushed up its eyelids to check for trademarks.

"What is it?" I asked.

"It's a fucking abomination!"

Sante backed up, aimed *lis* rephazer at the creature, and squeezed the trigger. A stream of light left the weapon, igniting a face. White hair turned red—then black—then disappeared. The body flashed for a split second like a Roman candle before crumbling into a loose pile of gray ash on the stone floor. The smoke was still clearing and Sante was already spreading the hot ash around with the tip of *lis* boot. "I'm looking for its brain," *le* explained. When *le* found it, it was a tiny silver capsule about 5 millimeters long.

"What are you going to do with it?" I ask.

"Destroy it," and *le* adjusted *lis* rephazer to a concentrated pinpoint. Even with concentrated rephazer fire, it took nearly a minute to melt the capsule into an oozing stream of hot metal."

"Okay, what was it?" I demanded to know.

"The Janaforma call them terminal clones. They can't exist without a biological home base supporting them. The biological unit uses them, entering and leaving at will. Destroying the brain, that biological unit will never be able to use this clone again."

****

"Let's go find Cle," I said.

The dungeons of Herzayzen contained over a thousand inmates in various stages of reprocessing. The robotic Igors had everything under perfect control—machines servicing machines and sentient beings alike—hardly noticing the occasional quickening of the latest recalls. The basic android staff ignored us completely as we scanned the gruesome chambers.

We did not have time to determine if Jana Revba's victims were remnants of friends or foes. Of course, we found androids, but we also found Humans, Ganats, Esquimaux, Naub and a surprising number of Tyrowsians conveniently dumped into the hell of Herzayzen. No one we encountered was alive—as we normally define the word. I wondered how a creature that shared Simon Forma's dream of the beautiful and perfect Janaforma, could have fallen so far into the depths of depravity. If a divine spark of creativity ever motivated Jana Revba, we found no evidence of it at

Herzayzen. What we found instead, suggested this genetic da Vinci had grossly missed his mark. Those dark urges—the diseases of the soul that twist and distort the mind—had dominated inside these prison walls.

We discovered a morgue-like holding tank for the newly erased. Freshly shaved bodies lay on long tables in head-to-heel, lifeless precision. In another chamber, we found approximately fifty creatures handcuffed and shackled to the floor, sitting in their own excrement. The smell was nauseating, rank, and vile. Like bald infants, in a too-crowded, day-care center, they sat shoulder-to-shoulder amusing themselves with a few scattered objects waiting for their new minds. First, I spotted the empty shell of what had been Piper, the hairdresser—her mind and her long, red hair gone.

Cle sat directly behind her chained to the floor by *cis* wrists. *Ce* was still wearing the same clothing *ce* wore the night *ce* left our quarters but nothing was left of it save a few tattered rags. *Ce* was filthy and dried blood caked *cis* scalp. *Ce* pulled and yanked not knowing what *ce* was struggling against in *cis* empty mind. *Ce* still hated anything on *cis* wrists. New hairs crisscrossed like patches of peach fuzz between the deep wounds where the Cerribeame torturers had burned *cis* mind away.

Sante and I wept in utter grief.

Cle sat with *cis* legs apart toying with four wooden blocks in front of *cim*, shifting and turning them with both hands. *Ce* was involved in what *ce* was doing with the full focus of *cis* concentration, as if *ce* were desperately attempting to make sense out of the Universal letters imprinted on the blocks. I put my hands on *cis*, helping him put the H and I block together. "Hi," I said.

Cle looked up at me with a dumb, vacant expression. *Ce* did not know me, but was able to imitate my voice. "Hi?" *ce* parroted.

Silent tears were streaming down Sante's face and dripping off *lis* chin. Taking the mediscan off *lis* utility belt, *le* swept the length of Cle's body. "Cle is dead. The iridic scan shows only minimal activity in the brain."

"I don't care. We are taking Cle out of here."

Sante swallowed hard. "You're our cartographer. You brought us here to discover the truth and now we know it. I still say it should end here. Cle is dead. I'm telling you this not as your lover but as a physician. We can't make this tortured body into Cle again. "

"I'm taking Cle out of this shithole, with or without your help," I announced with stony resolution.

"So be it; we are one. Let's make it happen."

We had no way of helping any of the others because we carried no communicators. We were afraid to use the functioning multidexes at Herzayzen because we might have alarmed the programmed staff to the fact that we were intruders. Besides, who would help us? I felt my cynicism mounting. I was sure the power structure that supported Herzayzen Prison had emanated from a larger base than Jana Revba's twisted mind. My experience suggested that greed always lurked behind evil, conveniently subjugated under the heading, "business as usual."

I continued to run the show and decided that we should leave the forcefield activated and all other mechanics of the place undisturbed. "Once we are free in space we will have time to reevaluate," I said.

Sante broke the cuffs that imprisoned Cle. "Put this on," said Sante handing Cle a spare breather off *lis* belt. Cle took it, wondering what to do with it.

"Come on, Sante." I was exasperated with *lis* sudden lack of empathy. "We have to dress *cim*." I put the goggles and breather on Cle. I smiled at *cim* as if we were playing a game and *ce* cooperated.

"I'm sorry," said Sante. "This is impossible for me." Sante took a vitarattha out of *lis* pocket and pinned it on the remnants of Cle's shirt. We moved quickly, threading our way back toward freedom. We ran out into the smoggy atmosphere, heading toward the glass-topped parapet. It was not easy getting across the glass a second time because Sante had to carry Cle. By the time we crossed, I had ripped the sole of my boot. With a little coaxing, we persuaded Cle to step onto the small lift pedals attached to the magnetic rope. Cle hide *cis* face against my shoulder while Sante cast a loop around the three of us. All the pitons held and we descended in record time.

We hit the ground and dropped the rope and braces, abandoning it with all the other trash relegated to this world. We raced over the open fields of trash and I stopped several times to adjust my flapping sole. We headed toward the enormous mountain of old tires where we hid the whitesuits. "There, right ahead," panted Sante's muffled voice from under *lis* breather.

Sante and I worked furiously threading the extra whitesuit on Cle's uncooperative legs. When we tried to put the helmet over *cis* head, *ce* began to fight. *Cis* arms and fists beat the air and *ce* tore at the helmet as if *ce* was drowning. The back of *cis* hand came up, cracking me in the jaw—smashing my teeth together in pain.

Sante attempted to calm *cim* by touching *cim* in several places but it did not work. "Damn!" Sante said. "There's not enough mind left to calm." Instead, *le* took a syringe off *lis* belt and emptied a cartridge of medisleep into Cle's neck. *Cis* knees collapsed and *ce* sank to the ground.

"Hurry," said Sante. "That's only good for about twenty minutes."

****

We put on our jetpacks and pulled down our visors. We supported Cle's weight between us and linked the whitesuit belts for safety. In a coordinated effort on the jetpacks, we lifted off the planet Herzayzen and into the peace of Sante's space. Cle began to wake up as we climbed into the safety of the pulsar. The ordeal and the medisleep had left *cim* exhausted. Sante scanned Cle again and said, "We can fix *cis* body as if it never happened, but Cle is still gone. This body is simple raw material, a potential waiting for a soul."

"Forget *cis* soul; what about *cis* scalp? *Ce* has open wounds and the wounds are clogged with hair."

"We don't have enough water to bath *cim* and I don't have the right equipment to clean *cim* the way *ce* needs to be cleaned." Sante ended up wiping Cle's head with sterile wipes, applying a layer of antibiotic ointment, and then lightly wrapping it with gauze. Then *le* took a prefilled syringe of antibiotic, and emptied it into Cle's arm. Cle had grown so inured to pain that *ce* didn't even blink.

"Do you consider yourself a spiritual person?" I asked Sante.

"Not any more. Why do you ask?"

"I thought you might know a prayer or Trinity witch incantation, something that would call Cle back. Cle loves you; Cle will come back if you ask *cim* to come."

"Even if I had the power, I would not ask *cim*. I don't have the right to ask *cim* and neither do you. Whatever happened to Cle in Herzayzen Prison was horrendous. If *ce* returned now, *ce* would bring all *cis* raw trauma with *cim*. I am not wise enough to help *cim* through it. I couldn't even help Cle with *cis* Sutcay Tay trauma."

I made a bed for Cle on the rear banquette. *Ce* cooperated fully with us and when we put *cim* to bed, *ce* stuck *cis* knuckles in *cis* mouth and began to nurse. *Ce* was peaceful as if nothing bad ever touched *cim*. "I wanted a child," said Sante with a vacant expression. "I never guessed it would be Cle."

"I need to ask you something," I said. "Once you told me you would tell me about your first experience in space. You said you would tell me after we made love, but, I would like to hear about it now, if possible."

Sante remembered. "I'm not sure it makes sense anymore. It was a feeling of incredible peace—a feeling of oneness and connection. I knew space was where I belonged. That was the gift space gave me." *Lis* face turned sad and *le* laid hands on Cle's sleeping body. "I don't know if I'll feel anything that good ever again."

****

Whatever Sante lost *lis* psychic sense of cosmic direction was still keen and *le* flew the pulsar back to Aeternus and landed it at Vitarattha R & D without aid of navigation. We decided to go see Admiral Vista who lived at the OSSS Club. *Cis* apartment was in the rear of the compound where it was quiet. We went around the building, instead of through the main entrance to avoid anyone seeing us. Sante tapped on the window of Vista's apartment and a moment later *ce* opened the door.

Sante put *lis* finger across Vista lips and pulled *cim* outside the door.

"Mother-in-heaven, I can't believe you succeeded!" Vista whispered in joy. *Cis* eyes seemed to feast on the sight of Cle. "Oh! No! What have they done to you, my precious child?" Cle shrank from Vista's obvious angst.

"Cle is gone," said Sante. "This is genetic emptiness waiting for a soul."

Vista bit back tears. "Then, you were too late."

"I'm sorry," said Sante looking personally responsible and more defeated than ever.

"All that genius wasted!" mourned Vista. "They've won! They killed more than our Number One Janaforma; they've destroyed our last hope." Tears washed down Vista's face. I saw something new in *cim*. Something I did not know was possible for a Janaforma. Vista was awash in the symptoms of hopelessness and disgust. It was the first symptom of FSP.

"There's more bad news," said Sante. "I killed someone. As Cle once said, 'It is difficult to keep death at the door.'" Vista merely raised *cis* eyelids, *cis* expression suggesting—it was bound to happen.

"I killed a terminal clone that I believe belonged to Jana Revba." That statement confused Vista and Sante began to tell Vista everything.

"Do you know where Rebecca is?" I interjected along the way. "We thought she would be the best to handle the evacuation of Herzayzen."

"That's my bad news," said Vista. "Rebecca has disappeared."

"There's a plan afoot to recall all the Janaforma," said Sante. "In a stampede, sometimes everything and everyone in the vicinity goes down."

I began to think about what Rebecca said to Sante, about trusting people and how few people knew the truth. "Rebecca was right. We need to trust a lot more people. We can use the multidex to spread the word and we can pray the media is free enough to tell the truth about Herzayzen Prison. Let everyone weigh it on The Triangle for a change. When they do, we will get the support we need from people who care."

****

We began to make plans. We bought food, medical supplies and new utilitarian clothing and then we returned to Vitarattha R & D for protection. While Vista reconnected the control boards on the pulsar, Sante and I gave Cle a shower and took showers ourselves. Sante laced a milkshake that *le* bought for Cle with a narcotic. When Cle fell asleep, Sante closed the open wounds with a laser. As we ate, we struggled to prepare a document we could release over the multidex but, without Cle, we were getting nowhere fast. Cle woke up and began whimpering. We offered *cim* food and *ce* refused to eat. We took *cim* to the toilet and *ce* sat on it and played with the toilet paper, spinning it around and around until Sante put *lis* hand on Cle's and said, "Stop!"

"Stop!" barked Cle like a perfect parrot.

"Maybe *ce* is thirsty," I said and I gave *cim* water. *Ce* drank the entire glass of water and then held up the glass with this hopeful idiotic expression on *cis* face. *Ce* drank the next glass of water too and then vomited all over the front of *cis* clothes. It took another hour to clean up the mess and by that time, Sante and I were exhausted. Cle fell asleep, but Sante and I were still trying to decide what to say in the document we wanted to release on the multidex.

"Come on," said Sante. "I want to show you something." We went down a short hallway and stopped at a door. "This was Kerisa's office," said Sante. "She was the real inventor of the vitarattha, but she always shared credit with Reyneldi and Dyne." *Le* laughed, remembering something. "She used to say the vitarattha was the scientific manifestation of the motherly instinct—like a mother's arms and that's why a vitarattha feels so good when a person activates it. She was an incredible person. The best in Cle, those things we love most in *cim*, came from her."

We went inside Kerisa's office. A few mementos still sat on her desk and on some dusty shelves—a couple of photographs—one of the beautiful Kerisa herself smiling happily between Dyne and Reyneldi and another of a cherubic Cle—perhaps *ce* was five years old. Beside the picture was a rock painted blue with a sparkly star in the center. I picked it up and put it in my pocket. Then I decided to take the pictures too. "Someday, I will tell the new Cle who the old Cle was and about *cis* parents," I said and I began to cry. "I'm so sorry that I forced you to go to Herzayzen Prison. I know I'm stubborn. It's taken me all this time to realize—but now I know you're right. Cle is never coming back."

"I've made peace with the new situation," Sante said. "You made the right decision and I'm glad we recued Cle. Cle is still a 3C Janaforma; the genetic potential is still there. It may not be exactly what we pictured our life to be, but it is an acceptable alternative. Who knows? Perhaps in time, this consort might need us as much as we need *cim*. It's for sure that *ce* will have the sex drive of a consort. Even if *ce* decides to leave us, *ce* might be willing to give us a drop or two of *cis* genetic material so we can reproduce." Sante tried to smile. The Janaforma lifegiver that rarely slept was near exhaustion. "This isn't over yet," *le* promised.

Vista walked into the room. "The pulsar is ready," *ce* said wiping *cis* dirty hands on a rag. "Do you have the document finished?"

"We haven't even started it," I said.

Vista appeared worried. "You haven't changed your mind?"

"No, but we're not Cle," said Sante. That was the truth. None of us possessed the verve for language that could equal Cle's talent. Still we had to try. On a portable multidex, we prepared a spool and recorded our message. It took the combined efforts of Sante, Vista, and me to write it, while we alternated efforts at babysitting Cle. Upon completion, Sante ejected the prepared message from the multidex. "Let's get into space," *le* said tucking it inside the breast of *lis* jumpsuit.

"I'm not coming," said Vista.

"Don't be foolish," I said. "The Tyrowsians know you are involved. You're carrying Janaforma self-sacrifice too far."

"No," insisted Vista. "I thought about it while outfitting the pulsar. I want to stay on Aeternus. My fight is here."

Sante argued with *cim*, but Vista's mind was set. Was it FSP or did *ce* weigh it on The Triangle? Whatever the reason, *ce* was adamant and refused to leave Aeternus.

"I'm a lot stronger than you," said Sante. "I could force you to come with us."

"Yeah, I know you are," said Vista. "You are the most ruthless Janaforma I've ever met and I mean that with reverent respect."

How strange to hear Sante described as ruthless. Once, I thought *le* was the most angelic creature I ever beheld. That Sante was gone exactly like the demigod Cle. It was proof positive to me that when the divine wrestles in the mud with Humans and Tyrowsians, wings were going to get broken.

We all embraced. Vista was now familiar to Cle so Cle had no objection to Vista's embrace or the kiss on the forehead. Cle yawned. *Cis* stomach was full at that moment and all he wanted to do was sleep. *Ce* had no memories to spur on *cis* sadness and keep *cim* awake.

Vista sniffed and wiped *cis* tears off Cle's cheek. "Take care of this child," *ce* said.

We never saw Vista again. Two cycles later, the Tyrowsian Constabulary discovered *cis* body when they broke into Vitarattha R & D. Vista had committed suicide moments earlier. The Tyrowsian media called Vista the first Janaforma victim of FSP.

****

The pulsar shot out of hanger 34 and this time our escape was not so slick. For a split second, the pulsar was at exactly the right angle to an incoming light wave. The wave and pulsar collided causing the velocity of the light wave to alter and create prism-streams of light to shoot off in every direction. Under normal circumstances, this phenomenon meant nothing, but when Aeternus Space Command saw prism streams of light changing at sharp angles and no authorized ship was supposed to be inside that particular space window, then they knew an interloper had breached Aeternus space. Sante shook *lis* head and said, "They had to see that. I'm going to skip inside the Lanlorn Asteroid Belt and hide there.

Inside the asteroid belt, only the red and amber of the sensor panel gave us light. Sante and I had begun holding Cle and cuddling *cim* until *ce* fell asleep. This time I was holding *cim* and *ce* began sucking *cis* clenched fist. Maternal responses flickered to life in me. Overcome with my desire to love *cim*, nurture *cim*, and reclaim *cis* lost soul, I submitted to my urges. Unbuttoning my blouse, I offered *cim* my breast. All the hungry tension relaxed in *cim* as *ce* took my nipple into *cis* eager mouth. *Cis* throat gurgled with happiness as *ce* began to nurse. A genetic link to basic survival was still alive in *cim*. At that moment, I was grateful to the Tyrowsians and the horrible Cerribeame for leaving Cle's need intact. Protective peace flowed between us; my loin filled with ancient contractions and my heart ached with wanting.

Sante said nothing, merely watched from the corner of *lis* eyes as *le* pretended to stare out the window of the pulsar.

Cle's childlike serenity was short-lived. *Ce* put *cis* hand between *cis* legs as an uncontrollable itch began to annoy *cim*. *Ce* squirmed, losing my nipple. *Ce* groaned with a confused, new agony of wanting. *Cis* erection, *cis* exigent need for sexual connection would not go away, demanding full attention.

Sante suddenly seemed engaged and *le* exclaimed, "A soul has moved inside *cis* body and you've found its thread. We must pull the soul forth and weave it into a new life." *Le* opened my pants slipping *lis* hand down between my underwear and flesh verifying the truth in the wetness there. *Le* brought out *lis* hand first touching it to *lis* lips, sanctifying it, and then offered it to Cle. Cle tasted me, savored it, sliding *cis* tongue back and forth over the primal memory of lust.

Cle looked eager and alert for the first time and Sante said, "Cle?"

Speaking like a rote liturgist, Cle reeled off, "Sante! Sante! Sante!" *Cis* words rang like a bell before matins. Cle stared at me with wounded eyes. *Cis* mouth poised—waiting for *cis* brain to form new thoughts, struggling to find the proper words. *Ce* grew impatient with *cim*self—stuttered, "ah-pa … ah …ma,"—shaking *cis* head in frustration. Words seemed trapped within *cim*. *Ce* choked, trying to free them. *Ce* sighed, going limp between us in total frustration.

Sante's eyes filled with tears embracing Cle for the first time since we found *cim*. "I love you my precious consort," said Sante.

Cle melted into Sante looking up into *lis* eyes. "Recreate love?" Cle cooed with childlike innocence. *Cis* speech was perfect.

"I'll show you how," whispered Sante and *le* began to manipulate Cle, speaking to *cim* with perfect oral grace, showing *cim* how to love, by example. I remembered Sante had worked as a sexual surrogate. "Yes," *le* admitted. "I have played the conduit countless times before." Sex was the bridge Cle used to reclaim *cis* life. "Relax," whispered Sante, urging Cle on like Cyrano in the bushes to make the proper moves. Cle gasped when Sante took *cim*. Then *ce* sighed with delight, fusing everything into pleasure as *cis* mind opened to love. Sante and I held Cle tight until the end, until love reunited us.

****

Later, Sante loaded the special spool into the multidex. "Bring Cle here," *le* said to me. Sante took Cle's finger and pressed send on the proper key.

Instantaneously, the message we prepared with Vista's help appeared everywhere in the Orion Spur. Sante laughed. "Cle's next multidex bill is going to break *cis* bank account."

We read the document once more as it appeared on our screen.

< *Hataeasta* > and *ra tukcah*!

I was your Number One Janaforma. I was kidnapped, tortured, and my mind stripped clean of memories yet through love and my loved ones, I still can bring you this important message. The Cerribeame are real and Tyrowsian business interests across the Orion Spur use the Cerribeame to bend life to their twisted purpose. Herzayzen prison holds all the evidence to support my claim. Plans are underway for the extermination of the Janaforma people. Only through Community action, fueled by love, can we stop this evil plan.

To my Tyrowsian brothers and sisters, a special message: Time traps us all on the unfolding hub. When we pretend time is unreal, *hataeasta* is perverted. It is time to be responsible for our actions through time—for time entangles us until death. Let us move forward in love by examining our assumptions of truth—knowing that the search is merely a push-up for the mind—realizing the effort will make us strong.

Signed, Jana Cle, Number One Janaforma

I later heard that when the message appeared on the multidex screens across Aeternus, what Tyrowsians always wanted to happen did. Time stood still. Off-World News, "Orion's Most Important Network," picked up our story and every news-droid in the business quoted and misquoted portions of the story; but the word did get out. Enough curiosity still existed in the universe to stop and listen. From the safety of our pulsar, we watched and listened as our letter began to echo all over Orion space.

****

The Aeternus Constabulary dispatched a ship to Herzayzen to investigate our claims. The media arrived too and for two cycles, we watched The Horrors of Herzayzen replay over the multidex. Meanwhile, the Cerribeame were sweeping across the universe on a preprogrammed death mission for Jana Revba. It was impossible to determine the life span of the Cerribeame. However, Sante guaranteed me that somewhere there was a band of Cerribeame specifically programmed for us.

"Is this a psychic prediction?" I asked. *Le* merely shrugged.

A few cycles later, a Ganat Cerribeame ship landed at Herzayzen. It was one of the old opalescent tugs used as a medical supply ship in another century. It was business as usual for the crew as they began to unload their cargo of individuals. The media was as startled as the Cerribeame, who were not android and could react with the speed of true Ganats. They fled, escaping into space. The media began to suggest the implications ran deeper than an old Tyrowsian man named Jana Revba and a few programmed killers. Real people were involved in real murder at Herzayzen.

Detective Shreeher was among the first wave from Aeternus to land on Herzayzen. He was the one that recognized Rebecca on a slab in the holding room and revived her from her drug-induced stupor. The one thing she lost was her hair. Rebecca remained at Herzayzen, working with Shreeher, to find hospitals for the inmates and to encourage the androids along toward jumping.

After a few cycles, Shreeher asked for assistance from the Orion Spur Alliance because the job was enormous. He did not get much help. One of the popular excuses for apathy that came out of Herzayzen was, 'Some messes are too big to clean up.' Herzayzen certainly fit that bill.

Five cycles later, the public was already growing tired of Herzayzen. Every talking head on the multidex had debated The Horrors of Herzayzen. The media fished around for a fresh angle and it did not take long to find one. The newly commissioned Admiral Jana Devina stepped into the spotlight of twinkling-fame to oblige the hungry media.

A force of Janaforma—Devina named them The Janaforma Elite—organized several rescue missions against the Ganat Opals as the media now referred to the Cerribeame. The media interviewed Devina and she said, "I won't rest until every last Ganat Opal is destroyed." She took off her cap with the logo 'Get that Ganat!' and waved it in the air.

The speedy Cerribeame females were formidable opponents for the Janaforma. Several old style space battles ensued between The Janaforma Elite and the Ganat Opals. Devina won every one. We knew she would. She had made herself into a genetically engineered killing machine. Sante wept as *ce* watched footage over the multidex, declaring her the antithesis of everything the Janaforma stood for.

The media showed us with exaggerated fanfare the many encounters between the Janaforma and the Ganats and always, Devina's smiling post-victory face. The war became a media event. The Horrors of Herzayzen were *keirtoyyan hataeasta**. Suddenly the OSSS, under pressure from the Ganats, declared Devina a disruptive rebel and a price was put on her head. Devina had confused a legitimate Ganat medical ship with one of the Cerribeame ships and destroyed the medical ship and everyone aboard.

Inside the marble buildings of Noble City, the capitol of the Orion Spur Alliance, politicians hammered their fists in excitement and complained about "the crisis on Aeternus." The big wheels assembled and not an empty luxury suite could be had anywhere, up or down the main boulevard of Noble City. A committee assembled with an enormous budget and a

*"forgotten"; language origin, Cuneate
mandate from the Orion Spur Council to investigate possible Tyrowsian

involvement with Jana Revba. The budget was big because everyone knew large grinding-wheels needed frequent and generous oiling.

Aeternus was in the spotlight. People who never heard of Aeternus suddenly could point to it on a star chart. One of the media's favorite new twists was comparing Aeternus to Calypso and how the Ganats lost their planet to Tyrowsian business interests. When the big wheels began to turn, Ymotano and Mi Cochon were the first to go. I do not know where Ymotano went, but he left Aeternus in a hurry. Later, Stevie Stress would tell jokes about Mi Cochon and say that he was such a glutton for punishment that he took a job as mayor of Philadelphia. Meanwhile we wondered why no one was paying attention to the Janaforma anymore. Aeternus was quiet. Static filled the communication wavelengths from that area of space. We decided to land and have a look around. Sante performed a fly-by over the Space Security grid. "Request permission to land?" *le* singled several times but there was no reply. Sante landed in the middle of the empty grid without permission and said, "Close canopy." No one answered because no one was on duty. We took off again and returned to Vitarattha R & D, landing there.

****

At Vitarattha R & D, we jumped out of the pulsar and looked around. We soon realized there was no tube service. We walked for miles dragging Cle between us. The deserted streets were dark and locked into permanent night mode. The closer to the old core we got, the more it became apparent that Aeternus was in deep trouble. Evidence of vandalism was everywhere, shattered store windows, litter, and graffiti-covered walls. Somewhere faraway we heard a high-pitched scream. It echoed through the emptiness and then died away leaving no clues.

We saw an old Tyrowsian biodroid. She was carrying a bulging suitcase under one arm and a multidex under the other. The price tag was still on the multidex. "Hey wait a minute," shouted Sante as she raced by. "What's happening?"

She stopped—sparing us the focus of one desperate eye. "The government's falling! The inner core'al blow without the Tyrowsians running it!"

"The inner core?" asked Sante.

"Sure," she said. "It's old. No one can run it but the Tyrowsians," and she raced off like a lunatic into the night. It was the same all over Aeternus. Life was scrambling to survive. The lobby of the Hilton was empty of personnel—android or otherwise. Electricity was out and with no stairs, no way existed to get up to our apartment.

We walked through underground areas. Someone had smashed the windows of La Carrefore Boutique and the manikins lay nude, disrobed of their designer frocks. Cle whimpered endlessly. Sante and I took turns trying to soothe *cim*. "We have to get off the streets," Sante said.

"Let's try Patra and Liart," I suggested.

We arrived at their place just as they and some others were leaving. Everyone was overjoyed to see us. We all cried except Cle. We joined other Janaforma and decided to open an emergency headquarters at Space Security Headquarters. Patra and several other Janaforma volunteered to go to the inner core of Aeternus and attempt to stabilize running systems and get full life-support back online.

I worked with Liart and Vertain trying to get the multidex working on emergency systems. When the electricity came on, we all cheered. The picture on the multidex widened across the screen and opened to Off-World News emergency service. "Flat screen will have to do," said Vertain. "We don't have enough energy for a hologram." A news droid was reading an open letter from the president of the Orion Spur Alliance calling for "calm in the crisis on Aeternus."

****

Thanks to the Janaforma, Aeternus held that cycle.

The Orion Spur Council sent an interim viceroy to prop up the Aeternus infrastructure. The Council's lackluster choice was a mousy Tyrowsian named Rownard who became famous for saying, "Bad things should not happen to nice people." As soon as Rownard ensconced himself in the comfort of 3 Lily Pool Lane, a contingent of Janaforma visited. They sat around and drank tea. That's when Rownard first made his famous statement, "Bad things shouldn't happen to nice people," but he used it often after that.

The Janaforma reaffirmed their position to Rownard saying they would not return to space to serve any living soul until the Aeternus government met the demands set forth in The Proposal. A standoff ensued. The renaissance went into a holding pattern because Rownard pleaded for time. That's when he used a variation of, "some messes are too big to clean up." He coined, "A mess this big is going to take some time to clean up." Still, the Janaforma had new hope. A deadline of fourteen cycles was set.

Rownard used this time to freeze all Janaforma capital and business assets. "Just until the matter can be settled," he suggested to the media. At the end of fourteen cycles, he said, "I've come to Aeternus to offer a new vision." Absurdity moved closer to insanity when Rownard suggested the Janaforma go back to work until the government had time to review all complaints.

Delay destroyed the trust. The Janaforma were infuriated with Rownard and appealed directly to the Orion Spur Council. The absurdity escalated. The Council stated that it could not interfere in the internal political workings of Aeternus although the Orion Spur Council had been the one to appoint Rownard. The absurdity moved fully into insanity.

The bald Rebecca came back from Herzayzen and attempted to help. The Janaforma drafted another letter, restating the original demands of The Proposal, sending copies to the Orion Spur Council. The council countered, demanding Admiral Jana Devina be arrested as a prerequisite to any debate on the issue. No Janaforma would move against Devina. A short time later, Devina's second in command found her body. She had committed suicide. The media reported that she was the second Janaforma victim of FSP.

All talk froze. Meanwhile it was business as usual. With Devina out of the picture, the Cerribeame were free to attack Herzayzen Prison. Shreeher and a few members of the media barely escaped with their lives.

****

Life was one *keirtoyyan Hataeasta** after another. I sat on the floor, in circle after circle talking of Vista, Devina, and others. The Janaforma circle was smaller now. Janaforma leaders either were dead martyrs or reduced to quiet sadness, like Sante.

It was just after Devina's *keirtoyyan Hataeasta* that hope rose like a phoenix from the ashes yet again. The force of many against the big wheel somehow jarred it and information began to trickle out of the ancient AIRS institute on Calypso. When Off-World News announcement, "Janaforma genetic records will be made public," it was a cause of much celebration.

****

On the planet Calypso, on the appointed morning, several interested parties waited for the Artificial Intelligence and Robotic Systems to open its doors. Excitement was high. Sante said, "A circus-like atmosphere hung in the air. It was noisy. Several Esquimaux children ran barefoot through the reflecting pool in front of the building. The media complained that the children were getting the cameras wet and a fight broke out between the media and the Esquimaux parents. The streetguards came raging down the walkway and restored order with the removal of the children hustling them off for mindstripping." That day, the story of Esquimaux child abuse became a bigger media story than Jana Revba's records.

Another news story quickly displaced the story of abused Esquimaux children. A group of 50 Tyrowsian mystics, living in space pods, outside Aeternus, had committed suicide. This was happening all over the Orion Spur in what the media began calling, "the new Fundamental SocioPsychic Epidemic among Tyrowsians." I remembered how Sante had cried for those space-pod mystics. *Le* did not have many tears left these days. *Le* never complained that life had dragged *lim* down to its level; but when the announcement came that Calypso planned to release Janaforma genetic

---

* memorial service; language origin, Cuneate

records, Sante was excited for the first time in ages and *le* was there that morning on Calypso with the Esquimaux children. *Le* saw the brutality of the well-armed streetguards who snapped bones with glee. *Le* was the one who administered first aid to the fallen in the street. The experience embittered *lim* even more against Tyrowsians. "You're right," *le* said to me. "There is no hope for a universe that can destroy its own children."

Lis bitterness did not deter *lis* purpose. *Le* returned from Calypso with nine carriers filled end-to-end with copied spools. Unfortunately, Simon Forma and Jana Revba files were indecipherable, encrypted in an alien language. It did not daunt Sante. *Le* expected the problem. It took *lim* three months to translate the first four words that began with, "Library of All Creation." Sante cursed the fact that Cle was not there to help. Sometimes *le* would look at Cle and then look away as though the sight of Cle caused *lim* pain.

I tried not to mind the loneliness while Sante worked; but I began to think again of Clidmore and Kinsey. They had evacuated Aeternus during the crisis—had gone to Wonder World to wait it out. Sante and I had a serious conversation and I told *lim* how I felt. *Le* listened to me as *le* always did. A few cycles later, Sante, Cle and I caught the Morpheus shuttle to Wonder World with our hats in our hands. Sante and I had come to Wonder World to join the Clidmore and Kinsey expedition that would explore the Square of Pegasus.

I finally shook hands with my idols in a small unimpressive building while the sound of merry-go-round music played in the street below. Clidmore and Kinsey had been following the story of Aeternus on their multidex. They knew about us and immediately offered us jobs. It was an opportunity, the kind I always wanted as a cartographer. We soon discovered we would have friends along the way. Vertain, Patra, and Liart signed up a few cycles later along with hundreds of other Janaforma. These people would become our extended family for the rest of our lives.

"I guess Cle was more psychic than *ce* realized," said Sante. "The Janaforma are leaving Aeternus for good. It's merely taken us a little longer than *ce* predicted."

Sante and I took Cle to see all the sights of Wonder World while we were there. *Ce* was the perfect age to enjoy it. Ce was precocious—the perfect mimic. *Ce* had the language abilities of a ten-year-old child, the emotional age of someone five, and the emerging libido of a teenager. *Ce* questioned Sante and I about everything and made fun of the way I wrote information down on scraps of paper. Without Sante's help, Cle was becoming too much for me to handle

At Wonder World, I saw the real Amtaee Htsoiure play his big drums. At Future World, we searched the stalls looking for some sign of Bell. We found her or perhaps she found us. All I know for sure is we met again. She appeared different. She no longer wore the green silky skirts of the Trinity witches. She was dressed as a gypsy in a costume of purple, gold, and blue.

"Ah!" she said upon seeing us. She looked at Cle, taking both cis hands in hers. She touched the lines of *cis* palms. "Through the cleansing of this soul's sacrifice, what once was can be again," she predicted. "Your fortunes are still the same. I see the possibility of yet unraveling the mysteries."

"And Dulce?" asked Sante.

"He is free," she said, "Thank you for that. Oh, and by the way—" She smiled. "The Trinity curse is lifted. You are guided by your true stars."

****

We returned to Aeternus for the last time. I packed my meager belongings, my great-grandmother's paperweight, my mother's china, and my collection of Universal Geographics. Finally, no reason remained to delay. This goodbye was for keeps. Signing on with Clidmore and Kinsey would take us on a journey to the star regions of Pegasus. This commitment would take generations to complete. We were done with Earth and Aeternus too. Perhaps some messes were too big to clean up. For sure— this one was too big—even for the Janaforma.

EPILOGUE

I have left life in the Orion Spur behind. Each year the stars of home grow dimmer. From here, I look out toward many tomorrows. Stars, worlds, and lives flash by like dreams of *hataeasta*.

We hear news rarely out here, but we do hear that Aeternus has fallen into oblivion. Orion space is dangerous space nowadays. Space Security is defunct because no Janaforma remain to run it. With no jobs and not enough people, Aeternus has become a ghost port. As far as I know no plaques or monuments were erected anywhere to the Janaforma for their sacrifice and service—plaques and monuments require actual people who remember and care. Now and again, someone among us mentions Aeternus and conversation turns to those past cycles.

We grow stronger out here. We work together and we take strength from our togetherness. I value the personal commitment I've made to self-sacrifice, altruism, and loyalty. The Janaforma have taken me as their own and I embrace their love and Community.

I am happy to say Sante has made progress on decoding Simon Forma's files. Some of the interesting aspects of Janaforma genetics, so far, reveal that Simon Forma discovered a new way to overload the genetic units making them longer than usual. The longer units were loaded with recessive genes making the master genes unstable during meiosis. When a Janaforma mates with anyone besides a Janaforma, an inversion occurs. Pieces of the chromosome detach and reattach in completely different parts of the chromosome.

As long as Janaforma procreate within their genetic family, this inversion problem is not detrimental, but if they procreate with other than Janaforma, the shuffling during reproduction brings some genes out from under the metaphorical table. Like hidden cards, the recessive genes cause problems in the Janaforma offspring. So far, there is no solution to this problem; but I have hope. I have seen Janaforma do the impossible many times before. It is easier to have hope out here and believe we possess the power to unravel it all. I know two things for sure. There are more truths waiting; and there is life, but only after many deaths.

ABOUT THE AUTHOR

Martha Fawcett was born in Tiffin, Ohio. As a child, her dad stoked her imagination with talk of future inventions, space travel, and meeting alien species. In addition to writing science fiction, she now takes delight in the protocols and absurdities of politics, a June garden in the morning, highly polished gemstones, and the beautiful flow of life. She enjoys time with her husband Bill and their two children, Penelope and Adam.